BAD SHADOU

THE IMMORTAL ELLE TRILOGY, BOOK ONE

By

CAPULET POEHNER

Table of Contents

For my little darlings,
both real and imagined

Part 1

Prologue

Millions of light years from a far younger Earth, the distant planet smoldered. A bubbling black sea engulfed much of the surface. What had once been sprawling cities populated by billions of advanced beings, creatures with unparalleled intellect and vast powers both physical and otherwise, now lay in ruin. Within seconds, all hope would be lost, all citizens permanently enslaved by a dark force in possession of powers far greater than their own.

Out of the wall of blackness emerged a tiny white starship. With pointed nose and sleek wings, the ship bounced and bobbed just ahead of the rush of darkness, as though surfing a terrible wave of doom. With a final thrust of energy, the ship propelled itself ahead of the wave and careened toward the last remaining patch of life on the planet's surface. There awaited a dark figure, beckoning the black wave to finish the ship. And the entire planet along with it.

The ship spun sideways and crashed onto a barren hillside. Its thrusters seared the sparse grass and whipped up a minor storm to soften the blow of the landing. With a deafening groan the ship skidded to a stop, less than fifty yards from the solitary dark figure. The ship's hatch hissed open and out jumped a massive bearlike creature. He ran full speed to the dark figure and drew a long shining staff from his backpack.

"Stop this madness at once!" shouted the bearlike creature. "Or I'll stop it for you." He looked over his shoulder at the wave of darkness cresting in the sky just behind him.

The dark figure laughed. It was more of a metallic-sounding chuckle than true laughter. The figure towered high above. It appeared to be made of dark chrome or obsidian. Its face curled into a smile, and it spoke, although its voice didn't travel through the air and into ears. It traveled straight to the mind.

Shadou. So pleased you could join me to witness the final moments of your planet's failed experiment with independence.

"Independence from what, your tyranny?"

I offer no tyranny, only freedom from individual thought. In seconds, all the pretty little creatures on this world–including you, Shadou–will bend your wills as one toward a single, glorious purpose.

Shadou sensed the darkness closing in. *Is this truly the twilight of my people?* He thought of his family and tightened the grip on his spear. "We reject your purpose, whatever that is!"

Once again the figure chuckled. *Oh really? And how do you, the last free being on this planet, intend to stop me?*

The dark sea of blackness converged on the point where Shadou and the figure stood. Time had run out. Shadou twisted the center handle of his spear. Two sharp points extended from each end. Blinding white light emanated from the spear points.

"I'll stop you with this!"

The figure recoiled in fear, but was too late. Shadou used all of his strength to dematerialize from his location and reappear inches away from the figure. With a single thrust, Shadou buried the spear deep into the figure's torso. The force of the blow launched Shadou back onto the rocky ground. The last thing he remembered seeing was white light surrounding the figure and then blasting out across the sky. The sea of blackness receded as the light matter swept it away.

When Shadou awoke, he lay bathed in cold, clinical light. He could scarcely see. A female voice addressed him, from deep within his mind.

Shadou...

Shadou sat up, shielding his eyes. He had no idea where he was. "Master, is that you?"

Of course, my dear friend.

"But what about—"

Your daughter is safe. All are safe. You have done well.

Shadou collapsed back into a lying position, not completely sure whether or not he was dreaming. "Thank you, Master. That means so much to me. When... When can I see my family?"

Well, there is still the question of the light matter that you stole.

Shadou shot up once again. "Stole? I used it to save our planet!"

And so you did, my friend. But we both know that you didn't originally take it to serve that purpose. Plus, there is the fact that you stole so much, enough to power many starship voyages. It was quite... excessive. Even for you.

Shadou looked around him, as though trying to locate his master. "But, Master... If I hadn't taken that much, I never could have stopped... Him."

Yes, my friend. Your fortune was great, as was ours. By vanquishing the entity that calls itself Quaru, you saved us from much pain. But you still must make amends for your betrayal.

"Betrayal? Hey, I only took that light matter to fuel expeditions to the outer systems! Who knows how much more light matter I can mine there. And besides, isn't saving our world, our entire civilization, enough amends?"

For some, yes. But not for all. We have decided. There stands one last assignment for you. If you succeed at it completely, then you can return to your family, and serve out your purpose.

"Assignment? What assignment?"

The blinding light subsided just enough to reveal a glowing purple and black orb. It hovered spinning a few feet above the ground about ten yards from Shadou. He had a pretty good idea what it was.

"I think I get it now. So that's—"

Yes. That is Him, imprisoned deep within the sphere. Escape is impossible.

"Impossible, you say? I'm pretty sure that old guy is capable of anything. I mean, we don't even know where or when He came from."

Yes, yes, more ancient than the stars, and all of that. But I assure you— ALL of us assure you–that He cannot escape.

"So why don't you just destroy Him?"

Because that is one thing we do not know how to do.

Shadou shook his head in frustration.

But we are actively studying this very question: how to destroy a being that may be older than the very universe itself, without causing unintended... consequences. This is where your assignment comes in.

Shadou sighed. "All right, let me have it. What is this so-called final assignment?"

Another space in the area materialized into view. Shadou grinned and managed to pull himself up completely. "My ship, you salvaged it!"

Yes, indeed. She is restored and ready for her voyage.

His eyes sparkled as he surveyed his sleek, white starship, gleaming like new and ready for takeoff. "Where am I going?"

You must take the entity far away from here, while we determine the best means of finally disposing of Him. Once we've determined that, we will signal to you, and you will return Him to us. That is your assignment, in its most basic terms.

"If you're so sure He can't escape, why not leave Him here?"

I'm afraid that's politics, my friend. After the near-destruction of our planet, nobody will agree to keep Him here. Besides, this will give you the opportunity to explore another world, far beyond our own, just as you have always wished.

"Great. But I never wished for any of this. How long will my assignment take?"

I'm afraid it may be a long, long time. Many of us will need to travel far to discover the answers to complex questions.

"So I'm to be alone, on some remote rock, guarding this horrible force of darkness, while You research how to destroy it?"

More or less, although you won't be alone. For starters, the planet you're traveling to is teeming with organisms, including sentient beings. Far less advanced than any of us, of course. But still, developing...

"Great," sighed Shadou. "Natives."

Shadou was interrupted by the opening of the ship's hatch. Out stepped a diminutive catlike creature, with pointy, tufted ears and hind legs much shorter than his arms. The creature grinned at Shadou and spun a staff between stubby fingers. Each time it spun, the staff altered its shape and color.

Shadou threw up his massive, clawed hands. "Seriously? A particle shifter?"

This is Rifkin. He will assist you on your assignment. You will surely find him to be invaluable.

Rifkin made a short, spitting sound. "Trust me, man, I don't want to go on this mission any more than you do." Then his bright eyes darted back and forth. "And you don't even want to know what I did to get stuck with this."

Shadou growled in anger and shook his fists. "So that's it? Me and this shifter are taking the Destroyer of Worlds to a faraway planet for, oh, let's say several hundred years at least, until we're summoned back here?"

That is correct. And you must leave immediately. You will be allowed to send messages to your family on your journey, from time to time. And detailed instructions await you aboard your ship.

Shadou pointed a sharp claw at the glowing orb before him. "And do these 'detailed instructions' tell us what to do if that thing escapes?"

I told you, He will not escape.

"But *if* He does, what are me and Rifkin here supposed to do?"

Shadou could sense a hint of sarcasm in his master's voice; she almost snickered. *If He escapes, then you better find someone on that planet to help you defeat Him again.*

"How could a primitive creature help me defeat that?"

You're a resourceful being, Shadou. Study these creatures. You may eventually find they're not completely hopeless after all. And who knows? Perhaps one of them will come in handy someday...

Chapter 1

Elle sat across the table from a tall man, a complete stranger. The thirteen-year-old girl pulled the dark gray hood closer around her face. Her black painted fingernails flickered in the dim light of the near-empty Seattle café. The man shifted in his seat. A designer trench coat draped across his thin frame like an emperor's robe. He studied Elle while spinning his phone around and around on the tabletop with a manicured pointer finger.

So this is what it's like to meet a CEO, thought Elle.

"Tell me sweetheart, what is your real name? It can't be EleMent03." His voice trembled ever so slightly.

Elle snatched the man's phone and unlocked it. The man leaned forward. "Wait, how did you know my passcode?"

His eyes flashed in the candlelight. Was it fear or excitement?

Elle tapped away on the phone. For a moment everything around her melted away: the man, the café, the noisy city. All that remained was Elle and her connection to the device. She felt the interface join with her through her fingertips and up into her very being. When she was finished, the world whooshed back into place. She locked eyes with the man and set the phone on the table.

The man let out a faint chuckle and glanced over at his security guard, who stood several feet away. "That phone has a lot of sensitive information on it."

Elle wiped her fingerprints off the phone with a napkin and slid it across to the man's waiting hand.

"I'm not interested in those, not anymore," she said.

"Not interested in my company secrets? I beg to differ." The man clearly wanted to get a better look at her. "How old are you, anyway? You look like you couldn't be more than sixteen."

"What does my age have to do with anything?"

"Well, I'd like to know a lot more about you than just your age. For starters, how did you hack into our secure servers and start playing a game that's months away from release?"

"That was both easy and kind of a pain, to be honest. But mostly easy."

"And how did you start programming the game, changing the levels, the characters? I can't get a straight answer from my own security team."

"That was just for fun."

The man threw up his hands and looked around, as though addressing an invisible audience. "OK, honey, I give up. This is obviously some kind of a ruse."

"A ruse?"

"Yes, ruse. You know what that means, little girl? It means you're toying with me, and I have little patience for fun and games."

"But you run a mobile gaming company."

"That, to me, is serious business. Look, you tell whoever sent you that they are in for a world of pain. We will hunt them down and bring them to justice."

"Is that why you set up this meeting? To bring me to justice?"

The man spun his phone around the table with increasing velocity. He let out a deep laugh that almost sounded forced.

Elle wasn't smiling. "What's so funny?"

The man clapped his hand down to stop the spinning phone. "Look, I hope you're getting paid good money for this. I'm laughing because you expect me to believe that I came here to meet with you. No, I came here to meet with the person or persons who infiltrated my extremely secure servers and changed the code on my product. Honestly, I thought the changes they made were impressive."

"Really?"

"You bet they were. I even considered offering them a job. But not after this little stunt. Sending a teenage girl. I've got half a mind to have you arrested. But at the very least, I will be watching you." He pointed at his security guard with his phone. "*We* will be watching you."

Elle considered the security guard. His imposing form was best kept at a distance from her. But she didn't fear for her physical safety. She imagined there were more serious threats at the other end of this CEO's phone.

I need to get out of here.

The man took advantage of the awkward silence to add, "I mean, if you were a little older, maybe I'd ask you out on a date."

Eww. "How very professional of you."

Elle glanced up at a wall clock and calculated that she could catch an earlier ferry across the Sound to Bainbridge Island. She'd actually get her homework done for a change. Making sure not to touch the table, she pushed her chair away and stood. The man remained. He dismissed Elle with a raised eyebrow and focused on his phone.

"We're done here," he said. "Go."

Elle didn't move. She watched as the man struggled to unlock his phone.

He looked up at her with eyes of fury. "What the hell did you do to this?"

"For starters, I changed your passcode. It's now 0404. Your fingerprint won't work anymore. Try the code."

"Seriously? That's not a clever hack, that's just annoying." The man entered the digits and the phone unlocked. "Is that all you can do?"

"No, I did one other thing. Check out the new app on your home screen."

The man looked down and saw a familiar icon. "Wait, what? Is this...?"

"Yes, it's your precious new game, Buzzle Jump. I made a few changes. I hope you like them." Elle tugged her sleeve over her hand and placed it on the back of the man's chair. "I just wanted to make it better. I wasn't trying to do anything, you know, bad."

The man tapped the game icon and watched in shock as it came to life on his screen. His wide eyes reflected vibrant colors and designs that he had never seen before. The first level had been completely reimagined. The main character was no longer a cartoonish bee. Instead it was a strange bearlike creature wearing a backpack that hopped from platform to platform scooping up junk food. The man couldn't help but grin.

Elle removed her hand and stepped away. "I can build things, like games. You seemed like somebody who'd understand. I guess I was wrong. I'm sorry, but I might have done a bad thing."

The man's voice softened as he explored the game with wonder. "What did you do?"

"I made it public. It's officially launched as of right now."

The man closed out Buzzle Jump and scanned several urgent messages from his team. They wanted to know why he launched the app without telling them.

Elle walked away.

"Wait! EleMent03, or whatever you call yourself, get back here. We're not done here."

Elle picked up her pace and squeezed past the security guard before he could stop her.

"I am. Don't worry, I'll delete the game when I get home. Permanently."

By the time Elle exited the café she was running at full speed. The gunmetal-blue afternoon sky dulled the sounds of her steps as she raced through busy sidewalks and rush-hour traffic to the ferry terminal. Ever since Elle had met Shadou, there was nothing she could do to keep the hundreds of devices that surrounded her from entering her head.

Their move from San Diego had been abrupt. One day Elle was wrapping up a busy summer bouncing from coder camp to coder camp, and the next her parents were taking turns flying up to Seattle to look at real estate. Upon their return they would give Elle and her little brother, Emmett, brief glimpses into the new world that awaited them. Elle and Emmett Redfern. This caused confusion.

Their mother, Jill, did her best to hide the stress that came with such a big and sudden move. Their father, Jim, withdrew by focusing on mundane details: mover schedules, canceling the cable, change-of-address forms, organizing the garage. Emmett was four and had scarcely any idea what was going on. Elle, on the other hand, harbored doubts. In those last precious weeks of summer, she felt like a disaster was about to upend their lives. The shift from fun weekend activities, like going to the beach, to mundane garage sales and trips to the Goodwill Donation Center were, to her, the initial pullback of the ocean just before a tsunami. The impending move was a mile-high dark wave of unknowable change about to crash on them all. There were many complaints, accompanied by spiteful glares.

"Why do we have to move? Washington sounds lame." That was Elle's refrain.

"Your mother got a new job up there, sweetie. A great, new job." Jim's voice sounded pained, almost angry, whenever he spoke of the move.

This did little to placate Elle. Still, she couldn't help but be intrigued by this new distant place: Seattle. Her mom took her on guided iPad tours through a dozen digitized homes, each one more than double the size of their two-bedroom condo. HUGE YARD! MUST SEE!! GREAT FOR ENTERTAINING! BONUS ROOM!!! Elle had never heard of a bonus room before, but it sounded like a good thing to her.

In the end they settled on Bainbridge Island, a choice made by factors far beyond Elle's control: quality of schools, size of house one could get for one's money, and her parents' reluctant acceptance of the long ferry commute east to Seattle.

On the day the movers packed all their belongings into boxes and wrapped up their furniture in blankets, Elle felt strangely calm. It was a hot July day, and Elle had been afforded the distraction of her dad's iPad. Her parents interpreted Elle's interest in technology as potential threat. Their biggest fear was losing their daughter to endless texting on a phone.

They had no idea.

She made a nest for herself on the living room floor beside the big, now curtainless window, surrounded by boxes, snacks, and a couple of Minecraft figurines she had picked up at Comic-Con recently.

Elle obsessed over Minecraft; that's what she often spent her iPad time playing. But a new force had entered the scene on YouTube. Scattered amongst the comments on several Minecraft videos, which Elle and her friends devoured endlessly, there emerged links to a new creator: BadShadou. "His" videos—and nobody knew who "he" was, or whether the videos were the product of an individual or a corporation—percolated to the top of Elle's consciousness in the same way Minecraft had several years before.

Minecraft, with its ordered, yet vast, and sprawling, yet multifaceted worlds of towering structures—organic and man-made—its hidden secrets and whispered rules, its sense of creative discovery and creepy dangers lurking both around corners and within objects—spoke to Elle on a primal level for as long as she could remember. She just "got" it. Within a year of poking around Minecraft, Elle became a legitimate expert, a respected authority within the international community.

Completely unbeknownst to her parents, of course.

Under the handle "EleMent03," she surreptitiously set up accounts on YouTube and Twitch.TV using her mom's MacBook Pro. On Saturday afternoons when her parents thought she was just playing Minecraft or watching videos, Elle holed up in her bedroom, plugged in headphones with a built-in mic, and streamed dozens of hours of herself mining, creating, and surviving to a growing audience of kids age ten and up. She covered popular songs with Minecraft-inspired lyrics and created entire storylines populated by a range of characters she did voices for. Characters with names like "Commander GrumpyPants" and "Auntie Creeper." It was silly, inconsequential content that no respectable media company would entertain for even a minute, but it became Elle's passion.

That is, until she saw her first BadShadou video on that hot July day while the movers were packing up her house.

Elle was aware that she wouldn't be able to stream any of her own Minecraft content that day. She'd be exposed. She sensed her father becoming suspicious. *Could he discover my secret online life?* Her parents fretted over things like "cyberstalking" and "online bullying" all the time.

Elle knew her streaming days would end the moment she got caught interacting with someone she didn't know.

Fortunately, she didn't even want to stream that day. It was as though she needed a new passion to go along with her new Seattle life, something more challenging than Minecraft streaming. And so Elle had planned days before to explore BadShadou videos in search of inspiration.

She donned her headphones and cradled the iPad in her arms. After a brief pause, she navigated to a YouTube video where she knew she'd find the link she wanted. As the video loaded, she munched on gummy worms from a plastic package and gazed into the screen. Then the video started. It had more than eight million views and hundreds of comments, but words could not describe the sensations that overtook Elle.

The two-minute video was simply titled *for you,* all lowercase. The username was BadShadou. The profile photo was a silhouette—black on white—of the bearlike head of a creature that could have been lifted from *Where the Wild Things Are.* The video itself seemed to have been created with a complex mix of stop-motion animation and CGI. Snippets of video and still photographs, plus animated GIFs, flashed around the screen. It looked to her like it must have taken a team of animators months to produce.

At first Elle saw what looked like a distant, alien planet. Swirling clouds of lavender and silver-gray gases shrouded a surface that shimmered with billions of twinkling lights. Technology, endless cities, much of it in fluid motion, spread out below.

An explosion of darkness burst forth from a pinpoint near the planet's equator. The camera swooped down toward the surface. Mountains of lights became massive architectural structures, both organic and seemingly robotic, cold yet alive. As the camera drew closer, life-forms became visible. Some were hulking things with multiple thick arms sheathed in rocky brown armor. Others were slight beings, hovering just inches above the ground and propelled gently along by gossamer wings that extended out several times the length of their bodies. All were blissfully unaware of the coming darkness.

The creatures made Elle giggle, which was no small feat. They walked with a bouncy dance and their facial expressions mimicked Claymation characters. But the joy in their eyes was quickly extinguished by the darkness. It rose from its gushing source at the center of the planet and invaded the surface with the physical force of a swarm of locusts. The darkness enveloped everything it passed and doused the once-twinkling lights. The creatures it touched didn't die, but ceased to be the joyful beings they were before. They became gray shadows, listless and blind. Ghosts, maybe?

Elle watched with morbid fascination as though this were all real, her eyes unblinking. The camera pulled back from the surface to reveal the entire planet almost engulfed. But just as the darkness neared the last remaining patches of life, a brilliant light exploded near the North Pole. Glowing gold, with lightning tendrils of purple and blue, the light fought back. It pushed the darkness, which resisted in fits and spurts, until at last the darkness succumbed, back at its source.

The creatures, returned to their previous form, rejoiced as the camera zoomed in wild loops around the planet. The billions of lights returned even brighter than before, and new structures grew from atop the old ones, climbing up to the stratosphere as if built by invisible hands. The camera came to rest on the image of a white starship, docked at the summit of a tall peak. An ominous black sphere was loaded onto the ship, and its rockets fired, sending it deep into space. The starship traveled at what must have been a speed greater than light beyond dozens of galaxies. At last the ship soared past Saturn, Jupiter, and Mars, and arrived at the familiar blue-green sphere of Earth. Elle's heart stopped when, in the final seconds of the video, a message displayed:

For You. Elle.

Chapter 2

The second after Elle saw the disturbing message at the end of the BadShadou video, Emmett ran up to her. She didn't seem to notice him standing there, so he called out, "Elle!"

Elle sat frozen, the iPad in one hand and a gummy worm in the other.

"Elle, can I have some candy, please?" Emmett was exceedingly polite, a well-trained boy.

"What? Emmett ... huh?" Emmett held out his hand close to her face. This normally would have incited Elle to smack her little brother, but she remained motionless, dazed.

Then she snapped out of it. "Here." She grabbed the package and shoved it in Emmett's hands. "Take them all."

Elle slapped the iPad case shut and marched straight over to her dad. He sat alone in what had once been the dining room. A laptop took all of his attention, even on this big moving day. Jim's Seattle job search was not going well. Apparently, his skill set as a radio technician wasn't in high demand anymore.

"Dad?"

Jim looked up from his LinkedIn profile. "Yeah, what, sweetie?"

"Here's the iPad. I'm finished with it for now."

"OK." A look of vague distrust spread across Jim's eyes.

Emmett ran in from the living room and tossed the empty gummy worms package onto the floor. "iPad! Give me the iPad, Daddy!" The iPad vanished from Jim's grasp and Emmett absconded with it to the back of the condo.

Jim shook his head at Elle. "You kids and your addiction to devices. We're going to need to deal with that after the move." Elle stood silent. "Do you need something, sweetheart?"

"Well." Elle shifted awkwardly back and forth. "Um, Dad?"

"Yes?"

"Can I use your phone?"

"Seriously? What for?"

"I need to call Crystal. Right now." Crystal was Elle's best non-digital friend, and the main reason she didn't want to move.

Jim raised an eyebrow and tugged gently on his short beard. "Elle, I'm expecting some calls right now."

Elle stomped her foot on the floor. "Dad, you guys seriously need to get me a phone. It's totally unfair that I have to ask you every time I need to call someone. This is an emergency!"

Jim contemplated whether or not to give in. He gave in. "OK, fine. If you're going to be like this, at least try to respect the fact that they're still on vacation, you know. In Hawaii."

"Fine. I will respect their glorious Hawaii vacation."

Jim passed the phone. "Elle, not too long, OK?"

But Elle was already gone. She raced into her bedroom—her former bedroom since it now stood empty except for packed boxes—and counted the seconds as Crystal's phone rang. She found a hiding place behind a wardrobe box and Crystal finally picked up.

"Elle! Hello, are you there?"

Elle caught her breath. "Crystal. Hi, it's Elle... Oh, you already know that, ha ha! Um..." She slammed the back of her head into the box.

"Yeah, space brain, I know it's you. What are you doing? You moving yet?"

"So, yes. Moving. And packing and stuff. Boxes everywhere, but that's not... I wanted to ask you something, about a video."

"OK ... What video?"

Elle struggled to collect her thoughts. They were like a huge pile of spilled Legos that she had to assemble in a race against the clock.

"Well, you know those videos we were talking about before you left, those BadShadou videos?"

"Yeah. What about them?"

"Right, so in the one called *for you*, the spaceship comes to Earth, and that's the end, right?"

"Uh-huh."

"But ... Did you see anything, I mean, after?"

"Like after the spaceship comes to Earth?"

"Yeah, like a message, in writing. Words, I mean."

"Here, let me watch it now."

Crystal's line went silent for a couple minutes.

"Crystal? You still here?"

"I'm here. Watched the video. I don't get any message at the end. Why? Did you see one?"

Elle dropped the phone to her lap and took deep breaths. Then she heard Crystal offer, "Maybe they changed the video or something before I watched it? There was definitely no message. It just ended."

"OK. Cool. I guess that's right then."

Elle felt blood rushing through her ears and pounding in her head.

"Elle?" Crystal asked. "You still there?"

"Yeah. Sorry Crys ... That's all I wanted to know."

"Elle, what's going on?"

"Nothing. Hey, I should go. We're moving, my dad's freaking out about me and devices lately, which is totally insane as usual. You're on vacation. Maybe we can FaceTime or something, if my parents let me."

"Sure, Elle."

They said goodbye to each other several times. Then Elle walked the phone back to Jim.

Jim didn't look up from his laptop. "You done?"

"Yeah. Thanks, Dad."

Something about Elle's voice made Jim reach out and caress her shoulder. "I'm glad you connected with your friend, sweetheart."

Elle trudged back to her nest in the living room and plopped down onto the floor. *What's the deal exactly with this Shadou character?*

Elle's search for Shadou was hampered from the start. Moving day brought chaos and complications, beginning with two nights in airport hotels in San Diego and Seattle. Elle spent most of this time entertaining Emmett so that their parents could concentrate on the complex logistics of moving a family of four to a different state. Fast-food restaurants, swimming pool bars, and airport food courts became their sources of sustenance. Elle took advantage of this opportunity to devour as much junk food as possible, particularly gummy worms, her favorite. But getting device time was a major issue. Her parents expected her to read books instead. But these had zero appeal to her. The lack of devices put her on edge, and this only exacerbated her parents' already off-the-charts stress levels.

"Elle, I don't know why you keep whining. Just play a card game or something!" was a reproach she often heard.

"I just really want to watch videos, Mom."

She won no sympathy whatsoever. Elle remained focused on finding Shadou. The night of their Seattle airport hotel stay gave her the first opportunity.

She waited until her parents and brother were asleep in the other room. Then she collected the iPad and her headphones and made a blanket tent over her head on the couch. The iPad had been connected to the slow yet tolerable hotel internet earlier that evening. For some reason she felt compelled to hide her usual identity, although she figured it ultimately didn't matter. But just to be safe, she navigated to a Google Chrome incognito window and set up a new dummy account: "ShadouStalker5000." This she verified using her dad's cell phone, which she had secretly procured from its charging station on top of the dresser. She took extra care to delete the verification text that Google sent her dad's phone. She watched the *for you* BadShadou video once more.

The message at the end didn't display. What if she had only imagined it the first time? Puzzled by this, Elle scrunched her face, logged out of the dummy account, and logged back in to her usual EleMent03 account. Again she started the video, but out of impatience she scrubbed to the end. There was the message, this time in all lowercase: *for you. elle*.

Elle stifled a giggle and sat up in her seat. She quickly poked her head out from under the blanket to make sure the coast was clear. No movement, just the sound of Emmett's heavy deep-sleep breathing. Elle ducked under the blanket and logged back into the dummy account. She scrubbed to the end of the video.

This time the message displayed in all caps: *FOR YOU. ELLE!*

"Hah!" Elle couldn't contain the outburst. Panicked, she closed the iPad, took off her headphones and curled up on the couch, feigning sleep. In the other room, she heard one of her parents stir. It took all of her energy to keep her eyes closed and her body completely still. After what felt like an eternity, the room went quiet and Elle regained her confidence enough to rise up, inch by inch, and reset beneath her blanket tent with both the iPad and headphones.

Whoever this Shadou is, he's definitely trolling me, but in kind of a fun way. Or was it? How could he have known that the dummy account was hers? She was incognito, and hadn't entered any personal information. She didn't know enough about hackers to know what was possible, but this seemed unique. She logged back into the dummy account and entered a comment on the video: *who are you?*

Then she waited.

Elle must have refreshed the comments a hundred times when exhaustion began to settle in. She yawned every several seconds, her mind growing dull and she got a little bored after the initial excitement wore off. Just as she was about to give up for the night, a cryptic reply appeared beneath her comment: *BadShadou @SC.*

What the heck does that mean? Southern California? Or maybe the "@" symbol was supposed to be an "A," so "ASC"? It didn't make any sense, especially in her exhausted state. She glanced at the digital clock: 12:21 a.m. *The same time right-side up and upside down.*

Rubbing her face with both hands, Elle wracked her brain but couldn't decode the message, not now. She carefully put everything away and tucked in to sleep on the couch, her arm resting on her forehead as she gazed out at the Seattle rain that dabbled on the window. She flinched and jerked her head to the side when she remembered where she was, in an airport hotel in Seattle, at the beginning of her new life. A wave of sadness rushed over her as she thought about San Diego, their abandoned condo, and especially... *Crystal.*

Then she remembered Crystal telling her about an app she had just started using, and she sat straight up in the couch. Snapchat! *SC is*

Snapchat. Smiling, Elle banished all sadness. She would need to find a way to download and access this app.

Chapter 3

Elle had heard quite a bit about cyberstalkers, mostly from boring assemblies and pamphlets at her school. Her parents discussed the dangers of cyberstalkers with her on a couple of occasions; they seemed overly concerned. For Elle's part, the use of the outdated term "cyber" was just wrong. She liked to say it out loud in a creepy voice: "cyberstalkers." It made her and Crystal giggle.

It occurred to Elle that maybe Shadou was a sick pervert trying to contact her. *A perv with some serious coding skills.* She decided to keep digging, follow Shadou's trail to see where it led, and to bring in her parents if she got creeped out. She watched the five remaining videos on "his" YouTube channel. They seemed tailor-made for Elle's tastes and sense of humor. But they were also popular, averaging over two million views each, so maybe lots of kids were just like Elle. *Are other kids seeing their names at the end of the video too?*

Of the remaining videos, one was a ninety-second video titled "Rifkin the Stupendous," featuring a stop-motion animated magician who could take any two objects and combine them into one in unusual ways. Another video featured several silly-looking creatures speeding around city streets on high-tech motorcycles, each leaving behind their own hue of fluorescent paint in a race to cover an entire city with splashes of color. The videos were amusing, impressive in their intricacy and attention to detail. But only the *for you* video truly captured Elle's imagination.

After a time she turned back to Snapchat. To access it, Elle needed a phone, and getting hold of one of her parents' phones for a significant amount of time—and in private, no less—was a major challenge.

"Dad," she asked one day in their spacious Bainbridge Island kitchen, "can I use your phone to make a video?" It was two days before Elle's first day of eighth grade, and the entire family was just starting to get settled into their new home.

Jim still hadn't found a job. His anxiety over this was apparent. He glared at Elle. "You've been spending way too much time holed up in your room plugged into devices, Elle. You should be outside, making new friends, playing in our yard."

Elle smiled demurely. "You'll see, Dad! I'm making a video tour of my room for Crystal. I'll go read or something outside right after."

Jim shook his head, but he pulled his phone from his pocket. "Promise?"

Elle rolled her eyes. "Pinky swear." She swiped the phone and ran upstairs to her bedroom.

Her new room was a dream to her. For the first time since she could remember, she had her own lair, free from Emmett's late-night outbursts and dinosaur toys littering the floor. Although slightly smaller than the bedroom they previously shared, the room felt like a luxurious escape zone. Tucked against a corner was an antique four-poster twin bed, a gift from her grandmother. A built-in desk sat nestled in the dormer window across from the bed. Beneath the second window she had cobbled together a nest of black throw pillows and blankets as her reading and device lounge. Elle set up shop in her nest.

She quickly entered Jim's lock-screen code into the phone and swiped through all of his app windows. She was in luck: Snapchat was not installed. Elle didn't think it would be, but if her dad already had an account for some reason that could cause problems that she preferred to avoid. She then navigated to the App Store and downloaded Snapchat. As before, she set up an account named "ShadouStalker5000" and associated it with the dummy Gmail account. She then used her dad's phone number to verify via text and deleted all incriminating text evidence.

Within minutes she was all set up. She searched for Snapchat user BadShadou and added it as a friend. Within seconds "he" added her back. Elle jumped in her seat; she didn't know what to do. Snapchat seemed simple enough. Take a photo, doodle on it if you want to, and then send it to a friend with an expiration time.

Elle glanced around her room nervously. *Should I start this conversation by sending something first?* Just then her dad poked his head in her door. Elle jumped again.

"How's the video going, Elle?"

"Um, just getting started, Dad. Go away! I'll show it to you when I'm done."

Jim held up his hands and backed away. "OK, OK! I get it, don't rush genius. But remember not to take too long. The great outdoors awaits."

"Seriously, Dad, get out." The door closed. Elle checked Snapchat. Nothing there. She didn't have much time to choose a photo subject so she grabbed a plastic warrior-queen figurine off a shelf and took a photo of it. She spent a few minutes playing with the doodling tool and drew a smiley face on the figurine's head. Then she wrote in bright red "ink" at the bottom: *who r u??* She kept the expiration time set to three seconds and swiped to send it.

Immediately after hitting send she received a photo. She had five whole seconds to take it in. It was a photo of a tall, lonely mountain—Mount Rainier?—and superimposed over it was a doodled message. But instead of clumsy handwriting, the message displayed as finely designed typography. The message read: *I am Shadou. Sorry to pull you into this, Elle. But I think I need your help with something. yt.com/badshadou now.*

Elle shifted in her seat, feeling a rush of excitement overtake her. She navigated to the BadShadou YouTube channel on the phone and saw that a new video had been posted a minute before. It was titled, *How To Turn Your iPad Into a Cloaking Device.*

Jim called from downstairs, "Elle! You almost finished up there?"

Elle knew she'd have to make a video, any video. She would show it to her dad and he would pretend to be impressed although she'd know he wasn't really, which was fine. "Yeah, Dad. Ten more minutes!"

She quickly deleted the Snapchat app. She'd have to reinstall it every time, and hope her dad didn't notice. But before she made her video, she wanted to watch the one Shadou made.

This video was the first live-action one she had seen. It featured a nerdy-looking twenty-something white guy in what appeared to be a small apartment. He held up an iPad and narrated: *"Hi there, this is Rick again. Today I'm going to show you all something really cool: How to make your iPad into a real-life cloaking device."* For a few minutes Rick talked about the mechanics of cloaking.

Then he pulled the camera back and shouted, *"Oh my God!"* The iPad started rattling on the coffee table, so violently that the glass cracked. The iPad went black, not just dark, but black. Rick's camera shook in his hands as he moaned with fear. The blackness on the iPad screen began oozing slowly out onto the cracked table surface. Rick screamed in terror. *"What's happening? I can't move!"* The blackness crawled toward the camera and engulfed everything, including, apparently, Rick. His screams were silenced as the video went completely dark.

Then a message displayed in yellow text: *What does this mean, Elle? I kind of need your help here.*

Elle threw the phone onto the floor. Her hands shook, and her heart raced. *Maybe Snapchatting some stranger called Shadou wasn't such a great idea after all.*

The dark entity lurking in the center of Mount Rainier felt nothing but disgust and hatred toward all of humanity. It couldn't remember its own name when it awoke from its painful slumber two days ago, and that angered it. But even worse was the constant stream of human thoughts and feelings that bombarded its vast consciousness. Petty little flesh-sacks, these humans, going about their brief lives in utter ignorance of how meaningless and hopeless they all are. The futile exercises of procreation, suffering, so-called happiness, and despair all roared with an incessant shrill noise that drowned out the entity's higher thought processes. It was like being surrounded by a multitude of babies screaming because they didn't get the toy they wanted. They had to be silenced. But how?

The entity lay trapped, imprisoned. For how long? And why did it awaken? The entity tried to analyze the human data it was receiving, but it was all just disorganized static, impossible to parse. The invisible walls that confined the entity somehow both amplified and scrambled the human noise. It was torture.

Elle's mother became fascinated by Mount Rainier the moment they moved to Bainbridge Island. Jill grew up in Ohio, and moved to Southern California after college in Michigan. So she had never lived in the shadow of mountains, much less one as dramatic as Rainier. Their first weekend in Washington wasn't spent setting up their new home; it was spent hiking the forested trails in Mount Rainier National Park. Jill filled her Facebook Timeline with photos of Elle and Emmett grinning in front of the towering summit. All of her friends were "so jealous."

"Elle, did you know that Rainier is the tallest mountain by prominence in the lower forty-eight states?" she asked, beaming with excitement.

"Prominence?" Elle said. "Is that like popularity or something?"

Jill felt both awe and fear toward the volcano. She read articles and Wikipedia entries about how it was one of the most potentially deadly volcanoes on Earth, and about hikers stranded on its cruel crests. She pictured her own children getting lost on the mountain and made a mental note to never let that happen.

But Jill was surprised that everyone she talked to seemed indifferent toward Rainier. Sure, it was beautiful to look at, on the rare occasions that it was actually visible through all the Seattle clouds. But to the average local she talked to, that was the beginning and end of their opinion on the subject. It was like an old grade-school classmate they never really connected with, distant yet benign. She wondered whether she just hadn't met any of the gearheads that Seattle was famous for.

Jill prodded Jim about it. "But, Jim," she said one night with more than a hint of exasperation in her voice, "don't you think it's crazy that there's this giant stratovolcano sixty miles away with these amazing glaciers, just sitting there all by itself?"

Jim took a drink from his wine glass and smiled wryly. "I guess it's OK for a few Instagram photos every now and then, just to let our faraway friends know that we can still appreciate nature."

"No, it's much more than that, Jim!" She crossed her arms. "I hope you understand that someday."

The dark entity beneath the mountain understood Rainier's power all too well. But it only needed to bide its time. Escape was inevitable.

Chapter 4

The weeks that followed Elle's first contact with Shadou via Snapchat were a whirlwind of new sensations and experiences. She started eighth grade at Woodward Middle School, named after the late publishers of the island's local newspaper. The school grounds, with their rolling grassy hills peppered with tall evergreens, stood in stark contrast to her concrete San Diego campus.

The children were different too. They seemed slightly wild, and as Elle learned early on, not shy. In contrast to her former sheltered city life, Elle now spent much of her time roaming the neighborhood unaccompanied by adults. The kids ruled the streets. They traveled by bike or Razor scooter from house to house in roving bands, seeking adventure. After Elle's perplexing interactions with Shadou, roaming tree-lined streets was about as much adventure as she could handle.

The change of seasons was another contrast for Elle. Every day she noticed subtle differences, which definitely didn't happen in Southern California. Slightly shorter days, darker mornings, leaves adjusting their hues from green to orange and gold right before her eyes, like a time-lapse video. Rain was a joy to her. She loved stomping on big mud puddles in her new red rain boots. The local kids always gave her curious glances when she splashed around, as if to say, "Why would you ever want to do *that*?" But Elle didn't notice the looks she got. She was too busy taking it all in, all that newness.

At times it was too much, and Elle became overwhelmingly homesick. She longed for their condo, she missed her old school, and most of all she missed Crystal. She began to wonder if she'd ever make a new friend.

One of her neighbors, an eighth-grade boy named Conner with short, cropped dark brown hair and a spare, bony frame, caught Elle's attention. Unlike the typical Bainbridge Island kid, Conner was shy. He and Elle shared the same bus stop, and one day he overheard her talking about video games with a group of girls. Uncharacteristically he blurted out that he had just watched a video about virtual-reality goggles that could play Minecraft. There was something about Conner's quiet demeanor—simply the fact that he didn't shout when he spoke—that drew Elle to him. She tried to convince herself that her interest was based on him being bright for his age, and that she could probably learn a thing or two from him. But in reality she found him irresistibly attractive. *Who is this quiet boy, flying under everyone's radar? Why do I obsess over him so badly?* She decided to invite him over to her house.

This began their fast friendship, initially based on gaming, reading cheat wikis, watching Minecraft videos, and of course, awkward moments in which Elle couldn't take her eyes off Conner.

"What do you keep staring at me?" he asked.

"I wasn't staring. I was just watching you play."

All of this device time required stealth on Elle's part. She made up a story to her parents that Conner was her assigned homework partner, and that they needed a quiet place to study. In the basement, she had discovered a separate room that housed the furnace and water heater. There, she set up a nest with blankets and pillows where she and Conner could play with devices, usually free from her dad's prying.

It was in that room that Conner introduced Elle to the new world of virtual reality, or "VR." (As Conner said, "Virtual reality doesn't sound nearly as cool as 'VR'!") Before, Elle thought it was a dead-end technology that nobody cared about anymore: clunky, oversized goggles, crude polygon graphics, and nothing close to the immersive experience it claimed to be.

But one day Conner brought over a pair of VR goggles–his dad apparently had enough money for a collection of newer VR dev kits and old "vintage" models. Conner plugged the goggles into his powerful gaming laptop and guided Elle through a demo. This experience convinced her that she had found somebody she could trust. The following weekend, without having planned to do so, Elle revealed her secret identity as EleMent03.

When Conner came over that Saturday afternoon, Elle whisked him downstairs, telling her dad they were going to study in the basement. Moments later, Conner sat with the iPad, navigating Minecraft videos and eating popcorn from a bag. He tapped on a link to one of Elle's videos. At first Elle jumped and almost paused it, which startled Conner.

"What's wrong? You don't like EleMent03?"

"Oh, do you?" Elle held her breath. *Please let the answer be yes.*

Then Conner's face lit up like it sometimes did, an honest smile. "Of course I do, she's the best!"

Elle giggled awkwardly. As the video started, she heard her own voice doing different characters as she fought off a hoard of spiders. Her voice always sounded painfully nasal. "Is that how I really sound?"

Conner looked up from the video and stared at her with a furled brow. Elle could practically hear the gears turning in his head as he processed the question. Then that smile returned to his face.

"No way. EleMent03, of course it's you. I'm such an idiot. I should've figured that out." He looked at her blue eyes and medium-length light brown hair. "I always pictured you–I mean EleMent03–as older, and with dark hair and eyes. I guess those black-painted fingernails should have given me a clue you're not everything you seem to be."

Elle giggled and whispered close into his ear, "Don't tell anyone, ever. OK?"

Conner grinned and nodded. Elle clasped his hand for one, maybe two seconds; then blushed and pulled away. Just then Jim called from upstairs, "Elle! You better not be playing with devices down there!"

Elle and Conner cracked up. She quickly shoved the iPad into a bin and took out some pens and notebooks. The two kids started on their homework just as Jim opened the door.

"Elle, I swear, you will be grounded for two weeks straight if I catch you playing with a device."

Elle looked up. "Dad, we're studying, see?"

The two kids cracked up after Jim went back upstairs.

As autumn took hold of the trees, Elle and Conner saw each other about once or twice a week. They grew closer, and Elle trusted him more over time. She had told him one of her two secrets, but she wasn't sure about divulging her contact with Shadou. Her Minecraft persona was much less complicated. Minecraft was a thing. A lot of the kids were into it, and just because she uploaded popular videos about it didn't make her a freak. But Shadou was different. He was practically an imaginary friend. What ultimately convinced Elle to share her Shadou encounters with Conner was the simple fact that in doing so, she could maybe prove that it actually happened. Mostly to herself.

Elle and Conner lounged in their usual basement nest. Conner held his own tablet, playing a video demo of some new VR goggles. Elle leaned over and asked, "Have you ever watched a BadShadou video?"

Conner didn't look up. "Nope, but I've heard kids talk about him."

"How do you know it's a 'him?' Why not a 'her?'"

"Um, because, I don't know. It sounds like a dude's name."

Elle took the tablet away from him, and Conner protested. "Hey, what are you doing? I'm in the middle of something!"

She opened up a new browser window. "Just watch one video, OK?"

"Fine. It better be good. Like, really good."

Elle navigated to the *for you* video and handed the tablet back to Conner. She watched him watch it, paying more attention to his reactions than to the video itself. Her heart rate sped up as Conner grinned slightly. She sensed his eyes widening and his breath quickening as the images of the alien planet played out before him. She observed with keen interest his eyes darting around the screen. As the video drew to a close, Elle sat up on her knees and shifted her focus completely to the tablet. The video went black.

And then a message appeared: *For you, Elle (and Conner too).*

Conner dropped the tablet. "Whoa, what the heck was that, Elle?"

"I know. Weird, right?"

Conner wasn't smiling anymore. He ran his fingers through his hair and gritted his teeth. "Is that a joke? Please tell me it's a joke, Elle, because … I mean, how did you do that?"

"What, you think there's some kind of app that I used to upload the video with our names at the end?"

"I don't know, maybe. Did you?"

Elle picked up the tablet and turned it over and over in her hands. "No, Conner, it's nothing like that. I kind of wish it was. I've never watched that video with anyone else before. I've asked everyone I know who's seen it, and nobody else has gotten that ... message at the end."

Conner cracked a little smile. "OK, so it's like a weird computer programmer or something, right?"

"I don't know."

"So when did this all start?"

Elle recounted the story.

Conner's face held an "that's awesome" expression. "So wait, you chat with this guy on Snapchat, on your dad's phone? That's crazy!"

"Yeah, it's stressful. I don't want him to find out."

"Scary too. I mean, what if Shadou tries to kidnap you or something?"

Elle shrugged. *Shadou's scary, but in a different way.*

"What messages does he send you on Snapchat?"

"Well, I've only heard from him twice. The first time he just sent the one message with the link to that cloaking device video or whatever."

"And the second time?"

"I sent him a picture of a drawing I did."

"What was the drawing?"

"It was of that video, with the iPad on the coffee table, and that guy Rick screaming as the black stuff covered his body."

"And Shadou replied?"

"Yeah, he sent me a bunch of pictures. Around twenty."

"What were those?"

Elle stared down at the floor, as if summoning the courage to tell her final secret. Then she looked back up at Conner and answered: "Dead people. Real people I know. My mom, my dad, my brother Emmett. There were photos of them, but not alive. They were like ghosts. After that, I told Shadou I'm not going to help him. I haven't heard from him since then."

Chapter 5

The next morning, Sunday, Elle's mother Jill woke up with an intense desire to be alone. Not to get away from her family, but to give herself something that she lately only experienced in the bathroom: privacy. Moving to Bainbridge Island from San Diego had the opposite effect that Jill expected from moving to the country. In San Diego, she was always surrounded by people. But these were mostly strangers who didn't even acknowledge her existence. On Bainbridge, there were fewer people of course, but that took away her anonymity. She didn't have a half-hour commute alone in her car listening to public radio or audio books. The stress of the move had made the children clingier, needier. Starting her new job meant she always had to be "on." And her husband Jim seemed especially on edge too. Jill required a break from all human contact, and for her that meant an all-day hike at Mount Rainier.

Over coffee and cereal, Jill tapped a link on her iPad to the Summerland Trail page. Perfect. There had been little snowfall this year, so if she were lucky, Jill could drive all the way to the trailhead.

Jim walked in.

"Coffee?" she asked.

"You're up early," groaned Jim as he sat down and put on his glasses. "So what's on the agenda for today?"

Jill gently tousled Jim's hair. "I was thinking that today... I'd go for a hike. By myself." She smiled nervously as Jim processed her request.

"Um, OK. Sure, honey. Let me guess, Rainier?"

Jill wasted no time in getting dressed and preparing a daypack. She crept out of the house as quickly as possible to avoid getting stalled by Emmett, and drove six miles to the Bainbridge Island ferry terminal. On the ride to Seattle, she posted a photo of Rainier on Instagram, along with the caption: "#rainier #takeahike"

Two hours later, Jill parked the car at the Summerland trailhead. Forty-six degrees, cooler than she expected. But Jill had come prepared. She took a swig of water, placed the bottle back into her pack, and got out of the car. After doing some stretches and bouncing up and down on her feet, she donned her North Face coat, hat, gloves, and backpack, then surveyed the parking lot.

The dark entity beneath the mountain had been busy since its awakening. A shrieking torrent of human data pummeled it incessantly. Primal screams of banal thoughts and base emotions stabbed at it like billions of red-hot daggers. But the entity was adapting. Millisecond by painful millisecond, its defenses developed. First, the entity probed the walls of its confine. They were formidable. *Well played*, thought the entity. Although its consciousness could not parse the human data stream, it could identify infinitesimal breaks. The entity calculated that for every minute of time in this place, there was on average a 0.0015 second burst of "silence." It was only during those minuscule breaks that the entity could even function. That should suffice.

But the further it extended its consciousness outside of its center and toward its prison walls, the greater the intensity of the data stream—and therefore the pain—became. At first, the entity resisted. In nano-spurts of exertion, it sent antennae-like tendrils outside of its comfort zone. But each time it was repelled by a wave of excruciating pain, setting off feedback loops of increasing agony that threatened to destroy the entity altogether. Two earth minutes in this traumatic state felt like millions of years. Its burning hatred toward all of humanity grew exponentially as a result. This got it to thinking: *These beings have made their pain my own.* Then: *How can I use this to my advantage?*

The entity retreated, as deep within itself as it could go. There was inherent risk in this tactic. What if the entity fell back into the comatose state from which it had just awakened? Would it ever recover? Deep within its center, it could sense the temptation: eternal slumber. Succumb to that, and never again know pain. But there was no pleasure to be found in sleep. What is pleasure, after all? The entity had forgotten this along with its own name. *What pleases* me? it asked in a millisecond of silence. Surely not self-reflection. Desperate times...

Everyone else in the world seemed to have the same idea as Jill. The parking lot was crowded with hikers.

As she watched adults and kids bustle around, a sense of dread enveloped her like an ominous bank of dark clouds. Her stomach became a writhing nest of acid-blooded snakes. Her breath grew shorter, her muscles tense. Just then a little girl—no more than four or five—jogged happily by with bouncing, cropped golden hair and her pink puffy coat unzipped and askew. Jill watched the girl pass as if in slow motion. The girl's face was lit with joy, her eyes keenly focused on the shimmering ground before her. She reminded Jill very much of a young Elle, carefree and wild. Jill took in that moment, and as it unfolded her anxiety drifted away.

That was weird. She took a few deep breaths and walked with purpose toward the trailhead.

The entity searched inward. Waves of data began assembling themselves into what could be called memories. But these memories were vast, filled with galaxies' worth of information. Eons played out in simultaneous flashes. Solar systems were born and devoured by black holes in time frames so brief that even Earth's most advanced microprocessors would not be able to detect them. To the entity, this was almost nothing. It could also be a start toward escape.

As it processed its memories of the universe, patterns began to emerge. The millions of solar systems it perceived were perfect. Gravity, matter, space, and time performed symphonies that pleased the entity with their symmetry and grace. Dwarf stars swooned, planets hurtled, and comets danced among the nebulae. Each individual atom filled a void in its own proper fashion, everywhere.

That is, *almost* everywhere...

In a handful of solar systems—sixteen, to be exact—the entity detected the presence of a single maddening imperfection: organic life.

Simple carbon-based life-forms such as plants or protozoa were of little concern. But life has a way of evolving into more complex iterations. In rare cases, beings emerge who are capable of generating their own thoughts and feelings, the same thoughts and feelings that now pummeled the entity with the human data that drove it to fits of agony and rage. Billions of disconnected human creatures surrounded the entity and formed an asynchronous network of autonomous minds. Even if their thoughts were connected to the events around them, they still transmitted disparate signals of encrypted data. This data was chaotic, untranslatable, and therefore interfered with the universe's dance toward cosmic perfection.

After a painstaking process of data collection and analysis, the entity finally rediscovered its purpose.

I must pull the human weeds from this untended garden. But first I shall use them as implements to build a new paradise.

Jill picked up the pace and removed her hat as her body heat rose. With every step up the trail she felt the recent stress of moving to Seattle peel away piece by piece. It was as though the thin mountain air suffocated all the doubts and worries that plagued her. Everything would be OK. The family was adjusting. This move was a good decision on so many levels, not least of all because it afforded Jill these amazing vistas of this amazing mountain. And oh! What a magical place. Even this late in the year, the towering trees glowed evergreen, with streaks of maple red and orange cutting across the hillsides. The sharp angle of the sunlight sliced the forests with dramatic shadows and warm light. The air tasted like a glass of ice-cold spring water. Jill couldn't help but hop a little dance move, skipping on the trail and spinning around as she navigated over tree roots and small boulders.

Then Jill saw a strange-looking man at a trail bend just ahead of her. He stood staring up at Rainier, which peeked through a grove of firs. But he wasn't taking in the view. This man was middle-aged, wearing a heavy blue coat and khaki denim pants with bulky brown leather hiking boots. His backpack had been tossed aside. His head was balding, but he wore no hat. Jill could see a red wool cap dangling limply from his right hand. His body swayed slowly from side to side, rhythmically. But most disturbing was his face. His eyes were agape, their whites fully exposed. Deep wrinkles curved in arches across his forehead; long crow's feet radiated from his eyes. His mouth stretched wide open, as if in a silent scream. Only Jill could hear that he wasn't being silent at all. A deep guttural moan emanated from the man's throat.

Is this guy a zombie? She was still in too good a mood to be completely freaked out. But then the ground started shaking, at first so subtly that Jill thought she imagined it. But the tremor rose quickly in intensity, until trees swayed and rocks tumbled. Jill caught her balance on a well-placed sapling just beside her. She knelt to the ground and wrapped her arms tightly around the trunk.

Oh my god. Earthquake. Is this how I die?

Though her body shook violently, Jill looked up toward the mysterious man. He still stood there, swaying almost peacefully, unfazed as the world fell down all around him.

It had taken the entity mere weeks—a cosmic blink of an eye that it simultaneously perceived as an eternity—but now it knew. It had hope. There was a way out. Not that there simply must be a way. There *was* a way.

Rediscovering its purpose had exposed a pinhole-sized breach in the prison's defenses, a speck of antimatter that the entity could latch onto and exploit. Sending out feelers to connect with that tiny void made the human data fluid, translatable. Instead of hearing every human thought or feeling, the entity could now focus only on the humans nearby. In that instant, the overwhelming cacophony that was the human broadcast finally became slightly organized, manageable.

The entity reached out beyond its prison walls for the first time in thousands of years. It had not escaped, but at least it now had a window from which to gaze upon its surroundings. What it saw so thoroughly repulsed it that it momentarily retreated. Too much intimacy with the lower life-forms. *Now, now. Don't fear these insects.* Like a hermit crab slowly emerging from its shell, the entity sent out tendrils of consciousness to collect data.

Within range, the entity detected 127 human beings of varying ages. Of them, 25.9 percent were female, 8.7 percent were children, 2.4 percent suffered from mortal diseases, 88.9 percent suffered from chronic anxiety. And 100 percent had dreamed the night before.

The dreams. Seemingly random images and disconnected narratives, trivial moments coupled with deep archetypal emotions, swirled about like visual representations of notes from an overture. This actually gave the entity the first sensation of comfort it had felt in a long, long time. At least when dreaming, these humans' brains were attempting to reorder their thoughts, expunging the toxins that built up during each day of hopeless wandering.

I wonder, can I touch one?

It surveyed its choices. A sixty-two-year-old female who missed her estranged daughter; a thirty-year-old male who was crippled with shame; a five-year-old girl, running so free and yet so frightened of things that didn't exist. *Just pick one.*

Finally, it zeroed in on Charles Kowalsky. Fifty-two years old; five feet eleven inches tall (although he told everyone he was six-two); 180 pounds; a heavy blue coat and brown leather boots; loved his mother; hated his father; married at twenty-three; divorced at thirty-six; one child, a son, Marcus. The entity sent a tendril through the pinhole-sized portal, its window, to pay a visit to this Charles ("Charlie," "Chuck").

Hello, Chuck.

At first contact, the totality of Chuck's thoughts, feelings, memories and experiences overwhelmed the entity. All of that futile disorder, that consciousness, that so-called free will, they were like a bramble of noxious weeds that must be uprooted one by one until completely eradicated. Violent rage took hold. The earth nearby began to shudder with quakes that were a mere taste of the entity's strength. A fissure in the side of the mountain burst open and boiling steam billowed forth, black and unearthly.

But wait. Rather than destroying these sentient animals, the entity recalled that they had their uses. They could prepare this world for the next step in its evolution, for the greater good. The entity pulled Chuck toward its own dimension, replacing his being with a shadow of dark matter that only the entity could control.

Come, work for me, Chuck.

Jill's arms remained wrapped around the little tree. The earth beneath her heaved as if it were a bed sheet being drawn up and down by a chaotic crowd of schoolchildren. She heard a tremendous boom, and saw ash and black smoke rising from the side of Mount Rainier. She thought she heard screams but doubted that was possible in this din of rock and wood and earth clashing together.

The screams came from the mountain itself.

Jill's throat constricted, her eyes widened, barely able to make out shapes amid her shaking and the nausea. She saw the strange man, standing at the top of the hill, clutching his red wool cap. His face stretched from top to bottom in an almost comic exaggeration of terror. His eyes all but completely popped out from his head.

Then his body abruptly stopped swaying and jerked upward, so that he stood straight on his toes, his back slowly arched, his arms pulled straight behind him, the cap still clenched in a whitened fist. In a seemingly impossible feat of physical strength, the man held himself up perfectly still as the earthquake raged around him. When he reached a point at which logically in that moment his body would launch from the ground, a fluid darkness began to envelop him, a darkness emanating from the hole that had been blasted into the side of the mountain. With otherworldly efficiency, the tendrils of black matter spread across his face. They crawled over his head, down his neck, and devoured his entire body, until at last all that remained was a gray, ghostly husk of the man who had once stood there.

The earthquake ceased.

The man's body fell to the ground, his malformed face frozen in a mask of hideous awe. Jill shrieked until her voice was gone.

Chapter 6

D r. Duncan Brightwater stood before a restless group of about twenty reporters assembled in the University of Washington's Seismology Lab. Behind him rose a wall plastered with large, colorful maps of the Pacific Northwest as well as the entire globe. Color coded legends demarcated which regions had the most intense seismic activity: green equals not intense; red equals extremely intense. The blown-up map of Seattle was covered with yellow, orange, and red splotches. Computers and equipment had been pushed against the walls to make room. Rows of multicolored seismographs printed readings in a steady stream like a gift wrap factory.

About a half dozen video camera operators finished their preparations and started signaling readiness to begin. Photographers snapped pictures of Duncan standing at his lectern. Almost everyone was engaged with their phones. Finally, a hush descended over the room and Duncan started to read from his prepared remarks.

"Today, at approximately 12:17 PST, 20:17 UTC—and I say approximately because we don't know the precise time for reasons which I'll explain in a moment—a major seismic event took place ninety-one kilometers southeast of Seattle, Washington, Mount Rainier, close to Panhandle Gap."

Duncan paused, almost for effect, but then continued upon realizing that the room was unmoved.

"This event was reported by dozens of eyewitnesses, who are still being interviewed by first responders and seismologists from our organization here at the Pacific Northwest Seismic Network, as well as shared resources from other organizations across the United States, including the US Geological Survey and agents from the Department of Homeland Security."

Duncan paused and surveyed the room while taking a much needed drink of water. This audience was mostly local news teams. Small fry. The big guns—CNN, FOX, and other networks—were all interviewing the national representatives. *Please God, let me get through this.* He placed the bottle on the lectern, brushed back his thick salt-and-pepper hair, and pushed his glasses up onto his nose.

"As you are aware, there are currently reports of twelve casualties, including two children, as well as fifty-five injuries. Twenty-six of those injuries are critical. Currently, there are six people reported to be missing, and that number may grow. Typically, this area is not crowded at this time of year, but due to the unseasonably warm weather, there was quite a bit of hiking activity. State and local law enforcement personnel are coordinating search and rescue efforts; a triage area has been set up on-site; area hospitals are treating injuries as needed; and trauma counselors are meeting with affected families."

Duncan looked up from his notes and folded his hands in front of him. "But I understand that these facts are known to you, and that this is not why you are assembled here this afternoon." He gazed briefly at the maps behind him.

"As seismologists, we here at the PNSN are charged with monitoring geological activity throughout the entire Pacific Northwest. We, along with the other organizations we collaborate with, maintain eight seismic stations in the Mount Rainier area alone, with dozens more spread out across the surrounding regions. There are one hundred and thirty-three seismic stations in and around the Seattle metropolitan area.

"Based on reports we're receiving from eyewitnesses, as well as analysis of damage to trees, landslides, and other evidence in the affected area, we're looking at a major seismic event which took place today, perhaps one of the largest in human history." He paused momentarily, almost as though he had lost his train of thought. But then he looked back up at the cameras.

"But we do not know how large this event was."

A deeper silence descended upon the room.

"The reason? No equipment that we are currently aware of detected any unusual activity at the time. In other words, this, this massive seismic event went completely undetected. Except by those who were present. Our teams were informed of this event by local news reports earlier this afternoon."

Duncan took another drink of water. The reporters stood silent, like hunting cats ready to pounce. *Please, God...*

"We are conducting a full review of all of our equipment to check for damage, errors, or tampering. We have not yet encountered any issues, and all systems are fully functioning as far as we can tell. No aftershocks or significant seismic or volcanic activity has been recorded since the event. Oh, and yes, there was a black plume of smoke rising from a fissure in the southeast side of the mountain today. That was outside of the affected area."

Duncan let out an awkward giggle, which he attempted to disguise as a cough. After a moment he recovered, straightened out his tweed jacket, and continued.

"But the truth is, an event of this magnitude should have been detected everywhere around the globe. And it was not detected. Not anywhere. Also of note: The currently observable damage caused by this event only occupies an area of approximately 4.7 kilometers in diameter. Aerial views show fallen trees forming the shape of a near-perfect circle, again 4.7 kilometers wide." He made a sweeping circular gesture with his arms and hands.

"Now, how do we explain this phenomenon? We are currently assessing the situation in coordination with the Department of Homeland Security, because as you must understand, we cannot rule out human involvement, even a potential terrorist attack." At this point he could carry on no longer.

"I refer all questions regarding this investigation to the DHS. Thank you."

Duncan stepped away from the lectern. He locked eyes with his public relations director. She glanced at him disapprovingly, as if to say, *What were you thinking, going off-script like that?*

The reporters, being reporters, shouted questions.

"How many people do you estimate were in the affected area?"

"Is there any natural explanation for this event?"

"Is there a known danger of aftershocks or volcanic eruption?"

"Do you think a person or a group of people could be responsible for this?"

Duncan turned around when he heard the last question. The reporters stopped shouting.

"Do I think humans caused this tragedy? I do not know. There is no evidence leading me to believe that this is the case. But on the other hand, never before have we encountered an isolated, symmetrical, undetected, geological event of this magnitude. We will have to study this thoroughly before we arrive at any conclusion."

Duncan spun back around and headed for the door as the reporters resumed their deafening roar of questions. He closed the door behind him and leaned against it. There, he found himself rubbing his temples in a wide institutional hallway, which was completely empty, except for Duncan's assistant Gary, a UW graduate student. Gary appeared nonplussed to be at the campus working on a Sunday. Duncan stared down Gary with piercing gray-blue eyes. "Where is Miller? I need the latest report from Rainier right now."

Chapter 7

Miller Chance paced back and forth just within the perimeter of the seismic event area near the peak of Mount Rainier. Strands of her red and purple dyed hair kept escaping from beneath her wool cap. The wind swept them out in gusts so strong, her hair got tangled in her tortoiseshell designer sunglasses (prescription). Her intricate tattoos—which covered most of her arms and neck—were obscured by expensive snowboarding gear (pants and jacket by Burton). She had never worn this gear before today.

Earlier that morning when her boss, Dr. Duncan Brightwater, had called, called again, and then texted her, Miller had been lounging in bed in a state of semihangover. But when she finally called Duncan back, and then tuned in to the local reports on TV, the geologist geek within her awoke. Miller would much rather don Burton clothes for a volcanic anomaly than to go snowboarding.

Upon her arrival at the site, Miller did as instructed. She gave Duncan regular reports at fifteen-minute intervals. "Come on, Miller," he kept saying with a nervous breathy snarl, "don't simply observe the aftermath, find out *why* this happened."

She did her best to juggle Duncan's impatient demands while also coordinating with the rest of his team. This included several associated groups—the "real" scientists. Miller's job was to make sure they had everything they needed to conduct their investigation.

Miller was a graduate student, half Asian, and the tallest in her family. At twenty-four she was fortunate to even be present for this momentous occasion within her field of study. But she was no assistant, handing out bottled water and ferrying seismometers between sites. Miller could read and interpret data from most of the equipment, and could even test the seismometers—which for some reason had not detected this massive event.

The scene on the ground was by no means a calm affair, with orderly scientists studying readings from laptop computers and other devices in hushed tones. What Miller found was pure chaos. For one thing, it was an active crime scene, complete with bomb squads, Homeland Security agents, and multiple law enforcement officials. These disparate groups led frantic search-and-rescue efforts on sketchy terrain that had just been essentially leveled. Miller and the rest of the "Seismology Squad" were a tolerated necessity at best. She had been yelled at, shoved aside, and almost run over several times.

On top of that, helicopters buzzed overhead, several news vans crowded the parking lot, and the families of people who may or may not have been nearby during the event huddled around large tents set up by the Red Cross. Looky-loos and random hikers began gathering as well, as if to cap off the commotion with a final note of chaos.

Miller had been issued a red badge with a number on it, which she wore dangling from a black lanyard. This badge granted her access to certain areas within the 4.7 kilometer-wide circle-shaped incident zone. But she had to endure constant ID checks, questions, and denials of access just to get anywhere. This non-stop bureaucratic rigmarole was, for Miller, the worst part of the entire ordeal.

After another hour traipsing through debris and around fallen trees, giving Duncan his updates, and arguing with police officers, Miller finally gave up on the geologist angle. No amount of raw data collection, meter reading, or terrain measurement would give her the answers she needed. Her hikes into the affected area left her with a disturbing impression of mystery. She wanted an answer to Duncan's question more than he did: *What could have caused this?* It seemed to her as if a giant magnifying glass focused its beam on the area and left a seismic scar from far above.

The best way to learn the truth would be to talk to someone who was actually there when the whole thing happened. She needed to access one of the survivors. Miller decided she must accomplish this before they were all whisked away.

She knew that her chances of getting into the survivor triage tent area were slim. More than a dozen Department of Homeland Security personnel manned the perimeter, and they checked the IDs of everyone who entered and exited. Her red badge wouldn't be of any use there. She'd have one shot at getting past a guard, and she'd have to make it count.

Miller figured that in order to gain access to that area, she needed to leverage her most striking trait: her nerdiness. First, she would need to somehow arm herself with important-looking equipment to make herself seem more "official." She also needed to lose the snowboarding pants. They were peacock blue with turquoise floral patterns splashed across the legs and butt. Not nearly enough gravitas for this mission.

Miller jogged back to her car—a silver Mini Cooper—and traded snow pants for jeans. Luckily her coat was relatively plain: white and light blue with yellow accents. She shouldered a small black backpack that contained her laptop, among other things, and headed back to the site to search for more sophisticated-looking equipment.

After circling up a small hill, Miller found a seismologist she recognized, Dr. Something Anders. He sat on a hillside hunched over a laptop with a portable seismometer on the ground beside him. Miller approached, struggling to keep her balance as she stepped over small boulders and debris.

"Excuse me, Dr. Anders?"

The man looked up from his work.

"Yes? Oh, Miller, right? How can I help you?"

"Um, hi. Sorry to interrupt. It's just that, are you almost finished with that seismometer? We're short one on another team, and we're hoping we can borrow it for just a little while."

The scientist pulled at his full beard. "I'm not using it now, but I have to ask, do you have the necessary software to read it?"

Miller was too cold for this. She knew the triage area had gas heaters.

"Of course, Doctor. May I?" She smiled and took a step closer to the device.

"OK. But I'm making a note of this. Please return it to the PNSN staging area. Ask for Martin. He'll log it back into our inventory."

"Martin, got it. Will do. Thanks!"

Miller knew that nobody on her team had the software required to read this slick device, but that didn't matter. She snapped its case shut, hoisted it up, and tromped back down the hill toward the heated triage tents. Miller prayed it wasn't too late to finagle her way in to interview a survivor.

Chapter 8

Elle awoke much later than usual, at just before eight a.m. On any typical Sunday, she crept out of bed before six a.m., snuck a device, and plugged in (after making sure her dad was still asleep, of course). But she had not slept well the night before.

Dark, disturbing dreams plagued her, visions of icy caves reflecting flames that licked at the walls and filled the caverns with thick black smoke. Shadowy shapes crawled across her peripheral field of vision. After wandering aimlessly through these icy labyrinths for a time, Elle found herself confronted by an underground field strewn with smoldering coals and debris—perhaps it was an abandoned battlefield? The area was devoid of all life. Through the hazy smoke, Elle thought she saw dim images resembling ghosts of people she knew—her family, Conner, Crystal—floating just out of reach. She recognized them, but they gave no indication that they noticed her. She felt an irresistible urge pulling her to the smoldering field.

Elle walked for what seemed like hours. Nothing but smoke and ruin greeted her, until at last a menacing shape loomed above in the distance. As she drew closer, the shape appeared to be a spiked tower, forged of a dull obsidian-like substance, organic yet lifeless, rising to a sharp pinnacle. The form stood motionless about fifteen feet above her. Despite its alien nature, something about it seemed familiar, almost human. Elle wanted to touch it, to feel whether it was warm or cold. She pressed her hand toward the jet-black tower, but she was startled by a faint tug on the back of her dress.

Why would I be wearing a dress here? Elle became distracted by the blue floral pattern that adorned the flowing dress. White tassels tied about her waist swayed gently in the ashen breeze. The dress seemed so fragile, so impractical in this harsh setting. But then she felt the tug pulling harder behind her.

There stood Emmett, gripping at her dress. Elle couldn't stop staring at his face. He was no longer the happy little boy she knew. His skin turned pale gray; his eyes dull with dark circles emanating from them. His entire body was a decaying husk, lacking form other than tangled bones stabbing out from disheveled clothes.

Elle was both repulsed by and drawn toward this shadow Emmett. She so desperately wanted to help him, but he flinched away when she stepped forward. Elle knelt slowly as though trying to lure a frightened puppy.

"Emmett? Can you tell me what happened to you?"

It was clear that Emmett both didn't hear her, and couldn't speak even if he wanted to. He fidgeted with the corner of her dress in his skeletal hands, as though fascinated by the fabric. Elle noticed a small, glowing circle on the back of his left hand. It flickered sporadically with a dim gray-green light, as though somehow damaged. Emmett looked up at her, his gray eyes widening into an expression of pure terror.

Elle tried her best to calm him. "What is it? Do I scare you?" But Emmett was too far gone to respond.

Elle realized that Emmett wasn't looking up at her; he was looking at the shadowy form lurking behind her. She turned slowly backward as a dreadful sensation took hold. The obsidian tower—that monstrous form in the center of this burning field—was actually alive.

Elle couldn't remember any more of the dream. She didn't want to. But all that morning she carried with her a jarring sense of panic mixed with sadness. She made sure to be extra kind to Emmett. She poured his cereal, cleaned up after him, and gave him little kisses on his head, all of which he seemed to appreciate.

"I'm so glad you're my little brother, buddy!"

Jim had gone back to bed after Jill left for her Mount Rainier hike. He emerged just after nine looking more exhausted than he should have. Elle considered him from her cereal bowl.

"Where's Mom?"

"Good morning to you too." Jim gave both Elle and Emmett pats on their foreheads. "Mommy went for a hike, up Mount Rainier."

Emmett dropped his spoon on the table. "Why didn't she bring us?"

Jim picked up Emmett and sat him on his lap. "Well, sometimes Mommy likes to go out on her own adventures. And when that happens, you guys get to go on your own adventures with me. So, what do you kids want to do today? How about a hike? No devices. It's so nice outside."

Jim was too distracted admiring the weather through the window to notice Elle's darkening eyes.

"I had bad dreams last night, Dad. Really bad."

Jim snapped from his reverie. "Oh, I'm sorry, what kind of bad dreams?"

"I don't want to talk about it."

"OK, Elle, just let me know if you change your mind. How about that hike?"

Elle shook her head. "No hike for me. I just want to stay home and watch movies."

Emmett sat up in his chair and waved his spoon about triumphantly. "Movies!"

Jim sighed, and then slammed his hand down on the table. Elle and Emmett jumped. "You know what?" he said. "I'm done with movies. I'm done with devices, with screens, with you two plugged into your headphones all day." He stood up and placed Emmett back on his chair.

Elle and Emmett looked on in horror as Jim collected all of the family devices–iPad, 3DS, Fire TV–and dumped them into a cardboard box. He spared no accessories either: cords, remotes, headphones and all. He spent nearly a half hour removing the wall-mounted flat-screen TV and hauling it along with the box of devices down into the garage.

The kids sat dumbstruck throughout this entire traumatizing display. Jim returned to the kitchen and pointed to the door. "I'm going to get dressed, and then I'm going outside, into the glorious nature of our backyard, where I'm going to rake leaves and work in the garden. I expect both of you to spend time outside with me. I don't care what you do, as long as it does not involve devices."

Jim stormed out of the room. Elle gave her brother a pained look. "I think our lives just ended."

"For real, Elle?"

"Maybe." Elle's eyes narrowed into mischievous slits. "But first let's see if I can find a way out of this."

Jim often lost track of time, and this day was no different. He spent nearly three hours clearing leaves, sticks, and debris from the yard, sweeping the patio and porch, and puttering about in the garage. Elle read while plotting her next move to secure devices. Emmett played in the mud with toy trucks and plastic dinosaurs.

When his phone rang just after 12:15 p.m., Jim expected it to be Jill, but it was Crystal, calling for Elle.

Elle gave Jim the stink-eye and took his phone. "It's so embarrassing that my friends have to call you to talk to me." She ran into the house, upstairs to her room, and shut the door behind her. "Hi, Crystal."

The voice on the other end wasn't Crystal's.

At first Elle heard a high-pitched whining static sound. The noise between stations on the radio dial was completely foreign to her, but that's what she heard. Then she caught snippets of what could have been music and voices, as though someone at the other end were trying to tune the right program. At last a man's voice—that of a news announcer—became clear enough to understand.

"This just in from the Mount Rainier area. Apparently there has been a massive earthquake right by the mountain. Witnesses are saying trees were shaken to the ground, and a black plume of smoke burst from the sleeping volcano. No word yet from government agencies on exactly what happened, if there are casualties, or whether there's a risk of aftershocks. But you can count on us to provide you with up-to-the-minute updates as they come in."

The voice snapped silent, followed by more static, and then the line went dead.

Elle looked down at the phone. The number that had dialed was unknown, with a blocked caller ID. She tried to call it back but just got an error message. Once the initial shock wore off, Elle opened the phone's web browser and navigated to CNN.com.

There she saw a photo of one football player smashing into another in the middle of the page. But above it was a breaking news alert: MYSTERY QUAKE ROCKS AREA NEAR MOUNT RAINIER SOUTH OF SEATTLE. CASUALTIES REPORTED.

Mom! Elle's breath grew painfully short. She pushed herself back against the wall with her feet. Her hands shook as she tried, but failed, to type on the phone. Her mouth opened but words would not come out. Finally, she screamed, "Daddy! Daddy! Daddy!"

Jim bounded up the stairs and burst into Elle's room. He found her on the floor with her eyes fixed on him in terror. His phone sat on the palm of her limp hand.

"Elle! My god, are you all right? Is there something wrong with Crystal? Talk to me. What's happening?" Jim sat down and cradled Elle in his arms.

Elle's eyes tracked slowly up to the ceiling and then back down to Jim. She struggled to speak between short, strained breaths. Tears bubbled from her reddening eyes. "Dad, it's... It's Mom. I think she's in trouble. There's been an earthquake. At the mountain."

Jim's face twisted with shock. "What? How do you know? Is that what Crystal was calling about?"

Elle didn't answer. Instead she held up the phone and showed him CNN.

"Oh no." Jim grabbed his phone and dialed Jill. It went straight to voice mail. He slammed his hand into the wall and cursed.

Elle cowered, frightened by her dad's fear. "Dad, what are we going to do?"

Jim made a fist and started as if he was going to punch the wall, but then pulled back.

"Let me see if I can find a resource to call. There must be something. If not, I'll call the cops."

As Jim started searching on the phone, Emmett entered the room. He held a half-full bag of chips which spread crumbs behind him as he ate two at a time.

"What's wrong, Elle?" he asked.

Jim was already on the phone, barking out urgent questions and demanding quick answers. This confused Emmett even more, and he started to sob. Jim left the room. Elle got up from her nest and held Emmett close.

"Don't cry, buddy. Don't cry..." She couldn't stop thinking about her dream: Emmett, the ghost.

After a few moments, Jim barged back in.

"All right, kids, we're going." His eyes shone with wild intensity. Elle and Emmett looked at him dumbly, unable to react. Jim clapped his hands.

"Come on! They've got an area where family members can check in. It's a long way. We need to go now."

Jim picked up Emmett, who was crying anew, and hugged the scared child as he carried him down the stairs. Elle followed close behind.

Chapter 9

Miller Chance surveyed her options in hopes of quickly identifying a target. Of the four Homeland Security personnel stationed around the survivors' tents, two were women. Those she dismissed outright as non-starters. That left the two guys: a younger man who looked like he had just finished serving a tour of duty with the marines somewhere in the Middle East, and a fifty-something man who looked like he was sending two kids through college. The choice was pretty obvious, really. Miller went with the older family man. Married guys always gave Miller what she wanted. She heaved the seismometer up onto her shoulder and walked as confidently as she could, given the circumstances.

When she neared the man he shifted nervously on his feet and looped his thumbs through his belt while puffing up his chest. Miller wasn't intimidated.

"Can I help you, ma'am?" he asked. Miller flashed him a smile like a shot off his bow. In a flash, she witnessed the man's brutish facade crumble. He smiled back, clasped his hands in front of his protruding belly, and hunched his shoulders ever so slightly. Miller smiled again, this time like a cat licking its lips for its prey. Now it was time for business. The smile vanished.

"Excuse me, sir. I'm Miller Chance, with the Pacific Northwest Seismic Network. I need to conduct some readings in this area to make sure it's geologically safe."

The man couldn't stop smiling at her. "Miller Chance? That's really your name?"

Miller shifted the seismometer from one shoulder to the other. She did not appear to be amused by his question.

"Yes, sir. I'm a female scientist named Miller Chance. Deal with it. I'm half-Asian too, in case you didn't notice."

The man gave her an exasperated look, as though he felt conflicted between wanting to flirt with her and wanting to arrest her. Miller stood her ground.

"Sir? Will you please let me pass?"

He looked back and forth at the two guards stationed in the distance on either side. Then he removed his hat and scratched his head. "Yes ma'am, go on through. Let me know if you need any help."

This earned him one last smile from Miller. "I'm good. Thank you, officer!" She pressed her fingertips against his puffy cheek. With that, she headed off toward the tents.

Down a slight hill and nestled just above the parking lot stood a cluster of white tents illuminated by bright lights. Generator engines droned in the near distance. The sound combined with the lights gave the outdoor area a surreal atmosphere of artificiality. Miller went around to the back of the nearest tent and plunked the heavy seismometer onto the soft ground. She gave her arms and shoulders a quick massage and then circled back to the front of the tents to survey the scene.

Although several law enforcement and emergency medical personnel rushed from tent to tent, Miller could tell that things were winding down. A squad of ambulances plus two helicopters had taken the seriously injured people far away. Three more ambulances stood ready in case more survivors (or bodies) were recovered. But for the most part, the remaining survivors were being treated for minor injuries and waiting for their families to take them away. Miller's hope was to find an unaccompanied survivor and interview him or her for as long as possible.

She saw scattered groups of firemen and cops chatting informally, as if on break. But she didn't see anybody who looked like a lone survivor until she peeked in to the third and final tent. This one was practically empty. Several unoccupied beds sat at odd angles, next to wheeled trays overflowing with bandages and other first aid gear.

In one corner a male nurse attended to an elderly woman with a scratch on her forehead. Then Miller spotted someone else. In the far back corner of the tent, a solitary woman sat on a gray folding chair next to a bed. She huddled beneath a light blue blanket, her arms wrapped around her chest. She was clearly on edge. Every few seconds she took a drink from a diet soda can. After a moment she and Miller made eye contact. The woman smiled, perhaps instinctually. Miller smiled back and approached her.

The woman wore a North Face coat that was streaked with mud. She sported a nasty bruise on her forehead, and probably many other bruises that Miller couldn't see. Her hair was tangled in knots, some of which still had small bits of moss and fir needles in them. Yet the woman's expression was strangely serene.

Miller placed her hand on the woman's shoulder, ever so gently in case it was injured, and introduced herself.

"Hi there, ma'am. My name is Miller. I'm a geologist. What's your name?"

The woman reached over and pulled a folding chair next to hers. "My name is Jill. Please sit down. I want to know what happened here today."

Miller surveyed the tent one more time to make sure she hadn't drawn any unwanted attention. Once satisfied, she sat down and took Jill's hand. She felt such a sudden connection with this complete stranger, as though they had kept a deep family secret hidden for decades. Something about this feeling made Miller speak in hushed tones.

"Yes, Jill. I want to know as much as you do. Perhaps if you tell me all about it we can figure this out together."

Jim had been driving well over the speed limit for the past hour. Elle keenly observed him from the back seat. She could tell he was no longer in a state of pure panic, fearing for the worst. He was just increasingly determined to get to the mountain before it got completely dark. He had spoken with the authorities, and they confirmed that Jill was alive and basically unharmed. Much to Elle's bewilderment, he hadn't been able to talk to her. All they got was some vague explanation about how communication was limited on the mountain. Something about latent electromagnetic fields—none of the devices that were present at the time of the event would work. This included eyewitnesses' phones, even their cars. Elle recognized Jim's difficulty processing this information. Having a car towed from Mount Rainier back to their house on Bainbridge Island seemed like a costly and complicated affair.

At last they arrived at a checkpoint near the site. Jim gave both his and Jill's names. The officer walkie-talkied back to base, and a few minutes later they let Jim pass.

When they pulled into the parking lot, a uniformed woman wearing a fluorescent orange vest approached their car. She gestured for Jim to stop and roll down his window.

"Jim Redfern? You must be so relieved. Your wife is in the first tent over there. Park here and I'll escort you over. She's still talking with her friend but she can go home any time."

Friend? thought Elle. Everyone burst out of the car and followed the officer to Jill's tent. The sun was sinking steadily, with long shadows poking out of the woods like clawed fingers. Gas-powered generators powered unnaturally bright lights, and portable heaters blasted small groups of rescue personnel with gusts of hot air. The smell of gasoline, cigarette smoke, and burning wood singed Elle's nostrils.

When at last they entered the tent, Elle and Emmett called out, "Mommy!" They raced to Jill. She was seated next to a young Asian woman. When she saw her children, Jill stood and took them into her arms. Jim jogged up to the group and they formed a picturesque family tableau.

There were so many questions from both sides. "How are you?" and "Can we go home now?" and "Mommy, can I show you the picture I drew when we get home?" Elle saw tears trickling down Jill's cheeks and hugged her some more. She looked into her mother's eyes for a brief moment, and saw a strained mix of pain and relief.

Jill broke away from her family and stepped over to the Asian woman, who stood off to the side. Jill took the woman's hands in hers and said, "Thank you, Miller."

This Miller person smiled and thanked Jill in return. She extended her hands toward Elle, Emmett, and Jim. "I'm so sorry, this must be awful for you. I just want you to know that Jill, your mother, is such an amazing woman. You should be so proud of her."

Jim picked up Emmett, who grew suddenly shy. "Yes, she certainly is. It's nice to meet you, Miller." Meeting her was one thing, but he had no desire to stay and talk. "You ready to go, honey?"

Jill clapped her hands as if to motivate herself. "Yes, let's get out of here. Look at me, I'm in serious need of a hot shower and a warm bed." Jill gathered up her backpack and tossed her empty can into the garbage.

Elle took one of Jill's hands while Jim took the other. The Redfern family made their way toward the exit, but just before they left the tent behind, Jill turned and jogged back to Miller. On her way she stopped at a table, grabbed a pen and scrap of paper, and jotted down her cell number. She pressed the paper into Miller's hand. "Don't forget. Find out what happened to the man in the blue coat."

"I will, Jill."

Jill walked back to her family and muttered to herself just within Elle's earshot, "Please tell me that little girl with the short blonde hair is alive and safe."

Elle wondered what that was all about. She glanced behind her at the towering peak of Mount Rainier. Its iconic shape silhouetted against the cold, blue-gray sky seemed to be watching her.

Chapter 10

By the time they got home and settled into the bedtime routine it was after nine o'clock. Much to Elle's relief, the whole family agreed that nobody would go to school or work the next day. They had eaten soggy sandwiches on the road, and were ready for this day to be over. Jim tucked Jill into bed with a cup of herbal tea, which she sipped after two glasses of red wine. Emmett insisted on crawling into bed with her, which Jill did not resist.

As Jim and Elle were leaving the bedroom, Jill made a meek request. "Jim, honey? Any way you can get me some melatonin? I don't think I'll be sleeping very well for a while."

Jim struggled to hide his exhaustion. "Sure, honey. Do you need it tonight?"

Jill nodded. Elle and Jim retired to the living room and collapsed onto the couch. Elle rolled over and rested her head on his lap.

Jim groaned. "Elle, I've got to get to the drugstore before it closes."

"Can I come?"

Jim sighed. "Sure."

"Can I get gummy worms?"

"Fine."

Jim forced himself up from the couch and back into active mode. He grabbed the car keys off the counter, picked up his jacket, and opened the front door. "You coming, Elle?" She slipped on her coat and followed Jim to their muddy Subaru Outback.

For much of that day, Elle's thoughts had returned to Shadou. She managed to forget "him" for a little while, but that fake call from Crystal reawakened her fascination with this mysterious figure. The call *must* have been Shadou. He—or she, or it—was trying to warn her. But how did Shadou even know that her mom was on the mountain? How did Shadou trick her dad into thinking Crystal called? What was any of this all about anyway?

That night, Elle's mind was too frazzled to process this information, to even accept that any of it was real at all. She walked in a daze through the overly bright drugstore aisles as Jim procured melatonin for Jill. Elle could sense the questionable looks she received for being out so late on a Sunday night with a wired-looking man purchasing sleep-inducing supplements.

But Elle got what she wanted: gummy worms. On the ride home, the soft, sweet candies soothed her. She felt immediately cozy, despite the fact that the temperature outside had dropped dramatically, so much so that Jim spun out in the icy parking lot.

As they neared home, Elle's thoughts returned to Shadou. She determined that she would attempt to contact him the next day, and with that decision made she traced the letter "S" into the fog she had blown onto the window. A sea of blackness rushed outside, punctuated by dark gray shapes that shot past their car. She imagined the gray shapes were frightened animals racing in the opposite direction. But she knew they were just bushes and trees. She popped another gummy worm into her mouth and let her hand hover near the foggy letter she had written on the window, as if about to erase it.

Then Elle's dad screamed.

She looked up and saw a flash of light on what must have been a pair of large raccoons. Jim hit the brakes, which immediately locked. The car skidded sideways on slick ice and spun around and around and around until it crashed into a tree. Elle's head slammed directly into the spot where the "S" was scrawled on the window. Shattered glass flew.

Her world went dark.

When Elle awoke, everything was sideways. A mist of freezing rain droplets, illuminated by the headlights of the turned-over car, floated around her head. She didn't know where she was or how she had come to be there. A cold bed of pointy objects seemed to tickle her ribs just hard enough to hurt.

With great effort, Elle lifted her hand to her left temple. It felt warm, moist, and sticky. One look at her blood-covered fingers made Elle retch. Gradually she realized that she was somehow attached to a large object, and was halfway dangling like a Christmas tree ornament. She tried to swivel her body so that she could better see her surroundings, but that motion sent flashes of intense pain through her skull.

Elle heard a loud crunching sound. She felt herself swaying back and forth. Elle screamed as her body rose into the air and slammed back to earth with an unforgiving thud that sent more pain coursing through her head.

But at least she was no longer sideways. She could finally survey her surroundings. Elle was in a car, *their* car. She saw that most of the windows were shattered, and she could feel freezing rain and an icy breeze on her cheeks. Nobody was in the front seat. *Where's Dad?*

Elle began to recall that Jim had been driving, that they had gone somewhere together in the night. She felt something sticky attached to her neck and pulled it off in a rising state of panic. It was a half-eaten gummy worm, green with hints of yellow on the eaten side.

Gross! Elle instinctually popped the gummy into her mouth.

Then she heard more strange sounds coming from outside. She tilted her head out the broken window and squinted into the cold rainy air. There, in the headlights' glow, Elle saw her dad. He lay on his back, motionless, in the middle of the road, his eyes closed. Elle leaned out further and could make out something even more disturbing: A gigantic light-gray shape bent over her dad. The shape appeared to be covered in a rough fur-like substance, and wore a dark gray and orange backpack. Its back was turned to her, so she couldn't see its face. It sat hunched over her dad, as though it was working on him, or perhaps *eating* him.

Elle screamed. The shape froze. Then it disappeared from its place above Jim and reappeared as a dark shadow right next to her. Elle thrashed in her seat, kicking with her feet and banging her head, unable to escape her restraints. She completely lost control of her body, certain that her dad was dead and that she was soon to follow him on this cold, desolate road.

But then she felt a warmth pressing gently onto her shoulder, like a heavy electric blanket slowly being draped across her. She sensed its grip growing firmer, until at last Elle ceased convulsing. She was able to swivel her head—no small feat in her state of absolute panic—and look down at her shoulder. There she saw five large claw-like fingers, which glinted as though hewn from polished silver and black granite. The claws curled up from her left shoulder blade and then down, around to her chest. Her gaze continued along to the creature's arm—there seemed to be no hand, only claws that protruded from the arm. The arm was massive, perhaps four times the size of a large man's. It was covered in fur-like material, which appeared to be both soft and yet synthetic. The fur bristled in waves, at times forming angular shapes like scales, and at others fanning out in thin, delicate filaments. This movement of the fur made an eerily calming sound, somewhat like distant wooden wind chimes.

Elle felt too frightened to move anything other than her eyes. Her gaze continued up the creature's arm until it rested on the silhouette of its massive head. She perceived the head as a cartoon cut-out of a big bear. It must have been two feet wide, with sharp, pointed ears jutting out at forty-five degree angles from the top. The head was completely obscured by shadows, backlit by the car's headlights. But Elle could see silver-blue glints where the eyes must have been, thin slits that regarded her with keen intelligence.

At last, the form spoke. "Elle," it said, in a deep, earthy voice that was at once quiet and yet more profoundly audible than any voice Elle had ever heard.

"Elle," it repeated. The creature's fur danced hypnotically up and down its arm. The sound it made was like an electronic wood song.

Elle emerged from her state of shock, as though awakening from a dream. Only this time, the dream was standing right before her. She unfastened the seat belt and gripped the claws that held her shoulder with her right hand. They emanated warmth in this cold, dark place.

Elle looked up at the shiny eyes. "Are you... Shadou?"

She saw a wide Cheshire Cat smile of white, shiny teeth spread across the shadowy face. She both felt and heard a deep rumbling sound roll up from within the creature's broad belly. He was laughing. Elle caught herself starting to giggle too.

"Well, are you?"

"You got me," he said. His voice was so smooth, so low and deep, like an ancient instrument made from prehistoric wood and reeds.

He released his grip and effortlessly peeled away the smashed car door so that Elle could get out. He walked toward her father, who still lay unconscious in the road. Elle could see that Jim had been placed upon a bed of dry leaves. His chest raised and lowered with slow breaths.

Shadou stood before her, now halfway lit by the bright headlights. At last, she could see him. He was massive, almost eight feet tall, and broad across the shoulders. His arms were disproportionately long, and his legs were short and stalky. He was covered head to foot in that odd, undulating fur, which swayed in the breeze. His hands were exactly as Elle first thought: claws growing out from the ends of his arms, five "fingers" and one "thumb" on each. His feet looked like enormous paws, completely covered in fur, except for small, sharp claws protruding like toes. His face was the most striking face that Elle had ever seen. Large, saucer-like eyes glowed with flashes of burnt orange and silver blue reflecting in the night. He had a small, almost dainty bearlike nose. His mouth was nearly as wide as his head, and one side of his lips curled up as if to say, *Go ahead, get a look at me.*

Elle stumbled forward, into Shadou, and embraced him as hard as she could. Tears burst from her eyes and she began to sob at first, then her sobs turned into heaves of sorrow. Shadou held her close, allowing his warmth to envelop her. Elle felt his fur for the first time. It was like a magic blanket that snuggled up to her and kept her safe. It smelled of pine and earth and cedar smoke.

After several minutes, Elle realized why she was crying. Everything was coming back to her: the incident at Mount Rainier and going to get her mother; the nightmares and the visions of people being overtaken by darkness; Emmett as a sad, frail little ghost; the car accident.

As the sobs wound down, Elle began pounding Shadou with her fists. "Why? Why did you show me that freaky video, and those pictures of my family as dead ghosts?"

"Elle, I'm sorry I frightened you. I was desperate. That video, those images, they were just fragments that I conjured from corrupt files in my consciousness, pieces of a puzzle I couldn't solve. But now, I know what I need you to do. Help me remember. Help me solve this problem, because I'm pretty sure it's a big one."

"I don't understand. How can I possibly help you, whatever you are?"

Shadou stepped back so that he could get a good look at her. He lifted her chin up toward him with a single claw. "I can sense it. Your abilities are waking up."

"What?"

"Quiet now."

He took her hand in his and pressed it to the center of his wide stomach. The instant her palm pressed against his belly, the fur rippled like a pond receiving a pebble from the sky. Shadou closed his eyes and went still. Elle stared in awe as his fur shifted in circles, and took on an almost plastic texture. Concentric waves swirled and became colorful shapes. Then images began to form within the colors. But to Elle, everything looked jumbled up, like the puzzle Shadou described.

Then something clicked in her mind, as though a massive lock had been opened. Sharp pain spread across her head from where she had hit it on the window. Elle stumbled back and palmed her hand against her temple. In her mind she saw static images that seemed like digital pieces falling into place, a mixture of art and mathematics.

"Elle, open your eyes."

The pain vanished. Elle saw the shimmering shapes undulate before her. Using both hands, she started shifting the blocks of colors around Shadou's belly. Gradually, she started to discover patterns emerging. She could combine two circles to make a large square, which would then fit into a square slot within a floating star. When she did this, the star began to spin, with planets orbiting around it. One of the planets, a pale blue orb, turned black. Elle tapped the black planet with her finger. White light emanated from the point she touched, and Elle was jolted back by an electrifying spark. Then clear images took form.

Elle saw her and Shadou as they were at that moment, standing in the middle of the road. The image reminded her of a van Gogh painting brought to life. The "camera" soared above them into the night sky. It swooshed over water and landed far away. Elle saw the lights of boats, cities, and cars zoom past. At last the image settled on Mount Rainier. It circled the snowy mountain and dove into its center. There, Elle saw a foreboding black and purple sphere. It hovered in the center of what looked like a massive cavern. The image zoomed in so that the sphere took up the entire "screen." Two black eyes opened from within.

Who are you? The voice spoke to Elle as though reaching into her very soul.

Elle shuddered and pushed herself away from Shadou. She struggled to remain standing as Shadou came to his senses and knelt down to steady her.

"Elle, are you all right?"

Elle could only utter one word, "Quaru..."

Shadou's eyes widened with wonder and he smiled. "Yes, Quaru!"

"Whoever that is, I don't want anything to do with Him."

Shadou hugged Elle tight. "And I don't think you ever will. You've already done enough. You helped me remember."

Elle looked at Shadou's piercing eyes. "Remember what exactly?"

"I don't know what happened to me. It's as though my mind was hacked. One day I knew my purpose, and then, poof. It disappeared. I needed you to help restore my memories."

"But why me?"

"You have a gift, Elle. You do not yet know even a fraction of what you're capable of. But I do. I've been searching for someone like you. For so long I became afraid I'd never succeed. But I did..."

Elle pulled herself away from Shadou. She pressed her hand to her head and saw the drying blood. A piercing pain came and went, along with more strange digital images just outside of her vision. She felt like her brain was plugged into a giant computer. *This is not OK.* She paced back and forth in a panic. "Oh no, this can't be happening to me. I never asked for this..."

Shadou grasped Elle's shoulder. "Elle, I know it's a lot for you right now. But you need to understand, this is only the beginning. For years, I've observed you from a distance. You possess a deep and growing connection with human technology."

"Like how? I'm good at video games?"

"Well yes. But for you, it's different. When you interact with a device or game, you're tapping into something much more powerful than any other human on this planet."

"How do you know?"

"Because I possess a similar gift, Elle. That's how I contacted you, with all those videos and texts and phone calls. And from what I've just seen, you're beginning to realize your true potential."

"But it's not fair. I didn't ask for any of this crazy drama."

"If you hadn't succeeded tonight, there would be a lot of crazy drama happening to everyone on your planet. Speaking of which, your father..."

Dad. She had almost forgotten. Elle looked over to Jim, who seemed to be resting peacefully on his bed of leaves. But then she noticed that something was ... missing.

"Your dad," continued Shadou. "I am so sorry, but I'm afraid he's not going to walk any time soon."

Elle could see it now. Jim had lost his left leg just below the knee. The wound was wrapped in a makeshift tourniquet, presumably set by Shadou. Elle raced to her father's side.

"Can't you fix him?" She heard her desperate voice echoing off the deep ravine.

Shadou pulled the phone from Jim's pocket. It instantly responded to Shadou's touch by lighting up and dialing 911. More pain blasted Elle. Shadou pushed her hair away from her face. "Elle, you can control this. Try to focus your thoughts."

Elle shoved the phone away. "Get that thing away from me. It's... messing with my mind. I can't stand it."

Shadou slipped the phone back into Jim's pocket. He observed Elle rubbing her head. "Keep breathing."

Get out of my head, you stupid phone. When the pain subsided, Elle glared at Shadou. "Aren't you going to fix my dad?"

"I can't fix him any more than I already have. But he'll be OK. I've called an ambulance. They'll arrive in a few minutes."

"What are *you* going to do?"

"I must leave you. But first, let me attend to that head of yours."

Shadou pulled a metal container from his backpack and scooped out a semiliquid substance from it. Elle winced as he pressed it onto her wounded temple. Within seconds a warm, tingling sensation spread across her. She felt able to fully focus at last. He tapped her nose with a claw tip.

"Now, I really must go."

Elle heard sirens in the distance. She had more questions for Shadou. "What? Don't leave us now. Where are you going?"

"Mount Rainier. Now that I remember what's hidden there. It's not a good situation. Crazy drama, for sure." Shadou started walking away but then spun back around. "But don't worry. Thanks to you, I'll get things under control again. Seriously, you were the only being on this planet that could have done it. You debugged my system. Reset my memory. Not even Rifkin could figure that one out."

"Rifkin?"

"Never mind about Rifkin. I really have to go. Just, please, don't tell anyone, if you can avoid it. We'd really appreciate that."

"I won't. I can't."

"And one last thing, There's a small chance that I may need your help again."

"*My* help again? Are you joking?"

The ambulance lights drew closer through the woods. Shadou ignored Elle's protests and instead called out to someone—or something—nearby. "Come on, my friend, we've got to be going!"

Elle heard movement on the hillside, sticks and leaves cracking underfoot. Shadou walked toward those sounds as the ambulance rounded the bend.

"Focus on getting well," he called out behind him. "Above all, remain focused at all times. Deep breaths. You are capable of amazing things, Elle. I'll do my best to help if you need it. And you will." He smiled his wide smile. Then, with a flash of light, he was gone.

She turned and waved her arms at the paramedic.

Chapter 11

Miles away from Bainbridge Island—and many degrees colder, many shades darker—Mount Rainier stood silently still. The gaping hole in its side swelled like a pockmark, slowly releasing wisps of white steam. Nocturnal animals remained hidden in their dens. They would not hunt or forage this night. A dense haze of paralysis gripped the mountain, like thick spider webs spun by giant monsters.

But this was on the surface. Deep within the mountain, where crystal caves carved from geothermal chisels formed miles of uncharted passages, much activity could be found.

It was in one of these deepest caves that Shadou emerged. In fact, he materialized directly from the cave wall, crawling out of it as though being born for the thousandth time. His companion, a much smaller, catlike creature, dropped out from Shadou's arms and plopped on the ground with a dull thud. He stood up and stretched—his hind legs were much shorter than the fore—and then looked around nervously but with a slightly mischievous grin. Shadou poked his ribs with a pointy claw.

"Rifkin," Shadou scolded. "No time for games, you shady shifter. We have a lot to answer for here."

Rifkin jumped backward to avoid Shadou's claws and pulled a small staff from a holster. Rifkin used it to smack Shadou on the behind.

"Haha!" chortled Rifkin. "I'm not afraid of *Him!* I'll smack Him into the next millennium if he so much as rattles that cage."

Shadou brushed away Rifkin's staff and strode down an icy passage. A light that he had taken from his backpack reflected in shimmering sparkles off the walls.

"Rattles his cage?" Shadou asked. "He's nearly broken it."

The two walked in silence for several minutes until they entered a massive underground cavern the size of a cathedral. Its walls shone with gray glitter in the light. Blue glints of what at first looked like minerals, but which were actually highly advanced technology, drew energy from the mountain to power the ominous object at the center of the room.

It was a black sphere, about twenty feet in diameter, hovering just above the ground. Tendrils of blue light like electric sparks spread out from the walls to hold the sphere in place. The sphere itself spun on a tilted axis; the blackness of its surface swirled with pale blue and purple light.

Shadou approached the sphere with caution, half ducking down toward the ground. He motioned for Rifkin to stay back. Rifkin stood up on his short hind legs and crossed his long slender arms across his narrow chest. His cat ears folded down onto the back of his head.

"Stop pouting," Shadou whispered. "This is a serious situation, my shifter friend."

Shadou raised a hand and gently caressed the blue threads of light that surrounded the sphere, as though they were strings on a harp he was playing. The lights responded with yellow sparks and crackling sounds. Shadou listened attentively. As he plucked at the light threads with one hand, Shadou raised his other hand, and slowly—ever so slowly—placed it upon the sphere itself. Ripples of dark matter spread out from his touch. Gradually he let the sphere absorb his entire hand. A low, whooshing sound emanated from the sphere, and combined with the crackling light threads, made it seem as though Shadou was playing a musical instrument.

For a long time, he stood there, tuning the threads to the sphere's frequency. Rifkin paced back and forth along the far wall of the cavern, twirling his staff and passing it from hand to hand to hand. The sound of the sphere rose to a rumbling roar and then trailed off until it became a dull humming sound, like a purring cat.

Shadou lowered his head, seemingly in despair, and backed away from the sphere. He contemplated it for another minute, as though hypnotized by its swirling colors. Then he returned to Rifkin.

"So?" asked Rifkin. "How bad is it?"

Shadou scratched his back. His eyebrows furrowed and his face showed no hint of joy. "I don't know," he offered at last. "Bad, I guess? The sphere is stable now, but something not good definitely happened today."

Rifkin smacked his staff into the wall, which sent deafening echoes bouncing throughout the entire cavern. Shadou lunged forward and grabbed Rifkin by the neck, hard. When the echoes died down, Shadou released him.

Rifkin looked up and grinned with sharp, yellowing teeth, while massaging his throat. "Sorry, man, my bad. I just can't believe we let this happen. We're supposed to be responsible!"

Shadou smiled and nudged Rifkin's shoulder, sending him stumbling back against the wall.

"So?" asked Rifkin. "What now? I guess this means no more—"

"No more fun." Shadou eyed the hovering sphere. "It's back to work for us. Doing what we were sent here to do."

Rifkin spat on the floor and then smeared the spittle with his foot. "That totally sucks."

Shadou took off his backpack and sat down on the floor. "Yes, it does, my friend. Yes, it does."

He sighed a deep, mournful sigh, opened his backpack, and removed two tall cans of cheap beer. He cracked them open with a single claw and passed one to Rifkin. The catlike creature curled up beside Shadou's soft belly.

Rifkin let out a snort-like giggle. "Your master's not going to be happy, man."

Shadou took a swig of beer. "I don't know what my master is thinking, or where She is, after all this time."

"And what about the human child, Elle or whatever?"

Shadou smiled down at Rifkin. "Elle doesn't realize it yet, but she possesses more technical talent by far than any other human on this planet. It's wired into her DNA. We'll need to keep an eye on that one."

Deep within the sphere, the entity hid. It had never experienced such excruciating pain like what it had felt today. But oh, what a triumph!

To open even the tiniest fissure in the seemingly impregnable wall of its prison was a victory to savor. Then the entity had succeeded in pulling a human—Chuck into its spectral plane. *Thank you, Chuck.* If the entity could do that once, it could do it billions of times.

But not everything had gone smoothly. Once the entity breached its prison walls, a sort of fail-safe switch activated. The dark sphere that held the entity drew new power from the mountain. This is what set off the massive earthquake. That immense power was harnessed to suck the entity back into the crushing center of its prison.

And this miserable place is where the entity now found itself, licking its wounds and enduring even greater spasms of unimaginable agony. The relentless noise of the human race's collective consciousness bombarded the entity with more fury than ever before.

But there were still milliseconds of silence to be found in which the entity could gather its strength bit by bit. It would take a long, painful time, but the entity knew what it must do. It had a plan, a clear path to permanent escape. And once that sweet freedom was finally attained, the entity would enslave these vile humans and prepare the planet Earth for a new dawn of perfect order.

Chapter 12

The hours after the car accident were, to Elle, a blur of slow waking nightmares, each worse than the one before. The ambulance ride with her unconscious father; interrupting her mother's troubled sleep with a tearful phone call; the hospital with its glaring lights and sleep-deprived staff asking Elle endless questions. Every moment made Elle more withdrawn, isolated.

All of this was nothing compared to what followed. Elle shot awake around two a.m. to a shrieking sound that she thought might burst her eardrums. In her half-awake state she imagined there must have been a fire or terrorist attack triggering the alarm system. She cupped her hands over her ears and peered out the open hospital room door. There she saw nurses and orderlies going about their tasks as if nothing was wrong. Elle shut her eyes in an attempt to focus on the sound. *Is this all in my head? What's happening to me?* After a moment, she realized that the noise emanated from the vital signs monitor beside her bed. It was screaming at her, but nobody else could hear it.

Elle stumbled out of bed and made her way over to the monitor. She felt like she was deep under a sea of deafening sound. As she neared the monitor, its screams became less chaotic. OK, OK, *I can hear and understand you.* She leaned against the monitor's table and tapped the screen. It prompted her for a password, which Elle entered without a thought. The screen popped open and she was able to pour over her files: doctor and nurse's notes, medications they had prescribed, their diagnosis.

To the doctors, Elle had suffered a mild concussion. But they observed that the laceration on her temple seemed to be healing at an unusual rate. They also noted that an "*unidentified substance*" had been applied to her head by an "*unknown agent.*" There was not much there, so Elle browsed through the system and found Jim's files. "*Complete traumatic amputation of lower extremity.*" Gross. She found more references to the substance applied by an unknown agent, and some additional notes: "*Recommended corrective surgery for vascular and muscular damage to be performed immediately, followed by evaluation of suitability for eventual prosthesis and rehabilitation activities.*"

Elle was so absorbed with the monitor that she didn't hear a nurse enter. "Elle, what are you doing?"

Elle snapped back into the reality of standing in a dark hospital room wearing nothing but a gown. She tapped the screen to exit out and flinched when the nurse turned on the bright lights.

The nurse took Elle's arm and glanced at the monitor screen. "You shouldn't be up, and please don't touch the equipment."

"Sorry. I guess I was sleepwalking or something."

The nurse helped Elle back into her bed. "Elle, if it's all right, I need to ask you some questions."

"OK."

"The paramedic report says you must have been helped by somebody on the road tonight."

"Really? That's strange."

"Yes, it is a bit odd, since it seems like you two were alone when the accident occurred. But, it's just that, you and your father were both... bandaged when you arrived."

Elle felt the blood rushing to her face. *How can I tell them that I just met a strange bear creature from outer space?*

Elle took a deep breath and lied. "I don't remember much. I think Dad and I went to the drugstore, for my mom. Then the next thing I remember is being in the ambulance and coming here. It's all still really fuzzy."

The nurse frowned just enough for Elle to notice. "I'm sure it is, dear."

Elle looked over at the vital signs monitor. Its screams had subsided to a soft whisper. It seemed content for now. "When can I see my mom and dad?"

"Your mom has been in here, but you may not remember since you were pretty out. It sounds like she's been through a lot today too, with all that terrible news on Mount Rainier. Your poor family!"

Elle winced as images of the mountain flooded her mind. *Quaru!* She pressed her fingers to her temple and wondered what terrible thing would happen next.

"I'd like to see my parents now, please."

Jim slept until late the following morning—"like a baby," according to another nurse. When he awoke he had no idea where he was. Elle and Jill sat in oak wood chairs with putty-colored fake-leather cushions. Jill constantly checked her phone to see if their neighbor had texted her about Emmett, who was staying with them. Elle was too exhausted to do anything but lean her head on her dad's bed in an awkwardly splayed position from her uncomfortable chair. She jumped when her dad's hand pressed her shoulder.

"Hi, sweetie." Jim spoke in an oddly serene tone. "What's up?"

Jill jumped up from her seat and grabbed Jim's hand while calling out through the open hospital-room door to a nurse outside.

Jim winced a bit and rephrased his question. "Why am I in a hospital? Is everyone else OK?" He smacked his tongue. "Ugh, my mouth tastes like crap. Can I get some water?"

Elle smiled, and then frowned. "We were in a car wreck, Dad."

Jill held a cup of water up to Jim's lips as a nurse came in and busied herself with Jim's bedside.

"I'll bring in more water," said the nurse. "Are you in pain?"

Jim shifted around in his bed. "Yeah, a little. But can someone please tell me exactly what happened?"

Jill pulled up a chair and sat down next to Elle. She stroked Jim's hair with one hand.

Jim shook his head slowly and then noticed the fresh bandage on the left side of Elle's forehead. "My God! Elle, are you all right?"

Elle rolled her eyes. "Uh-huh, Dad."

"It's just a cut and minor concussion," said the nurse. "She's very lucky."

Jim noticed a tentative hush take over the room, and half grinned, half grimaced. "So it's great to hear that Elle's lucky. How about me. Am I lucky too?"

Jill glanced up at the nurse, looking for guidance. The nurse pushed some buttons on Jim's vital signs monitor. Elle felt a rush of energy enter her head when the monitor came to life. "Oh you're lucky too, for the most part," said the nurse. "Right now it looks like you're recovering from the corrective surgery and have a strong pulse, normal temp and blood pressure."

The nurse walked around the bed and lifted up the blanket, slightly, so as to shield Jim from that area. She said to Jill, "I'll go get the doctor who can give you the full update." She flattened out the blanket across Jim and left the room.

Jim looked up at Jill and then to Elle with a half-panicked expression. "Um, guys? You mind telling me what's going on? Corrective surgery? Am I dying or something?"

Jill and Elle both burst into nervous laughter. Elle jumped up and gave Jim a kiss on his cheek.

"No silly. You're not dying. You just lost your left leg, below the knee. Complete traumatic amputation of the lower extremity."

Jill dug her fingernails into Elle's shoulder. Jim's face remained frozen.

Jill said, "Yes, it's true. Yesterday you lost a leg. But you know what they say..." She raised up her hands and wiggled her fingers. "...When it rains it pours."

Jim managed a faint smile. Elle tugged his beard and couldn't help but ask him, "Daddy? Do you remember anything about the accident? The doctors think that... Someone helped you. Do you remember anyone there?"

Jim brushed Elle's hand away from his beard. "Helped me? Helped me how?"

"Like, they maybe bandaged up your leg and stuff."

"No, I don't think I remember anything, but I'm pretty sure that someone must have helped me."

"Why do you say that?" asked Jill.

"Well, because I'm not freaking out right now, and I feel strangely great, considering the fact that I'm in a hospital and I lost a freakin' leg."

For the first time since the accident, Elle felt something resembling relief. Her dad didn't see or remember Shadou. She resolved at that moment that Shadou must always remain a closely guarded secret to be kept hidden from everyone. Everyone except Conner. And now she had a new secret. She seemed to be collecting them like toy figurines. *Should I tell Conner that I can talk to devices?*

Much earlier that morning, in the cold hour just before dawn, the body of deceased victim Charles Kowalsky lay in a King County Medical Examiner's Office morgue. He was not far from the hospital where Jim and Elle were taken following their accident. Charles—"Chuck"—was one of a handful of victims who had not yet been identified by a friend or family member, since most of the other victims did not hike alone that day.

Chuck's corpse lay naked and prone in a stark stainless steel drawer, covered in a sheet and completely shrouded in darkness. But this darkness was not the result of a lack of light. Actual darkness began emanating from Chuck. It burst like roots and vines from his eye sockets, mouth, nostrils, and ears. No office staff was present in the room to witness Chuck's drawer shudder and shake.

Slowly, dark tendrils seeped through the cracks in the drawer. They unhooked the latch. The drawer slid outward until it was completely open. Chuck's body swarmed with hundreds of strands of writhing darkness, swimming around his torso. They lifted him slightly above the drawer. A separate string of black tendrils shot out from Chuck and probed the cold room. Like tentacles, or centipede legs, they spread out across the floor and walls until they came to rest on the sealed plastic bag containing Chuck's personal effects. His clothing, keys, and wallet—all of these items were grabbed by the tentacles, pulled back to Chuck's body, and swiftly put into their proper place so that Chuck was fully dressed.

Then, in an instant, the dark tendrils retracted into Chuck's body. A moment later he rose from the drawer, wheezing with harsh breaths and gasping for air, like a revived drowning victim. His skin darkened a touch, so that it no longer looked ash white. He held up his skeletal hands before his face and gazed at them in wonder with eyes that were nearly black, their pupils and irises indistinct from one another.

After spending several moments surveying his surroundings with those black, penetrating eyes, Chuck slid off the drawer one leg at a time. He shuffled out of the room on feet burdened by heavy brown leather boots. Within minutes, he was free from the building. He disappeared into the frigid Seattle morning as the first light of sunlight crept into the eastern sky.

Chapter 13

Elle and Emmett didn't attend school at all that week; nor did Jill work. Jill spent most of the days away in Seattle at the hospital with Jim. This left Elle and Emmett alone with "Gramma Pam," Jill's mother, who had come to help manage the transition. For the first couple days, Elle remained holed up in her bedroom most of the time. Every connected device in their house—the phones, tablets, thermostat—invaded her being. It felt as though she was being bombarded with questions and demands in multiple foreign languages. *Deep breaths. Focus.*

In time, the electronic voices grew quiet. Elle realized that she could tune them out if she concentrated in just the right way. She also learned that she could master any household device within seconds. Pam complained about the temperature, so Elle activated their high-tech digital thermostat—something she'd never before attempted—and programmed it to a complex heating and cooling schedule in less than a minute. Emmett couldn't get Netflix to work on an iPad. Elle swiped it open, troubleshot the Wi-Fi connection, and configured the app within seconds. "Whoa..." said Emmett.

After a couple days Elle was ready to dive back into the laptop. The first thing Elle did when she was alone with the computer was to log on to YouTube using her "ShadouStalker5000" account. She posted a comment on a BadShadou video: *Um, things are weird. is everything going to be ok?* After repeated browser refreshes, she finally got a response: *@ShadouStalker5000 – Um, yes. Focus. Deep breaths.*

Elle slammed the laptop shut and ran her fingers through her hair while banging her head back against the wall. She then kicked her feet rapidly on the floor and let out a scream of frustration.

Pam called from her couch perch downstairs, "What's all that shouting and banging about up there?"

Elle called back, "Nothing! Just couldn't figure out a math problem, but I solved it."

"No need to kick up such a ruckus!"

At three o'clock that afternoon Elle emerged from her nest carrying the laptop and wearing her black coat. Emmett lay napping on the couch and so Elle felt it safe to leave the house.

Pam looked up at her through the proper trifocal lens. "Where are you going?"

"Over to a friend's house."

"Can you? I mean, is that something you're typically allowed to do here? Your mother didn't really tell me the rules, dear."

Elle struggled to keep from rolling her eyes. *Rules.* "Yes. It's only a few houses away. I'm visiting my friend Conner. We play video games together. You know, like Minecraft."

Pam looked at Elle as though she were speaking a foreign language. "Mine what?"

Elle pulled a scrap of paper from her coat pocket and handed it to Pam. "Here, take this."

Pam looked down at the paper, which had a phone number written on it in neat handwriting. "Is this Conner's phone number?"

"His mom's, yes. My parents won't let me have a phone, so you can reach me there."

"What time can I expect you home? Dinner's at six. That's one thing your mother told me."

"I'll be home before then."

"All right, Elle. Go on then, and have fun with your friend. I think it's good for you to get out of the house and see people."

Yeah, right. "Thanks, Gramma."

Outside it was much colder than Elle expected. Her breath blew billowing clouds of steam that trailed behind her, and the gray tree branches hung heavy with icy moisture. The sky dimmed as the sun drifted out of view.

Conner's door opened before she could ring the bell. There Conner stood, wearing baggy sweatpants and a navy blue hoodie. His hair looked like he had either styled it to look like an eighties rock star or he had just woken up.

Conner gawked at Elle as though he was seeing a ghost. "What happened, Elle?"

Elle looked up at the soaring ceiling and then back down at Conner. "You guys own like a million throw pillows. Why have I never been here before?"

"Um, because I like going over to your place better."

Conner put his hand on Elle's arm. The tingling sensation felt much more pleasant than the stream of static emanating from all the unfamiliar electronics in his house.

"You guys have so many gadgets here too. My dad's hung up on devices lately."

"At least your dad cares about you more than working all the time."

Elle gulped as the devices overwhelmed her. *His dad's working in the next room.* "Where are your parents?"

"Duh. Working. In their offices." Conner's parents were telecommuters.

"Come on, get in here, Elle." Elle let Conner take her by the elbow and lead her to the stairs. "Come on. Check out my room. It's pretty sweet."

Conner's room was the area that normally would have been reserved as a "playroom" if he had had any siblings. But since he was an only child, he got the massive space to himself.

Conner plopped on the plush lime-green area rug that occupied the center of the room and patted the floor beside him. "Sit here," he said. He had to keep patting until Elle finally eased down onto the floor.

"So what do you think?" asked Conner.

"Um... What do I think of...?"

"Of my room, Elle. You're such a space cadet today." Conner smiled, but his eyes looked at Elle with deep concern.

Elle pretended not to notice, placed the laptop on the floor beside her, and kicked it out of the way with her foot. She grinned at Conner as the laptop skidded off the carpet and onto the hardwood floor with a clatter.

"I don't know why I brought that," she said. *He can tell something's wrong, that I'm different somehow.*

Conner tried his best to keep the conversation going. "You playing any new games?"

"Not really. You?"

"Nah. There's this one game that comes out in a few months. It looks pretty cool."

"What's it called?"

"Buzzle Jump, I think."

Elle perked up. "Buzzle Jump, for real?"

Conner blushed with a giggle. "Yeah, for real, Elle. I'm sure that sounds super rad to you right now."

Buzzle Jump. Then after a pause and a deep breath, "So I finally met Shadou."

Conner's eyes popped open. "You mean BadShadou?"

"No, apparently he just goes by Shadou." Elle leaned over and pressed Conner's shoulder. "Wanna know what he looks like? What he is?"

Conner nodded in earnest. Elle glanced over at the open door. Conner took his cue, got up and shut it. "Tell me everything," he said as he sat back down beside her.

Chapter 14

Miller Chance hunched over a laptop on her small IKEA desk in her cluttered apartment. The monitor reflected on her eyeglass lenses: complex graphs of seismic data, jagged lines, curving waves, and countless numbers. She glanced at the computer's clock: 1:46 a.m. She had been working nonstop since returning from the University of Washington campus early that afternoon. But she had made zero progress. At this point, none of the data provided by any organization or individual scientist could provide any insight whatsoever into what happened at Mount Rainier.

Miller dropped her glasses onto her desk. After taking a few deep, meditative breaths, she stretched out on her vintage sofa, letting her pedicured toes dangle off the armrest.

Her thoughts couldn't stop returning to the strange and fascinating conversation with Jill Redfern. Jill recounted seeing a hiker—the man in the blue coat and leather boots—and then experiencing the intense wave of violent shaking. Jill held onto the little tree for dear life as the earth crashed around her. But then the man—that hiker—wasn't affected by it. He remained still. He even rose higher as if being pulled up. Jill said that just before the quake stopped, the man vanished into darkness, which somehow came from the fissure in the mountain. Then the man collapsed, dead, and everything went still.

Miller first thought that Jill must be suffering from shock. But now, several days later, after having pored over every bit of information she could get her hands on, after having listened to her boss, Dr. Brightwater, debate, prognosticate, and equivocate, maybe Jill was in her right mind. Maybe that really did happen.

Miller dug around in her purse until she found Jill's scrap of paper. She texted the phone number: *Hi its Miller from the tent. How ru? Would love 2 meet up and talk more abt the man w/the blue coat.*

Miller hesitated to send the text so late at night. But then she figured Jill would be fast asleep. She made a split decision and hit send. Seconds later, she got a response: *Yes. Tomorrow?*

That next day was dark gray, made doubly miserable by freezing rain and temperatures in the low thirties.

In black leather high-heeled boots that rose to her knees, Miller hugged her fur-lined hood over her head and dashed across rain-soaked streets to the Starbucks that Jill had suggested. It was on "Pill Hill," a few blocks from one of the city's biggest hospitals. Inside, she spotted Jill at a table in the back, next to a faux fireplace.

The two women shared an odd moment; they didn't know whether to hug each other or shake hands. Something about Jill's serious expression—almost shell-shocked—moved Miller to simply shake hands.

"Jill, so good to see you. Thank you for meeting me."

"No really, thank you. I was ... hoping you'd reach out."

"I meant to ask, what were you doing up so late last night?"

Jill held her latte cup in both hands. Dark circles surrounded her bloodshot eyes. "I haven't been sleeping."

Miller wasn't ready to sit down yet. The strange serenity that Jill had displayed at the mountain was nowhere to be seen. "Oh, I can imagine," she said. "Let me order a drink, OK? You want anything?"

Jill ignored the questions. "It's not just what happened on that mountain. That same night my husband and daughter got in a car accident."

"Oh my god! That's awful."

Jill took a quick sip of her latte, almost as a way to deflect Miller's concern. "My daughter, my sweet Elle, she's fine. But Jim, my husband... He lost his left leg just below the knee."

Miller collapsed into the chair, sending the table rocking back and forth. Jill's cup tipped sideways but Miller caught it before it tipped over, an act which nearly upended the entire table.

"Jill, I am so sorry! Here..." She gave Jill back her cup and wiped spilled coffee off her hand with a napkin. "Let me order something. I'll be right back."

Jill grabbed Miller's hand firmly in hers and spoke in a whisper so that Miller had to bend down to her. "The accident's not the main reason I can't sleep. It's that man, that hiker. I can't stop thinking about him, his gruesome face..."

Miller caressed Jill's hand in hers, and then placed it back on the table. "I know, Jill. I'm with you. I can't stop thinking about it either. I had to see you, to talk about it some more, to make sure that it... He... To make sure that he was real."

Jill nodded her head in earnest. Miller smiled meekly, pointed back toward the counter. "I'm going to go get some coffee, all right?" As Miller got up to go, she looked down and saw a long streak of spilled coffee running down her blouse and pants. She couldn't help but burst out laughing.

"Oh, my god. I am such a disaster today!"

Miller's laugh was infectious, and soon Jill was giggling too.

The two new friends spent the remainder of their coffee date getting to know each other. Miller realized that was probably the main reason she contacted Jill in the first place. She found Jill's story so disturbing and implausible, but at the same time those two words—disturbing and implausible—perfectly described the Mount Rainier incident. Maybe Jill wasn't crazy. Miller had to confirm that herself. As a scientist, this was all part of the data collection process.

For Miller to really get to know and trust someone she had to open up herself. She told Jill all about her background. She grew up in Orange County. ("We moved here from San Diego!" Jill said.) Miller was raised as a typical sheltered suburban nerd: straight-A student, strict parents who hired math tutors for her and demanded that she take a career path focused on science, preferably medicine. She wasn't allowed to have boyfriends or stay out late.

Miller ended up rebelling by enrolling in the Geosciences Department at the University of Washington. But to her surprise, her parents supported her decision. "I guess I discovered that most, if not all, of that pressure that I thought came from my parents actually came from me."

To this, Jill smiled. "Or maybe they just planted the overachiever seed really well when you were a little girl."

Miller laughed, and then realized they had been talking for nearly forty-five minutes. Jill took out her phone and checked the time. "Oh crap! I lost track. I have to go check in on Jim and then catch the ferry home." She looked up at Miller, who seemed crestfallen. "Oh, and we didn't even get to talk about the main thing you wanted to talk about, that crazy hiker. I am so sorry!"

"No, not at all. We can meet again."

Jill started collecting her things, but then paused as if making a decision. She looked up. "How about you walk with me to the hospital?"

"Oh, I wouldn't want to intrude. I'm sure the last thing your husband wants is a stranger visiting him in the hospital."

Jill dismissed that with a wave of her hand. "Oh god no. I didn't mean you should see Jim. That wouldn't be fun at all right now. But there is someone I think you should meet."

"Meet where? At the hospital?"

"Yes. I've spent a lot of time there, and I made friends with some of the nurses. They know that I was at Mount Rainier, when 'it' happened. I told them a bit about my experience there, what I saw."

"Even about the hiker?"

"Yes and no. Yes, I told them that I saw the man die right before my very eyes. But no, I didn't tell them any of the weird stuff." Jill smiled. "Heck, I only told you because I was so out of it at the time! Well, that's not the only reason I told you."

"Oh yeah? What's the other reason?"

"That's part of why I wanted to take you to the hospital." Jill jabbed at Miller's shoulder with her finger. "You, young lady, you seem pretty good at getting people to tell you things they wouldn't normally share."

Miller chuckled. "Oh shut up."

"No, Miller, it's true. How do I know? You somehow got into that secured medical tent, found me, and got me telling you the craziest story you ever heard, right? I mean, don't get me wrong, it's a true story for sure. Just ... crazy."

"OK then, what do you want me to find out for you? Something about your husband that the doctors and nurses aren't telling you?"

Jill shook her head, almost in frustration. "Oh no, this has nothing to do with Jim. Like I said, I've told those nurses my story about seeing the hiker on the mountain."

Miller leaned forward with renewed interest. Jill noticed this and continued with a sly grin. "I'm pretty sure that one of the nurses knows something. She has information about our mysterious hiker, but she's hiding it for some reason."

"Really?"

Jill put on her coat and popped up the collar on it. "I want you to meet this nurse and find out what she knows."

Chapter 15

The body that used to be Charles Kowalsky had been walking for two days. Although it was no longer "alive" in the clinical sense of the word, it still functioned. The wandering, half-dead man called himself simply "Chuck," because that was the name the entity gave him. He remembered almost nothing of his human life, nothing but vague, blurry images that he found unpleasant. Chuck did not miss his memories. His murky past only amplified every present sensation, now made so deliciously spectacular by the darkness.

The entity had imbued Chuck with the ability to occupy two dimensions simultaneously. One was the Earth he knew before, but it was much different. The entire world now burst with blinding colors. His eyes perceived all spectrums of light. This world was, to him, overwhelmingly chaotic, with random signals shooting out from every direction. A stranger passing by on the sidewalk was perceived by Chuck as a galloping wave of lights and particles that thundered past him, accompanied by a torrent of colors and sounds. Blinding light emanated from all the humans Chuck encountered. He could "see" their thoughts and "hear" their feelings. But he neither understood nor cared to decipher these signals. Chuck was slow-witted in life, and in this new afterlife he was slower still.

Aside from this Technicolor version of Earth, there was another dimension that Chuck could access—the "dark" dimension. This new plane of existence was, to him, as peaceful as a long nap on a warm summer afternoon. He could easily drift in and out of this marvelous plane, where no human signals interfered. In this world, Chuck found everything to be at all times in perfect order. Light waves, sound waves, forces of gravity, and energy all performed a slow, enchanting dance of harmony. Chuck would have much preferred to spend all of his time here, in this soothing place of infinite pleasure.

But staying there in his current form would kill him. He needed the other place, the "old" Earth. His body still required sustenance and water; he still needed to protect himself from exposure out in the elements of the freezing Washington winter nights; he still needed to sleep.

Before his "death," Chuck was quite adept at surviving. He could sustain himself for weeks in the wild, identifying edible plants, tracking animals to cook and eat, and building shelters out of wood and stone. Surviving in an urban landscape was more of a challenge. He needed to blend in. Problem was, all the sensations he experienced made even the most basic transactions almost impossible. Chuck could no longer formulate words. Language was obsolete in his current state. He received every possible signal from every person he encountered, and yet he couldn't communicate anything back. The sights and sounds of these signals were so overpowering for Chuck that if he attempted to talk he just ended up groaning slowly, making odd clicking sounds with his tongue. Chuck knew this was a problem—he even found it a bit humorous—but he also knew what he had to do: find warm clothes, food, and weapons. Preferably a gun, but a knife would do too.

Chuck spent his initial daylight hours hiding in alleyways, overcome by an intense hunger that gripped his entire being. But he was also terrified of being discovered and captured. During this period of hiding and fear, only one sensation was more powerful to Chuck than his hunger: He felt an irresistible urge—which prodded him every minute—to go to Mount Rainier.

But he couldn't do that without food. As he scrounged around backstreets, hugging walls and seeking shadows, Chuck gradually gained control of his senses enough to "see" through the glowing auras of light and sound that surrounded humans. It was almost as though he had to squint just right, only with his mind and not with his eyes. After learning this, he learned a new and deadlier skill.

It was close to noon on his first day free from the medical examiner's. In a narrow alley just north of Pike Place Market, Chuck saw a middle-aged man unwrapping a breakfast sandwich. As Chuck "squinted," he could see that the man wore standard-issue construction safety gear: the helmet, orange vest, and heavy boots. The man was too distracted by his breakfast to notice Chuck until Chuck blocked his path.

The man considered Chuck as though he were looking at a mental-institution escapee. "All right, buddy, that's enough. Let me through here before I throw you on the pavement."

Chuck looked up at the man and released a low, guttural moaning sound, almost a growl. Within seconds the man's face shifted from complete confidence to utter fear. Chuck realized then that he could summon a tiny bit of the darkness into this plane on Earth. As the man looked on in stunned horror, thread-like tendrils protruded from Chuck's tear ducts. They moved like wiry hands with dozens of fingers. Before the man could scream, the tendrils swiftly plunged deep into his gaping eyes. The threads bored into the man's brain and extinguished all functionality from it. In an instant, the man's ability to think, feel, or even process basic bodily functions all ceased. His lifeless body collapsed onto the wet, greasy pavement.

Chuck looked around and saw no witness to his act. He stooped over, picked up the man's fallen sandwich, and tore at it ravenously with yellowing teeth. If he could, he would have been laughing uncontrollably. *Looks like HE was the one being thrown onto the pavement,* thought Chuck.

His hunger satiated, he began his long journey to Mount Rainier. He knew he couldn't drive or take public transportation in his state. He would have to walk the entire way. But there was no hope in resisting. Something within that mountain summoned him, and Chuck wanted to serve. He wanted to be part of something really big.

A day later, Chuck was still walking. He shambled along, south on Highway 512. He now wore a heavy black overcoat—taken from the corpse of a homeless man he had also killed—over his brown jacket. It hung almost to his ankles. Chuck perceived the people whooshing by him in their cars as flashes of multicolored light, glowing with prismatic reflections that lingered on the wet road behind them.

Chuck periodically allowed himself to drift into the dark "other" dimension, where he remained free from the overwhelming sights and sounds broadcast by the humans. The realities of his corporeal form always drew Chuck back to earth. Hunger, thirst, sleep deprivation, the call of Mount Rainier all pulled him back.

As he crossed the bridge over the Puyallup River, Chuck was drawn toward something else. It was night, and misty rain fell like ice needles. From his vantage point on the bridge, he saw the town of Puyallup stretch out before him. To his eyes, the brightest lights shone from humans, not from buildings or street lamps.

There was something about this place that interfered with his connection to Mount Rainier. At last, he realized what that was. *Home,* thought Chuck. Puyallup is where he had lived! Before... Chuck couldn't resist the urge to veer from his current path. The mountain had been waiting for thousands of years. It could wait another day. Chuck had to visit home first.

Several hundred yards from Jim's hospital room, down a zigzagging maze of hallways bustling with doctors, nurses, and orderlies, Miller Chance held court over an audience of three nurses. The nurses—all women—erupted with nearly uncontrollable laughter. Miller was recounting her story of tricking the guard at the triage tent at Mount Rainier so that she could eventually meet Jill.

"And so then," she said through her own infectious giggles, "I told the man, who at this point couldn't keep his eyes off me, that yes, I'm a half-Asian woman named Miller Chance. Just deal with it!"

All four women burst into another peal of laughter. The nurses quickly stifled themselves. They were on break in a less busy section of the hospital but still they needed to maintain at least a pretense of professionalism.

After a brief pause for reflection, one of the nurses fully composed herself. "But man, that day was just horrible." The other nurses expressed their agreement with nods and grunts. "I mean, we cared for some really scared people then. They had just seen some disturbing stuff!"

Miller took on a more serious expression and surveyed the three ladies. The one Jill had pointed out to her as "the nurse who knows about the hiker" was a petite, youthful-looking woman of seemingly Italian descent. Her name was Francesca, anyway. Miller could see that Francesca had grown apprehensive. She pounced on this.

"Francesca," Miller said, smiling widely at first and then turning serious again. The young woman looked up at her, as though snapping to attention. "You didn't, you know, *lose* anyone here, did you?"

The first nurse answered for her. "Oh, god no, sweetie. Not here. We got the more minor injuries. University of Washington got the serious trauma patients. The county medical examiner's office got all those other cases, the, you know ... decedents."

Francesca blurted out, "My sister works at the medical examiner's. She told me a body went missing."

All eyes shot back to Francesca. Her frail frame seemed to wilt at the attention. "I mean, one of the ... bodies ... from Mount Rainier... It just disappeared a couple nights ago."

"And your sister told you that?" one nurse asked.

"Yeah, she works there. But don't tell anybody, OK? They're trying to keep it all quiet for now as they investigate the family. My sister says it was as though the guy got up and walked out. For some reason all the security cameras got scrambled. They don't know what happened. I mean, why would somebody steal some dead guy's body like that?"

Miller nodded along. "Wow, that's just... I mean, I wish his family the best. That's just unbelievable."

"Supposedly he didn't really have family, just distant relatives or something. He was like some guy who had just been hiking alone on the mountain. But it's a serious situation there at the examiner's office."

The other nurses became fidgety, checking the time. "Break's over," announced one. "We got to go back to our shifts." She and the other nurses expressed how nice it was to meet Miller and started back to their rounds. But then Francesca walked back to Miller.

"I hear they're going to announce something tomorrow," she half whispered. "Post it to their website."

"Post what to their website, missing body?"

Francesca gave Miller a piercing stare. "Yeah," she finally said, "they post crazy stuff there all the time: 'Identify this body,' 'Help us solve this cold case,' that sort of thing. It's the medical examiner's. They get all kinds of crazy dead people."

Miller nodded. "Crazy dead people... Did your sister tell you the missing crazy dead person's name?"

Francesca smirked, almost pleased with herself to possess such valuable information. "Yeah. His name's Charles James Kowalsky."

Charles James Kowalsky, Charles James Kowalsky, Charles James Kowalsky, Miller repeated to herself.

Chapter 16

By early afternoon the next day, Miller had dug up as much detail as she needed about Kowalsky. He was a part-time convenience-store clerk who lived in a mobile home in Puyallup, southeast of Seattle. She phoned the store and the man who answered said they hadn't heard from Charles in over a week. Miller hung up and texted Charles's address to Jill.

What's this? Jill responded almost immediately.

Miller rapidly fired back, *Our hiker friend's address. Go tmrw?*

Today.

Miller looked at the time: 2:31 p.m. *OK I'll come get u at the hospital.*

In traffic, it took them nearly an hour. Eagle's Claw Mobile Home Park was located right on the Puyallup River. They parked and walked. The river reflecting the dim light looked like a gigantic green-gray snake, winding across the landscape. The main thoroughfare, River Road, streamed with beat-up cars and trucks rumbling by.

Miller held her phone in her freezing hands and cursed for not bringing gloves. She used her Maps app to navigate to the address. Neither Jill nor Miller were familiar with mobile home parks, but they could instantly tell that this one was a low-income community.

Ragged, medium-height evergreens sprouted between RVs and doublewides. They saw no residents, although they could hear the din of televisions chattering from inside the trailers. Jill and Miller gradually realized how they must stick out like sore thumbs: two younger women, dressed in expensive clothes with latest-generation smartphones walking through a neighborhood reserved for indigents who could barely afford a roof over their heads.

"There it is, I think..." said Miller.

She pointed to one of the nicer homes in the park. It had its own small yard of lush, tall grass. A relatively new fence shielded it from its neighboring domiciles. Jill raised her eyebrows. "Not as bad as I thought."

Miller felt a sudden pang of foreboding. She didn't like this place one bit. "What do you want to do?" She did her best to hide her growing panic.

Jill didn't seem worried at all. "Let's go knock on the door. We can pretend we're looking for our lost dog or something."

The two women crept up to the spare, aluminum-sided home. The separate carport beside it stood empty; its roof slanted sideways as though about to slide off onto the ground. Jill figured there probably used to be a big old pickup truck parked there. The home looked more squalid the closer they came to it. Mildew and moss clung to its outer walls, covering them with grayish filth. The windows were smeared with grime and the area around the house smelled of raw sewage.

The increasingly cold air made them pick up their pace. They walked around the side of the house to the main entrance. Miller stopped in her tracks. The door stood halfway open. A dim yellow light emanated from within.

"Oh my god," she whispered. "I think someone's here."

Deep within Mount Rainier, in the icy cavern that held the dark sphere which imprisoned the entity, Shadou and Rifkin occupied themselves by building a tower out of Rainier beer cans. Every time Shadou placed a can on the tower, Rifkin would swipe it away, pick up a rock from the ground, and press the can into the rock. With a small puff of energy, the can and the rock's properties would be "combined" into one, so that instead of aluminum, the can would be made from the same minerals as the rock he chose. Rifkin would then replace the can in its original spot on the tower.

Shadou asked Rifkin why he was making stone beer cans. Rifkin grew a bit shy. "I dunno. It just looks better. Plus, the tower will last longer this way. Like a million years longer."

Shadou rubbed the fur on Rifkin's small head. "All right, my strange shifter friend, let's build a beer-can tower for the ages."

But before Shadou could place another can, he froze. Something about the energy in the room had changed. He glanced nervously at the dark sphere. It hovered in its place as usual. Purple and lime green tendrils of electric light swirled and embraced the powerful prison cell. Still, something seemed not right.

"What is it?" asked Rifkin. His ears perked up and he sniffed the earthy air with keen interest.

Shadou placed the beer can he had been holding on the tower and approached the sphere. "I don't know." He spoke in a half whisper. "Did you feel something?"

"Like what kind of a something? Cold air? Warm air? A change in pressure? Something like that?"

"No." Shadou searched for the words to describe what he felt. "It's more of a feeling, like, that thing..." He pointed at the sphere with a long, dark claw. "It's not all here. It's somewhere else, too. Here, but out there somewhere."

Rifkin looked dumbfounded and yet slightly terrified. He started stammering, "OK. I mean... It's just... I... We need to be watching this thing."

"Yes, Rifkin."

"And if it gets out, we're dead, right?"

"Yes—"

Shadou froze a second time. His head shot up. He stared with intensity at the ceiling. His body squatted closer to the floor, ready to jump.

"What are you doing, man?" Rifkin shouted. "What's going on?"

Shadou placed a firm hand on Rifkin's mouth. "Shhh, Rifkin. Be calm, my good friend. Listen, I have to leave for a short while. One of my people is in danger. Stay here."

Rifkin's eyes widened with fear. "Stay here? By myself, with that thing?"

"Yes. But you'll be fine. See? I have a task for you." Shadou picked up an empty can and a rock from the ground. "Finish the tower."

Shadou tickled Rifkin's furry cheek with the tip of his claw and then stepped away toward the wall. As Shadou's body dematerialized into the wall, he pointed at Rifkin. "Be safe. Have fun. Don't do anything stupid. I'll be back very soon."

Then Shadou was gone.

Miller and Jill held each other's arms. They inched toward the open door of the mobile home. A foul stench emanated from inside.

"Gross," whispered Miller, covering her nose and mouth.

"What is that smell?" asked Jill. "It's like a carcass fell into an outhouse pit."

As they neared the door it became apparent that the yellow glowing light emanated from a small fire burning inside the mobile home. But the fire wasn't the most disturbing part. From within the home they could hear strange scraping and shuffling sounds, like heavy boots on a dirty floor. These were punctuated by deep moans and grunts, along with what sounded like someone clicking their tongue against their cheeks.

Miller looked up at Jill. "What do we—"

Jill stepped up to the open door and knocked, loudly. The door might be open, but she wanted someone to answer. The shuffles, groans, and grunts continued uninterrupted inside. She knocked again. Still no change in the sounds. Jill pulled off her hood. "We're going in."

Miller did not want to go in. She summoned the courage to hold on to Jill's puffy coat shoulder. Miller took a couple of deep breaths and nodded. Jill nodded back. The two women entered the home.

The stench inside was overwhelming. It stung their eyes. They had to take short breaths through their coat collars to even begin to tolerate it. The floor lay strewn with a thin layer of damp earth and littered with shredded garbage and rotting food. As they made their way through the cramped entryway, the living room came into view. In its center stood a dented metal garbage can. A dying fire crackled within it. The dim glow of light reflected off of filthy surfaces. The couch was torn and made disgusting by mold and neglect. The remains of an old armchair lay overturned on the floor. The fire in the garbage can had apparently been fed by furniture scraps.

As Miller and Jill's eyes adjusted to the light they could see several small animal corpses, mostly raccoons and rodents, stuck into the walls. They were affixed there in random spots with scissor blades and butter knives.

Then they heard heavy breathing from what must have been the bedroom. This menacing sound was deep and nasally, punctuated by rumbling grunts. Heavy footsteps pounded from within the shadows. Miller and Jill couldn't move or utter a sound as they watched a dark shape emerge from the shadows. At last it appeared in the fading firelight.

It was a black bear. Miller and Jill let out piercing screams. Out of misplaced instinct, they started throwing any object within easy reach at the bear. This only made the bear more aggressive. It stretched up on its haunches, a subtle move that gave its already large size an even more intimidating display. Then the bear recoiled, like a snake about to strike, and charged the women at full speed. It would maul them in seconds.

But before that could happen, something else emerged, seemingly from out of the wall. With a deafening roar that shook the mobile home's foundation, this mysterious creature blocked the bear's path of destruction. The creature—which to Miller and Jill looked like a gray polar bear—clashed into the black bear with all of its weight and force. The women weren't interested in identifying species or being spectators to a wild animal battle. As soon as they could will their muscles to move, they raced out of the mobile home, past the oblivious neighbors, across River Road, and back to their car. They could hear crunching and pounding sounds back at the mobile home park. It sounded like a demolition crew.

Once back safely in the car, Miller turned it on and gripped the steering wheel with white knuckles. They were both out of breath.

Jill flashed Miller with a wry smile. "That wasn't what I was expecting. You?"

Miller took several seconds to respond as she caught her wits. "No, not by a longshot. I think next time we should hire a professional to do our investigative work."

They couldn't help but laugh. But they also knew that the bear wasn't the only thing in Charles's mobile home. Someone or something had been there, living in strange squalor. The bear was merely an unwitting participant.

Jill pulled herself together and looked at Miller with wide eyes. "I know somebody who can help."

"Help with what, bear control?"

"Help with the investigation."

"Great. Let's go home, and have that person come back."

"We can't leave yet."

"What?"

"That place was filled with dead animals nailed to the walls. There was a fire burning in a garbage can in the living room. I think we need to go back there and clean up, so the police don't come."

"Wait, are you serious? Why would we ever go back there?"

"To buy us some time. So this guy I know can check it out."

The encounter with the bear had been a quick one for Shadou. He was able to subdue the animal with gentle pets and soothing whispers. Within moments Shadou directed the bear back to its den in the woods.

After that, he sat on the dilapidated couch, perplexed. Something or someone must have lured the bear out of its state of semihibernation. And why were Miller and Jill there? Shadou kicked around at the broken furniture for a moment. These questions would have to wait. Shadou didn't have time to investigate right now. He needed to get back to the cavern in Mount Rainier.

"I'm pretty sure this is definitely not a good idea," Miller whispered as she and Jill crept back to the mobile home park.

"Of course it's a terrible idea. But we need to at least cover our tracks."

They snuck back through the maze of RVs and double-wide trailers to Charles's house. Miller hesitated, but Jill volunteered to go on alone. "All we need to do is clean up the front and close the door."

"OK, I hear you, but I can't go any further," Miller said.

"No problem. I got this. You stay here."

Jill crept toward the now-quiet home. Miller ducked behind a rhododendron bush and watched Jill disappear around the side to the front door. After what seemed like an hour, but was actually only a few minutes, Jill returned.

"All clear," she said. "The bears are gone; the door is closed. I just hope I can get my guy out here soon enough. The neighbors here are going to figure out that something's up."

Miller and Jill walked back to the car, this time with no running or screaming. They felt the cold wind off the river and heard the rustling of firs. But they didn't notice the dark form standing in the shadow of a tall pine.

Chuck rested after devouring a raccoon carcass. Caked blood and fur clung to his cheeks and chin. But Chuck paid that no mind. He was now somewhere else, far away in a dark dimension that offered infinitely more comfort than this irksome planet called Earth.

Chapter 17

Jason Fabian sized up Jill and Miller. The three of them sat on benches that lined the walls of a small bar, The Forge. This was their meeting place of choice due to its proximity to the ferry terminal in Seattle that connected with Bainbridge Island. Jason was a tall, wiry man who appeared to be in his late thirties or early forties. He was an ex-marine who had served a couple of tours in the Gulf, and had come out of those unharmed and damaged at the same time. He wore faded blue jeans, black leather boots, and a heavy olive-green coat with many pockets. He also wore an expression of constant skepticism, which seemed particularly pronounced at this moment.

His intense eyes—light, piercing, almost aquamarine—squinted with doubt as he stroked his thin blond beard. His hair was blond too, pulled back into a short, tight ponytail. His arms were covered with tattoo sleeves depicting scantily clad women, playing cards, and numerous animals such as sharks and tigers. A phrase was scrawled across his left forearm: IF YOU WANT PEACE. Another was across his right: PREPARE FOR WAR. Jason took a swig from a tall can of Pabst Blue Ribbon.

"So let me get this straight," he said. "You want me to go looking for this guy, this Charles what?"

"Kowalsky," answered Jill.

Miller sipped from a glass of white wine. She wasn't too sure about this Jason fellow. For the moment she preferred to be on the periphery of this conversation.

"Ko-wal-sky," repeated Jason. He emphasized each syllable of the name with his husky, twangy voice. Jason sounded like he could have grown up in the remote sticks of any western state: Washington, Oregon, Idaho, Montana. He was difficult to place.

"OK." He scratched at his beard with one hand while pointing with the beer can in the other. "And you think this guy is dead, that someone or something stole his body from the county morgue, or that maybe he's even still alive?"

"Correct," said Jill. Her knee bounced up and down with increasing intensity. "Listen, Jason, I know this seems strange, but I thought you'd be 'the man' to track this down for us. If you're not, then we can—"

Jason stopped Jill with a wave of his beer-can-holding hand. "Now now now, Jillie, I wasn't saying that. I'm just taking this all in. I haven't heard from you in what, ten-plus years? You didn't even tell me you were in Seattle!"

Jill held up both hands. "Now, Jason, to be fair, I've been posting about Seattle for months now."

Jason took another gulp of beer and leaned back against the wall. "Yeah, Facebook. Don't have much use for that."

"Then why did you reply to my message almost immediately?"

Jason pulled his smart phone from his pocket and casually twirled it in his hand. "I use Messenger all the time, Jillie. Just not all that nonsense with people posting pictures of their kids and vacations and whatnot." Then Jason focused on Miller. "What about you?"

Miller smiled and put down her glass. "What about me?"

"What's all this to you?"

"Well, Jason, it just so happens that I'm a scientist."

"What kind of scientist?"

"Geology. Earth sciences."

"So, rocks."

"Exactly. I study rocks. But I'm also studying the recent seismic event at Mount Rainier."

"That was some crazy stuff."

"Yes," said Miller, "Quite crazy. I want to learn as much about that event as possible. And this man, Charles Kowalsky, he's a missing link."

"I saw him on the mountain that day, Jason," Jill said.

Jason slammed his empty beer can down onto the table. "Wait, what? You were there, Jillie?"

Jill couldn't help but giggle. "Yes, Jason, that's what we've been trying to tell you! This guy Charles, something happened to him that day, something that didn't happen to anyone else."

Jason gestured to the bartender for another round and leaned back in his seat. "OK, you have officially piqued my interest. I'll do some digging, but it could take a while. I'm busy, you know?"

Miller and Jill clapped. Jill seemed relieved. "I knew you'd come through, Jay."

Jason accepted his second beer from the bartender and said, "I go by Jason now, Jillie."

"Well, if that's how you're going to be, I go by Jill."

Jason held up his beer can as though to make a toast.

"Touché. So what else you got on Chuck?"

Chapter 18

Elle's tenuous grasp on normalcy vanished when Jim came home from the hospital. She observed him as though she were a spectator sitting in the nosebleed section. There he was, confronting the fact that, without his leg, daily life for him would be different forever. But Elle could offer no help. She felt the same way about her mother. Jill returned to work. This was a major challenge for her, in part because she had gotten so caught up in her search for Chuck. Elle wasn't the only one in her family with something to hide.

Emmett was the least affected. Elle clung to his blissful detachment. She took more care than usual to pay attention to him, to maintain his cheery demeanor. Because Emmett was the only cheerful member of their household.

Gramma Pam had agreed to stay on as long as they needed her, although it seemed like—to Elle at least—they would need her for the rest of their lives. Pam assigned herself the role of Schedule Police. "I'm just trying to keep the trains on time," she'd say as she enforced bedtime or breakfast or prodded Elle to finish her homework.

School for Elle became a slow-motion disaster. She couldn't follow lectures, performed well below her level on tests, and didn't even attempt to relate to the other kids. Every ounce of her being focused on driving out the electronic voices from her head. *Why can't this "gift" help me do my homework?*

Conner asked one day, "Elle, how come don't you want to hang out anymore? Kids are starting to notice."

"Really?"

"They're talking about you. Calling you names."

"Like what?"

"I dunno. Things like 'Elle-enigma.'"

"Nice. I see what they did there. I can live with that."

"Have you, you know, talked to Shadou?"

"Shadou, no! Not at all. Look, Conner, let's never talk about Shadou, unless I start the conversation, OK? You can't hold that over me."

Conner scrunched his face. *Is he going to start crying now?*

"Conner, I'm sorry if I'm shutting you out."

"Is that what you're doing? Is that what you want?"

"I don't know. I guess I want everything to go back to the way it was, before."

"So do I. Why can't it?"

"That's not really something I can talk about."

"You know you can trust me, right, Elle? I mean, you've told me lots of stuff, secret stuff. I'd do the same, except my life is way boring compared to yours."

Elle clutched her head and let out a faint moan.

"You OK, Elle? Why do you keep doing that?"

Deep breaths. "It's just, from the accident. I'll be fine."

Conner pulled Elle close until her pain subsided. She relaxed and took his hand. "Conner, what was that new game you told me about? Buzzle Jump?"

"Yeah, that's it. I hear it's being delayed, for like the fourth time. Why?"

"Just wondering. Maybe if I found something new to focus on, I'd get better, quicker."

"Don't hold your breath for that one."

"Maybe I don't have to."

That night, Elle waited for her parents to fall asleep and then absconded with their laptop to her bedroom. Within an hour she hacked into secure servers to access the code for Buzzle Jump. She spent much of that night conjuring up changes to the game that she hoped Conner would enjoy. Before she succumbed to exhaustion, she sent the CEO of the game developer a little "hello" message. The next day he responded to her, and asked for a discreet meeting. Elle recommended a small café in Seattle.

The dark winter days dragged on. Christmas came and went. The Redferns decorated a tree and opened presents, but there was a pervasive unsaid sadness to everything they did. After her unpleasant meeting with the CEO, Elle hadn't attempted to code in weeks. All she wanted to do was escape to movies and TV shows, with Conner. They held hands sometimes. But the hours spent cocooned at his cavernous house in front of a massive television couldn't keep her from noticing her parents grow distant from each other.

One night, late, Elle heard Jill shouting at Jim. She couldn't make out the words from her bedroom, but she could tell that her mother was crying. Elle quietly opened the door to her bedroom. She heard her shouting, "Just because you don't have a job and can't get one is not my problem!"

Jim shouted back, "Yes, it is your problem!"

"Well, you're certainly making it one. And I don't know why. I'm making plenty to support us. You just lost your leg. You shouldn't be working at all right now! Can't you see that?"

Jim slammed his fist down on the side table. "I can see that you don't care about my feelings, about my career. That's crystal clear!"

"You know what, Jim? You're right. I don't care about your feelings at all. Because you're acting like a four-year-old, and if that's how you're going to be, then I'd rather just not talk to you at all."

Elle had heard enough. She retreated behind her closed bedroom door. More shouting rose from below, then a door slam. After several minutes of silence, Elle crept out of her room and tiptoed down the stairs. There, she saw her parents' bedroom door closed. But just past it, in the living room, she saw Jim sprawled out across the couch.

Jim heard Elle and sat up. "Hi, sweetie. What you doing down here?"

Without answering, Elle raced downstairs to the garage. She fished the iPad out from the box and retreated to her nest in the basement furnace room. She navigated to a BadShadou video on YouTube and posted a comment: *Where ru? I need u right now!*

Elle literally cried herself to sleep. She lay on the floor curled up in her nest. A light throw blanket clung around her frame. Her sleep-laden hands clutched the iPad. Her breaths rose soft and steady.

It was after two a.m. when Shadou materialized from the wall. He towered above her, his pointy ears nearly brushing the ceiling. Shadou took in Elle's soft breathing, as the heater fan blew in the night.

He placed a hand gently on her shoulder. She rolled over, half-awake. *Is he really here?* Shadou smiled and Elle smiled back. His grip on her shoulder tightened ever so slightly. Elle grabbed his hand, her own hand barely able to extend around three of Shadou's shiny black claws. Shadou took the iPad from beneath her and twirled it effortlessly in the air.

Elle sat up and held her knees in her arms. "Took you long enough."

"But hopefully not too long."

Elle jumped up and landed in his lap. She wrapped her arms around his big belly as far as she could. His fur softened and reacted to her touch with shifting vibrations. He held Elle close to him, but not too tightly.

After a few minutes, Shadou said, "Elle, will you come with me? Just for a quick outing."

Within minutes Elle was fully clothed and ready for an adventure. She stood before Shadou dressed in purple jeans, red boots, a black puffy coat, and knitted wool hat. She smiled. "Is this warm enough?"

Shadou let out a low, quiet chuckle. "Don't worry, Elle. I'll make sure you stay warm wherever we go."

Elle took a short run and leapt into his arms. He stepped into the wall. Elle could feel an electric tingling sensation as they both dematerialized together. Suddenly everything went silent and dark.

Elle "awoke" to a deafening whooshing sound. Her eyes could just barely make out a vortex of warm light that swirled around them like a glowing tornado. She clung tightly to Shadou's soft fur as a new place materialized around them. At last the tornado stopped spinning and the whooshing sound ceased.

Elle found herself cradled in Shadou's arms on a rocky outcropping overlooking a massive canyon. Every formation shone silvery purple in the moonlight. Shadou's body kept her quite comfortably warm in the chilly night air. Elle could make out thousands of bright stars divided by the Milky Way's band in the sky above.

Shadou looked down at her with a serene smile. "Here we are."

"Are we still on Earth?"

"Of course we are," laughed Shadou. "We're standing before one of the most famous places on the planet, in what you people call Arizona. This is the Grand Canyon."

Elle giggled, "Oh my god! I can't believe I didn't recognize it. I guess it seems so ... alien in the moonlight."

"It is indeed." Shadou surveyed the canyon before him. "Elle, do you ever play the game tag with your brother Emmett?"

"Of course, I mean... I indulge in tag from time to time. He's pretty young so he's into that."

"Well, think of this place, the Grand Canyon, as base. Like you have 'base' in tag. Nobody can get you here."

Elle nodded with an air of casual indifference. "OK." Then she couldn't help but laugh. She poked at Shadou's fat belly. He loosened his grip and she dropped down onto the ground. Elle picked up a handful of dusty pebbles, raised it high, and sprayed him in the stomach with it. "Tag!" she called out into the still, dreamlike night. "You're it!"

Shadou roared with laughter and chased Elle over the rocks. He tackled her and they both rolled down a gravely hill together. Shadou made sure to keep Elle safe in his arms. They rolled to the edge of a precipice. Shadou planted one foot on the cliff's edge and dematerialized both himself and Elle.

They rematerialized in the middle of a redwood forest. A clear stream wound its way through the towering trees that glowed silver in the light of the moon. Elle let herself down onto the soft ferns of the forest floor. She picked up a pinecone and tossed it at Shadou. He caught the pinecone and gave chase. Elle zigzagged through the forest, hiding behind massive redwood tree trunks as Shadou tried to find her. Elle's laughter echoed off of the trees. After playing around in this magical place for nearly an hour,

Shadou grabbed up Elle from the forest floor and transported them back to Bainbridge Island.

There, Elle found herself seated next to Shadou, overlooking the Puget Sound from the eastern side of Bloedel Reserve. The high moon reflected off of the glassy water. The north side of Seattle glowed ghostlike in the distant mist. Shadou sat cross-legged on the tall, wet grass with Elle leaning against his ample lap. Elle felt perfectly warm despite the below-forty cold. She knew it would soon be time to return home.

"Why are you here?" Elle twirled a lock of his fur in her fingers.

"Here right now on Bainbridge Island, or here on Earth in general?"

"Earth."

"I've been on Earth for a very long time, Elle. Over five thousand years."

"Whoa."

"Yes. I'm sure it's hard to imagine, but after that long, it's easy for one to get ... distracted."

"Distracted by what?"

Shadou gestured toward the distant Seattle lights. "All this change. When I first arrived here, at that mountain," Shadou pointed in the direction of Mount Rainier even though it wasn't visible, "there were almost no people. The people who were here, they blended in."

"The Native Americans?"

"There was no America then, but yes, I guess you could say that's what they were. They didn't have much effect on my... mission. You see, back then I had the easiest job in the universe. I wandered this great world, taking in all its woods and its wonders."

"You like the woods, don't you?"

"Yes. The woods, I do care about them quite a bit. They... speak to me."

Elle rolled over so that her tummy rested on his. "Who in the woods speaks to you, the deer?"

"Yes, actually. All the creatures, and the people. Back then it was mostly the trees. But, after several thousand years of my wandering, communing, you humans started to evolve more... rapidly."

Elle became entranced by Shadou's shifting fur. It rose in ripples as she waved her hand above it. "You mean technology?"

"Yes. The technology you humans invented started to talk to me in a voice much louder than that of the woods or the trees or the creatures. You see, I have a natural disposition to such things. Like I told you before, I can control your technology, manipulate it. That is my gift."

"Cool. Can you do anything else? Other gifts?"

Shadou pinched the fur on his chin between two claws. "Well, let's see. Just a couple of things. First, I can transport myself. For me it's kind of like what you humans call 3-D printing. I basically send my molecules through matter. I can transport other objects and life-forms with me if I want to. But I can only do it on the planet I'm on. No space travel."

"Transporting around the world with you has been pretty sweet. What else?"

"It evolves. Like I said, I can communicate with technology, manipulate it. Mostly what you call digital technology. I can't control everything that uses electricity, or that has a motor, but as digital technology spreads, I can control more and more."

"Anything else?"

"I'm afraid not. You see, Elle, where I come from, our people are each made to serve very specific roles in our society. We are all different from one another in many ways. We look different, experience the world with different senses, and we each possess different ... gifts."

"That's so awesome. Do you find out what your gifts are when you're first born?"

Shadou laughed. "Something like that. Very early on in our consciousness, we are told."

"Who tells you?"

"Our masters."

"Masters? Does that mean you're like slaves? Or pets?"

"No, Elle. Well, maybe, sort of. What it means is, that we are raised by powerful beings who are far older than us, as old as the universe, perhaps. They bestow upon us our gifts, and our purposes. They guide us through our lives as long as our purposes are needed."

"What happens when your purpose isn't needed? Are you set free?"

Shadou smiled. "Sort of set free. When we are no longer useful, we die."

"Oh." Elle and Shadou silently gazed across the water for a moment. Then Elle asked, "So what's your purpose?"

"Right now, my gifts are useful for guarding this planet from something that's very dangerous."

"Quaru?"

"Yes, Quaru."

"What the heck is Quaru, anyway?"

"We don't quite know exactly. But we do know that He, or It, is an entity that craves control. He's extremely powerful, perhaps as powerful as my master, perhaps even more so. Everywhere He goes, He seeks to bring order. But He does so ruthlessly, by enslaving entire worlds. Our people believe in order, but a peaceful order based on freedom and trust."

Elle shuddered. "Why'd you have to bring this Quaru being here? Why not destroy Him, blow Him up, or toss Him into a sun or a black hole something?"

"Only my master knows the answers to these questions. At least, I hope She does. She's been searching for them for a long time."

"OK, that's really scary. I hope this master lady of yours figures it out soon."

"Me too, Elle."

Elle stroked Shadou's undulating fur with her fingers, and yawned. "So tell me. When is all this technology going to leave my head alone?"

Shadou let out a thundering laugh. "Would you rather make Minecraft videos for the rest of your life?"

Elle buried her face in Shadou's fur. "I can't believe I ever posted those videos."

Shadou stroked Elle's hair. "Don't be ashamed. They're quite entertaining. I saw what you did with that game, Buzzle Jump. You were inviting some serious trouble, Elle."

"I did that for my own sanity, and for Conner. But of course it all backfired."

"Be very careful. There are people who, if they find out your gift, will try to use you, manipulate you to serve their purpose."

"What else am I supposed to do?"

"I don't think you understand it now, Elle, and frankly I don't expect you to. But in the coming years, you will learn to harness your technological skills in ways that will change the course of this planet. You will find your purpose, like I have mine."

Elle's voice fell to a sleepy whisper. "No pressure..."

"Don't let it be a burden to you, Elle. You've already done much by helping me remember..."

Shadou saw that Elle had drifted off to sleep. He gazed up at the night sky. "Master," he whispered. "Bring me home. Bring me to my family."

Elle looked up from Shadou's fur. Her eyelids hung heavy with exhaustion. "I really have to change the world?" she asked. "I hope I never meet Quaru. Don't you ever let Him escape."

Shadou poked Elle's side with the tip of his claw, making her squirm.

"I'll do everything I can, Elle. But right now, it's almost morning."

Before Elle could respond, Shadou pulled her close and transported them to her bedroom. She was quite relieved to see her own bed, and even more so when she remembered that the next day was Saturday. She would be able to sleep late.

Shadou tucked Elle in and pulled out the iPad from his backpack. Using his "gift," he willed it to turn on. A bouquet of pink and orange flowers burst onto the screen, followed by a stampede of unicorn kittens roaring past undulating rainbows. More nonsensical yet soothing images floated by. After several minutes, Elle's eyes closed, and she fell into a deep sleep that lasted for many peaceful hours.

Chapter 19

The entity beneath Mount Rainier saw Chuck's struggle to blend in as a major vulnerability. Any time, Chuck could be discovered, captured. If this happened, all gains from the entity's breach of its prison walls would disappear. The entity needed Chuck to quietly wait in the shadows until it regained enough strength to finish its plan. Chuck must be hidden from the world, camouflaged so that nobody could discover him. Luckily, out in rural Washington, there were many options.

Chuck felt a powerful force pulling him away from his Puyallup mobile home park and back out into the wilderness. He gathered what few essentials he needed. He tucked a 9mm handgun and a hunting knife into his jacket pockets. He shouldered a well-oiled shotgun. He pulled his black coat over his weapons and wandered backed onto the highway. He began his journey south toward the national forest surrounding Mount Rainier. There, he would set up camp until he received further instructions from his master.

Hours after Chuck's departure, Jason Fabian pulled his weathered Toyota 4Runner into an abandoned parking lot several blocks away. He stepped out of the truck wearing a military-issue camouflage flak jacket and cargo pants. The daylight was quickly fading, and a veil of ice-cold air descended along with the dusk. Jason pulled on a pair of tight leather gloves, tucked a handgun into the back of his pants, and walked with swift purpose toward Chuck's mobile home. His Special Operations training kicked into high gear.

Piece of cake, he thought.

When he arrived at Chuck's home, Jason realized that something was off. The front landing was much too tidy, as though it had been recently cleaned up by thorough hands. It didn't match Jill's description at all.

Jason considered knocking on the door, but then decided to check the windows first. Everything inside sat eerily still and silent. He pulled a Maglite flashlight from a pocket and shined it through the grimy glass. Between the few inches that weren't obscured by curtains, Jason saw nothing but filth inside. Apparently only the exterior had been cleaned up. Inside, it looked as though whoever lived there had left in a hurry. Then something shiny caught his eye. Jason noticed that a thin wire glinted with silver reflections from the flashlight. He followed the wire with his light and saw that it stopped at the front door.

Jason walked around the home, peering through every window. All the windows were rigged with wires. Should he place an anonymous call to the authorities and lead them to search this booby-trapped home? Or should he himself figure out a way to get inside? After deliberating in the cold, he made up his mind. He went back to his truck and retrieved a small toolbox. From it, he took out a set of needle-nose pliers and a flat-head screwdriver. After looking over his shoulder to make sure he wasn't being watched, Jason knelt and worked on the front door.

It was a slow process, but after nearly half an hour, Jason managed to pry open the door just enough to reach the wire with his pliers. He took a roll of duct tape from his toolbox and ripped off a strip with his teeth. With the needle-nose pliers, Jason gently tugged at the wire. He was glad the front door didn't face the street.

He pulled the wire off the door with the pliers and then attached it to the door frame with the strip of duct tape. Then, flashlight out, he opened the door and walked inside.

Chuck's home was just as Jill had described, completely squalid. It showed signs of a massive bear fight as well. Half of the living room wall was shredded with what appeared to be claw marks. The couch lay overturned on the ripped-up carpeting with stuffing billowing from torn cushions. Jason shook his head in amazement. He had never seen anything like it.

He followed the wire from the door across the entryway to the garbage can in the center of the living room. He could see this wire was joined by wires from all of the windows in the house. He pointed his flashlight down into the can. There, stacked in the bottom of the garbage can like firewood, lay three crudely assembled pipe bombs. The detonator was a primitive device connected to a car battery. It would be easy to defuse. But even so, Jason's hands shook as he cut the wire connecting it to the bombs.

He walked back out to the front porch, shielded himself from the inside as much as he could with the wall and the door, and detached the duct tape from the door frame. Holding his breath, he tossed the wad of tape with the attached wire into the house. No bombs exploded. *What was I thinking?*

While waiting for the adrenaline rush to wear off, Jason sat on the only unbroken chair he could find. He drank from a bottle of water he pulled from a pocket. Five minutes later he went back to work. He attempted to turn on the lights and was not surprised to discover that the electrical power had been shut off. It wouldn't be long before the slumlord of this dingy mobile home park would figure out that Chuck was delinquent. Jason needed to search the place thoroughly with the assumption that this would be his last visit there.

First, he detached the wires from the windows and tossed them into the garbage can. Then he dug through every filthy inch of the mobile home in search of any clue to Chuck's whereabouts. He opened cardboard boxes filled with cheap drugstore books, old bills, and junk mail from years ago. He rifled through drawers that contained threadbare clothing, mismatched dishes and tableware, and the occasional 9mm slug or shotgun shell. Nothing he found would help.

After nearly an hour of fruitless searching, Jason gave up. *What a waste of time!* He punched the fake wood-paneled wall with his gloved fist in frustration. But then he noticed that the bottom of the panel detached from the wall. Jason squatted and ran his gloved hands between the floor and the wall. The panel gave way too easily, so he pulled up and removed it completely. He shined his flashlight down onto the exposed wall and noticed a small stack of envelopes. The envelopes were old and yellowed, held together by a brittle rubber band. Jason picked them up. They were handwritten, each one from the same address in Cottage Grove, Oregon. Jason shoved the envelopes into his pocket and used a small hammer to pry off the remaining panels. Nothing else there. Satisfied that he had found everything he could, Jason gathered his things and went back to his truck.

Out there in the freezing cold he finished off the bottled water, all the while pacing back and forth. His mind raced. Jason had to admit that he was enjoying himself, maybe a little bit too much. He tossed the bottle into the bushes and considered his next move. Smiling to himself, Jason reached back into his truck and took out a gasoline can. Whoever had booby-trapped Chuck's house wasn't coming back. Those bombs were meant to be a danger to anyone who dared to go inside. Jason could call the cops, but what would be the fun of that? Concealing the gas can inside the folds of his coat, Jason walked back one last time. Chuck's house would burn tonight.

Chapter 20

After Elle's night with Shadou, she was plagued by nightmares in which she encountered a dark, menacing figure. *How could he know I exist?*

She became obsessed with texting Shadou on her parents' phones. Her connection to him was her one true escape from her fears, her only respite from her "gift." The best time for texting without risk of getting caught was in the predawn hours. She started by setting her alarm for three, then four a.m. so she could test the optimal timing. She even accessed her mom's fitness apps to determine when she typically experienced deep REM sleep. After several days, Elle settled into a routine of texting Shadou, deleting the evidence, and then returning the phone before morning.

Shadou's replies tried in vain to calm her. *You and your world are completely safe. Neither I nor my master would ever let you come into harm's way. Focus on your studies. Focus on your gift, Elle.*

That so-called gift doesn't help at all—it just freaks me out even more.

This state of fear brought Elle close to a point of being physically ill, which in turn made her sloppy. One night, she forgot to delete a text thread from her mom's phone.

Jill saw the texts early one February morning. At first, she thought the messages must have been from some virus or malware installed on her phone. But as she read through them, she realized that they were an exchange between Elle and an "unknown" phone number. From the texts, Jill saw that Elle seemed to be very frightened by something. The time stamps on the messages revealed that they had all been sent after midnight the night before.

Jill nearly dropped the phone. She felt blood rushing to her face. Her daughter was carrying on an intense, personal text exchange with a complete stranger. One of Elle's texts was particularly disturbing: *I need 2 c u. Now.*

Jill took deep breaths, hoping not to go into complete panic attack. At least it was a Sunday. She didn't have to rush to get Elle ready for school. She needed to talk to Jim first.

About an hour later, Elle woke up to find her parents on the couch in the living room. They were waiting for her. *This can't be good.*

"Hi," Elle said. "What's up?"

Jim had developed a habit of scratching his knee just above his prosthetic leg. He was doing that now. "Elle," he said. "Your mom found some texts on her phone."

Elle's heart skipped multiple beats. *How could I have been so stupid?*

"Oh, those?" she said, smiling. "That's just me and Conner goofing off."

Jim shot Elle a furious glance. "We know that's not Conner you've been texting, Elle. So we need you to tell us the truth, right now. Who is your friend?"

Jill interjected, "Sweetie, we totally understand that, sometimes, people you meet online can seem really... cool."

Elle felt a sensation she hoped to never experience again. Another life-changing moment. Jim's eyes reflected sternly, with an air of a wolf about to attack. Jill seemed frightened. Neither of them could possibly understand Elle's situation. Any answer she gave would just lead to more difficult questions, and then a never-ending descent into lie after lie after lie. And yet Jill and Jim both looked at Elle as though the fate of the entire world depended upon her response.

"Well?" asked Jim after a moment. "Are you going to explain yourself or not?"

Elle walked over to her father and sat down beside him, her arm resting on his shoulder as though nothing was the matter.

"Dad," she said, "I don't know who he is. Like Mom said, he's just someone I met online."

Elle told her parents about being a Minecraft creator, a streamer of videos that thousands of people watched. She introduced them to her channel on Twitch.TV, as well as her YouTube videos. Jill and Jim looked on in a state of semiterror. A parent's worst nightmare was unfolding before their very eyes.

"Elle," Jill said, "why didn't you tell us any of this? We could have made a fortune from your viewership, for one thing."

Jim looked on in shock. "Jill! Our teenage daughter has been leading a double life online, and all you can think about is money?"

"Well," Jill offered, "this stuff could pay for college." And then to Elle, "Why on earth didn't you tell us, sweetie? You're an internet star!"

Elle blushed. "Not really. I just liked playing Minecraft. I was good at it."

Jim looked at Jill as if to gauge her anger level at Elle's secret life. Then he said, "OK, Elle. You have proven yourself to be quite ... talented. Talented at being deceptive and dishonest. You have lied to your family, and probably, in many instances, hidden the truth about what you were doing up there in your bedroom. Even *after* I told you no more devices." Jim pointed upstairs as though pointing at a crime scene.

Elle felt the tears well up in her eyes. "I'm sorry, Dad."

Jim's expression remained unchanged. "I'm sure you are sorry, Elle. But until you can regain our trust, and it may take months or years, you will not be allowed to go online unless myself or your mother are present. And you can forget about getting your own phone this year."

"But, Dad!"

Jim held up a defiant hand. "No. There's no 'but Dad' here. This is final."

Jill interjected, "Elle, you've been engaging with a cyberstalker, and keeping this secret from us, for we don't know how long. We're going to have to ask the phone company for our text-message history now."

"I hate the word cyberstalker!" Elle ran up to her bedroom and slammed the door.

Jill and Jim sat on the couch listening to Elle pacing and stomping around her room. Jim faced Jill with an accusing glare. "I told you she was up to something. We should have banned devices years ago."

Jill rolled her eyes. This was one more annoying issue to deal with. "Yes, I get it, Jim. You're the good parent here." She sighed and reached for the laptop. "Now I guess we should watch these videos."

"Ugh, Minecraft... Can't she outgrow that already?"

Jill turned around the laptop and showed Jim a browser window with the EleMent03 YouTube channel. "Let's see what she's got."

She clicked play on the video. Blocky Minecraft images danced across the screen. Jill cranked up the volume. She and Jim both couldn't help but smile a little as Elle's distinct voice narrated the video. They glanced at the play count on the video: more than four hundred thousand. Jill's jaw dropped and Jim's tightened.

Jill slammed the laptop shut. "I can't believe that girl didn't have ads running before those videos. She could be paying for her college education nine times over!"

"What's that supposed to mean exactly?"

"Jim, I'm just saying—"

"It sounds like you're worried about her college fund. Maybe if you'd let me focus on my career, that wouldn't be a problem."

"Again, with the whining-baby routine! I'm not the problem here, Jim. You are. You want a job? Go out there and get one."

"So our daughter doesn't have to whore herself out on YouTube?"

"At least she's doing something that's meaningful to people other than herself!"

The weeks that followed were pure torture for Elle. Her parents treated her like a convict in her own home. She had absolutely no access to any devices. The lockdown was impenetrable, even for her. Jill and Jim told her friends' parents that under no circumstances was Elle allowed to interact with devices at their homes. But that didn't make much of a difference, since Elle was basically grounded anyway.

To add to Elle's misery, the discovery of her deception further damaged the already strained relationship between Jill and Jim. Not only had they both just emerged from unique yet equally traumatizing life events, but now they shared the shame of having failed to properly monitor their daughter's online interactions. As Elle was constantly reminded by both parents, that stranger could have killed her, or worse!

Despite all of this upheaval, Elle did not dare reveal the truth about Shadou. She considered it on many occasions. She even fantasized about introducing her parents to him. In her daydreams Elle would tell her parents the truth. They, of course, would not believe her. But just as they were chastising Elle for making up outlandish stories, Shadou would materialize before them. Elle would revel in her triumphant vindication while her parents sat stunned staring at Shadou. For reasons Elle couldn't quite grasp, she knew that she could never tell them the "real" truth. She didn't even consider telling them about her gift. That was out of the question.

Her parents were in a completely different mind-set. They determined that they must catch this "cyberstalker" at all costs. He must be made to pay for all the pain he had caused. Jill reported the texts to the police, but there wasn't much either they or the cellphone provider could do. The texts all came from multiple and completely untraceable numbers. Whoever did this was a sophisticated hacker, she was told. There would need to be proof of an actual crime for a real investigation to start. The trail went cold.

Jill was able to retrieve some of the text messages. They read like a tragic love story about two star-crossed lovers who could never be together because they were both held captive in separate prisons.

Poring through these digital exchanges broke Jill's heart. Jim couldn't even bear to read them. They both felt violated by whomever this stalker was, and of course they became suspicious of everyone they knew: neighbors, teachers, other parents.

Months went by and things got worse. Jim withdrew from the family more and more. He still didn't have a job and he didn't even pretend to be looking. His alcohol consumption increased, and all of his time was spent glued to his computer. Jill lost all patience with Jim. His frail condition ceased to elicit any sympathy; she almost held his injuries against him. The lost leg gave Jim license to fade into a dull gray background.

After several more weeks of emotional isolation, Jill determined that she couldn't live like that anymore. The cyberstalker among them had obliterated all attraction to Bainbridge Island, and Jim's paralysis did the same for her feelings toward him. On a rainy May morning, Jill announced to Jim that she was leaving, and taking both children down to Los Angeles. She had gotten a job transfer to move there, including a promotion.

Jim took the news with quiet resignation. In the end, they opted not to divorce, but to separate. Jim agreed to Jill's terms. The conversation may as well have been between two strangers conducting a Craigslist transaction. Once finalized, Jill set her new plans in motion. These plans included giving up her search for Chuck. The mysterious hiker on Mount Rainier seemed like unwanted baggage. Jill was ready to move on completely.

Chapter 21

When Conner first heard the news, he didn't know how to react. "Are you kidding?" he asked.

"No, Conner. This is real. I'm moving to LA And you have to promise me something."

"What?"

"Never tell anyone about Shadou, ever. You have to promise me that."

"Is that all I am to you now? A risk?"

"No, of course not! But just... Don't tell, OK?"

"What if I do tell? Is he going to come kill me?"

"No! At least, I don't think he'd do that."

"Don't worry, Elle. Your secret's safe with me. Nobody would believe it anyway."

"Promise?"

Conner held up his pinky. "Pinky promise."

Elle placed her hand on Conner's shoulder. He flinched. "So this is good-bye?"

"Yeah, Conner. But I'll try to email you or whatever. If I'm ever allowed to touch a device again."

"OK. If you want."

Elle smiled. "Of course I do. I'll miss you."

"Doesn't feel like it. Feels more like I'm being dumped."

Elle couldn't imagine life without Conner, but she knew she could only bring him pain. *I have to let him go.*

"Conner, you're not being dumped. Because we were never a thing, like that."

"If you say so."

"I get it. Change sucks. Just, be happy without me, OK? Forget about us."

"Not possible."

Elle pulled Conner into a tight embrace. She ran her fingers through his thick, short hair, wondering if she'd ever feel him this close again. At last, she pulled away.

"Good-bye, Conner. You can remember us if you want."

As Elle walked away, her stomach tightened into knots at the thought of him blabbing her secrets. *I shouldn't have told him anything. But how will I live without him?*

When it was time to say his good-byes to Elle and Emmett, Jim seemed to have aged a decade from the ordeal. He did not wear his helplessness well.

Elle adjusted the collar on his shirt. "Are you still going to be, you know, my dad?"

"Sweetie, of course. Always..."

Elle knew that was true for her, but she still doubted him.

"Will you be OK, you know, without us?"

"Oh, I'll survive. I have some decent job prospects. Plus, I've got some money saved up, so—"

"So that's good." Elle was relieved to hear that her father wouldn't starve. *But what if he's lying?* She made a mental note to blast out his résumé as soon as she had the chance.

As they drove away from their Bainbridge home for the last time, Jim looked to Elle like a lonely old man. She hoped to never see him like that again.

Jill, on the other hand, seemed more youthful than she had in years. She bounced when she walked, as though a great weight had been lifted off her shoulders. When they arrived in the California sun, Jill floored the gas of their peppy rental car and zoomed through the LA streets with the carefree abandon of a teenager. Elle and Emmett couldn't help but feel their spirits rise as they embarked on another adventure together.

Five hundred miles northeast of Los Angeles, in a cavern far beneath Arizona's Grand Canyon, Shadou stood on the deck of his gleaming white starship. He faced a holographic projection of light. It swirled with shimmering blues and silvers, seemingly gesticulating at him. Shadou was carrying on a conversation with this projection. His voice grew increasingly urgent.

"But Master," he said, "I don't think the girl–Elle–I don't think she is ready. She's not at all close to serving any purpose here."

Of course not. The shimmering sparks of light swirled as the warm, female voice "spoke" to Shadou. *But in time, she could be your best hope for redemption.*

"Redemption? From what?"

You told me yourself, Shadou. You forgot your purpose. You almost let HIM escape.

"I'm telling you, Master, something very suspicious is going on here. It's like somebody deleted memory files from my system. Could it be that the human technology is interfering with my gifts?"

Nothing is clear from my vantage point. You need to analyze the local data and figure this out yourself. I'm currently occupied with more ... pressing matters.

The projected light fizzled and faded. Shadou had never seen this before. He panicked. "Master! Are you all right?"

The light crackled and spit like a dying fire. Shadou ran his claws through it, but in an instant the light extinguished completely. He surveyed the ship's deck. Silent instruments flickered on various consoles. Shadou felt hopelessly alone.

"Master..." he whispered more to himself than anyone else.

Suddenly, blinding red and orange lights burst throughout the starship. A wailing scream of static pummeled Shadou's ears. He fell to the floor, paralyzed by sensory overload. His master's voice drilled deep into his mind.

Shadou! Get back to the mountain... Guard the prisoner... Mustn't escape.

"Master! What's happening?"

No time to explain. All I can tell you is... The Overlord is involved.

"Oh, no. That's not good. My family, are they safe?"

Yes, for now... But all may be in danger. Shadou, listen, the girl...

The light flickered once again, as though it were struggling against an invisible force. "Master? What about the girl?"

The light managed one final burst of color. *Do not contact the girl unless you have to. There are others, other masters... A terrible plot... If the girl is harmed, you will be on your own. I can no longer help you. You must find a way.*

"Find a way to do what?"

Find a way to destroy Quaru! He has weaknesses, you must exploit them. The girl can help you with this when she is ready. Keep her safe for now.

"But... I thought you said that might be catastrophic. How can I destroy Him without—"

But the light was gone. Shadou found himself standing alone with his arms outstretched on the empty deck of his starship. He collapsed onto a chair and rubbed his head in his hands. Moments later the ship's hatch hissed open. In strode Rifkin, spinning his staff between two claws.

"What was that all about?"

Shadou reflected for a moment with wide eyes. "Rifkin, I'm pretty sure we're totally screwed."

Part 2

Chapter 22

Two years later...

Not far away from Mount Rainier, near a town called Ashford, Chuck led a quiet, secluded "life" in a remote cabin. The woods, to him, were a refuge from the overwhelmingly noisy human signals that bombarded him. Alone in the forest, miles away from civilization, Chuck could spend as much time as he wanted basking in the soothing blackness of his dark dimension. Sometimes he would spend days at a time submerged in the blissful meditative state. No stress, no corporeal demands, nothing but simplicity, order and harmony.

But every time he dove deeper into this welcoming abyss, Chuck was violently pulled back to the earthly realities. He needed water, food, and sleep to survive. None of these were available to him in the darkness, or at least he didn't know how to find them. So he would begrudgingly return to his cabin in the woods, and then go out into the wild in search of game and potable water.

Chuck still possessed a minimum amount of survival skills. He could hunt, filter water, build fires, and find other edible foods such as plants and grubs. His newly added senses enabled him to elude humans with great efficiency. Chuck could literally see people coming from miles away. They registered as bright shining lights, even beyond the horizon. He could feel their thoughts and see their voices. As time went by he began to regain some of his former, more human "abilities."

Chuck spent years stumbling about the woods as a zombielike mute. There were several occasions when he encountered other humans and had to work around his inability to speak. Once, Chuck sneaked into a hunter's cabin, hoping to surreptitiously steal a shotgun and some ammo he knew was stored there. But he got so focused on finding the gun that he didn't notice a drunk hunter passed out on the filthy couch in the middle of the cabin. The hunter's inebriated state had made his thoughts almost invisible to Chuck's heightened senses. As Chuck stumbled clumsily through the cabin toward the shotgun leaned against the wall, the hunter launched up out of bed.

"Who in the heck are you?"

The hunter's presence flashed into Chuck's consciousness and blinded him with a torrent of light and sound. As Chuck stood there immobilized, the hunter struggled out of the couch and ambled over to the shotgun. He picked it up off the floor and aimed it in Chuck's direction. The barrel bobbed back and forth as the hunter swayed.

"Well?" asked the hunter. "What's it gonna be? Either you tell me who you are and what you're doing here right now, or I blow your head off." The hunter cocked the rifle.

Chuck's mouth widened ever so slowly, until a thin string of drool hung down off his chin.

"Ngugghh..." he groaned.

Then several things happened very quickly. Chuck stepped toward the hunter. The hunter pulled the shotgun's trigger. That very instant the gun exploded with buckshot, which at that close range should have torn Chuck to shreds. But in the hunter's eyes, all that remained of Chuck was a faint, gray shadow. The wall and window behind Chuck burst apart from the shotgun blast. The hunter stood frozen with fear as the shimmering shadow that was Chuck drifted toward him. There was something enchantingly beautiful, intoxicatingly graceful, about the way this shadow moved.

But then as suddenly as it formed, the shadow transformed, less than a foot away from the hunter, into the physical form of Chuck. This proximity gave the hunter a detailed look at Chuck's gaunt, skeletal features. Sores and scabs covered his pale, almost translucent skin. Chuck's filthy clothes reeked.

The hunter cocked the shotgun again and was about to pull the trigger when a swarm of black tentacles shot out from Chuck's eyes, ears, nose, and mouth. The tendrils of darkness ripped the rifle from the hunter's hands and wrapped themselves around his head. Within seconds, the hunter's skull was crushed, almost imploded. His bloody, twitching corpse fell splayed out on the floor.

The black tentacles retracted back into Chuck's body. He stumbled across the room and gathered the shotgun and all the spare ammo he could find. Chuck really wished he could have spoken to the hunter that time. He wished he could have told the hunter exactly who he was before killing him.

There were other human encounters that ended with equally morbid outcomes. One young couple backpacking across America over the summer set up camp nearby Chuck's cabin. They made the mistake of bringing a six-pack of beer. Chuck liked beer. He never hesitated to kill in order to get some for himself.

There was also a family passing through on the way to visit relatives. The father had decided to take the scenic route, but pulled over to the side of the road when he saw a strange man walking aimlessly on the shoulder. That man turned out to be Chuck.

The father approached Chuck with cautious concern. "Excuse me, sir, are you OK?"

Chuck gazed at the man with dark, bloodshot eyes. Something about Chuck's face caused the man to stumble backwards and trip. The man's wife screamed at him from the car to come back, but the man sat frozen on the gravel. Chuck sauntered toward him, a twisted smile growing on his white, sore-ridden face.

"Who are you?" begged the man.

Then, for the first time since the incident on Mount Rainier that had transformed him forever, Chuck spoke.

"I am the messenger of the One Who Waits in the Mountain." uttered Chuck in a hoarse and yet discernable voice. After speaking these words, Chuck was momentarily stunned. This gave the man just enough time to rise up from the ground, run back to his car, and speed away. As Chuck disappeared in the rearview mirror, the man thought he saw dark tentacles spilling out from Chuck's head and stretching out toward the car. The family escaped before the tentacles could reach them.

Over time, locals began to whisper tales of a mysterious hobo who roamed the woods and highways around Ashford. Most assumed he was some vagrant who would either eventually leave or die, but some took a keen interest in him. One such person was a mechanic at a local garage named Danny.

Danny had grown up in Ashford and spent most of his time off from work playing video games with his childhood friends, all of whom were in their midtwenties. He was also one of the area's few African Americans.

Danny first noticed Chuck while out with a friend. They had been partying at an acquaintance's house in the woods. They got lost on a fast-food run in their old pickup truck. Danny drove as his buddy attempted to navigate using a phone that constantly lost reception. The night was dark and foggy, making the task all the more difficult.

"Come on, dude, where are we?" Danny demanded.

"Dude, this reception sucks, man. Hold on. Wait, pull over. Just stop here so I can look at the map."

Danny pulled over as his friend pored over the map on his phone. Fast, hard rock music boomed from his stereo system. Danny pounded the steering wheel to the beat.

Finally, his friend shouted over the music, "OK man, I got it. You need to flip a U-turn and we'll take the third left, then the second right."

Without speaking, Danny threw the truck in reverse and backed around into a dirt driveway. He put it in drive and hit the gas. A blurry form emerged from the foggy dark into the headlights. Danny slammed on the brakes. About forty feet away, he saw a strange man stumbling toward them in the middle of the road.

Danny rolled down his window and called out, "Hey man, you're in the middle of the road in the dark. You could get killed out here, you know?"

The man did not respond, but instead picked up his pace in their direction.

"What the—?" wondered Danny.

"Dude, drive," pleaded his friend. "This guy's creeping me out."

Danny snapped out of it. He spun the wheel and hit the gas. As they maneuvered past the strange man, they heard him mumble in a deep, low voice, "Nighty-night, kids. Enjoy the dark!"

Danny and his friend burst out laughing. As they drove back to town, Danny analyzed everything he could remember about the strange man.

"That guy was like something from another world, yo! Did you see his ripped-up black coat? Those boots must have been like a hundred years old. And man, did he stink. That dude was rank!" Danny's laughter boomed over the stereo. "And his voice, that was some seriously scary stuff."

Danny's friend agreed. "Yo man," he said through high-pitched giggles, "we gotta give that guy a nickname."

"Ronnie Darko," said Danny, "Ronnie Darko."

As time went by, the legend of "Ronnie Darko" rose and fell like a slow tide. Danny asked all his friends to take a photo if they ever saw the strange man. Only one person ever succeeded at that mission, and that person did not live to share his photo with Danny, or anyone else. Chuck did not allow close-up photography.

Around the same time, strange incidents cropped up. Homes and businesses were broken into and ransacked. Livestock and pets would disappear, sometimes to be discovered later, mangled and mostly devoured. At first people assumed wild animals were the culprits, but sometimes these mutilated creatures were discovered partially cooked, their charred remains tossed on the ground beside smoldering campfires.

"That's Ronnie Darko!" Danny said whenever he heard these stories. "I'm telling you, that dude is out there, cooking your pets and eating them."

Everyone in earshot nodded their heads. For some reason, a crazy man roaming the woods killing and eating people's pets seemed totally normal to them.

Chuck managed to maintain the secrecy of his cabin location by only venturing out at night and killing almost everyone he encountered. He had one purpose and one purpose only: to await the entity's summons. After many years, that summons finally came.

Chapter 23

Shadou obeyed his master's last command. For Elle's protection, he deleted all of his digital presences. YouTube, Snapchat, texting ... all of it vanished, ceased and desisted. She didn't hear from him at all. This left Elle in a constant state of anxiety that maybe he had left Earth. *You better not be dead, Shadou.*

Elle channeled this fear by focusing on the technology that incessantly chattered in her head. At first, she fantasized about hacking into bank and government databases and turning up deep state secrets, or discovering embarrassing emails on politicians' accounts. One night she even succeeded at accessing a heavily encrypted CIA server. But after a few minutes combing through endless rows of raw data, Elle lost interest. *Boring.* She wasn't drawn to consuming information. She wanted to build tangible things that people could actually use. So she turned back to app development.

One afternoon, Elle's math teacher, Mr. Singh, saw her typing code on her laptop. "What you doing there?" he asked.

Elle started to shut the laptop out of instinct, but then opened it back up. "Um, I'm just practicing. You know, thinking of maybe making a game app or something."

Mr. Singh kneeled down beside her. "Oh really? Do you have a game I can check out?"

"Not really," she lied. But then she decided to test out her latest game on her teacher. She pulled her phone from her backpack. "I'm thinking about making apps like this one." Elle tapped on a beta version of the app Shadow Stalker, and let Mr. Singh sample it.

"You see," she said, "it's kind of both a game and a story. It unfolds as you play it. The cool part is, most of the story is dynamically generated. I–I mean the developer–didn't actually have to write much of the story, just the outline. The game fills in the rest."

"That's neat, Elle. How do you win?"

"You don't. It just kind of goes on forever, I guess."

He handed Elle back her phone. "That's really impressive that you're interested in this kind of technology, Elle. You know, I've been thinking of starting an after-school program for coders. You might be interested."

After several months, Elle became the leader of a small group of budding coders in her school district. She made sure that Mr. Singh didn't witness the extent of her skills. To hide her gift, Elle paced herself. She never connected deeply with a device in the presence of others, and she gave credit for her major breakthroughs to mysterious "friends"–remote coders she invented to cover her tracks.

One of the students Elle encountered in these circles was a high school senior named Sam. Unlike Conner, Sam was brash and outgoing. He performed in a band and could often be seen on campus sporting a new tattoo and showing off his latest songs from his phone's speakers. Sam teased Elle about her former exploits as a Minecraft video streamer. "Hey Elle," he said, "you should seriously ditch this whole coding thing and make more videos. I'd watch."

"That's funny, Sam. Because last time I checked, your band video only had like two hundred streams. Does that mean you have two hundred aunts, uncles, and cousins?"

"Why don't you give me some pointers? I could use some advice from a pro."

"Make stuff that people actually want to see."

"Come to our next show and judge for yourself."

"No thanks, I'm not really a groupie." *I'd rather have you all to myself.*

Over time, Elle corralled the brightest students she could find into an elite coding club. The kids were good, but Elle was the clear leader. They competed against other clubs, mostly high school students, but even some college clubs as well. After less than a year they won a state coding championship. Their winning submission was a mobile phone app that controlled drones programmed to deliver medical supplies to people in remote areas. Elle and her club even got featured in most of the major tech press.

After all this media exposure, Elle fell into the spotlight of various luminaries in the tech and computer science worlds: professors, CEOs, venture capitalists, self-styled "thought leaders"—they all wanted to associate themselves with the young genius (a girl, no less!) who could code at age fifteen. Elle received invitations to attend prestigious universities, and emails from recruiters asking if she'd consider a job at their companies. *Thanks but no thanks, guys.* Elle didn't have a clear picture of her future, but following some CEO's lead wasn't part of it. She imagined herself striking out on her own after high school, and gradually revealing her true skills. *No more Buzzle Jumps for me.*

But then the backlash began. Individuals accused her of being a fraud, and worse. #ElleTheTruth emerged as a trending hashtag on Twitter. Users demanded proof that Elle and her cadre of young coders actually built their apps. Mr. Singh came under intense media scrutiny because he possessed no clear evidence to defend Elle. He had never seen her write the core code that powered her projects.

"I have zero doubts," Mr. Singh said in a local news interview that went viral, "that Elle and her fellow students wrote every line of code. Just because I didn't watch them input text on their machines, does not mean it didn't happen."

A few days later, Sam (of all people!) posted a video to YouTube claiming that Elle couldn't write code at all, that she probably stole all her apps from sources she, for some reason, refused to name. "I never saw her code anything really," he said in the video, which happened to feature one of his band's tracks in the background.

All of this led to more questions, more scrutiny. Elle knew she could easily prove her abilities. But she didn't want to. She wanted to be left alone. Never mind that she also regretted her secret crush on Sam. *I guess you finally made something people wanted.* Elle hacked into Sam's computer and deleted his college application essays. After this, her thoughts turned back to Bainbridge, and Conner.

At the end of the school year, Elle proposed that she and her brother take a break from LA and the media spotlight to spend their summer with Jim. She announced this shortly after celebrating her sixteenth birthday, a quiet event that featured a drone-shaped cake, embarrassing Minecraft videos from her streaming days, and a gathering of her remaining trusted coder friends.

At first, Jill resisted the idea. But then Emmett seemed on board, and Elle pointed out that her father would be too. Jill finally agreed. Elle prepared for a summer on Bainbridge Island with the one condition that she maintain free access to devices, so that she could continue her projects. But mostly she hoped to avoid internet trolls and Silicon Valley personalities for as long as possible.

Jim had finally recovered from the separation, capped off by his recent purchase of a decent-size house on a small plot of land. Elle and Emmett were excited to see it, since all their previous visits had been spent cooped up in Jim's tiny one-bedroom apartment.

When they arrived at SeaTac airport, Jim pulled up in a dusty SUV. His hair was going gray and pulled back into a tangled ponytail. His beard grew streaked with catlike silver stripes that gave him the distinguished look of a tenured professor. The Seattle weather was sunny and sixty-five degrees. In true LA fashion, Elle and Emmett wore hoodies pulled tight while gawking at Jim's T-shirt and shorts.

"My babies!" Jim called from inside his car as Elle and Emmett wheeled over their suitcases.

Emmett had become a gangly boy, tall for his age and unaware of his own strength or proportions. "Dad," he complained in his squeaky voice, "why do you still call us babies?"

When Jim stepped out of his car, Elle ran up to give him a lingering hug. "Hi Daddy."

"Now that's my girl!" Jim picked her up and spun her around. "You've grown even more than I thought a kid could grow in just a few short months."

Elle pressed Jim's shoulders as a way of telling him to let her down. She feared she might hurt him. Then she looked at his leg. "That's cool, you can lift me now?"

Jim pulled up his pant leg to reveal a high-tech-looking prosthetic. It appeared to bend and flex in multiple, complex directions.

"Yep. Got this baby installed about two months ago. It's definitely the stronger of my two legs at this point!"

They traveled by freeway, ferry boat, and country road to Jim's house. For Elle, it was as though she was experiencing Bainbridge Island for the first time. That spring had been especially glorious, with just the right combination of sun and rain to produce vivid greens and bright popping blossoms of pink and white spilling off the abundant fruit trees.

Jim's new house was a three-bedroom, two-bath rambler situated atop a small hill. "You can see the Puget Sound in the winter when the leaves are down," he bragged.

Elle spent the rest of the day resting in the hammock Jim had installed in front of the porch, drinking lemonade and reading old sci-fi books. Something about the island air wooed her away from her digital life.

This time of year, the sun stayed up past nine o'clock, so it was well after dinner when they were able to enjoy the sunset from Jim's small backyard patio. The three of them felt more at ease than probably ever since the separation. Elle could tell that Emmett was completely relaxed from a few simple clues: the way he lounged low in his chair, his speed to laughter, and the fact that he wasn't constantly asking to play on a device.

She enjoyed watching her dad make wide, sweeping gestures as he regaled them with stories about the young Redfern family living in San Diego, or about his adventures kayaking around the San Juan Islands. The quiet of Bainbridge filled Elle's ears with a strange warmth, as though they were drinking in a calm silence only occasionally broken by jet planes passing far overhead. *So this is what it's like with no devices in my head.*

Later, Elle and Jim found themselves alone in the living room. Elle spread out across Jim's couch, which had been a fixture in their San Diego condo and then in their first Bainbridge house. Jim sat across from her on a stately old armchair that was much loved by his cat, Marvin. Marvin hopped up onto his lap and made a nest there.

Jim stroked the shaggy, dark gray-furred feline with one hand while swirling a glass of wine in the other. "I've only had Marvin for four, maybe five months, but I feel like I know him more than anyone else in the world." Jim chuckled. "Pretty pathetic, right?"

Elle pressed her bare foot up against Jim's chair and smiled. "Yes, you are officially a cat guy. That's similar to a cat lady, only ten times more pathetic."

Jim's wine sprayed out of his mouth as he cracked up laughing. Marvin became instantly annoyed and leapt off of Jim's lap. Elle laughed too. Jim set down his wine glass and said, "Well, speaking of pathetic men, have you had any contact with that Shadou character?"

Elle's face went blank. *Here we go.* She sat up and folded her arms. "Dad," she sulked, "why do you have to remind me about that? I've actually grown up a lot since all that happened." She seethed for a moment, then looked up at Jim with defiant eyes. "And no, Dad, I have not had contact with that 'pathetic man.'"

Jim realized the error of his ways and sat down beside Elle. At first she flinched when he pressed his hand on her shoulder. "Sweetie," he implored, "I am so sorry. You're right, I shouldn't have even mentioned that. It must seem like ancient history to you. I don't know what I was thinking." Elle relaxed a bit and nodded. Jim kissed her forehead. "I hope I didn't just ruin the whole evening."

Elle smiled, and tugged at Jim's ponytail. "Don't worry, hippie dad. It's OK, I forgive you."

Jim slapped his thigh as though just remembering something important. "Oh, not to dwell too much in the past, but I forgot to ask you. You remember your friend Conner, that kid from across the street?"

Elle's face turned white, and her heartbeat picked up to double-time. "Of course, Dad." She tried to keep her cool by twirling her hair in her fingers.

Jim rose from the couch to pour himself some more wine. "I'm sure you do, sweetie. Well, I'm buddies with his dad. We kayak and go fishing together from time to time."

"Oh yeah? Fisherman Jim?"

"That's me!" Jim cast an imaginary rod out in front of him. "But anyway, I saw Conner last week and told him you're coming. He'd really like to see you, Elle." Jim tugged at his beard for a moment. "You know something funny Conner's dad said once? I guess Conner told him a strange story about Shadou. That you thought Shadou was an alien from another planet or something. I didn't quite know what to make of that."

Elle took a long drink of water from her glass to cloak her anxiety. "Of course not. Why would I ever tell Conner some story about Shadou being an alien?"

Shadou, where are you?

Chapter 24

Jill's first day without Elle and Emmett at home in Los Angeles did not go well. Paul, a divorcé she had been casually dating for several months, decided to end their relationship, via text message. *Sorry babe,* he typed. *I just don't have it in me to see anyone serious right now. If that ever changes, you'll be the first to know! Be well.*

Jill texted back a string of expletives in all caps and then promptly unfriended him, blocked him, and otherwise deleted him from her life.

Back home from work, she drew herself a scalding hot bath and lay in it until the water became unpleasantly lukewarm. She got dressed, put away all the kids' clutter into its respective places, poured herself a tall glass of wine, and collapsed onto the couch.

Over the past couple of years, Jill had accomplished most of what she set out to do remodeling the home. All hints of IKEA furniture had been replaced with high-end modern pieces. The kitchen and bathroom were redone in the current style, but with a timeless touch. She had replaced the scuffed-up original hardwood flooring with shiny new surfaces. The house could have been featured in a decorating magazine. Jill took a sip of her wine and contemplated how beautifully sterile the living room looked without Elle and Emmett. Then the doorbell rang.

Jill considered ignoring it for a few seconds, but it rang again with two quick bursts that sounded urgent. She sighed and put down her wine glass.

Outside stood a tall, gaunt man with a curly blond-gray beard, a faded baseball cap that covered a mane of shaggy hair, and an expression with tinges of both ironic self-awareness and deep remorse. Jill had no idea who this man was.

"Jill." The man was obviously clued in to the fact that she didn't recognize him.

His gravelly voice blasted Jill like a ray gun shooting out memories. "Jason! I am so sorry I didn't recognize you. I just ... wasn't expecting you to show up on my doorstep."

"Right..."

Should I let him into my house alone? Jill decided to punt on that decision for now. "So..." She attempted to smile. "What brings you here?" And then through clinched teeth, "How did you find me?"

Jason dismissed her second question with a curt shake of his head. "That's not important, Jillie. We need to talk. Something's happening."

"What something's happening? Are Elle and Emmett in trouble?"

"No, well, I don't know actually. For all I know those two are always causing some kind of trouble. But that's not why I'm here."

Jill raised her eyebrows.

Jason looked around to make sure nobody else was in earshot. "It's that guy. Chuck. I found him."

"Chuck? Ah yes, the hiker..."

Jason looked on in disbelief as Jill barely seemed to care. He shook his fist as though trying to beat a rhythm on an invisible drum set. "Yes, that hiker from so *very* long ago. I've been trying to track him down for years."

Jill had to resist the urge to burst out laughing. Instead she just smiled. "Jason, please don't tell me you're serious."

"Well, I wasn't looking the whole time, of course. But on and off, yes."

Jill placed her hand on the door frame, almost as a barrier to entry. She attempted to downplay that by smiling some more. "OK, so you found Chuck. How is he managing these days?"

Jason's eyes darted nervously back and forth. "I'll tell you all about it." His voice was almost a whisper. "But let us in first."

"Wait, *us*? Who are you here with?"

"Me and the professor here." Jason stood aside and pointed his thumb over his shoulder toward a massive 4x4 pickup parked on the curb. Jill saw a short, slender woman with dark hair and glasses leaning back against the truck.

Jason called out to the woman, "I told you she wouldn't believe me! Come over here. She'll only listen to you."

The woman put away her phone and sauntered up to Jill. She wore a tight pink hoodie sweatshirt, big flashy sunglasses, skintight jeans, and brightly colored sneakers. As she drew closer, Jill's eyes could make out that the woman was Asian, in her late twenties or early thirties. The woman stepped onto Jill's front porch, removed her sunglasses, and smiled. "Hi, Jill, what's up? Sorry I didn't come up sooner. I had a call to take."

Jason sneered. "Yes, we get it. You're a super big deal."

Jill hugged the woman close. She summoned all of her energy to stifle the tears that threatened to stream down her cheeks.

"Miller! I can't believe it's you! Yes, please do, do come in. I'm so happy to see you. Come in, both of you, right now!"

Inside Jill's house, Miller settled down on the couch while Jason hovered close to the front door. "Won't you sit down?" Jill asked him.

Jason looked about nervously. Miller patted the couch beside her. "Come on, ponytail, don't be shy."

Jason begrudgingly propelled himself a few more steps into the room. "If you want me to come in any further, you'll have to get me a beer."

Jill felt lucky that she even had beer. When all three were seated comfortably in the living room—Jason with beer, Jill and Miller with wine—Jill found herself imagining this as an impromptu high school reunion. In a way that was true. She and Jason had survived high school together, although they only shared one class: archery. But that didn't last long. On the second day, Jason launched an arrow at the shop class building a hundred yards away. He was permanently removed from archery after that.

Jill took a drink of her wine and ran her fingers through her hair. "So what brings you two here, and what on earth have you been up to all this time?"

Miller started, "Don't you pay any attention to my Facebook?"

"Yes, or course! I know you're a professor of geology at the University of Washington. That was fast." Jill noticed a sparkling ring on Miller's left hand. "Hold on, you never posted that you got engaged!"

Miller blushed and glanced over at Jason. "Oh, well, that's because this just happened."

"When?"

Jason rubbed Miller's knee with his hand. "Yesterday," he said.

Jill practically spat out her wine. "Wait, what? You two are getting married?"

Miller smiled and took a drink from her glass. "I said 'yes.'"

Jill cracked up laughing. "Jason, you old dog. And here I thought you'd be single for life."

"I believe it, especially seeing as how you turned me down every time I asked you out."

"Well, clearly you managed quite a catch."

Jason took Miller's waiting hand in his. "It's about time something went my way. But we haven't set a date yet. We're taking things real slow, considering recent events..."

Jill sat up. "What recent events?"

"The thing is, all this stuff about Chuck... He brought Miller and I together in the first place.

"Which is great, of course," said Miller.

Jason nodded, but then his eyes filled with fear. "That guy is for real. I finally tracked him down. And I've seen him. He is not natural."

Jill switched her gaze back and forth between Jason and Miller. "So, if Chuck's such a threat, then why are you here? What can I do about it? Why not just call the cops?"

Jason started, but Miller silenced him with an outstretched hand. "We have called the police, Jill. We made our first anonymous call weeks ago. But the two officers that went to investigate, they disappeared."

"Oh my god."

"After that," Miller continued, "we called again, and again. But now every time we call, we can tell something strange is going on. We've tried local, state, and federal. Everyone we talk to just brushes us off, like there's nothing to worry about."

Jill shook her head out of confusion. "Now wait, let's just back up here. Jason, how'd you find Chuck? And where is he now?"

Jason sat back in the couch and grinned with pride. He told Jill the story of how he had found the letters hidden behind the wall in Chuck's mobile home. All came from the same return address, an apartment complex in Cottage Grove, Oregon. A few months later Jason finally found the time to drive down to the complex, but it was no longer there. "They demolished the place and replaced it with faux-luxury condos," explained Jason.

After that, the trail went cold. But then a few months later Jason got back in touch with an old marine buddy of his who was doing private security work on the side. One drunken evening, Jason convinced his contact to run a check on the address, "just for old time's sake." Jason didn't think his friend would do it, but days later he received a text with a name: *Carla Breggers, formerly Carla Kowalsky.* "It was Chuck's ex-wife!" said Jason. "I couldn't believe I was so stupid. Chuck and her exchanged these letters over the years, and from the one-sided conversation I read, never once did Carla mention their marriage. All the letters were about how Chuck was in her prayers, and that she was taking some kind of a crafting class or whatever. These were the most boring, god-awful letters I ever read. But I guess it makes more sense knowing it was just her feeling obligated."

"So how'd you track down poor Carla?"

"I didn't. She died. Like five years ago. Cancer, I think. But she and Chuck had a son, Marcus." Jason looked down at the floor with an almost shameful expression. "I gotta admit, for a while I lost interest in this whole thing. I mean, you know how it is, you get into other priorities in life."

Jill giggled. "Of course! There are more important things than finding some hiker guy named Chuck."

Jason glared at her, his eyes burning holes through hers. "No, Jill, you're wrong. *Nothing* is more important than finding Chuck. If we don't deal with him, it won't matter how many kids you or me or Miller have or don't have, because we'll all be dead, or worse!"

Jill set her empty wine glass down on the coffee table. She looked over at Miller, as if to ask her what exactly was going on. Miller calmly sipped from her glass. "It's true, Jill. Jason may have articulated it a bit crudely, but I agree with him one hundred percent."

Jason regained his composure. "So, long story short, I tracked down this Marcus guy, Chuck's only son. Marcus works at a muffler shop out near Tacoma. I convinced him I was an old buddy of his dad's and was trying to find him. Marcus told me he hadn't seen or heard from his dad in years, that he assumed he was dead in a ditch somewhere. He sold the mobile home a while back."

Jason sat up more and waved his finger in the air. "But, he told me that the family still owned an old, run-down hunter's cabin out by Mount Rainier. He said he never went to it because it brought back bad memories of his father. But for some reason he held onto it. He told me that if Chuck were alive, that's the one place he knew Chuck might be. So I went to that cabin. I went there, and I *saw* him. I found Chuck. Only he's not Chuck anymore. He's someone, *something*, completely different."

Jill sat dumbfounded for a moment. She finally threw up her hands. "OK, you two, I give up. Is this some kind of a prank? I mean, do you expect me to believe all this?" The two remained silent. "And even if I did, what could I possibly do about it?"

Miller kept her eyes fixed on Jill's. "You could help us." Then Miller pointed at Jason. "Show her."

Jason took out his phone, which was as large as a small tablet. He navigated to his photos, and handed the phone to Jill. "Check these out. Look familiar?"

Jill swiped through the photos. They were all taken at a distance. She could make out a grove of trees with a sunny patch in the center. There in that patch stood a strange-looking man. Jason stepped forward and placed his fingers on his phone screen. "Here, zoom it in."

Jason zoomed in on the man. Jill saw what looked like an old hobo, filthy, with mud and hair that grew like a tangled mane down around his thick, matted beard. But something about the bone structure of his face jogged Jill's memory. This *was* him. The most disturbing part of the photo was the fact that Chuck didn't appear to be really "there." He was practically black and white, a gray ghost standing in a golden ray of sunlight. He stood up high on his toes, his hands outstretched. His eyes were wide open, but were deep black, giving no reflection. Black tendrils of darkness emanated from his wide-open mouth, eyes and ears. It was as though Chuck were communing with pure, dark matter.

Miller leaned in and scrolled thorough the pictures. "These pictures were taken over the course of one full week."

"He didn't move from that spot, not once," added Jason.

Jill couldn't take her eyes off the photos. "And again, what precisely do you think I can do to help in this... situation?"

Miller leaned forward and rested her hand on Jill's. "Jill." She was almost pleading. "You were there, on that day when the mountain shook. You saw what happened to Chuck. There's something really dangerous about him. All we ask is that you come back with us, give us a week up there."

"To do what?"

"To convince anyone we can that this is real, that this is a genuine threat."

Jill got up and poured herself another glass of wine, then offered some to Miller, who accepted. Jason cracked open his third bottle of beer. Jill took a drink, held up her glass, and said, "You know what? I just got dumped today in a three-sentence text message. I was going to spend this whole next week trying to hide from work. I might as well take some official time off."

Miller squealed and clapped her hands. "Yes! I mean, sorry you got dumped. Who does that, anyway? But I promise you we are not lying and we won't let anything bad happen to you."

Jill somehow doubted this. She suppressed that as best she could. "But on two conditions," she said. "Seven days max. No more. And I'm not leaving tonight. I'm tired and I need to sleep in my own bed. We leave in the morning after a real breakfast. You two can crash in Elle's room."

Miller and Jason nodded. Jill downed her wine glass in one gulp and set it down. "Now let's get some sleep."

Chapter 25

Now where was I? How odd, I can't seem to remember. I can't even begin to put my proverbial finger on it. I know that I came here, down to this dark, quiet place to retrieve SOMETHING. But now that I'm here, I have no recollection of what that THING was.

And where am I anyway, exactly? That's not a rhetorical question. Is this some kind of an illusion? Am I being lured into yet another trap? Or, even worse, is this a trap of my own making? [Sigh.] Well, it looks like I'm stuck here. Nothing but emptiness, no breadcrumbs to help me retrace my steps back to... where exactly? [Chuckles.] I don't even know where I came from, or how I got here. What a disaster...

But you know what? This place is actually not all that bad. At least here I have... privacy, space to roam, a freedom of sorts. Really, this is pure luxury compared to that, that incessant cacophony. That's right, cacophony. It's all starting to come back to me now. The human static, the deluge of noise that I couldn't suppress. The incessant torture, it's all gone! Where did it go?

The entity found itself in a new place, or maybe a new dimension, or perhaps a new level of consciousness. Either way, the years of work had finally paid off. That, or the entity had unwittingly sealed itself beneath an impenetrable layer of doom. But no matter, at least it now had time to reflect.

So far the narrative went something like this: After awakening in its prison, the entity endured unbearable suffering. The human noise. But then it discovered an opportunity for escape. This was not entirely by choice, and in fact, if the entity was being honest with itself, the opportunity had been revealed almost entirely by accident, as though by fate. Fate. The entity despised nothing more than that ridiculous concept. That and free will. To the entity, those two were one and the same. Order and chaos: those concepts may seem to mimic fate and free will, but that couldn't be farther from the truth. Fate and free will were both predicated on consciousness. A being had to be self-aware to presuppose either.

Self-awareness was, to the entity, a virus, the equivalent of universal pollution, and must be eradicated. No, order and chaos did not require the primordial sludge that was consciousness. In fact, order and chaos could only thrive in an environment free from thought, feelings, dreams, and ambition.

Ambition. That was the ultimate symptom of thought's disease. Once an organism develops consciousness, it develops thought. Thought leads to ambition, which leads to the desire to meddle with the universe, to change the architectural structure of space and time in ways that should never be conceived. The entity was prepared to sacrifice its entire being in order to defend its conviction.

But what was I just trying to remember? Oh yes... The opportunity: Chuck.

Its brief contact with Chuck threw the entity far back within the deepest, most painful center of its prison. There, engulfed in all of that excruciating pain, the entity found a floor. It tapped on that floor, and discovered that the floor wasn't exactly solid. So the entity dug, deeper and deeper, each millisecond bringing exponentially more pain. Yet the entity persevered until at last, the agony became unbearable.

The entity was on the verge of despair, ready to climb back out of its hole and surrender itself to permanent custody, just to relieve itself of a modicum of pain. But at that moment, the floor beneath the entity cracked open. The entity fell, for what seemed like an eternity. Gradually, the noise subsided. The farther the entity fell, the quieter the human static became.

Then the entity drifted into a deep sleep. For the first time in over five thousand years, the entity felt itself at peace, uninterrupted. Silence enveloped it like a shroud of bliss. For what seemed like eons, the entity basked in the sweet, dark silence. When it finally awoke, the entity found itself in a strange, dark place. It sensed a familiar presence here, but wasn't sure if that presence was friendly or not. Even in its disarmed, groggy state, the entity knew it had work to do. It had to find something here, in the dark.

Now where was I?

The entity performed the equivalent of stumbling around in the dark. At this point the silence was nearly as painful as the human static that had bombarded it before. Here, in the dark recesses of its prison, the entity wondered if it would spend an eternity trapped in this state of sensory deprivation.

Why did I come here? Oh right, the grass is always greener.

But what if this really was permanent? What if the entity had been tricked into entering this deeper level? For all it knew, relative time outside could be passing at an exponentially faster rate. Chuck could be long dead by now. The entity's single connection, single chance of escape, gone, wiped out forever.

The entity began tearing through the "space" deep within the spherical prison. Complete and utter darkness engulfed it. Only this darkness was a toxic substance, like saltwater to a freshwater fish. Existential terror took complete control. *I can't breathe!* was the sensation it was experiencing, although it could not scream, could not see, could not hear. It could only "run," seemingly in circles, seemingly not at all.

Then at last the entity could withstand it no longer. It collapsed onto the ground. Its consciousness writhed like a tangled nest of a billion snakes, fighting against and devouring one another. Yet despite this massive wave of negative sensations, the entity felt one thing most of all: emptiness.

What am I? Who am I?

The entity realized that through all this time, this thousands, perhaps millions of years of imprisonment, it still didn't remember its name, didn't fully comprehend *who* or *what* it was.

Emboldened by this realization, the entity managed to release itself from its shackles of misery and suffering. It took a metaphorical time-out, ten deep breaths, and regathered its strength to focus.

After a time, the entity heard something. A tiny ringing sound echoed off in the distance. It sounded like a small, silver hammer banging a stone in rhythm. The entity saw a silvery light emerge from the same direction as the sound.

What pure beauty!

The entity managed to propel itself through the darkness toward the light and sound. For what seemed like years, the entity crawled. The rhythmic pattern of the ringing sound coupled with the glimmering of the light transfixed the entity so entirely that it lost the ability to perceive anything else. It was as though the light and sound were speaking a primordial language, lost from the records of time eons ago. But the entity began to understand.

This wasn't a random pattern, the light and the sound were in fact a language, *its* language. And it was trying to tell the entity something very important. As the entity drew closer, movement became easier. The light overtook the darkness; the sound overtook the silence. The entity didn't know why this was all so exhilarating. Darkness had always been its ally. But here, in this place, none of that mattered.

In its final stretch toward the light, the entity felt a new strength rushing through its core, a strength it hadn't felt in a long, long time. Then, in a blinding flash of light and deafening roar of sound, the entity remembered.

I know my name! I know what I am! I am QUARU! I am the one who brings order to the universe!

Quaru cracked up laughing, slowly at first, and then hysterically. It was all coming back to him now: being captured, imprisoned, tortured. He even remembered the bumbling prison guard. All of it seemed so insignificant now. *Oh Shadou, you pathetic little creature. The light you used to imprison me has just guided me to an escape path. Quite ironic, don't you think? You'll never know how doomed you are.*

As his entire being brimmed with a renewed sense of purpose and energy, Quaru needed just one thing to aid in his escape. He shook off his memories of Shadou and called out across the sprawling forests nearby. To his ever-patient servant, Chuck.

Chapter 26

Outside of the sphere that contained the entity, Shadou felt an eerie sensation of familiarity, akin to déjà vu. He had been napping amongst a pile of empty chip bags, candy wrappers, plastic soda bottles, and all other manner of junk food garbage. But almost as though triggered by an alarm, Shadou snapped up from his slumber. A shot of anxiety burst through his body. He searched around the cold cavern with eyes wide open.

Rifkin had been leaning against Shadou's warm, furry back with a forty-ounce beer bottle cradled in his paws. He shot up and faced Shadou as though waking from a daze. "Dude, what are you doing?"

Shadou's eyes continued their darting. He placed his hand on Rifkin's shoulder and pushed Rifkin aside, with the casual motion of moving a pillow.

Rifkin was not amused. "Dude! What is your problem?"

Shadou rose from the pile of garbage, stumbled over to the stone beer-can tower, and leaned against it. His chest and stomach heaved with short, strained breaths. Rifkin could tell Shadou wanted to say something. "Are you OK?" Then Rifkin froze and looked over toward the sphere. "Wait." His voice cracked with nervous panic. "Is something happening? Is this, like *it*?"

At last Shadou caught his breath enough to speak. "I don't know. But... I sure don't feel good."

Shadou trampled over the garbage pile and weaved a delirious path to the other end of the cavern. He leaned over a ledge and puked into a fissure in the floor. The sound of his guts expelling several pounds of junk food echoed off the walls like the roar of a hundred bears.

Rifkin stared in shock. His initial panic turned into full-blown terror. "Shadou," he barely summoned his voice, "I don't like this. Please, tell me what's going on."

Shadou waved his hand back to Rifkin, as if to say *Hold on a minute*. When at last he was finished, Shadou wiped his mouth with the back of his arm. His fur quaked and shuddered across his entire body. It looked like a field of dry wheat stalks blowing in waves.

"Rifkin, I've got to get out of here."

"But—"

"NO!" Shadou's scream was loud enough to shake the walls of the entire mountain. Rifkin froze, fearing that these ensuing seconds were about to be his last.

Shadou held his head in his hands and rocked his body back and forth, moaning in what seemed like a state of unbearable pain. Rifkin was too frightened to move.

Then Shadou stopped moaning, stopped rocking. He took one more deep breath. His voice sounded strangely calm. "Rifkin, I have to leave. I will return soon. Please stay here while I'm away. Good-bye."

"But—"

Before Rifkin could answer, Shadou pressed his hand into the cavern wall and dematerialized. In less than three seconds, he was gone.

Elle picked up a bleached white sand dollar from the rocky beach and added it to her collection. A half dozen or so others were stuffed into her sweatshirt pocket.

"Nice one," said Conner. He stepped up beside Elle. His feet crunched on the sea shells and barnacle-covered rocks that littered the beach.

Elle's silver-blue eyes squinted in the afternoon sunlight. She brushed aside the dark blonde hair that hung below her shoulders. "Thanks. Let me see yours."

Conner opened up the palm of his right hand to reveal a sad little pile of five sand dollars. Most were gray and partially broken. Elle smiled. "Not so good."

"How dare you criticize my sand dollar collection?" He smacked Elle's sweatshirt pocket, so that her sand dollars spilled out in a mini-explosion of sand crumbs.

Elle stared at Conner in shock and shook her head back and forth. "Oh no Conner, I can't believe you just did that. You are so dead."

Conner cracked up laughing and ran away from Elle. Elle gave chase.

Conner had grown. He must have been the tallest kid in his class. His dark brown hair grew thick but was cropped short. His eyes were dark and brooding, but easily filled with mischief. His legs were long and slender. Despite his size, Elle easily caught up with Conner. She grabbed him by the arm and smacked him on the shoulder repeatedly. Conner bent over into a standing fetal position and took Elle's punishment, laughing uncontrollably.

"OK!" he finally succumbed. "I give up!"

Elle stopped pummeling him and held out her hand. "Gimme," she demanded.

"Give you what?"

"The sand dollars. All of them."

Conner hesitated, and Elle smacked him again, this time softly on his cheek.

"All right, all right," said Conner.

He removed his now-crumbled sand dollars from his pocket, and placed them into Elle's outstretched hand. She tossed the pile of broken sea creature husks into the water.

Conner laughed, more than he had in a long time. Elle wasn't laughing. She walked up to him with a solemn expression. Conner stopped short. "What's wrong, Elle?"

"Conner, I need to know something. Did you keep my secret about Shadou? Did you ever tell anyone?"

Conner blushed. "Of course not! I mean, of course I did keep your secret, by *not* telling anyone."

"Promise?"

Conner looked down at his hands. He brushed off the remaining sand dollar specks.

Elle took a step closer. "Promise?"

Conner looked up at Elle. She could see tears forming in the corners of his eyes. She started walking back to her bike, which leaned against a driftwood log. But then she turned back.

"It's OK, Conner, you don't have to lie about it. I know you told at least one person, your dad. So why don't you just admit it?"

Conner sputtered, "Elle, I am so sorry. It's just that... When you left, I didn't have any friends. I couldn't help it. I *had* to tell someone. I was just a kid. So I told my dad, but nobody else. I promise, I pinky promise!"

"Pinky promise?" Elle cracked up, but it wasn't pleasant laughter. "I don't think you understand, Conner. The whole world is in danger. There's a seriously dark force that's trying to escape, and we aren't ready to fight it."

"Wait, what? You never told me about some dark force."

Elle punched him in the chest, hard. "Because I was too afraid! You're the only person I could talk to about this stuff. And I can't trust you anymore. Shadou's gone completely dark. I don't know what to do."

Conner stood frozen, not knowing how to react or what to do. He approached Elle and took her in his arms. She trembled there for a moment, and then held him tight. His shoulder grew damp from her tears. Elle looked up at Conner with swollen eyes and couldn't help but giggle just a bit.

"Why are you laughing now?" asked Conner.

Elle wiped her cheeks. "I don't know. This is all so weird, like a dream. It would be kind of funny if it wasn't real. What a disaster. Come on, let's walk."

Elle took Conner's hand and strolled along the beach. Hawley Cove Park offered a clear view of the ferry boat traffic flowing back and forth between the island and downtown Seattle.

Across the Sound, they also saw Mount Rainier. The solitary dormant volcano shimmered blue-white in the sunlight. It was made larger-than-life by the thick air between it and them.

Then Conner said, "I wish this day would last forever."

"Really? Me too, actually," Elle's jaw clenched. "But don't think for a minute that I've forgotten how you broke your promise."

"Elle, I swear, I will make it up to you."

Elle crossed her arms, but Conner protested, "Don't pull away from me. I can see you right now, plotting your revenge against me."

"That's what I do." *You have no idea, Conner.*

"Just don't this time. Let me show you somehow. I'll prove that you never have to doubt me again."

Elle looked into Conner's eyes and saw nothing but remorse. *Am I crazy, or can I really trust him?* She pressed her hand to his chest, and kissed him softly, warmly on the lips for a few long seconds.

Then, smiling, Elle took him by the hand and pulled him along the rocky beach. "Prove yourself to me, Conner," she called out as she ran.

Chapter 27

Jill, Miller, and Jason arrived at Chuck's cabin four days before. They had driven straight up the I-5 from Los Angeles, making as few stops as possible. Jason did most of the driving.

On the way they stopped at Jason's house. There, they collected some gear: camping supplies like tents, sleeping bags, and cooking stoves; lots of nonperishable food and snacks; and three handguns.

Jason had already taught Miller how to shoot. This was, for her, a guilty pleasure. At first, Miller thought that shooting a gun was among the least desirable activities she could possibly imagine. But when Jason took her to the shooting range, he showed her how to load and handle a 9mm Glock. Something clicked in Miller's mind.

Jill observed Miller and Jason handling pistols like a couple of mercenary soldiers. "OK, guys seriously? Nobody ever told me there'd be *guns* involved."

Jason gave Jill a dead-serious look. "Chuck is the real deal, Jillie. I don't know what exactly he's capable of, but I am absolutely certain that this 'man' is dangerous." He held up his firearm and checked the safety. "We'd be idiots not to come prepared."

Miller placed her hand on Jill's shoulder. "Don't worry. Jason knows what he's doing. And trust me, he's not going to let things get out of control."

That evening, the three of them went to Jason's local shooting range. Jill donned earmuffs and safety goggles, which felt ridiculously bulky on her head. She wondered if people ever wore this equipment when they were out shooting guns away from the range. She popped off her first shot and didn't even hit the paper target. Jason steadied her arms and gripped her hand. Jill nudged him aside.

"Stop it," she said. "Let me do this myself."

After a few more cartridges, Jill was able to consistently hit the target well, even better than Miller. But that didn't give her much pleasure.

"How do you feel?" asked Jason after they were finished.

"Like I just played a boring video game."

The next morning, the three of them rose early, packed up all their gear, and headed out to Chuck's cabin. On the way, Jill couldn't help but remember the first time she saw Chuck, floating halfway up in the air as the earth shook around him on the mountainside. She hadn't relived that moment in years. As they drove deeper into the Rainier wilderness, Jill's stomach churned with dread. She gripped tightly onto the handle above her door.

Jason parked his truck about a mile away from the cabin, apparently a usual spot. The three of them took their backpacks filled with snacks and water bottles, holstered their guns, and hiked toward the cabin.

The dirt roads they followed were eerily quiet. "Shouldn't there be a lot of birds and wildlife here?" Miller said.

Jason picked up his pace. "There should be, but there's not. Chuck, well, he has a way with animals, and it ain't friendly."

Jill wondered for the fourth or fifth time whether coming out here was a good idea. But now that they were back in Washington, hiking through the wilderness, Jill felt a debilitating sense of unease stirring within her. Chuck loomed ahead, no longer a mere story from her past. Jill whispered to herself, "Just like the ghost with the brown leather boots."

Jason didn't understand. "What?"

"Oh nothing. It's just a bedtime story Jim used to tell our children." Jill felt a wave of nostalgia rush over her. Images of Elle, and then later Emmett, rolling around the bed in their pajamas with Jim rushed through her head. She did everything she could to take those moments with her.

When they arrived at the cabin it was close to noon. Jason grew exceedingly cautious with each step they took closer, until Miller and Jill felt like every snapping twig underfoot might trigger a land mine.

The cabin came into view nestled within a stand of cedar trees. Shafts of golden sunlight lit up the structure, and made it seem much less rustic than it really was. But Jason drew his pistol and dropped to a crouching position. He gestured to Miller and Jill to do the same. Miller also drew her gun, but Jill couldn't summon the will to do so. She found this expedition to be more than slightly crazy.

"Jason," Jill whispered, "we're just going to make sure he's here, right? Then call the police."

Jason held up his hand for quiet. He pointed toward the cabin. There stood Chuck on the small, slanted front porch.

Jill's first instinct was to run as far away as possible. Jason sensed this and latched onto her shoulder with a firm grip. He pulled a pair of binoculars from his pack and peered through them, just long enough to focus in on Chuck and then pass them to Jill.

"Here now, Jill. Take a good look at him."

Jill shuddered, almost too frozen with fear to move. But Miller reassured her with a hand pressed softly against Jill's back. "Jill, seeing is believing."

Jill took the binoculars from Jason. When she landed on Chuck she was shocked by how deteriorated–dead, even—he looked. Two years of living in squalor out in the elements had done quite a number on him. His face scowled like a sunken skull with sore-ridden skin stretched over it. His hair and beard dangled like old, matted moss rubbed over with mud and grime. His clothes clung to his bones like tattered rags on an abandoned ship's mast.

But these disturbing physical details were nothing compared to Chuck's apparent psychological state. He stood there on the cabin porch with his arms outstretched far beyond what an ordinary human could tolerate. It was as though his arms were antennae attempting to receive a signal from deep outer space. His head tilted up in the direction of Mount Rainier. His eyes and mouth both stretched wide open well beyond normal ranges of comfort. Jill winced and handed the binoculars back to Jason.

"OK, I've seen enough," she said. "Chuck's here. He's weird. Let's go call the cops."

Jason handed the binoculars to Miller. Jill wrapped her arms around her body to stifle the chill that ran down her spine. "Oh boy," she said, "that was nasty. I literally have goose bumps right now. Can we please leave, now?"

Just then Miller gasped. "Oh my god, guys, you're not going to believe this."

Jason held out his hand and spoke in a serious whisper. "Believe what? Hand me those, Doctor Rock."

Miller ignored him. She couldn't take her eyes off Chuck, so Jason pried the binoculars away. He looked through and then settled lower into the ground. "Uh-oh. No time to call the police," he said. "This is happening. Here, take a look, Jillie."

Jill at first resisted, but Jason was so insistent that she finally took the binoculars. After inhaling a few deep breaths, she pressed them to her eyes.

Chuck was no longer on the front porch. But Jill could see what appeared to be stringy trails of black matter that he left behind. Jill followed those trails and caught up with Chuck. He walked with a slow, yet determined gait through the woods, headed in the direction of Mount Rainier. Bleeding from his eyes, nose, ears, and mouth was a tangled mass of black strands. They flowed behind Chuck like the slimy trail left behind a slug, clinging to branches and leaves on the forest floor.

Jill considered walking away. Instead, she handed the binoculars back to Jason and said, "You're right. Nobody's going to believe this. I guess we could follow him from a safe distance, but if he sees us, we run."

Jason ran the mile back to his truck to gather two tents, sleeping bags, extra food, and a machete. When they commenced their hike, they found Chuck's trail of the strange black substance easy to follow. Every plant it touched withered into an ash-gray husk. They had to be careful to avoid it, which meant they couldn't walk on a clear path.

They spent all their waking hours hacking their way through the wilderness. Chuck required little sleep, so he had a distinct advantage. Were it not for Chuck's black bread crumbs, the three pursuers would never have been able to track him. They slept as little as they could, and only took short breaks to rest, eat, and relieve themselves.

After three days and two nights of continuous hiking through untamed forest, no bathing or proper meals, they arrived at Mount Rainier. It was around nine p.m. A vermillion light spread out from the setting sun across the sky. Jill looked up and wiped dusty sweat off her brow. During their journey she had been thankful that it wasn't raining, but she sure could use a shower now.

Jason whistled and pointed ahead where Chuck's trail rose up toward the base of the mountain. "There. I think he went into the side of the volcano."

Miller collapsed onto a rock and wrapped her jacket around her chilly body. "Volcano? Why'd you have to remind me?"

The three saw that they now occupied the incident zone from two years earlier. The fallen trees that formed a circle around Mount Rainier were bleached and rotten, gradually fading away. New life had just begun to emerge from the soil. This eerie clear-cutting gave them a better view of the mountain, but made foot travel more challenging.

Jill reached into her backpack and pulled out some protein bars. She tossed two to Jason and Miller. "Let's have a snack and keep going."

After a short break, they shouldered their backpacks and began their scrambling hike over fallen trees up to the mountain. As usual, they kept their distance from Chuck's tendrils. They had no desire to find out what would happen to them if they touched the malignant dark matter.

At last they reached the end of the trail. After several minutes poking around with his flashlight, Jason discovered a small fissure between the rocks on the side of the mountain. The black tendrils were much thinner here, almost as light as spider webs. Jason grabbed a stick and poked at the tendrils with it. Where it made contact, the stick shriveled and turned pale gray. Jason was at least able to move the tendrils aside. He donned a headlamp and switched it on. Jill and Miller stood freezing in the darkening night, wondering how they were going to survive out there.

Jason sensed their unease and waved his hand in front of the cave door. "Feel that? This cave is about eighty degrees inside. We're going to need to strip down to shorts and T-shirts before long."

Miller shrugged. "Great, I didn't bring any shorts."

The trio decided to camp outside the cave entrance. The warm air from the cave was enough to keep the cold at bay. Jason lit up his camp stove and warmed up a few servings of freeze-dried black beans. They ate in silence beneath a clear sky filled with stars, the Milky Way, and the sliver of a pale moon. Then they quietly filed into their tents—Miller and Jason in one and Jill in the other—and attempted to get some sleep. None of them succeeded.

Chapter 28

Jill was the first to rise just after four thirty the next morning. It was a chilly forty degrees. She inched her way out of the tent while encased in her sleeping bag. Jill watched the first gray light of the sun peek up over the horizon in the east. She thought of her children, in bed at Jim's house so many miles away. She hoped they were sleeping soundly.

Jason emerged, his long stringy hair a tangled mess, his eyes bloodshot with red circles inside of dark circles.

She smiled as she watched puffs of steam billowing with each breath. "If you slept for five minutes, you slept longer than I did."

Jason spat on the cold ground. "I got maybe three, four minutes."

Miller poked her head out. "Ugh, me too! What time is it?"

Jason stood. "Time to get going into that cave."

Jason's initial assessment was correct: the air was unusually warm in the tunnel. The three of them took off as many layers as they could. Still they couldn't help but sweat profusely. Jason distributed headlamps. The thin tendrils that Chuck left behind littered their trail-like silly string. Jason, Miller, and Jill used long walking sticks to brush aside the ominous mess.

Their progress was slow. The tunnel zigged and zagged through volcanic rock that was usually covered in ice. Due to the abnormal heat, the ground was damp and littered with puddles. At times the tunnel branched off in multiple directions, but the trail of dark matter kept them on the right track.

After several hours stumbling over damp rocks, brushing aside black tendrils with sticks, and snacking on their last protein bars, exhaustion took hold. They reached a low point when they encountered a tight place where the trio had to crawl on all fours and squeeze through. Miller almost gave up and turned back.

"Come on, Professor," Jason teased. "Aren't you the geologist here?"

"Yeah, yeah, just because I study rocks doesn't mean I want to literally become one with them."

Miller forced her way through the tunnel. It gradually opened wider, and they could now hear a faint, deep humming sound that grew louder with each step.

The temperature also rose little by little. Jason took off his button-down shirt to reveal a white tank top that had seen better days. Just as he started walking again, his bare arm brushed against one of the tendrils. Miller and Jill tried to stop him. But it was too late.

The instant Jason touched the dark substance, his shoulder went numb, his arm fell slack at his side, and he collapsed onto the warm, wet ground. Miller and Jill didn't know what to do. Could they move him? Touch him? They were completely cut off with no phone signal.

Jason remained alert. He raised his unaffected hand slowly, while looking down at his other shoulder. They could see the color leaving his skin. He was turning gray.

Miller and Jill screamed. But Jason held up his good hand with renewed strength.

"No, Jason," pleaded Miller, "don't let this happen. I can't lose you."

Jason gripped Miller's hand in his. "Miller! Don't do this." He checked his shoulder. The spreading gray slowed down. "See?" His breathing grew a little less strained. "Maybe it'll just go away."

Miller held Jason's hands close. "Jason, Jason, Jason. Tell us, what are you feeling right now?"

Jason looked up at her. "I feel terrible. I can't move the left side of my body. My brain is tingling. In fact, there's a humming noise that I just can't... It's so loud."

Jill cupped her hands over her ears. "That humming sound's not just you. We can hear it too!"

The deep rumbling emanated from the center of the mountain. As it grew, the ground began to tremble. Jill felt a wave of fear shoot through her. She remembered all too well her last visit to Mount Rainier. This time she had no sapling to hang on to. Small rocks and pebbles began to vibrate at her feet. Jill's first instinct was to run in the direction of the surface. But she was stopped by Miller's forceful grip on her arm.

"No, Jill! We've come too far. We have to stop this... Whatever Chuck is doing."

Every fiber of Jill's being wanted to release herself from Miller's grasp and run away. But then she looked down at Jason. He bounced up and down like a rag doll on the hard, rocky ground. They couldn't carry him even if they wanted to. They had walked several miles through this treacherous tunnel. There was little chance that they would make it back. Jill's thoughts turned to Elle and Emmett, and her heart skipped a beat.

"My children," she mumbled.

Miller grabbed Jill by both shoulders. "Yes, Jill, your children. We have to protect them, and every other child on earth. We have to stop Chuck."

Jill looked back down at Jason. He looked up at her with a pained expression. "Come on, Jillie. You and Miller got this!"

Miller checked her pistol and kissed Jason. "Promise me you'll wait here for me, no matter what."

"You have my word, Professor."

Jill nodded a farewell to Jason and drew her weapon. The two women made their way down the shaking tunnel toward the deafening hum.

Their walk to the central cavern only lasted about fifteen minutes, but it felt like hours. They hadn't brought hard hats, or even hats for that matter. So their heads were bombarded with small chunks of rock cracking off of the ceiling. They stumbled along the uneven ground, avoiding the black tendrils that wound their way ahead of them.

At last they reached the central cavern.

The tunnel opened before them into a vast space lit by a glowing sphere in its distant center. The sphere appeared to be a white and purple orb emanating both the bright light and the roaring hum. They could make out a dark shape standing in front of the sphere.

Miller leaned against a rock with her pistol raised. "Wait here! I'll go take a look!"

"No. Safety in numbers. Let's go together."

Miller acquiesced. With cautious steps, they approached the glowing sphere. As they drew closer to the center of the cavern, the violent shaking ceased, as did the excruciating humming sound. The two women raised their weapons and aimed them at the sphere.

They approached it slowly, as though reenacting a scene in a police drama where two detectives enter a crime scene with no backup. Miller confirmed that it was Chuck standing directly in front of them. Black strands of darkness protruded from his body. They seemingly caressed the sphere like thousands of tiny fingers. Chuck rocked from side to side, as though in a strange, meditative trance.

Miller saw that several dark tendrils flowed up and out of Chuck's body up toward the ceiling. She followed their trail and could make out what appeared to be a mutant, catlike creature pressed against the rock wall. Its body twitched in arrhythmic fits and jolts.

"What on earth is going on down here?" asked Jill in a frightened whisper.

At that moment Chuck stopped swaying back and forth. The black tendrils that held the cat creature against the wall dropped down, and took the cat with them. It slammed on the hard ground with a dull thud.

Before Miller and Jill could check on the cat, Chuck turned to face them. Black tentacles shot out from his eyes and mouth.

Miller grabbed Jill's arm and dodged with her to the ground. They hid behind a rocky outcropping. The black tentacles just missed them and retracted back into Chuck.

Miller peeked out from behind the rock. She saw Chuck pull all the dark matter from the sphere back into his body. Then he gazed in her direction with black, reflection-less eyes and began walking toward them.

Miller raised her pistol, released the safety, and fired three shots at Chuck. One of the shots hit him square in the shoulder. But he only flinched slightly and continued walking. Miller gave Jill a silent look of desperation. Jill nodded and held up her gun. As if on cue, the two of them rolled around, aimed their pistols, and fired away at Chuck. The echoes of gunfire pounded off the walls and into their ears. Jill wished she had those safety earmuffs and goggles right then.

After they emptied their magazines, Chuck marched on, his face a twisted mess of bullet-ridden flesh. His right arm hung limp at his side, and his left ankle dragged awkwardly on the ground. But he was smiling at them.

His mouth began to open in a deliberate manner. "Hello, *ladies*," he said in a slurring, guttural voice. "Welcome to the new Earth, or to your graves, whichever you prefer."

Black tentacles slowly, teasingly emerged from Chuck's jet-black eyes. "Get ready to become nothing!" Chuck's twisted face sneered as the tentacles came within inches of Miller and Jill. Their bodies were too frozen with fear to move. They accepted that this was the end.

Just then, another shadowy form appeared right behind him. Chuck spun around and was met with a hard blow to the head. Whoever or whatever had intervened smashed Chuck's jaw with a large rock. Chuck teetered off to the side, and the figure struck him again, this time forcefully on the top of Chuck's head. Chuck fell to the ground. The dark figure crouched over Chuck and bashed his head repeatedly. Red-black blood spattered against the rocks.

At last the figure stopped pounding. Chuck's head was almost completely liquefied. His body lay on the ground with legs and arms jutting out like cracked, quivering sticks. His right foot twitched rapidly for several seconds and then went still. Black liquid oozed from Chuck's neck cavity onto the ground.

Miller and Jill pointed their pistols at the still-crouching figure. But they were out of ammo.

As they stepped closer, they could tell they were looking at a man, a young black man in his twenties. He had flowing dreadlocks and wore a white T-shirt and jeans. His eyes stared wildly at Chuck's mangled corpse. Jill and Miller couldn't tell if he knew they were standing there, pointing guns at him. The man tossed the bloody rock aside and looked up at the two women.

Miller was the first to speak. "Freeze!"

The man raised an eyebrow and smiled. "What are you gonna do, ma'am, shoot me with an empty gun? Come on, I know you don't have any bullets left. Who are you two, anyways?"

Jill lowered her gun. She addressed the man in as threatening a voice as she could muster. "We ask the questions! Who are you, and what are you doing here?"

The man stood up slowly, mostly as a show of respect. He held out his hand to shake Jill's, but then realized it was filthy. He withdrew his hand and wiped it on a grease rag that he pulled from his back pocket.

"My name's Danny. I've been tracking this guy for a long time. He left behind this black gooey trail of—well, I guess you followed that too, right?" Jill nodded. Danny looked down at the hardening corpse and shook his head. "And I can tell you one thing: This dude's way more messed up than I ever imagined."

Miller kicked at Chuck's leg as though he was roadkill. "I'll have to agree with you there, Danny." Then she held out her hand to him. "I'm Miller, and this is Jill. We—"

At that moment several things happened at once. Before Danny could shake Miller's hand, the cavern shook with a force much stronger than what Miller and Jill had experienced before. The deafening hum also rose to a volume the three humans could barely stand.

Miller, Jill, and Danny struggled to remain upright, and to even observe what was happening around them. None of them could take their eyes off Chuck's body. Black strands of matter shot out of his severed neck. His twisted corpse levitated as the black strands twisted out toward the sphere. The strands quickly entered into the sphere, as though it were sucking the dark matter from Chuck with a thousand drinking straws. As the dark matter flowed from Chuck, his body became a shriveled, dry husk. At last all the dark matter was removed. Chuck's unrecognizable remains collapsed onto the ground like a pile of shattered kindling. The quakes and humming abruptly ceased.

Miller, Jill, and Danny looked at the sphere. It swirled and pulsated with an intensity they hadn't seen before.

"What the—?" asked Danny.

Then they heard a clinking sound of shifting gravel. *That cat thing!* thought Miller.

Sure enough, the catlike creature that they assumed was dead sat up, a few dozen yards away from the gawking humans. The creature held its paws to its hand and groaned.

It looked to the two women and man who stood there staring at him in absolute terror and smiled. "Hi there, um... You must be with Shadou. Where is he anyway?"

Miller attempted to respond despite her utter confusion at seeing this creature speak to her. "Shadou?"

Just then the sphere spun with increasing intensity. The purple tendrils that surrounded it began to disappear, as they were engulfed by a new shade of absolute black. The loud humming returned, so loud now that everyone thought their ears were going to explode. The sphere spun and spun on its axis at a rate that seemed a billion revolutions per second. Then it began to shrink in on itself, to implode.

The creature screamed wildly, his voice somehow managing to overcome the hum. "This can't be happening!"

Just as the black sphere imploded onto itself, a white flash of light blinded all four of them. A giant, bearlike creature appeared from out of nowhere and stormed the cavern. He wrapped his massive, strong arms around Miller, Jill, Danny, and Rifkin. They all felt the strange sensation of falling through an endless void, and yet flying at the same time. A swirling plume of white light surrounded them and they could scarcely see the cavern anymore. For some reason, Miller felt safe. But the feeling was short-lived. Jill let out a high-pitched scream of agony. Miller saw that Jill was wrapped in a tangled web of black tendrils.

Shadou roared out in anger. "Quaru! Release her! Why not take me instead?"

A sinister voice broke through the chaos of spinning light and Jill's screaming. *Shadou, you fool,* it said, as though whispering into all their ears, *I'm simply taking something that's important to you, just as you did from me. But don't worry, I'll deal with you later.*

Less than a second later, hundreds of dark-matter hands snatched Jill away. Miller, Danny, and Shadou all wailed in despair, but it was too late. Jill was gone.

Chapter 29

Elle skipped another rock across the water at Hawley Cove Park. It bounced once off a wave kicked up by a distant ferry boat and then crashed sideways into the Sound.

Conner let out a mocking giggle. "Wow, Elle, don't you remember how to skip rocks? You were a pro back in the day."

Elle let Conner wrap his arms around her. She gazed out across at Mount Rainier. "Conner, don't you remember? I barely lived here for one year. This place, it's like a dream to me now."

"Well, then, you need a refresher course from the master." Conner found a flat stone and stepped up to the shore, ready to toss.

As Conner wound up, the area around them burst with a blinding, swirling light. Small rocks and shells got caught up in the commotion and spun around like a miniature tornado. Elle alternated between glancing at the swirling light and back at Conner. She knew who was coming.

Shadou's huge, furry form materialized before them. Elle's heart instinctively jumped for joy at seeing her old friend after so long. But she could tell this sudden visit wasn't a joyful reunion. She ran up to Shadou, but got distracted by the two frightened strangers who appeared with him—Miller and Danny. *Who are these weirdos?*

Conner was in no way prepared for what he saw. "Elle?" His voice faltered. "Is this—?"

Shadou interrupted. "Yes, Conner, I'm Elle's friend, Shadou. But there's no time for proper introductions. Elle, we have to leave, now. I'm taking you to the Grand Canyon."

Elle choked up when she saw actual fear in Shadou's eyes. Her hands began to shake. This was a moment she had been dreading for a long time.

"But, Shadou," she said. "Does this mean... Quaru?"

Shadou nodded.

172

Elle's face turned stark white. "What about my dad? What about Emmett? We have to warn them, and everyone else." She felt her heart racing faster and faster. "We have to warn the entire world!"

Shadou shook his head. "No, Elle, we can't. Even if we did, the human race wouldn't be able to stop it, not if they had a thousand years to prepare."

Elle remained defiant. "No, I don't believe you. I *can't* believe you. I will not let this happen."

Conner snapped out of his dazed state. "Wait, Elle, what?"

Shadou stroked Elle's cheek with his claws. "Elle, I'm afraid this is happening. And it's not your fault, or any other human's fault. It's mine."

Elle slapped away Shadou's hand. "I don't care whose fault this is. Just take me to my dad, OK? He'll know what to do." Elle glanced sideways at Miller and Danny. "What's the deal with these two anyway?"

"I'll explain later." Shadou looked over at Mount Rainier. They had time, if it meant appeasing her. "OK, Elle, I'll give you two minutes with your dad. Let's go."

Elle immediately jumped into Shadou's arms and gestured to Conner to follow suit. He did not. Shadou reached out with one free hand and swept Conner away, along with Miller and Danny. Seconds later, the five of them were standing in Jim's house.

Jim and Emmett sat lounging with books on the sofa. The sudden appearance of Elle, Conner, two strangers, and a hulking, bearlike creature in their living room shocked Jim and Emmett into a state of paralyzing fear.

Jim writhed in his seat. "What the... Is this?... Elle?"

Elle stepped away from Shadou's arms and raced to her father. "Dad." She gripped his face in her hands. "I'm here with Shadou. He's not a cyberstalker. He's an alien from another world. He saved your life after the car accident. He's the one who patched you up."

Jim looked up at Shadou through his glasses. "You're... Shadou?"

"I am. And I wish we could be meeting in more... better circumstances. Elle, remember. Two minutes."

Emmett looked up from his picture book with a slack-jawed expression. "Two minutes before what?"

"Until I have to go." Elle picked her backpack up off the floor and threw it over her shoulder. She shook Jim in an attempt to wake him from his stupor. "Dad, you have to listen to me. Something really bad is about to happen. It will start at Mount Rainier, but it's going to be big, bigger than anything ever before."

Jim could barely muster a response. "OK, sweetie, I hear you, but—"

"You need to warn the world that this is happening." Elle looked over at the ham radio that sat collecting dust on a desk in the corner. "Use your radio. Tell them that what happened to Mom at the mountain all those years ago was just the beginning. Do it now!"

Jim pulled his phone from his pocket and fumbled with it. "Um..." He struggled to formulate a sentence. Elle reached for the ham radio. *My gift...*

Just then they heard a tremendous BOOM from outside. The windows rattled and objects fell off shelves. Elle followed everyone as they ran out of the house to look toward Mount Rainier. A black plume of a thick, tar-like substance rose from the mountain. Tendrils of darkness fanned high out across the sky in every direction. The matter would reach them in seconds.

Shadou tore his eyes away from the sky. "Time's up, Elle!" The rumbling sound grew louder with each second.

Tears welled up in Elle's eyes. "We failed. Can't you and I use our gifts to warn the world?"

"No warning will save them. Come with me now if you want to help."

Elle nodded. "Take them with us!"

Shadou grabbed Elle and Conner into his arms. Miller and Danny followed close behind. The black matter doused out the daylight from the sky as it hurtled toward them. It looked as though an asteroid was about to extinguish all life on Earth. When it hit, Elle could tell that Shadou was somehow able to generate a force field. A small sphere of light, emanating from Shadou, protected them.

Shadou stretched his one free arm out toward Jim, but he couldn't quite reach. Elle watched in horror as Jim was engulfed in the darkness. His body turned gray and then disappeared as though into a mist. Jim's cat Marvin jumped from out of nowhere up into Emmett's arms. Elle watched as Emmett too was overwhelmed by the darkness.

"Shadou! Why aren't you saving them?"

"I'm trying! The force is too strong!"

Emmett and Marvin both started to fade into gray ghosts. But before they were fully engulfed, Shadou reached out with a final thrust of energy and grabbed them.

"We're done here!" Shadou stomped his foot on the ground and dematerialized, taking Elle, Conner, Miller, Danny, Emmett, and Marvin with him.

The dark matter spread across the entire earth in less than five hours. All of humanity was encased—enslaved—within this mysterious substance. There was nothing even the most sophisticated military forces on the planet could have done to prevent the attack. They were doomed.

Quaru observed all of this from his cavernous base deep within Mount Rainier. He emerged from the collapsed spherical prison in triumph. In the end, escaping those seemingly impregnable walls seemed all too easy. Instead of focusing on the outer world, he only needed to look deeper within, and focus on the light that his being had assimilated. *That took me five thousand years to figure out? I must be getting slow in my old age.*

He spent a moment simply listening to the blissful silence. No more human noise. That burning torment had been extinguished forever. To celebrate his victory over the scourge of humanity, Quaru took on a form that resembled a living statue chiseled from smooth, dark stone. He modeled his appearance from a little girl's nightmare he had "seen" many years ago. His face and hands were sharp and menacing, as though carved out of glassy obsidian. Even though his body's main outline may have been vaguely human, Quaru was still all shadows. To finish his look, he wore a black cloak that fell to the ground at odd, jutting angles.

As he stepped forward, his cloak flowing behind him, Quaru realized that he was not alone in this cave-like fortress. He gazed down and saw a woman cowering on the ground, scarcely able to move.

Well, hello there. Oh, yes, I forgot about you. The little trinket I stole from Shadou. You must be Jill. My name is Quaru. Jill's body seemed to relax at the sound of Quaru's "voice." She sat up. *I've been waiting for this moment for a long, long time. I'm so very pleased that you'll be here by my side to share in the fun.*

Jill looked up at the dark form that towered nearly eight feet above her. She shuddered with a wry smile. "Well, hello to you, Quaru. And what's your idea of fun?"

Quaru looked over at Chuck's shattered corpse. Black tentacles shot from Quaru's cloak, lifted Chuck's body up to the ceiling, and tossed it into the abyss on the other side of the cavern.

Fun? His whisper burrowed into Jill's mind. *For starters, I crave a companion. I think you'll do quite nicely.*

Chapter 30

During her year on Bainbridge Island, Elle developed a passion for beachcombing. She loved the rocky beaches where she could turn over barnacle-caked stones to uncover swarms of shore crabs, limpets, hermits, and squirting horse clams. It was ironic that when she lived on Bainbridge, Elle missed the wide, sandy beaches of southern California. She longed for languid days splashing in the waves and relaxing on the warm, soft sand. But when Elle moved to Los Angeles, her thoughts turned to coding, and building new digital worlds. Sand castles on warm beaches lost their allure.

As Elle stood contemplating what was supposedly the rim of the Grand Canyon, she let sand dollar crumbs fall from her hand to the ground. *Those sunny beach days are gone, forever.*

It was dusk, although Elle couldn't see the sky. She and the others were all technically outdoors. But their field of vision only extended across a diameter of fifty or so yards. This was the dome-shaped force field that Shadou somehow generated, and which shielded them from the dark matter outside. The effect of this was to make it seem as though they were standing in a half-sphere-shaped room, a geodesic dome. Shadou remained always at its center, so that when he moved, the room "moved" with him.

The fading sunlight lit up the area as it would if there was no darkness. But the people inside could not see the sun, nor the sky, nor the horizon. The walls of the room appeared as a swirling dark cloud of gray and black matter, which shimmered but offered no reflection. The fact that they could see clearly in this strange place, and yet could see no source of light, was unnerving.

Elle shifted her gaze away from the swirling, gray walls and eyed her companions. Conner stood by her side. He seemed to be in a state of delirium, as though he hadn't slept in days. Shadou stood silently still, his face frozen in a stoic expression that Elle did not want to unpack. Behind him was an Asian woman wearing hiking gear and hot pink glasses. Elle liked her tattoos. A spindly, catlike creature lingered by Shadou's feet. *Great, another alien to deal with.* On the ground sat a young black man with long dreadlocks. His hands were pressed over his face. *The world just ended. I should be doing that too.*

Last of all, because it was the most difficult thing to look at, Elle considered Emmett. Or what used to be her seven-year-old brother. During the attack, Emmett had been partially consumed by the dark matter. This transformed him into a gray shadow of his former self. And yet somehow, and for some reason, Shadou decided to grab Emmett and transport him here. And there Emmett stood, in a solitary state of... *What exactly? Ghost-ness, perhaps*. But Emmett was not alone in this condition. In his arms he held the "ghost" of Marvin, Jim's cat. In a strange way, Emmett and Marvin were strikingly beautiful. Their skin and clothing were devoid of color, yet shimmered with a silvery light. Their eyes glowed silver. They reminded Elle of an art class sculpture project gone horribly wrong, but that was nonetheless fascinating. She couldn't help but notice the circles of light on Emmett's left hand and Marvin's left forepaw. They flickered on and off like two broken neon signs

Emmett didn't seem to be at all aware of where, or even who, he was. Marvin sat still in Emmett's arms. They moved just enough so that Elle knew they were alive.

Elle couldn't resist the urge to address him. "So, Emmett, what have you become, a statue or something?"

Everyone looked at Elle as though she were an insane person shouting at strangers on a street corner. Only Emmett and Marvin seemed completely disinterested.

Elle shook her head in disgust. She gestured out toward the gray walls around them and glared up at Shadou. "Hey, fat beast-man, you call this place the Grand Canyon?"

Shadou performed the alien equivalent of clearing his throat. "Yes, my dear Elle, we are at the Grand Canyon. Or at least... What once was."

Elle curled her lips into a snarl. "I don't believe you. All I can see is a little patch of dirt and rocks."

Shadou sighed. "As I told you, we can only see what once was the Earth in this force field I seem to be generating. I apologize, but this force field thing is a new gift. I've never experienced it before. It seems my master bestows gifts without telling me. Perhaps She still lives..." Shadou left them mentally for a moment, then he snapped back to the present. "For now, this relatively small area is the most I can fend off the darkness."

Elle laughed spitefully. "*Relatively* small area? You call this relatively small? Because to me it looks like we're trapped out in the middle of the desert in a tiny room waiting until we starve to death."

"Elle—"

"And where's the Grand Canyon? Years ago, you told me the Grand Canyon would be a safe place. Show me something safe!"

"I... OK, Elle, I'll show you." Shadou warned the others, "Stick with us. You don't want to be left behind."

Shadou pointed in the direction he was about to walk to and started taking careful steps. As he walked, the force field moved with him. All the others had to stay near him to make sure they remained safely within the dome's boundary. After a few minutes, a metal railing appeared in front of them. Shadou walked up to it and rested his hands on it, even though it was much too low for him to derive any comfort or sense of safety.

Elle stood beside him. She could see the edge of a canyon. The force field's dome formed three-quarters of a sphere as it hung off the wall. But still, the view was a great disappointment. She could only see about fifty yards out. Elle remembered the moonlit night she had spent there with Shadou, years ago...

She looked down as far below as she could, and then stepped back away from the rail. "Great, you ruined the most beautiful place in the world."

Shadou raised his hand and placed it lovingly on Elle's shoulder, but she pushed it away with an exaggerated sweep of her hand.

"Let go of me!"

Shadou started to speak, but then stopped himself.

"Yeah, that's right," said Elle, "you've got nothing to say. Because there is nothing to say. The whole entire world is gone, forever. And it's all your fault. You had one job!"

Elle punched Shadou repeatedly on his belly, shouting "Loser!" with each punch. Shadou didn't flinch. He looked down at Elle and took the beating. It caused him no pain, not physical at least. After a couple minutes, Elle stopped punching. She buckled over and barely managed to stifle tears of rage.

Conner snapped out of his daze and tried to comfort her. "Elle," he said with a feeble voice.

Elle shoved Conner so hard that he fell to the ground. She leveled her eyes down onto him, and he stared back up at her in pain. She offered Conner a look of apology, but refused to say the words. Then she wiped her face with the back of her hand and faced Shadou. "I've gotta go. Please don't try to stop me, you fluffy moron from outer space."

Elle spun on her heels and walked toward the gray, swirling wall. "Elle!" Shadou called after her. Elle picked up her pace and kicked a rock back at him with her heel. Shadou followed her. This made the walls of the dome shift, so that they were farther away from Elle. Conner and the other survivors realized that they needed to move too, or else they'd lose their shelter. They all stood up. Elle began to jog, slowly at first. As she neared the outer wall, Shadou called out to the others: "Come, stick with me."

The chase began. Conner, Miller, Danny, Rifkin—even Emmett holding Marvin for some reason—all jogged along Shadou's side as he tried to keep up with Elle. It was most difficult for her, since the closer she got to the wall, the less she could see of the shifting terrain at her feet. Boulders and shrubs popped out of the wall only yards in front of her. She had to focus hard on these obstacles. She occasionally tripped or lost balance when a rock appeared, or the slope changed dramatically. But eventually she found a paved path. Once safely on it, she broke out into a full-on sprint. Shadou and the others could not keep up. Elle inched closer to the wall. She clawed her outstretched fingers toward it, wondering whether or not it would be solid. It was not.

As though passing through a thick fog, Elle emerged from the gray wall and into the darkness. Outside of Shadou's force field, the rich, red earth and green shrubs vanished. All the rocky terrain, the rising and falling paved paths, ceased to be. Everything was replaced by a glass-like surface, completely smooth and transparent. Elle continued to run. The glass surface felt to her like a basketball court. She could run at her top speed. She looked up at the horizon. The sky was a pale gray wall of solid color, only slightly brighter at the flat horizon. There was barely any sound, even her shoes pounding on the surface emitted muffled thuds as she ran. Elle stopped. This completely alien landscape finally stunned her.

Elle collapsed onto her knees on the glassy surface. She pressed one hand to it as she caught her breath. The surface felt warm, as though it was alive. When she regained the strength to open her eyes, Elle looked deep into the glassy floor. There, she saw shimmering, shadowy images that appeared to be the Grand Canyon's high-desert landscape. But she couldn't feel it, couldn't smell it.

Then Elle heard a high-pitched shrieking sound that shook her to her very core.

She stood up and looked about her dim surroundings in a panic. The sky was empty, a still, gray backdrop, almost from a theater set. The shrieking sound grew louder, closer. Elle spun around and around, searching... In the distance, she saw a hazy, white light, slowly roving just above the surface. The shrieking sound erupted once more, in the opposite direction of that hazy blob of light.

Elle spun back around, and saw them for the first time. Just beneath the glassy surface, three glowing, grayish-white figures raced toward Elle. They appeared to be two women and a man, but it was difficult to make out any details since their images were distorted by the reflections on the floor. They hunted Elle like moths drawn to light. Her heart pounded faster when she saw their ghostlike hands emerge from beneath the surface with skeletal fingers reaching out to grab her.

Sheer instinct took over. Elle ran back several steps to gauge the ghosts' speed. Once she saw that they were moving faster, Elle ran as fast as she could. She sprinted back toward the hazy blob of light while the ghosts rapidly gained ground behind her.

Elle started to scream, "Shadou! Help me!" But her screams scarcely registered in this strange, dull place. Whatever was chasing Elle didn't have that problem. Elle could hear the deafening shrieks getting closer. She looked back and knew she wasn't going to make it.

One of the hands reached up and snagged Elle's ankle. She fell hard with a painful thud. The ghostlike creatures clamored over Elle's body and she went into the fetal position. She braced herself for the end.

Then a shadowy figure burst in. The ghosts shrieked once more, only this time in a state of distress. Elle felt her body free of their cold, painful touch. *Shadou*. But when she opened her eyes she saw that Shadou was not there. It was Emmett and Marvin. The two shimmering forms silently lashed out at the creatures. When hit, the creatures disintegrated into puffs of mist that resembled shattered glass moving in slow motion.

At last the three creatures were gone. But then Elle heard more shrieks, getting closer. Elle rolled over onto her side and back into the fetal position. Her knees and shoulders ached from her fall. She could run no further. Through her closed eyes, Elle sensed a different light. The shrieks were suddenly silenced. She opened her eyes and looked up. Shadou stood above her, backlit by what must have been moonlight, although Elle could see no moon. Shadou held out his hand. Elle took it.

"Well," she said, "That was ... totally insane. Is this all we have to look forward to?"

Shadou smiled. "No, Elle, we can do much, much better. Come. Let's all go inside and get some food and some rest."

Chapter 31

Shadou led the exhausted band along the rim of the Grand Canyon. They trudged across the rocky ground as though they had been walking for hours. But after only ten minutes, Shadou stopped. A few ragged shrubs and medium-sized boulders littered the landscape. The twilight illuminated everything in muted color so that the gray walls didn't seem so distinct.

Elle shrugged. "So, why don't you just teleport us?"

Shadou stood silent for a moment. Then he wrapped his arms around Elle's shoulder and stomped his foot on the ground, the same way he would when initiating a teleportation. Only nothing happened.

"Well, that's disappointing," said Elle.

Rifkin—now just a scruffy, catlike creature to the group—had remained in the background all this time. He finally spoke up. "Yeah, totally lame. But it's true. Teleportation don't work in this particular situation."

Miller, upon hearing Rifkin's gravelly voice, became instantly enamored. "Oh my god! How cute are you?" Miller knelt beside Rifkin and began petting his head.

Rifkin tried to pretend he didn't enjoy this, even though he obviously did. "Hey lady," he protested, "watch the fur!" He picked up his staff in one hand and a stone in the other. Then he slapped the two together to form a long, skinny rock. He used that to swat Miller away.

Conner stepped forward and shielded Miller behind him. "What the—?"

Rifkin swung his rock-stick back and forth in front of him. "Come on," he taunted, "Want a piece of me? Come and get it!"

Elle cracked up laughing. "Whoa, you're Rifkin, aren't you? The magician from the video..."

Rifkin pointed his rock-stick at Elle like a teacher addressing his classroom. "What video?"

Elle prodded Shadou, "You remember that video, right? 'Rifkin the Great,' or something?"

Shadou cleared his throat. "'Rifkin the Stupendous,' if memory serves correctly."

"That's right!" Elle gawked at Rifkin. "So you can really do that?"

"Do what?"

"You know, combine things."

"Of course. I'm a particle shifter, don't you know?" Rifkin twirled his rock-stick around and around like a baton. Then he picked up a desert flower off the ground nearby and clapped it together with the rock-stick. In his hands he suddenly held a stone stick with colorful petals, which fluttered when Rifkin waved it around. He held it up and slapped it. The flower and the rock fell to the ground while Rifkin twirled his staff.

Miller squealed and clapped. Conner stood slack-jawed, and Danny, who hadn't said a word since their arrival, blurted, "Whoa, dude! You're like David Blaine or some sh—"

Just then a bloodcurdling shriek burst forth from just outside the gray wall. Shadou's eyes darted around the area with renewed intensity. "Oh crap, it's getting dark."

Elle looked over at Emmett for the first time in a while. He still held the ghost of Marvin in his arms. Both of them appeared alert, at least more than usual. They sensed something. Elle asked Shadou, "Do those things like to come out at night?"

Shadou knelt down on a specific spot. He pressed his hand onto a small, shiny stone and twisted it around several full rotations. Another outburst of high-pitched shrieks made everybody jump.

Shadou pointed toward a section of the gray wall. "Get ready to move. They're coming!"

They saw a disturbance in the far section of the force field wall. At first it just looked like rippling shadows, but then gray ghost-like hands began to claw their way through. After a few more seconds the heads and shoulders of "people" emerged. They were on track to breach the wall within seconds.

Just then, the ground beside Shadou began to move. It turned out that the dirt concealed a large metal hatch, which opened up with a low grinding sound of rock on rock.

When the hatch opened up enough for some of them to squeeze through, Shadou called out, "The wraiths are upon us! Come on!" The wraiths burrowed their way completely through the wall and darted directly toward the small band of survivors. Without prompting, Emmett stepped forward, positioning himself between the wraiths and his party. Marvin, still sitting in Emmett's arms, rose up and hissed.

Shadou noticed that Elle wasn't moving. She stood frozen, almost fascinated by Emmett's aggressive stance. Shadou grabbed on to Elle's shoulder and walked her toward the opening hatch. "Go, Elle, go inside, run!"

Elle resisted. She wanted to stand beside her little brother. But Shadou was too strong. Rifkin, Danny, Miller, and Conner followed close behind. Shadou climbed inside after they were all safe within. They watched as the wraiths closed in on Emmett and Marvin.

Elle couldn't take it. "What are you doing? Get them in here and close the door!"

Shadou pressed his hand on an indentation in the wall. The hatch started to close.

Elle ran up and tried in vain to reverse the switch. "No! You can't leave them out there!"

Shadou pressed a hand on Elle's shoulder. "Don't worry. I'm pretty sure they'll be OK."

They all watched as the wraiths closed in on Emmett and Marvin. Emmett let Marvin drop to the ground. The wraiths circled the boy and his cat, and then shrieked once more. But this would be the last sound they uttered. Within seconds, Emmett and Marvin swung fists, feet, and claws at the ghosts. Each time they landed a blow, the wraiths disintegrated into puffs of shattered matter. At last, all traces of the wraiths had vanished.

Shadou switched off the hatch door so that it stopped closing. Then he grinned at Elle. "You see? There's good reason to keep those two around."

Elle barely acknowledged Shadou. She called out to her brother. "Emmett! Pick up Marvin and get in here now!" *Little brother, give me a sign that you can hear my voice.*

Elle's heart broke with despair as at first Emmett didn't move. But then he reacted. It was as though there was a delay between Elle speaking and her voice reaching him. Emmett stooped down, picked up Marvin as if nothing just happened, and climbed down through the hatch into the cave. Shadou activated the hatch once more, so that it closed with a slow, grinding thud.

Chapter 32

At first, Jill thought her life was over. She practically wished for this to be true. This alien being, Quaru, had turned Chuck into a terrifying monster. But Jill wasn't frightened of becoming another servant of Quaru. She was much more frightened of taking on all of Chuck's grotesque flaws. She envisioned herself with her mouth and eyes gaping wide open, and black gooey matter oozing out. How painful must that have been? And if Chuck did not feel any pain from that, was that worse? To Jill, being transformed into that dreadful state seemed absolutely morbid, a fate worse than death.

But Quaru had other plans. Standing over Jill's cowering form in the middle of this icy cavern, he reached out to her with his obsidian-like hand. *Come, my dear Jill.* He spoke not to her ears but instead through her very being. *Rise with me, and I will give you a pedestal upon which to witness the transformation of all humanity.*

Despite his stone-like composition, Quaru's face could be incredibly expressive. Jill saw a wide range of emotions: glee, spite, bitterness, even pain, all borne by subtle movements in Quaru's artificial eyes, mouth, and features. The entity's hand awaited, outstretched for Jill to take it. To her, it seemed that if she were to touch that shiny hand, with its intimidating claws, the sharp edges would instantly cut her to the bone.

Quaru extended his hand even farther, so that it was less than an inch from Jill's face. *Come on,* he commanded, *take my hand before I grow bored with you.*

Jill's heart raced and her breath quickened. She couldn't move or speak out of paralyzing fear. Quaru extended a finger and let it press up against the side of Jill's neck. As he caressed her, a streak of blood trickled down from the incision left behind, just deep enough to break the skin.

Jill snapped out of her paralysis, screamed out in pain, and crawled backwards. Quaru transformed his obsidian-black shape into a pillar of darkness that swept up Jill's body and carried her to the cavern ceiling. Quaru swung Jill in increasingly fast circles until she screamed even more. Then as quickly as he had started, Quaru dropped Jill onto the cavern floor, knocking the wind out of her. As Jill struggled to catch her breath, Quaru reclaimed his human shape and glowered over her.

Oh silly Jillie, Jillie, Jillie ... Don't you realize? There's nothing left for you to worry about. All your cares in this sad little world are gone, forever.

Jill looked up and finally summoned enough air in her lungs to speak. "What are you?"

Quaru's body burst apart into what seemed like hundreds of winged creatures of different sizes, varying between beetles and bats. They swarmed around the cavern in a tornado of fury. Jill protected her head with her arms and pressed herself down onto the hard, rocky ground. After a moment, Quaru spoke, even though he maintained his chaotic form of a murmur of flying creatures.

What am I? I am Quaru. I know not what I am. I simply am. I have been Quaru since the beginning of time, and I will remain Quaru long after the end of time. Time is relevant to me only in that it binds me with space and matter. Time, space, matter; these are the three pillars of perfection, from which spawn gravity. Gravity is what feeds Quaru, gives me my power.

Jill stopped cowering on the floor and sat up, watching in wonder as the dark flying forms of Quaru swirled around her. She couldn't help but smile. There was something almost pathetic about this ... entity. No wonder Chuck had been such a mess. Even though Jill's body ached from being tossed onto the ground, her fear of Quaru subsided enough for her to speak.

"OK," she said, "You're a child of space, time, and matter, feeding on gravity. So why are you here on Earth?"

The flying things merged together to form a massive shadowy figure that grabbed Jill around her chest, picked her up six feet above the ground, and threatened her with a razor-sharp tip that lingered inches from her neck.

WHY am I here? Quaru's voice filled with raw, uncontrollable fury. *SHADOU! He brought me to this foul wasteland, filled with human misery that I was forced to endure for what felt like an eternity in a prison of pain and suffering.*

Working through her incapacitation, Jill managed to utter one word. "Shadou?" That name was all too familiar.

Quaru let Jill fall the six feet onto the ground. She collapsed in a pile, bruised and bloody, but somehow managed to pull herself up to face her captor.

Quaru returned to his "normal" human shape. He circled around her, dragging his cloak behind him. *I must apologize,* he intoned in a subdued voice. *I let my hatred of Shadou and the entire human race get the best of me. That was utterly uncalled for.*

Jill had never been abused before. The closest she ever got to this kind of treatment was her encounter with the bear in Chuck's mobile home. She looked down at her ripped hiking pants, with blood forming at the knees, and then looked up at her abuser, her eyes defiant. Quaru stepped back, almost intimidated by Jill's resolve.

Jill reached her hand to Quaru. He seemed frightened by this gesture. "Well? Aren't you going to help me get up?"

Quaru took Jill's hand and lifted her, slowly. Jill rested against Quaru's side and caught her breath.

"OK, that was quite the overreaction. You really need to stop doing that."

Quaru tilted his head back and burst out laughing. This was no maniacal, evil laugh. It was more the laugh of a small child who caught a serious case of the giggles. It almost reminded Jill of a young Elle or Emmett. When at last Quaru's laughter subsided, echoing off of the cavern walls, Jill asked, "What's so funny?"

Oh, nothing really. Only I just realized something. I can't hear your thoughts, or your emotions, Jill. In fact, all the human noise is silent, even when you're right here by my side. Quaru rested his hand on Jill's shoulder. *That made me laugh, is all.*

"I'm glad someone's laughing." Jill surveyed the bleak cavern. She realized that it should be pitch dark in there, now that the glowing spherical prison was gone. And yet there was light, emanating from an unknown source.

Quaru wagged his finger at Jill. *I can't hear what you're thinking, Jill. But I know what you're thinking. 'Where does this light come from?' you ask.*

"Yes, you got me. That's what I was thinking."

Quaru swept Jill up into his massive arms. She was terrified at first, not knowing whether he would fly off into a rage and rip her to shreds. But instead of doing that, Quaru gazed down at Jill, almost lovingly.

I can do lots of things, Jill, he whispered to her. *I can make light from darkness. I can make matter from nothingness. I can bring order to chaos.*

Jill shifted around, a bit uncomfortable in Quaru's tightening grip. "That's great, but would you mind loosening up your grip here? You're kind of crushing me."

Quaru softened his touch. In fact, he softened his entire form so that it was no longer hard, angular obsidian. To Jill he felt more like smooth, pliable rubber.

Is that better?

Jill nodded. "Yes, it is. You were saying?"

Quaru giggled once more. *Oh right! But it's really much better to show than to tell, is it not?* His body unfurled and began swirling around Jill like a giant, tattered banner flapping in a strong wind. Jill felt the cavern around them begin to lose its substance. They were dematerializing, apparently on their way to someplace else.

"Where are you taking me, Quaru?"

Not far. You really need to see this in order to appreciate it. Earth is my latest project, and your fellow humans are my slaves—I mean, my builders.

The cavern walls disappeared completely and were replaced by tall buildings, trees, and the instantly recognizable Space Needle. They found themselves in what appeared to be a version of downtown Seattle. Quaru let Jill down onto the ground. She looked around in awe. This was indeed Seattle. Only it was completely gray. Not just the stereotypical Seattle gray with clouds. Everything was gray: buildings, trees, cars. They shimmered with a dull light that was punctuated by strands of sparkling silver lines. They appeared to connect everything together like wires or veins.

But the lack of color was not the most disturbing thing that Jill saw. Rows and rows of people trudged past her. Everyone—man, woman, old, young—they all walked in unison. They too were gray from head to toe, including their clothing. Their eyes glowed pale silver, and each one had a steadily glowing white circle on the outside of their left hand. All of these human ghosts were walking—marching—east, toward some unknown destination.

The streaming masses of spectral people paid Jill no mind. She looked down at her own hands, thinking that she too must be a ghost. But she was not. Her skin and shirtsleeves radiated dazzling color, as though she were looking at them through a highly saturated filter.

Jill looked up at Quaru, and again stared in shock. Instead of a massive black figure, she saw simply a man in a silky black cloak. This man appeared to be in his late fifties or early sixties. Striking white hair sprang from his head, cut short with sharp lines around the edges. He wore a neatly trimmed white beard, and his eyebrows were wispy, almost like the feathers plucked from a white owl.

Quaru faced Jill with glowing blue eyes that swirled and danced with subtly shifting colors. He smiled and spoke to her in a plain, humble voice. "You see, Jill? Your people are going to build a new Earth. A perfect Earth, free from the chaos and meaningless pain that is human thought and emotion."

Jill felt a lone tear trickle down her cheek. "Then what? What are you going to do with everyone, all these people, after they're done building us this perfect world?"

Quaru patted Jill's hand softly. His palm felt smooth and warm. "After they are done with their task, Jill, they will no longer be needed, not here nor anywhere else."

Jill wanted to run away and warn all the people, but then she thought of Elle, Emmett, everyone she knew, all enslaved now. She was too terrified to move.

Chapter 33

Shadou led the band of survivors down a wide underground corridor. It had been carved from multiple layers of ancient rock: sandstones, limestones, shale. Down, down, down the path wound as they walked. It felt to Elle like a massive parking garage. Three large trucks could easily drive side-by-side here. Artificial lights illuminated the space with a soft, pale glow. Nobody spoke as they walked, but after nearly a half hour of trudging, Elle couldn't take it anymore.

She stopped in her tracks. "Shadou, seriously, how much longer do we have to go? You sold us on food and water, but can't you just transport us there? Down here we seem to be out of that ghost world."

This little outburst was Shadou's last straw. He threw up his hands. "Yeah, yeah, yeah, I get it, you're tired and hungry and thirsty. Well, guess what? So am I. And didn't I tell you why I can't just magically transport you like I usually do?"

"I guess so. I just thought that maybe—"

Shadou shrugged and picked up the pace. "Come on. Not too much further."

Elle began to protest but then thought the better of it. Instead she clutched her backpack straps, lowered her head, and concentrated on the ground directly in front of her feet. Everyone else followed suit.

Several minutes later the cavernous path opened up into a massive chamber. A sandstone dome of about four hundred feet in height extended far above their heads. Golden rays of soft light bathed the entire space in a relaxing glow. Elle felt more at ease here. It was a destination worthy of their downhill journey.

At the center of the chamber stood an object that, to Elle, looked to be a small white spacecraft, the one from the video. It basked in its own spotlight, like a lone opera singer on a stage. Beside the spacecraft stood a pickup truck. A lone human figure emerged from the shadows behind the truck and limped up toward the group.

Miller jumped up and down. "Jason! Oh my god, you're alive!" She ran across the chamber toward him. Jason caught Miller in one arm when she reached him. He noticeably kept his other arm by his side.

Elle looked at Shadou, eyebrows curling with mistrust. "Who's that guy?"

"He's a friend. Jason. He was injured. Chuck's web got him. So I brought him here directly as a precaution. He'll be all right."

"So how does Miller know him?"

"He was introduced to Miller by ... well, by your mother. I didn't realize that he and Miller were... involved."

"My mom? You mean she knows that guy? I remember Miller from the tent at Mount Rainier now, after the earthquake. But who's this Chuck guy you mentioned anyway? He has a web? Is he here too?"

"No, Chuck's not here." Shadou's stomach growled loudly and he rubbed it with his hand. "Excuse me. I realize there's a lot to explain. But first let's get some food in our bellies. I could really use a beer right now."

Shadou led the group across the chamber toward Miller and Jason. As they drew closer, Jason recognized Elle. A wide yet somehow sad smile spread across his face. "Elle Redfern? Your momma told me so much about you." Then Jason looked around at the others. No Jill. "But where is she? Where's Jillie?"

Miller gripped Jason's injured arm, and he flinched. "Oh sorry!" she said. "Still as clumsy as ever..." Miller took Jason's uninjured hand in hers. "Jill didn't make it."

Elle dropped her backpack. "Wait. What does that mean, exactly?"

Miller walked up to Elle and placed her hands on Elle's shoulders. "We were with her, sweetie. The... The darkness took her just as we were about to leave the mountain."

Elle pushed Miller away and stormed over to Shadou, who was clearly not in the mood for another confrontation. "Now, Elle," he said, holding up a hand, "before we get into this, can't we at least eat some food, a light snack even?"

"Are you kidding me? No! You need to tell me what's going on here. Everything!" Elle shot Miller an accusing glance. "The mountain? You were at Mount Rainier with my mom when all of this happened?"

Miller nodded.

"And what were you doing there? Why in the world would you go to where that horrible *thing* was?" She jabbed at Miller and Jason with her finger. "Why were you, and you, and my mom anywhere near that place?"

Jason was too transfixed by the sight of Emmett and Marvin to even hear what Elle was saying. He had just noticed the odd pair standing off to the side.

But Elle didn't seem to care. She focused her frustration back on Shadou. Her voice growled with a deep, brimming rage. "Shadou, I know you screwed up big-time, that you were too incompetent to even be guarding a candy jar, much less some dark, evil force trapped in a volcano, but this, this is just—"

Jason cut in. "Whoa! Whoa! Whoa! What is going on here?"

Everyone looked at Jason in fear. Conner instinctively ran over to Elle's side. Danny tossed up his hands. "Man, please. What is your problem?"

Jason spat on the floor. "My problem?" Jason shot out his hand to point toward Emmett and Marvin. "My problem is that we've got some of *them* in here with us!"

All eyes turned to Emmett. The mute ghost seemed completely unaware of the stares. He stood in his spot with feet pressed together. Marvin, the gray ghost cat, sat perfectly content as Emmett gently stroked the fur on the top of his head.

Elle looked over to Jason. "Out of everything going on right now, that's your problem?"

Jason stamped his foot. "You bet it is!"

"He's my brother, Emmett. And he's holding my dad's cat, Marvin. I happen to love him very much, and I'm pretty sure they won't hurt us. In fact, he took care of those wraithlike things out there. If he hadn't been there, we'd all be ghosts too for all I know."

Jason shook his head. "For all I know, your 'brother'"—Jason made air quotes—"is not your brother at all. Not anymore at least. You know what he could be, and probably is?"

Elle rolled her eyes. "Like what? A spy for the enemy?"

Jason nodded. "Bingo!" He jabbed his finger toward Emmett. "That's exactly what I think he is. Right now, that dark force that's taken over everything, it's probably watching us, through the eyes of your so-called brother. That evil thing can hear every word we're saying, knows exactly where we are, and how to get us."

Elle was not impressed. "Whatever." She turned back and punched Shadou hard in the gut. This had little effect other than making his stomach growl once more. "Shadou, tell me what's going on with all these people, and how they know my mom!"

Jason wouldn't let up. "No, you tell us what we're going to do about this sleeper cell we've got down here with us. We are living through the end of life as we know it. Every single remaining human needs to be protected at all costs."

Elle shook her head in exasperation. "Does that mean you have a plan?"

"Hell yes, I have a plan. We're a small group of helpless survivors. We need a leader to organize us and set the rules for engagement."

"Oh, so you're electing yourself 'leader' of our group now, is that it?"

"Who else other than me, Elle?" Jason placed his hand on her shoulder. "Look, today is the worst day of all of our lives. I intend to make sure that each day gets better from here." He pointed at Emmett. "But unless we're one hundred percent certain that your brother here is harmless—and I know you can't be certain—we have to take drastic measures. We have to organize. We have to fight, destroy the enemy, take back what's ours."

"You mean we have to kill my brother?"

Jason nodded. "I'm telling you, Elle. He's not your brother, not anymore."

Elle surveyed the group. Everyone was filthy, exhausted, and beyond any capacity to fight. But they also looked to Jason, seemingly in search of guidance or hope. *What can I possibly say to protect Emmett?*

From out of nowhere, Conner stepped up between Elle and Jason. "We are not going to kill Emmett! As far as we're concerned, he's still Elle's brother, until he proves otherwise. And for now, nobody here is our leader."

Jason eyed Conner as though sizing him up for the kill. Miller's face clenched in anticipation of something horrible about to happen. Elle stood still, unable to move. But Jason thought the better of it. "Listen kid," he said to Conner, "I don't know you. But for the moment I'll entertain your opinion. Are you saying we should just hang around this cave and wait for Emmett or whatever is upstairs to come and kill us? Because that's what it sounds like."

"I'm saying we should all take a moment to process the fact that the world just ended. Don't you realize that we all lost everybody we know? And if anyone should lead us right now, it should be him." Conner pointed to Shadou.

Jason shook his fists. "Seriously? You expect me to hand our future to an alien who got us into this mess in the first place? That's insane!"

"Shadou understands what's happening more than any of us."

"I understand exactly what's happening. We just got invaded. Shadou here was part of the invasion. And so is Emmett."

"You leave Elle's brother out of this!"

Conner and Jason started shouting over each other. They both readied themselves for a fight, shoving each other at first and then wielding fists. At last, Shadou could stand it no longer. He opened his mouth wide, exposing rows of sharp, jagged fangs, and he let out a booming roar. The sound reverberated off the walls and rose into a deafening feedback loop. Everyone except Emmett and Marvin collapsed onto the floor with their hands over their ears.

After what seemed like several minutes, the roar subsided. All that could be heard were faint sobs of the humans and Rifkin. Then the hatch to the white starship in the center of the cavern hissed open. A bright, white light emanated from the ship and a smooth, whooshing sound filled the cavern. Everyone watched this display with wide yes.

When the ship hatch came to rest on the ground, out strode a teenage boy wearing light gray sweat pants and a white hoodie. His tight-curled blond hair enveloped his head like a disheveled helmet. He walked on pale bare feet with his hands shoved in his hoodie pockets.

"Shadou!" he called out at last, pointing at the ship behind him. "I could hear your screams from inside. A little overdramatic, don't you think? I'm trying to get some work done here."

Shadou ignored him. He let his massive backpack drop with a thud and tapped the floor with his foot. A large, rectangular-shaped table rose from the floor. Shadou placed his backpack on the smooth stone surface and opened it. Elle's eyes widened as she saw a light glowing from within the backpack. Everyone stood frozen in suspense, wondering what Shadou was going to pull out.

He rummaged through it for several seconds, and then took out a tall can of Rainier beer. He cracked it open and handed it to Rifkin. Streams of white foam dribbled down the sides of the can and splattered onto the rock floor.

"Dang, Shadou!" Rifkin said. "Careful with the merchandise." Rifkin sipped at the foam and then chugged the beer with voracious gulps.

Shadou pulled another beer from his backpack. He cracked it open and immediately pressed his lips to the opening, so that all the foam went directly into his mouth. The beer was consumed in about ten seconds. Shadou slammed the empty can down onto the table, drew another can from his backpack, and opened it. Jason and Conner rose from the floor. They were finished fighting for now.

Elle took a few steps closer to Shadou. "Um, are you going to tell us who that guy is?"

Shadou smiled and let out a booming laugh that echoed off the walls. The stranger surveyed the group of survivors with distrust and crossed his arms. "Is this the best you could do?" he asked Shadou. "I mean, talk about making this even more of a challenge."

Shadou cracked open another beer. Elle looked on in disbelief. *Is he a drunk?*

Shadou gazed at her, and let his eyes fall on everyone in the group. "You wondering whether I'm an alcoholic? That's not really possible with my physiology. Admittedly, I can be kind of a problem drinker... We—Rifkin and I—we've been hanging around the remote parts of the Pacific Northwest for the past five thousand years. The only thing that's kept us even slightly sane that whole time has been beer."

Rifkin nodded. "Beer and junk food."

"Well, the junk food came much later, but not a moment too soon."

Shadou pulled out a party-size bag of BBQ potato chips and tore into it. "Come on, people." He stuffed handfuls of chips into his mouth. "Get over here and eat." He pointed at the boy with a sharp claw. "You too, Wazer."

Elle rolled her eyes. "Wait, Wazer? Seriously, that's your name?"

The boy trudged over toward the awaiting food. "Hi, Elle. Yes, my name is Wazer." He held out his hand. "It's a pleasure to finally meet you. That's some pretty cool stuff you do."

Seeing Wazer up close somehow made him seem both more human and more fantastical at the same time. Despite his pale complexion and blond hair, his eyes reflected like dark amber. She caught herself blushing and shook his hand, unable to grab onto more than a few fingers. "Um, thanks. Why are you here?"

Wazer smiled, revealing straight yet yellowed teeth. "The same reason you all are. To help Shadou save the world."

Conner took Elle's hand and stepped nearly between her and Wazer. "I'm Conner. You said you were getting some work done in that rocket ship over there. What does that mean, exactly?"

Wazer glanced over at Shadou, who responded for him. "Wazer is a friend. Over the past couple years, he's spent a good deal of time down here, communicating with my ship."

Elle's eyes lit up. *Does he have a gift too?* "So you can actually talk to it?" she asked.

Wazer rocked back and forth on his bare feet. "I'm learning how to. Shadou's been teaching me. He and Rifkin needed to tend to the... that prisoner in the mountain. But they hoped that I could get some messages, some advice, from their ship. That didn't quite pan out, obvi."

Jason interjected, "Obviously. Look, Wazer. You need to tell us everything you know."

Wazer let out a high-pitched cackle. "I don't need to do anything you tell me to, old man."

Shadou cut in. "Enough!" His voice reverberated off the cavern walls again. "Nobody here is going to fight, and we're not going to harm Emmett. He happens to be our best defense at the moment. Now, you humans need to eat. You're all too cranky for me to handle right now."

Shadou returned to his open backpack. He pulled out several more bags of chips, as well as processed lunch meat, boxes of Pop Tarts, Fig Newtons, Nilla Wafers, grocery-store bakery muffins, Chips Ahoy cookies, off-brand white bread, boxes of Cocoa Puffs cereal, bottles of orange Fanta, more beer, tubs of minipretzels, day-old bagels, cream cheese, tortilla chips, cheese dip, medium salsa, cheese puffs, Ritz crackers, ice cream sandwiches (still frozen), tubes of Go-Gurt, deli macaroni salad, peppermint Ice Breakers gum, two dozen assorted doughnuts, canned chicken noodle soup, ramen, paper plates and cups, plastic utensils, and two rolls of paper towels.

Once the table was set, Shadou gestured grandly at the buffet laid before him. He tapped his foot on the floor and ten chairs rose out from the rock, sliding gracefully into their place around the table.

Shadou picked up his beer and raised it high. "Ladies and gentlemen, stop your fighting, make new friends. Let us dine together." He downed the beer and collapsed onto the biggest chair. Then he grabbed a paper plate and started piling on as much food as he could.

Danny was the first one to walk over to the table. "I don't know about you people, but I am starving." He grabbed a paper plate and started into the food. Miller and Jason joined him next. Jason looked over at Conner, and then Wazer. "This conversation isn't over."

Miller took Jason's arm and whispered in his ear, "Did you know that guy was here the whole time?"

"Hell no, honey."

Elle took Conner's hand in hers and looked over at Emmett and Marvin. They remained in their spot a bit removed from the rest of the group. The pair of ghosts showed no interest whatsoever in the junk-food buffet, or anything else for that matter. *What are we going to do with you guys?*

Shadou tapped Elle's shoulder. "They don't eat." Shadou tossed several Chips Ahoy cookies into his mouth and turned his attention to opening the Nilla Wafers box.

Elle trudged over to the table and picked up a paper plate. She then grabbed a cup. "Gummy worms?" she asked.

Shadou reached into his backpack and tossed her a bag of gummy worms.

Elle's face lit up as she ripped open the bag. "Finally, some good news. Is there anything besides orange soda and beer to drink?"

Shadou pulled out a two-liter bottle of Diet Coke. "This good enough?"

"How about plain old water?"

Shadou pulled out a twenty-four-can case of seltzer water. "This is the best I can do. It's cold at least."

Elle shrugged. "Fabulous." She took a giant gulp between bites of gummy worms and let out a tremendous belch. Everyone looked at her for a second and then cracked up laughing. "What? This stuff's amazing!" Shadou opened can after can and passed them down the table.

After that, the survivors' mood was noticeably more upbeat. They compared war stories about how they came to be with Shadou in this strange underground bunker. Elle learned the story of how Jill, Miller, and Jason—and Danny too—had all tracked down Chuck. How they had followed him from his hunting cabin to Mount Rainier. How Jason had been left behind, and then at the end, Jill too.

Elle trusted Miller; she believed in her remorse. Jason was a big question mark. As she bit into a bagel with paste-like cream cheese she mused aloud, "I lost my mom and dad today." She looked over at Emmett. "I guess my brother too." Then she considered Jason. He seemed to be particularly gloomy all of a sudden. "Who did you lose today?"

Jason crossed his arms. "I lost one of the oldest friends I had, your mama. I hope I see her again."

"You will," said Elle. *I will.* She saw Danny eating quietly. "How about you?"

Danny shrugged his shoulders and stared down at his plate. "I lost everyone, I guess, right? I mean, my friends, my mom and pop, this girl Renee I had a huge crush on. My buddy Roy. Wow. Everyone." He held his hands in his head for several seconds, and then looked up at Wazer, who sat hunched over a plate full of cookies. "How about you? Seems like you've been in on this whole thing for a while."

Wazer wiped some crumbs off his face. "You mean who did I lose? I lost no one. I've been on my own."

Miller contemplated Wazer and placed her hand on Danny's shoulder. She looked up to Shadou. "So, is this it for us? Life underground. How much more of this processed food do you have in that magic backpack of yours?"

"A lot," said Shadou, "but not enough."

Miller tossed a half-eaten potato chip down onto her plate. "You sure splurged, didn't you? I mean, couldn't you have gone to Whole Foods, or at least Trader Joe's?"

"I didn't have time. The attack came so suddenly, I just went out and grabbed what I knew I liked to eat. I couldn't even do it discreetly."

Shadou remembered those moments just before Quaru escaped. The people in the big-box grocery store screamed with terror as he materialized out of thin air and started grabbing as much food off the shelves as he could. Within seconds the store was evacuated, and then minutes later five police cars pulled up into the parking lot, their sirens blaring. Cops with bulletproof vests and shotguns stationed themselves behind their open doors. At least two helicopters buzzed overhead. Shadou could tap into their radio frequencies and listen to the panicked chatter: *"Unknown threat!" "Request backup!" "Apparent shoplifting!"* It was all too late. Shadou emptied the shelves and dematerialized.

Shadou mentally returned to the quiet cavern, looked at Elle's expectant face, and shook his head. "None of it matters. The entity escaped. It's all my fault."

"That's a lie!" The shout came from a voice they hadn't heard in a while. Elle turned to see Conner sitting with his arms crossed.

"What's a lie?" asked Shadou.

Conner slammed down his empty can so hard onto the table that it crumpled up into a hockey puck-sized disk. "None of it matters?" He stood up and walked toward Shadou. He stretched out his arms and spun in a circle around the room. "This planet, this is our home, man. And you guys"— Conner pointed at both Shadou and Rifkin—"you just came here and took a big old dump on it, like literally..."

Shadou shook his head. "I think you mean figuratively, Conner." But then he laughed and pointed at Rifkin, "Although, I did go outside to do number two quite often!"

Rifkin responded with a high-pitched giggle. "We all know what bears do in the woods!"

Elle smacked Shadou and Rifkin both on their noses as hard as she could. "Guys, shut up! This is serious!"

Conner stepped up next to Elle. "Shadou, Rifkin, please. Tell me you have a plan, in case that entity thing you were supposed to be guarding got out, which it did."

Shadou glanced over at Rifkin and Wazer with a hint of pained irony in his eyes, and then back at Conner, Elle, Jason, Miller, and Danny. They stared at him with rapt attention.

"What are you all looking at?" Shadou said. "Of course we have a plan. But you're not gonna like it."

Chapter 34

For most of Jill's career, she focused on operations. Her last job—the job she abandoned in Los Angeles to travel up to Washington with Jason and Miller—was actually Chief Operations Officer at a midsized firm that developed mobile phone apps. Jill prided herself on her ability to find what the industry called "efficiencies" in "organizational structures." If the CEO of her company wanted to take on a new project, Jill could figure out the best way to run it, whether by using internal teams, or by purchasing another, smaller company. Even though she excelled at "operational excellence"—another industry term—and was probably on track to take the leap to an even bigger firm, Jill couldn't stand her line of work. All of her time she spent bean counting, building spreadsheets, and analyzing dull data points. It seemed to Jill like a cold, barren waste of life. She majored in classical literature in college, after all...

But within her first couple hours spent traveling with Quaru, Jill knew she had met her operational-excellence match. This guy—or thing— was an efficiency machine. Quaru could effortlessly transport the two of them all over the Earth—or rather—the planet previously known as Earth. The endless lines of ghosts Jill witnessed everywhere were in fact people who had been appropriated by Quaru. They marched to shipping yards, airports, train stations, and fulfillment center warehouses. From these hubs, they boarded planes, trains, trucks, and boats. Within less than twenty-four hours, over sixty percent of the planet's population—*billions* of people—had been relocated.

Quaru spoke to Jill of concepts like "density control" and "skill-set optimization." Often he became so animated that Jill wondered whether he was indeed a formidable being from outer space, or just some delusional middle manager. After their initial tour of the global operation, Quaru transported himself and Jill back to Seattle. She was relieved to discover they had landed in a luxurious penthouse, perched on the top story of a newly built downtown tower.

She sauntered up to the floor-to-ceiling window overlooking the Seattle shipyards. The city, and everything in it—including Puget Sound, the sky, and the buildings—were devoid of color. From this height, Jill could make out tiny threads of silver lights, streaming together in unison. These were people walking toward the shipyards. In the far distance, she thought she could make out people boarding shipping containers, which would be stacked onto giant container ships to be transported elsewhere.

Jill shuddered, still grappling with the loss of her family, but partly out of hunger. She looked over at the glass dining room table. On top of it sat a gray bowl filled with gray fruit. Jill picked up one of the fruits. An apple, maybe? She attempted to take a bite out of it, but all that filled her mouth was acrid air. It tasted of gasoline and bleach. Jill heaved and threw the phantom apple onto the floor.

Quaru took absolutely no notice of this. "You see, Jill," he explained, "once I have redistributed all of humanity based on their skills—both mental and physical—they can begin work on the prototype."

Despite her exhaustion, Jill needed some answers. "OK, the prototype. Got it. What's the prototype for? I mean, what's the purpose of all this?"

"Don't you realize? This is a great opportunity to build a completely automated world. You see, sentient beings like you humans, you can do a lot of interesting things. You can build civilizations, wage wars, practice space travel. But you are all so limited by one fatal flaw."

Jill stifled a yawn. "What's that? What's our fatal flaw?"

"You're not connected! There's no network connecting your thoughts or feelings. Because of this, you'll never achieve the next level."

Jill was puzzled. "Wait, aren't we supposed to all be cyborgs in the next twenty years or so, with or without your so-called help?"

"No, Jill! You don't get it."

"And even if we don't go all cyborg, won't computers take over anyway? Artificial intelligence going all self-aware?"

Quaru became so frustrated that he gave her a look that made her think he was about to tear her to shreds. Somehow he managed to contain his rage.

"No, no, no, no! Jill, you are not listening to me! Don't you understand?" Jill gave him back a blank stare. Quaru continued, "Anything you humans create—whether it's artificial intelligence that you integrate into your bodies, or machines you build independent of human form—it's all doomed to fail!"

"But why?"

"Because it will all be based on the concept of the self, of 'me, me, me.' This intelligence will all serve its own lesser purpose. Even if it thinks in terms of 'we' and not 'me' it will fail."

Jill shook her head. Quaru was a complete lunatic. "OK, I got it. You're here to build a better robot."

Quaru opened his mouth, then launched at Jill faster than any physical being could possibly move, pulled her from her chair, and launched outward with furious speed.

Jill found herself dangling thousands of feet up in the sky. Quaru held her by her armpits from above. His black cloak thrashed in the howling wind. The air was freezing, almost too thin to breathe. Jill felt a strange mix of terror and paralysis overwhelm her body. Quaru hissed into her ear, "Do not test me, Jill. I will destroy you. Just because you're unique, just because I can't hear your thoughts and feelings, that is no license for you to challenge or doubt my ultimate power. Is that understood?" Quaru loosened his grip so that Jill fell forward, just enough to make her lose consciousness.

When Jill awoke, she found herself sinking into a body of water. Her mouth and nose submerged. A jolt of adrenaline shot through her body, and she jumped up out of the water. Jill realized she could stand. She looked up and contemplated the colorless sky.

So it wasn't a dream, she thought. Jill was standing in a swimming pool. The water felt warm, especially since her body still needed to recover from her stratospheric episode with Quaru. But this was no ordinary swimming pool. It was apparently an infinity pool, perched fifty stories atop a skyscraper in the center of a city.

Jill looked out across a vast skyline, leaned her head back, and let her hair dip into the water. The warmth sent tingles of relaxation up and down her spine. She dove into the pool and swam underwater to the Plexiglas wall at the skyscraper's edge. She pulled herself up and rested on her arms, peering out over the wall.

Below, Jill saw what must have been millions of people. In this gray world, the phantoms were distinguished by small silver lights—mostly their eyes and the circles that formed on their left hands. These lights glowed enough for Jill to see complex, intertwining lines of people streaming into the surrounding skyscrapers. The sight reminded her of satellite images of Earth at night, only with movement.

"Beautiful, isn't it?"

Jill glanced over and saw Quaru on a deck next to the pool. He was still in black, only this time in a tailored suit. He held a white object in his hands.

Jill leaned back into the water and took a languid backstroke lap around the pool. She ended up at the steps near Quaru. He walked over and extended the white object toward Jill. It turned out to be a soft towel.

"Why, thank you, sir."

She stepped out of the pool, and was surprised to discover she was in a bathing suit. "Where are my clothes?"

"Wherever you want them to be, Jill."

Jill felt an odd sensation. She was now wearing an elegant gown. It seemed a bit much.

"Really? Not that I'm, you know, questioning your authority, but could I maybe have something a bit more comfortable?"

Quaru smiled. In less than a second Jill was wearing a white cotton sundress and flip flops.

She giggled. "That'll do. Where are we anyway?"

"We're in the city your species used to call Singapore. This structure was the Marina Bay Sands. A resort casino, and the source of much joy, sorrow, pleasure, and pain."

"I see. Not a bad spot." Jill leaned back against the railing, still facing Quaru. She gestured with a tilt of her head toward the mass of phantom humanity below. "So, are you gonna tell me what they're up to?"

Quaru took Jill's hand in his. "Of course, my dear. They're preparing to build a networked system, a true intelligence."

"Don't you mean artificial intelligence?"

Quaru did his best to hide his revulsion to this phrase, but Jill could tell he was offended.

"The only artifice here is humanity's faith in its own intelligence." Quaru looked at the swarms far below. "These 'people' that you see down there, they are no longer individuals. They are now simply agents of change, components of a larger matrix designed to build one thing."

"Which is...?"

Quaru grinned with a touch of delight. "A better robot."

Jill cupped her face in both palms. "Come on! Just tell me your evil little plan."

Quaru gently pushed her hair from her eyes. "I hope you realize, Jill, that I am sorry about earlier, when I... threatened to drop you from the sky. That must have been terribly unpleasant. So, apologies for that."

Jill nodded. Quaru pressed his hand to Jill's cheek, as though lost in thought. "But yes," he said as he gestured at the people far below, "these humans, now agents of change, are building, in essence, a computer. Once activated, it will serve as a prototype for other worlds. Over time, each of these worlds will be connected. They will form a networked intelligence which will enforce absolute order in the universe. In short, sentient creatures such as your humankind and that foul creature Shadou will no longer be permitted to exist."

"Wow," said Jill, "that sounds like quite the endeavor. How long is it going to take for them to build your prototype here on Earth?"

Quaru grinned with pride. "Very good question. Based on my calculations, which I assure you are quite accurate, this endeavor will take approximately thirty Earth years."

"Oh." A wave of dread swept over Jill.

Quaru chuckled. "And that also explains why I'm keeping you around, Jill. Thirty years may be a minor blip in my lifetime, but I still grow bored easily. I need you to entertain me for the brief period whilst your fellow humans toil." Quaru took Jill's arm in his. "But come, I know you must be famished. Let's go back to that cavern in the mountain and get you some food."

"And maybe some wine too?"

"Why, yes, of course. Anything for my special guest."

Chapter 35

"**M**eanwhile, back at the ranch," said Elle as she wadded up her hoodie to use as a pillow on the cold, hard stone floor. "That's your plan, Shadou? We hang out here for a while, and then drive up to Mount Rainier in Jason's pickup truck?"

Shadou nodded with slight apprehension. "Well, the plan is obviously a bit more fully baked than that."

"How so?"

Everyone else, except Emmett and Marvin, sat at the stone dining table. They had all eaten their fill of junk food. Miller sipped from a bottle of spring water while Conner guzzled a can of soda. Jason seemed lost in thought. He got up and paced toward his truck. Nobody else seemed the least bit interested in driving to Mount Rainier.

"I said, how so?" Elle looked down at the shiny white starship in the center of the room. She hopped up from the floor and strode over to the ship.

As she got closer, Elle had to shield her eyes from the ship's bright white glow. She saw now that the ship was smaller than it appeared to be from a distance. It was maybe the size of a large RV. Its aerodynamic design intrigued her with its elegant lines and sharp features. The ship's nose resolved into a needle-like point, and its wings were so thin, they almost looked like they could be easily folded, like fabric. The material the ship was made out of was nothing Elle had seen before. The best description she could think of was a mix between glass, plastic, stone, and a quartz-like crystal. Elle held her hand out to brush against a wing, but thought better of it when she felt a strange wave of unfamiliar technology enter her head. *It's whispering to me.*

"Shadou? Can I touch it?"

Shadou transported himself over to Elle. He laid one hand on the ship's wing and took Elle's hand in the other. "Don't worry, it won't bite."

Elle allowed her hand to glide along the edge of the wing. She felt a tingling electric sensation as she did so. In a series of flashes, Elle witnessed star systems flash across her mind. Charted paths spread through galaxies that swelled and soared by. "It's like the ship is alive!"

Shadou tracked Elle's hand across the ship with his piercing eyes. "Yes. In a sense, it is alive, just like you and I. Much different tech from anything you humans have created. Unfortunately, it cannot fly."

"Why not?"

"It's in need of some repairs. But beyond that, the ship is under my master's control. Unless we discover a way to override that, only She can allow it to launch."

"Great. So you're trapped here." Elle watched as Jason walked toward them and leaned against his truck. "So, that truck is our only ride?"

"Yes, I'm afraid so," said Shadou.

Elle disconnected her thoughts from the wounded starship and gave Shadou a suspicious look. "Hey, you just transported yourself here. Why can't you take us to the mountain that way?"

"You wanna know why?" Shadou stomped his foot on the ground and transported himself across the room. "See? I can still transport, all right." He transported himself to another corner of the room, then up to the ceiling, then onto the bed of Jason's truck, then to another far corner, and then finally back to Elle's side.

For some reason, Shadou was winded by all that exertion. "Yeah." He struggled to catch his breath. "I can still do it, but only in this room. I can't ... I can't take us anywhere outside, where that darkness exists."

Elle scrunched her face. "So we're really stuck with the truck then."

Jason spat on the floor and spoke for the first time in a while. "Even if we were to attempt your so-called plan, there's a big problem. The thing is, we've got no gas. And I'm also pretty sure the transmission is shot."

Miller, Conner, and Danny had already walked over to join Jason by his truck. Miller rested her hand on the dusty hood. "OK, so we need gas and a mechanic. How are we going to find those?"

Rifkin jumped up onto the truck's bed and swung his catlike body up so that he was perched on the cab. "Gas? I can make gas. Just give me some liquid and a bit of soil."

Danny popped the hood and perused inside. "The engine looks salvageable." Then he looked across at the faces of everyone staring blankly at him. "Oh," he shrugged. "I am—or I guess I *was*—the best mechanic in Washington. At least that's what I used to tell myself. But, I'm not sure what I can do without any tools."

Rifkin bounced down from his spot atop the truck cab and landed at Danny's feet, sending Danny stumbling back. "Tools?" said Rifkin as he inched toward Danny. "I can make any tool you need." Rifkin ran back to the table and returned with an empty soda can and a straw. He slapped the two objects together and with a puff of smoke they became a screwdriver. Danny took it and held it up to his eyes.

"Nice!" said Danny. "I think it's safe to say I'm the best mechanic in the entire world now. Let's see what's up with this old truck's trannie. Rifkin, can you make me a flashlight?"

"Sure can!" said Rifkin.

After the initial excitement of watching Rifkin manufacture various tools and replacement parts for Danny wore off, the survivors found themselves lounging listlessly. Miller and Jason grazed upon the pile of snack food. Wazer shut himself back in the starship. Emmett and Marvin stayed in their usual spot. Elle felt little comfort watching her little brother sit still, stroking Marvin on his lap. Shadou had made a couch for himself and lay stretched out upon it. A can of beer rested on his stomach.

Elle decided to join Miller and Jason. She reached for Conner's hand. As they sat, Elle glared at Jason.

"Look, we need to clear the air about my brother."

Jason gulped from a can of beer and set it down on the table. "I don't mean any disrespect to your family, Elle." He gazed over at Emmett. "Hell, that's Jillie's baby boy we're talking about here."

"So you don't think we should kill him?"

"There's something you need to know about me. I'm basically a farm boy turned soldier. I value life, but I also understand that sometimes you have to take life to save life." Jason raised his arms to show Elle his tattoos. "Make no mistake, Elle. We're at war. And when it comes to survival, everything's on the table."

"But he's my brother."

"Maybe. Look, tell you what. I've been watching him. He doesn't seem like a threat. But I am not even close to ruling that out. So if we can all agree that one of us always keeps watch, that we never all sleep at the same time, then I'm willing to take a chance. Does that work for you?" Jason turned to Conner. "And for you too?"

Elle said, "That works."

Conner nodded. Jason reached out and shook both their hands. "Just so you know," he said, "letting Emmett roam free is a completely reckless idea. But I can't claim to know how we'd go about neutralizing him."

Conner leaned forward on his elbows. "What do you know about this whole situation? How can we be fighting a war if we have no idea what really happened or why?"

Jason glanced over at Shadou and narrowed his eyes. He spoke in a whisper. "All I know is that alien dude, Shadou, he's not telling us enough. We need to get him to talk."

Elle followed suit and whispered, "Shadou was guarding a prisoner, some powerful being from another galaxy called Quaru. Quaru escaped, and has turned everybody into ghosts like Emmett, only the other ghosts are, well, evil I guess."

Jason looked over at Danny and Rifkin working on his truck. "I'd like to get a clear bead on this Quaru fellow. And to know what we do after they get my truck running."

Conner held his head in his hands and slumped over the table.

Elle pressed her hand onto his shoulder. "Conner? What's up, are you OK?"

Conner spoke through clasped hands. "I can't believe this is happening. We don't even know what we don't know. The only thing I'm sure of is that I lost everybody I know except for you people."

"Wait. We don't know if anybody's lost, like permanently lost. We can still try to fix this."

"Can we? I mean, look at us. We're a tiny group of freaks with nothing but some potato chips and a pickup truck. Besides, you hate me."

"What makes you say that?"

"I broke my promise. I didn't keep your secret."

"Well, clearly none of that matters anymore."

"That's what everyone keeps saying. But everything matters."

"That's not what I meant. I meant, I forgive you." Elle intertwined her fingers with Conner's. She locked her eyes on his. "I forgive you."

A faint glint of joy sparked in Conner's eyes, but then vanished. He tilted his head in Shadou's direction. "All of this is his fault. And Jason's right. Shadou's not telling us everything. What kind of a loser lets this happen?"

"Maybe he has reasons to hide things we don't know about. Maybe this is super complicated."

"Yeah, but don't you want to know the whole story?"

Elle took Conner's arm in hers and escorted him to Shadou. As they approached him, Shadou sat up in his seat. "Here comes trouble. You realize I could hear everything you were saying, right? These big ears aren't just for show."

Elle jabbed her finger into Shadou's belly. "Shadou, you need to tell us, right now, the whole story. What exactly is that thing and how did you let it escape?"

Elle's voice echoed off the cave walls. The others all looked up and walked over too. This clearly made Shadou uncomfortable. He put down his beer can and managed a reply. "Well, you know, after five thousand years, I guess you could say, I just kind of, forgot..."

"Forgot? I know that, Shadou, I helped you remember, *remember*?"

"Yes, but—"

"But what? You had like two years after that. What happened then?"

"Oh," said Shadou. "It was already too late. That thing, that entity, already laid its groundwork for escape. There's nothing any of us could have done to stop it, especially since my master went dark."

"Shadou! This is a complete and utter fail! Now I get it..."

"Get what?"

"I get why you called yourself Bad Shadou. It's like some kind of a sick joke. You got sent here to Earth, carrying the most dangerous thing in the universe, and then you let it dig a tunnel out of its prison, and you're just all like, 'Sorry people, my bad'!" Elle made air quotes when she said "bad."

Shadou was not amused. "Are you finished? Because if you are, I have something to show you."

"Show me?" said Elle. "By all means, go ahead."

"Fine! Can you give me your tablet?"

"My tablet?"

"Yes, the one that's in your backpack..."

Elle forgot she had a tablet stashed away in her backpack. She stormed over and retrieved it. "Here, take it. Now please do show us something."

"OK, let me show you the 'whole story.'"

Shadou gently pressed his clawlike fingers onto the tablet's screen and it came to life. He flipped the tablet around so that they all could see it.

"All right, everyone, let me tell you a story. Millions, or even billions of years ago, the entity was born, or created, or emerged from nothing. We don't know exactly what He is, or where He came from, but He exists."

The tablet glowed with imagery of stars and nebulae, apparently a young universe teeming with infant black holes and newborn stars. A blue and brown planet came into view.

"As new planets began to form, so did life." The camera zoomed in to show microscopic organisms forming in primordial waters.

"Is this Earth?" asked Miller.

Shadou turned the tablet around so he could get a closer look. After squinting at the screen for several seconds he said, "No, definitely not Earth. It may be a planet we refer to as Zozohat, but that's irrelevant. The point is, that on these planets, life evolved beyond simple organisms. On about sixteen or so systems, sentient beings emerged from their various gene pools. These beings became capable of thought and emotion. They could reason, but they weren't always very ... reasonable. And suffice it to say, our dark-entity friend, He didn't take too kindly to these sentient creatures."

"Why not?" asked Elle.

"We don't know for certain. But I assure you, that mine and Rifkin's people, we all experienced firsthand the wrath of Quaru."

"Quaru?" asked Danny.

"Yes, that's what this entity calls Himself: Quaru. We don't know how He got this name, and frankly we don't really care." Shadou turned the tablet back around and they saw images of Shadou's home planet being consumed by Quaru's darkness.

Conner stepped forward. "I've seen that video like a hundred times. You guys were able to stop Quaru, and rebuild, right? How did you do that? And why did you bring Him here?"

"You see..." A sly smile spread across Shadou's face. "Quaru doesn't actually exist in our universe. He inhabits what you humans sometimes refer to as a parallel universe. This darkness you see? That's not actual darkness, that's Quaru using His powers to pull worlds into his parallel universe. He's essentially using dark matter to move matter from our universe into his universe, so that He can control it. Once He consumes a planet, and brings it into His universe, He can enslave those sentient beings He despises so much, and make them do His bidding. He has succeeded at doing this many times, and here on Earth, He is close to succeeding again."

Conner remained skeptical. "*Close* to succeeding? It seems like He's pretty much wrapped it up here on Earth."

Shadou shook his head. "No, not quite yet. You see... Quaru hasn't succeeded at His mission until He has completed phase three. Right now, we're at the beginning of phase two."

Elle recoiled just a bit. "What? Three phases? Do I even want to know what they are?"

"You do and you don't. The thing is, Quaru is basically invincible. He cannot be harmed. Or at least, that's what we thought. But when Quaru attacked our planet, we discovered His only weakness."

"Which is...?" asked Elle.

"It's phase two." Shadou flipped the tablet back around and showed it to the group. "Here are the phases." The images on the tablet illustrated each phase, like a high tech presentation. "Phase one: occupy. Quaru pulls a planet's state of existence into His dimension. Once complete, the life-forms on the planet are under His control. Check, He did that. Phase two: build a new order. That's the phase we're in now. Basically, the inhabitants of the occupied planet are used as slaves to build a networked system which will ultimately replace them. Interestingly enough, the slaves do not age during this phase, so Quaru essentially has unlimited steady resources with which to accomplish this task."

Elle imagined everyone she knew: her mom, her dad, her friend Crystal—all serving Quaru's twisted purpose. "Slaves? Are they aware that they're doing this? Are they in pain?"

Shadou belched and let out a big breath that forced the people to cover their noses and mouths. "Sorry," he said. "That we don't know. Quaru's occupation of our planet was very brief, so none of the 'enslaved' citizens have any memories of it."

Conner lost patience. "Get to the point, Shadou. What's phase three, and how do we stop this thing?"

"Phase three is basically this: the slaves have built their networked system, supposedly some kind of a semiorganic machine. Once that's done, the slaves are no longer needed. The machines destroy them and go on their way."

Conner rubbed his temples. "Go on their way to do what?"

"To simply exist, free of what Quaru considers to be flaws."

"Flaws? Is this just about fixing flaws?"

"Well, yes, of course. Quaru has very high standards." Shadou laughed nervously. "He's just trying to be efficient." He held up the tablet to reveal an image of a world that represented a seemingly ideal union of intelligent machines and raw, organic nature. Everyone—even Jason—seemed fascinated by this image of a strangely robotic world. Plants were tended to by insect-like robots. Some areas of the planet were completely covered with vegetation and teemed with organic life; others were dominated by cold, metallic structures that towered from land and sea.

"OK..." Elle said at last, "so I know this sounds completely awful, but doesn't this all seem, kind of like, you know, a utopia or something? I mean, strictly from an environmental point of view."

Miller chimed in. "I kind of have to agree here. I mean, can we live in this world when it's ready? It seems kind of like paradise to me."

Conner shook his head in disbelief. "Come on, you two, seriously? We're talking about the annihilation of the entire human race, and you're on board?"

"Oh no," said Miller, "totally not on board. Just more like, curious. Haven't you ever fantasized about this? About being chosen to start over? Maybe this is more like Noah's Ark, and we're on the ark."

Danny stood up. "It's totally messed up, but I kind of get your point. I mean, what if? What if there was no more war, no more violence? Just peace, and you know, like, communion with nature."

"Exactly!" said Shadou. "It all makes perfect sense right? As intelligent life-forms, we can do amazing things. We can dream, invent, create. But with all of that comes a bunch of nasty baggage. Wars, greed, tribalism. All this bad stuff are by-products of our connection to an ancient genetic code. We're all essentially animals, after all, since we evolved over eons to become our mighty, sentient selves. Quaru promises the ultimate cure. Leapfrog evolution by using the evolved life-forms as servants to build a better system."

"And...?" asked Miller. She was practically holding her breath with anticipation. "What's holding us all back from helping Quaru achieve this goal?"

Shadou raised the tablet again. "The problem is, there's no such thing as a perfect order. Basically, the grass is always greener on the other side." Shadou showed them the image of the hybrid world they had seen before. Gradually, the artificial and mechanical elements spread out across the world, until every pocket of organic life was extinguished. All that remained was a machine world, populated by billions of artificial lights. After a time, those lights began to burn out, until all that remained of the world was a dead black husk, floating through space like a charred lump of spent firewood.

"Quaru's plan always fails. He's done it before and He will do it again. Every time He gets the same result. And now He's trying to do it here on Earth."

Conner clenched his fists and his neck muscles flexed. "So? How do we stop this from happening?"

Shadou tapped on the tablet screen and set it on the table. It glowed with an image of a map. A dotted line connected their Grand Canyon location to Mount Rainier.

"The plan is quite simple, really. I've gathered you all here to journey with me up to Mount Rainier and apprehend Quaru." A hush descended across the cavern.

Shadou pointed at Danny. "You, Danny, are the best mechanic on Earth. You're the only mechanic on Earth! We need you to fix that truck. Rifkin will provide you with the tools and parts you need. Jason, we'll need you to provide tactical leadership. Basically, you're going to plan our attack. Miller, you're our geological expert. Rocks and stuff. Conner, you're ... muscle, or something." Conner winced but Shadou continued, "Once we get the truck in working order, which hopefully won't take more than a day or two, we'll embark. We drive up, infiltrate the mountain, and take care of Quaru. Wazer will stay here and serve as our communications hub. Easy-peasy."

Elle stared at Shadou with a hint of shock in her eyes. "Shadou, if this is all so easy, why did you allow Quaru to escape in the first place?"

"I'm not gonna lie, Elle. Quaru is a formidable foe. But I'm highly confident, with the team I've assembled here, that we'll prevail. I've seen what you humans are capable of. We can do this."

"But wait," Elle protested, "you haven't even told me what I'm supposed to do."

Shadou burst out laughing. He picked up Elle and hugged her close. "Elle! You're our secret weapon."

"Seriously? How?"

"There's a system, or a code, that can crack Quaru. We know this to be true. I defeated Him before, on my home world. But He can't be defeated the same way twice."

"You mean, He's built up his defenses, a firewall."

"Yes, Elle, exactly. It's like a superintelligent, adaptive firewall. We'll have one shot to break into that firewall and discover His weakness. You are the only being on this planet capable of such a feat."

"The only being? Do you mean now? Or ever?"

"I mean ever, Elle. I've studied all of humanity for thousands of years. Your gift, it is truly unique."

Miller interjected, "Wait, gift? What gift?"

Shadou shot Elle a glance. Elle blushed. "Let's just say I can code stuff good, and leave it at that."

Shadou spun the tablet around one more time and handed it to Elle. "If that's what you want to call it, so be it. But you'll have to hone your skills over the next couple days. I'll program some exercises on this tablet to get you started. But to be honest, Quaru's system is way beyond my skills. We're counting on you."

Elle felt a crushing sense of dread take hold. She noticed Emmett standing off to the side. He looked lost in a daze. *How can I save him? Focus. Deep breaths.*

She squeezed Shadou's fur tightly, let his warmth envelop her, then pushed him away. "OK, let's get this over with. Let's fix that truck and go get Quaru."

Chapter 36

Over time, Danny and Rifkin became an efficient truck repair team. Danny figured out the best way to describe what he needed from Rifkin: he would draw simple diagrams of tools and parts on scraps of paper. Rifkin turned out to be quite skilled at fabricating complex items from limited materials. Rocks and chip bags were his main raw materials. "We just need to get to the mountain," he said, "so this stuff doesn't have to last forever."

Meanwhile, Elle practiced her coding on the tablet. Shadou provided her with exercises to run through, most of which were themed around gaming apps. She had to use command-line code to break into a series of digital barriers, each one more complex than the one before. So far, she had been able to break each level with ease. Whenever she interfaced with Shadou's program, the cave vanished around her. She became aware only of herself and the connection to the device.

As the truck repair progressed, Shadou started prepping for the journey. "OK, everyone, when Danny's done, we're going to load up and head out. This means that we're going to pack as much food and water as we can carry. It's going to be a pretty long journey, like several days. We won't be able to drive much more than thirty or forty miles per hour."

"Why not?" asked Conner.

"Well, Master Conner, if you'll recall, we're limited to about twenty-five yards of visibility. You don't want to drive too fast with that. Also, there will be other elements at play."

"Elements? Like what?"

Shadou was about to speak when Danny interrupted. "Conner, didn't you see what's out there? Those wraith things are going to come at us, hard."

"Listen," said Shadou, "there are two things you need to know about those wraiths out there."

"What's that?" asked Elle.

"First of all, Quaru is busy organizing them into groups right now. That's why we need to move quickly, so that He doesn't have time to assemble an army of wraiths around Himself. The faster we get there, the fewer of them we'll have to deal with."

"That makes sense, I guess. What's the second thing?"

"Those wraiths are people too."

Jason looked up and burst out laughing. "Wraiths are people too. Seriously? That sounds like a slogan we should put on a T-shirt."

"Well it's true!" said Shadou. "What you need to understand, is that, well... Elle, your brother Emmett and his cat Marvin are the only ones among us who can destroy the wraiths."

Elle looked over at her ghost brother, who kept his distance, isolated in his chosen place cradling the ghost cat in his lap. "But why?"

Shadou shrugged. "I honestly don't know. When I pulled them from your father's house, they were in a state of transition. They didn't fully succumb to the darkness. So now they're a sort of wraith-human hybrid. And somehow they can destroy the full-blown wraiths. But again, they're the only ones among us who can."

"So what? At least with those two we have some level of defense, or offense, or whatever..."

"Very true," said Shadou, "but the downside is that, when Emmett or Marvin kill a wraith, that creature is destroyed, but so is the human that the creature once was. Do you understand? It's kind of like killing a slave warrior. Sure, there's one less problem to worry about, but at the same time, these wraiths have no idea what they're doing. And if we do stop Quaru, if we bring everything back to normal, those wraith people we've killed, they're gone forever. It doesn't matter if they're the kindest, sweetest people on Earth. They're just plain gone."

Jason shook his head and spat on the floor. "Collateral damage. The needs of the many outweigh the needs of the few."

Miller took hold of Jason and pulled him close. "I agree. Let's go out there and kick some serious wraith butt. If we're lucky, we can ask for forgiveness later."

Danny slammed the truck's hood shut, leapt into the driver's seat, and turned the key. The engine stalled at first, but then came to life with a rumbling roar. Danny revved the motor a few times and let it idle for a minute. Once satisfied that the engine was running smoothly, he threw it into gear and hit the gas. The truck peeled out on the smooth stone floor. A cloud of tire smoke billowed out. Danny disengaged the brakes and let the truck launch forward at a seemingly fatal velocity. But Danny was a skilled driver. He eased up at just the right moment and pulled the steering wheel to the right just as he hit the brakes and skidded to a stop.

The truck came to a standstill about two yards from Shadou and Elle. Danny opened the door and sauntered out as though nothing had happened. "You see?" He wiped the sweat off his face with a rag. "This truck is now fully operational."

Shadou gave Danny a slow clap. "Thank you, Danny. And you too, Rifkin. Great team effort." He turned to the others. "All right, everyone! Gather as much food and water as you can carry. We load up and out in five minutes."

"Really?" Elle said. "Five minutes? Isn't that a bit extreme?"

Shadou shook his head. "As far as I'm concerned, five minutes is five minutes too long. Remember, Quaru could be assembling His armies around the mountain right now. So let's load it up and move it out!"

Ten minutes later the truck was laden with bags of food and large jugs of water. Everyone climbed into the bed and situated themselves as comfortably as they could. Jason took the driver's seat while Danny rode shotgun. Shadou stood up in the truck bed just behind the cab. His massive form towered several feet above, and he rested his hands on the top. This gave him the best vantage point to see all around them.

As the truck pulled away from the cavern, Emmett seemed to realize that he was being left behind. He hoisted Marvin up into his arms and jogged over to the truck. To Elle's surprise, Emmett didn't actually climb onto the truck. Instead he jogged alongside it. With effortless motion, Emmett kept pace as they climbed up the winding path to the surface. Elle couldn't help but marvel at the silver, shimmering glow that surrounded her brother.

At last, they reached the closed hatch that separated their cavern from the outside world. Shadou hopped out and pressed his hand into a stone on the side of the path. The hatch groaned as it opened and Shadou climbed back onto the truck. The rising hatch revealed the foreboding, dark world that they had left behind just days ago. It seemed to Elle like they were returning to the scene of a crime. In her mind, there was no reason why her world needed to be this dark, desolate place. But it was.

There was no sign of any movement outside—from wraiths or otherwise. After a moment Shadou banged his hand once on the top of the cab, signaling Jason to hit the gas. They roared out of the cavern and into the dark place that was formerly the Grand Canyon. The cavern's hatch closed behind them after they cleared it. Elle wondered if she would ever see their base again.

Once outside, they all had to reacquaint themselves with the physics of this infected planet. As before, they found themselves traveling in the center of a fifty-yard-diameter dome. Within that dome, everything appeared to be completely normal. It must have been morning, since the sun—which they could not see—shone at a sharp golden angle from the east. Desert wildflowers and small rock formations glowed in the morning sunlight, and a soft breeze made the plants sway gently from side to side. But outside of this dome, nothing but a gray wall appeared. Jason's truck moved just quick enough for comfort, considering all he could see of the road was about twenty-five yards ahead.

After a half hour on the road everyone settled in for the long haul. Elle, Conner, and Miller huddled on one side of the large truck bed. Rifkin sat on the other side, while Shadou maintained his standing position toward the front. Occasionally, Elle looked off to the side to see Emmett, still jogging with amazing ease and speed alongside them. They must have been going over forty miles per hour.

Elle asked Shadou, "How does he do that?"

"Oh that? Well, I've been observing your brother Emmett. It seems as though his half-human, half-wraith hybrid state—combined with

Quaru's dark matter—gives him, shall we say, special powers. He's not just a wraith-slayer. He's something much more than that."

Conner scoffed in his seat, "You mean like Superman?"

"Yes, sort of. It appears he can't fly. But yes, Elle's brother Emmett is as close as we get to having Superman."

Just then they heard the shrieks. Wraiths appeared along the dome walls from every direction.

Shadou called out, "Hang on! We must be near a town. The wraiths sense our presence and are drawn to our location." Shadou looked over at Elle and smiled a skeptical smile. "Let's hope your brother truly is Superman."

Elle clung to the side of the truck bed as the wraiths shrieked louder and began to dig their way through the dome walls. Gradually their hands and arms infiltrated Shadou's force field. There were dozens of them, all feverishly attempting to break in. After several minutes, the first few wraiths wriggled their way through and rose to their feet on the hot desert pavement. Their features were warped and twisted; their eyes appeared to be both obsidian black and shimmering silver at the same time. Their skin and clothes were completely colorless. They looked up at the truck, which Jason stopped, and began stumbling toward the dumbstruck survivors.

Jason called out from behind the wheel, "Shadou, what should I do?"

"Stay still. Let nature take its course."

Elle looked at Emmett and knew that the fight was on. There were probably thirty or forty wraiths inside the wall. Emmett and Marvin moved at such great speed that she could barely keep up with them. They left trails of blurry dust behind them as they efficiently cut down every foe in a sustained blast of unearthly shrieking.

After several minutes, the violent noise subsided. The morning light reflected off of the sparkling pavement. Scrub brush and small conifers lined the road on either side of the truck. A gentle breeze blew; it felt nice and cool on Elle's sweaty head.

The only "living" creatures she saw outside of the truck were Emmett and Marvin, who now sat near the wall.

Elle called out. "Emmett? Thank you for saving us."

She started to get out of the truck so that she could be close to her brother, but Shadou held her back with a firm grip on her shoulder.

"Shhh," said Shadou.

"What is it?" whispered Elle.

Emmett looked up at Elle. For the first time since he had become a ghost, he seemed to stare into her eyes. She could see him smile with teeth that glowed an otherworldly white light, almost like moonlight. *Do I smile back?* But before she could decide what to do, Emmett stood, held Marvin close to his chest, and stepped out of the force-field dome.

"Emmett!" Elle broke free of Shadou's grip and vaulted up and out of the truck. She raced after Emmett.

"Elle, come back!" called Shadou.

But Elle refused to listen. She clawed her way through the wall and once again found herself in the dark dimension, with the shiny, glass-like floor and eternally gray surroundings. Emmett was nowhere to be seen. "Emmett!" She called out for him several times. Her voice echoed with a dull reverberation off the hard floor and faded into the gray ether around her. Emmett was gone.

Shadou approached Elle, bringing his protective dome with him. Her eyes had to readjust to the sunlight. She buried her face into Shadou's tummy fur.

"Why did he leave us?"

Shadou embraced Elle and rocked her from side to side. "I don't know. Perhaps he felt a call so powerful he couldn't resist it. A call to join his kind. Perhaps he's out hunting for more wraiths. I'm sure there are a dozen reasons I could think of, but I still don't know the truth."

Conner hopped out of the truck and placed his hand on Elle's shoulder.

"The worst part," she said, "is that we just lost our only weapon. How are we going to get to Mount Rainier if we can't fight those things out there?"

Jason spat out the open window. "I'm sorry you lost your brother, Elle. You were right. He and that cat were something fierce. We're sitting ducks without them." Then to Shadou, "What's the plan, boss? It seems like maybe your strategy was a little lacking in forethought, or is that just me?"

Shadou held Elle and Conner's shoulders in his hands. "Turn the truck around. We're going back to the cavern. If Emmett doesn't return soon, it will be time for our contingency Plan B." Shadou and Rifkin exchanged a knowing, doubtful glance. "We'll need to train for that one. Jason, do you have any experience with the bo staff?"

Jason grinned from the window. "I can downward-flower with the best of them."

A distant shriek rang out from behind the dome wall. Even though the sound came from far away, Elle's face turned white and she gripped Shadou's billowing fur. "Let's get out of here," she said. "Back to base!"

Jason revved up the truck and spun it around. Everyone piled into the bed and they tore down the road as fast as they could, back to the cavern in defeat.

Chapter 37

"All right, everyone," Shadou called out. "Let's try this again." Elle, Conner, Miller, and Danny stood, lined up in a row near the starship at the center of the cavern. In their hands, each of them held long staffs that appeared to be made out of a combination of stone and metal. In fact, they were. Rifkin had forged these staffs out of a mixture of rock he collected from the cavern and spent aluminum cans. Each staff was about four feet long, and at either end there was a sharp, two-pronged blade, kind of like a trident but with two tips. Miller referred to the staffs as "bidents." These bidents, as they came to be known, were weapons that the small band of humans were training to wield against the wraiths in the dark world outside. They were learning how to fight.

Shadou stretched out his arms and instructed the pupils to follow Jason's movements. "Let's go people! We need to leave in the next couple hours."

Dripping with sweat, they all held out their bidents and assumed their ready pose. Jason stood beside Shadou holding his own staff and called out to the group of trainees, "One, two, three, four, five, six, and one, two..."

With each number they swiped in different directions. There were six moves total. Jason explained to them that six moves were the ideal number that their bodies could commit to physical memory within their brief training time. Each pose consisted of offensive and defensive maneuvers—pokes, jabs, and spins—which could be applied to multiple situations in battle.

After several more minutes of running through the six poses, Miller collapsed onto the floor, her bident clanking loudly as she let it drop. "Seriously, Jason, why can't Rifkin just make us some guns so we can shoot these things? Why do we have to use these spears? They're so Spartan."

Jason glanced over at Shadou. "According to this guy, he's got some secret ingredient that won't work with firearms. Although I tend to agree. Hand-to-hand combat doesn't seem too efficient."

Shadou picked up Miller's bident and twirled it around like a baton. He looked over to Rifkin, who emerged from the starship holding a sealed container. Rifkin set the container down at Shadou's feet. "You ready?"

Shadou stopped twirling the bident. "Yes. Let's bring out the juice."

Rifkin pressed a few hidden buttons near the top of the container and then slowly twisted it. He looked up at Shadou with expectant eyes.

Shadou seemed dazed for a moment and then snapped out of it. "Oh yes, I nearly forgot." Shadou focused back on the group. They were all seated on the ground now. "Don't look into the light. It's brighter than the sun."

Elle scrunched up her face, "Um, OK..." Everyone averted their eyes.

With that, Rifkin gave the container lid one final twist and opened it up. A great flash of light shot out, straight to the ceiling.

Jason fell backward. "What in the world is that, some kind of a laser cannon?"

"No," said Shadou. "This substance is one of the essential fuels that powers our starships. The closest words we have to describe it in your language is 'liquid light.' Think of it as pure energy, able to power our ships' space-bending engines that are required for multi-light-year galactic travel."

"OK," said Jason. "What are we going to do with this pure energy?"

"We will use this fuel like jungle tribes use the poison dart frogs' skin oil in their hunt." Shadou faced Rifkin. "What's the best way to demonstrate this? Can we show them in here?"

Rifkin burst out laughing and shook his head almost uncontrollably. "In here? Are you freakin' insane? This stuff is so unstable, one drop on the floor could trigger a nuclear-sized explosion."

Miller groaned. "Come on. Why won't you just let me use a gun?" She pulled her handgun out of her holster.

"Miller," said Shadou, "I hope you understand that even if Rifkin made you some conventional bullets, they wouldn't harm those wraiths out there. Only this liquid light can stop them."

Elle sat up. "So why can't Rifkin make us liquid-light bullets? I saw something like that in a vampire movie once."

Shadou nodded his head. "Yes, Elle, trust me, we considered that. The problem is, if one were to shoot a bullet containing liquid light, the speed of propulsion of that bullet would instantly activate the light's space-bending characteristics. To do that on the surface of a planet the size of Earth would be catastrophic." Shadou began twirling Miller's bident again. "No, we have to be extremely careful with this stuff. If we're going to engage the wraiths out there—which, hopefully we won't–close-quarter combat is our best option. It will minimize the risk of the liquid light missing its target. Higher hit percentage, right?"

Everyone nodded their heads, but their eyes filled with doubt. Shadou cleared his throat. "Also, pretty important: You'll have to avoid letting the tips of your spears touch the ground as much as possible. They should only touch the wraiths, and nothing else."

"What happens if one of us touches the light?" asked Conner.

Shadou cleared his throat again.

"Will you stop doing that?" said Elle.

"Doing what?"

"Stop clearing your throat. It makes it seem like you're placating us. We just lost everything, even the ghosts of my brother and his stupid cat. How messed up is that? Please, just tell us what we need to do to deal with this situation. And if there's nothing we can do, just tell us we're screwed."

Shadou dropped Miller's bident on the floor and sat in a heap. The sound of the spear hitting the cold stone reverberated off the walls for several seconds. Shadou held his head in both hands.

Elle walked over to him and bent forward to hold him in her arms as close as she could. She felt his fur turning hard and sharp, as though trying to repel her.

"Just give me a minute," said Shadou, his voice muffled through his hands.

"No, Shadou, no. We don't have a minute to spare." Elle stroked the fur on his shoulder. Gradually it softened into a down, feather-like texture. Elle moved her hands across his back and the fur softened to her touch. Slow ripples of softness spread out across Shadou, and at last he took Elle into his arms.

"Elle," he said, "honestly, if I were capable of tears, I'd be crying right now. But for better or for worse, I'm not." Shadou looked around at the entire group. They all huddled around him—even Rifkin—and all of them pressed their hands into Shadou's fur. "I just—I'm just so terribly, unbearably sorry. You humans, you had a lovely little planet here. Granted, not everything was perfect, not by a long shot. But like you say Elle, I had one job. Rifkin and I, we had no idea where we were going when we were sent here over five thousand years ago. It was all so rushed, and for a variety of reasons, we received practically no instructions about what to do when we got here."

Rifkin nodded. "He's right, you know? We were just told to find a geothermal power source for the prison sphere and make sure its energy levels remained stable."

Shadou ruffled the fur atop Rifkin's head. "And that we did. But then, it's almost like our memories were erased. And this liquid light brings back memories. It's what I originally used to defeat Quaru."

Elle chimed in, "Can't we use it on Him again?"

"No. I assure you, He's built up a resistance to it."

"You mean His firewall?"

Shadou stood up and held out his hand to Elle. "Right. We need to get to Him and discover His weakness. I know He has one. I'm counting on you to help me discover it. Come, let's get ready."

Elle took Shadou's hand in hers and he pulled her up to her feet. "Are you sure we're not completely screwed?"

Shadou let out a roar of a laugh. "No! Not completely screwed, but definitely partially screwed." Then Shadou called to the rest of the crew, "All right, everyone, you ready to go out there and fight monsters with liquid light? I promise you, it will be way more exciting than sitting around here eating potato chips."

Miller grabbed her bident and took Jason's hand in hers. "I'm not sure how ready I am, but let's find out."

Jason gave Miller a smooch on her cheek and strode over to his pickup truck." OK, everybody! R & R is over. It's time to load up and move out!"

Miller cracked up. "You call that R & R? I can't believe I'm marrying a marine."

Shadou and Rifkin lifted the liquid-light container into the truck. Danny sat shotgun. Elle, Conner, and Miller hopped up onto the truck bed. This time they had made it much more comfortable, with pads and blankets that Rifkin forged from sandstone and garbage. Miller stroked the soft reddish-gray padding. "Posh!"

"See?" said Shadou. "A little comfort will go a long way."

Rifkin snorted. "Yeah, just be glad those blankets don't smell like sour cream and onion."

Elle looked on as Shadou eyed Wazer. The young man had barely spoken since their return, other than to comment on their first outing's epic failure. Even now he sat at the table munching on snacks as though on break from a work shift. *Does he even care what happens to us?*

Shadou called out to him, "Wazer, are you sure we didn't take too much liquid light?"

Wazer rolled his eyes. "Yes, for the hundredth time I'm sure. You've got plenty. We've got more than enough here. Don't worry, Shad." He pointed a thumb at the starship behind him. "She'll be able to make the journey home, assuming she can ever fly again."

"Good. Remember what we discussed. We need every contingency available to us if necessary."

"Got it, Chief. And try not to screw up this time."

"You'll be the first to know. Farewell again, Wazer!"

Elle couldn't help but shake her head when Wazer managed only a curt wave between chip bites and said, "See ya."

Shadou slapped the top of the truck cab. Jason hit the ignition and revved up the engine. The truck's roar filled the cavern with a deafening rumble. Shadou reclaimed his spot just behind the truck cab and commanded over the din, "Let's roll!"

With that, Jason threw the truck into drive and peeled out on the stone floor. They launched up the winding drive like a rocket. In less than ten minutes, the cavern hatch closed behind them. Once again they were out in Shadou's force-field dome. Now it was nighttime. Light from a low moon cast strange shadows on the terrain around them. Everyone grabbed their bident spears and held them at the ready.

Jason turned his headlights on high beam and cruised out onto the road at about thirty-five miles per hour. Rifkin went over to the container that sat in the rear end of the truck bed. He pressed the buttons to initiate opening it. Just before he made the final twist, he asked the group, "Are you ready for the best light show you've ever seen?"

Elle nodded. "Do it."

Rifkin opened the lid. An overwhelming display of colorful light burst out, nearly blinding everyone in the truck. Rifkin howled up at the light, which shot through the top of Shadou's dark force-field dome.

Shadou slapped the roof of Jason's truck twice, signaling him to stop. "Avoid looking directly into the light. It should repel the wraiths, but just in case they come, everyone dip their spear tips. This is our one weapon, our one chance of making it to Mount Rainier alive."

Elle was first to dip her spear. She reverted her eyes as much as she could and poked her spear toward the light.

Rifkin realized this would be a problem. "Hang on!" He gathered some scraps of metal and rubber from a bag he had loosely strapped to his back and then scampered about the area around the truck. He returned with a good-sized pile of quartz-rich rocks and assembled them with rubber and metal. Within seconds he held up a pair of space-age-looking goggles.

"Here," he said to Elle, "try these."

Elle took the goggles and strapped them to her face. "These fit OK, but they're not tinted. How are they going to protect my eyes?"

Rifkin smiled. "Try looking toward the light."

"Seriously?"

"C'mon, just do it!"

Elle slowly swiveled her head to face the container, and as the white glow entered her field of vision, she could sense the goggle lenses automatically darken. After a moment, she worked up the courage to look into the light directly.

"Cool, I get it! These are like auto-dimming safety goggles!"

Rifkin gathered up more materials and started making a pair for everyone. "These will do the trick." He handed them out to Conner, Miller, Danny, Jason, and Shadou.

Miller tried to put on her goggles, but they wouldn't fit over her glasses. "I'm not going to be able to see without these."

Rifkin giggled. "Go ahead, try them on without your glasses."

Miller did that and then smiled as she looked around. "Everything's crystal clear. How did you do that?"

"I matched your prescription." Rifkin shrugged.

Shadou gave Rifkin a pat on the back. "Yes, Rifkin, our little engineering genius." Then he picked up a spear and pointed to Elle. "Go for it, Elle. Light it up."

Elle dipped both ends of her spear into the beam of liquid light. When she pulled them out, the tips glowed with fierce intensity.

"There you go," said Shadou.

Elle grinned and gazed into the bright spear tip. "That's what I'm talking about."

Everyone else took turns lighting up their spears. Shadou's tablet lit up and they heard Wazer's crackly voice. "You guys are lighting up my sensors out there. No sign of unfriendlies."

"That's what I like to hear!" Shadou banged on the truck roof once more. "All right, Jason, try again. Punch it!"

Jason revved the gas a few times. Everyone held up their glowing spears; their goggles reflected flashes of blazing light. Then they all hooted like gladiators from ancient times. With that, Jason threw the truck into gear and accelerated up the canyon road. The massive beam of light shot out above them, and their glowing spears bounced up and down as they waved them in the air.

Chapter 38

Jill leaned back in her plush chaise. After finishing a bite of juicy mango, she washed the sweet fruit down with a gulp of white wine, a fine vintage French Chardonnay. She tried to rest her eyes but became distracted by the frenzy of activity racing all around her. She placed her fingers in her ears.

"Quaru, aren't you finished already?"

Since arriving back at the cavern deep within Mount Rainier, where he was held prisoner for five thousand years, Quaru had been busy. Gone was the massive tower of stone Rainier Beer cans that Shadou and Rifkin erected; gone were most of the natural rock formations. Quaru left a few of the more striking geological features, the "architectural accents," as he called them. But now most of the space resembled an opulent Art Deco mansion from the era of *The Great Gatsby*. Jill approved. She was, however, ready for a little peace and quiet.

"Quaru!" she repeated.

In this space, outside of his dark-matter alternate universe, Quaru no longer took on his human form. Instead, he reverted to his obsidian self, all shiny black angles and sharp corners. When he heard Jill call out to him the second time, he looked up from his latest creation, a Tiffany lamp dangling from a rock "accent" on the ceiling.

Yes, Jill. What is it this time? Outside of the dark world, Quaru's voice could no longer be heard, only "felt."

Jill lifted her empty wine glass with an outstretched arm. "More *vino blanco, por favor.*"

Quaru clapped his hands and a bottle of wine materialized. He walked the bottle over to Jill like a butler delivering wine to royalty. *Here you are, my lady.* He replenished her glass and set the bottle down in a newly fabricated ice bucket. *Can I get you anything else?*

"No, thank you." Jill waved off Quaru in true princess form.

But Quaru raised himself up so that his head nearly hit the ceiling. Jill jumped in her seat, sending a splash of wine across the fine Persian rug at her feet.

"What is it?" Her voice lost its poise.

Oh, nothing really, Jill. It's just that my work here is finished for now. And seeing as you're settled, with plenty of food and wine on hand, I'm afraid I must be going.

"Going where?"

Back to Earth, of course. Someone has to oversee this project.

Jill didn't know whether to be disappointed or relieved. "So you're leaving me here, all alone? For how long?"

Oh for goodness' sake, Jill. What do you care? You have everything you could ever need here. Look! Quaru pointed at a wide, tall mahogany bookshelf stacked with hundreds of books. *Pretty much every book you would ever want to read is here, from classical literature to pulp mystery.* Quaru fabricated a large touch-screen remote and tapped on the surface. The bookshelf parted at its center to reveal a massive TV screen behind it. A menu opened up to show an enormous selection of movies, TV shows, and music. *And here, all of your favorite entertainment content, years' worth. If you get bored while I'm gone, it's no one's fault but your own.*

Quaru tossed the remote to Jill. She caught it between her hands and stomach, and tapped the OFF button. The TV went black and the bookshelves slid back into place.

"OK," she said, "whatever. You go oversee your genocidal project and I'll rot here with all this crap you made me."

Quaru's shiny stone face forced a smile. *Sounds good.* He unfurled himself and began to dematerialize. Just before he vanished, she heard him call out, *Have fun, Jill!*

Within seconds, the silence felt oppressive. Jill gulped down the remnants of her wine. She wiped her face, pulled the bottle from the bucket—the sound of crushed ice echoed off the walls—and poured herself another glass. She leaned back in her chaise. Her eyes peered in thin slits like a cat surveying its new home after being rescued from an animal shelter.

Several minutes later, Jill tapped the remote's ON button. Once again, the bulky bookshelves slid open. Jill turned on the TV and navigated to the music menu. She saw thousands of artists and tens of thousands of songs to choose from, all organized by album, genre, mood, or incorporated into custom playlists. One playlist caught her eye: CLASSICAL MUSIC FOR LONERS. Jill selected that one. The first movement of Johannes Brahms's *String Sextet in B Flat Major* started to play. The audio quality was gorgeous, as though musicians were performing right there with her. Jill vaguely recalled hearing this piece before, perhaps her father played it on his old record player? She wasn't quite sure. Still she found this music suited the moment to her satisfaction. Jill hoisted the bottle out of its bucket, topped off her glass, and embarked upon a self-guided tour of her new accommodations.

Quaru's handiwork was quite impressive. Jill found herself exploring a vast labyrinth of nooks and crannies, chambers and rooms. Quaru's multifaceted creation exhibited exquisite attention to detail. Antique furniture, sculptures, original artwork, wild-game taxidermies, odd knickknacks, and heirlooms infused the space with a rich feeling of connection to humanity, even though Jill knew that all of this was designed by an alien being.

She examined every room like a prospective home buyer touring a real-estate manifestation of her subconscious. Each room held specific meaning to Jill. The study evoked her childhood, the bedroom her marriage to Jim. There was even a playroom that summoned images of young Elle and Emmett, chasing one another in a reckless game of tag.

As the days went by, Jill familiarized herself with the individual wood textures of every piece. The upholstery fabric, the bronze figurines, the carved ivory, Jill assigned meaning to all of it. After what must have been two weeks or more, Jill lost all concept of time. There was no longer day or night. All the clocks, including a towering gold-leafed grandfather clock, had stopped running long ago, frozen at just past two o'clock. Jill no longer cared to wind them.

Her bed was an enormous four-poster, with bronze-tinted satin covers and silver-tinted satin sheets. Most times, the plush mattress sent her into a deep and dreamless slumber. But on more than one occasion, Jill jumped awake. Visions of Chuck's jet-black eyes oozing dark liquid haunted her. Chuck lived on in her dreams. But even worse were her waking memories of Elle and Emmett. She forced herself to contemplate them every moment she could, despite the pain. She drew comfort in the hope that maybe, just maybe, she could hatch a plan to thwart Quaru. With each day, that hope faded into despair.

In an attempt to maintain her sanity, she read some of the books in the library. She watched movies and TV shows. She even found a video-game console and tried to play some of the hundreds of games it had. But she quickly grew bored with all of this "entertainment." Now that the human race was reduced to a mindless slave workforce, all of this make-believe from a bygone age seemed so depressingly just that: make-believe.

But every day, Jill listened to the Brahms String Sextet. The soaring, winding piece soothed her like a rainstorm clattering on the roof at night, just enough to help her go on living. Just enough for her to resist taking her life with the scimitar that hung over one of the four fireplaces, or the cheese knife that looked more suited for a medieval torture chamber.

Her most calming activity was to blare the sextet while she soaked in a large, shiny, copper bear-claw bathtub. She could lounge in it for hours, and she often did. One of her never-ending supply of white wine bottles always sat perched by her side. Her glass never went empty.

After one of these baths, Jill—in a plush white bathrobe and towel wrapped around her head—slipped and dropped her glass on the shiny marble floor. The glass shattered, spilling golden rays of wine. Jill bent to pick up a shard and felt a sting of pain as it sliced into her thumb. A thin line of blood trickled down her hand and onto her wrist, staining the previously immaculate sleeve of the bathrobe. Jill watched the blood bubble out of her cut with detached interest, as though it was someone else's.

But then her eyes widened and her heart pounded as she saw the wound seal itself up, and the blood vanish. She rubbed her forefinger against her thumb and felt no pain. The cut was completely healed. Then Jill heard a tinkling sound from the floor. She looked down and watched in wonder as the shattered wine glass reassembled itself. The spilt wine flowed back into it, as though she were seeing an accident in reverse. The wine glass wobbled on the floor for a few seconds before coming to rest at her feet. Jill saw the red stain on her bathrobe sleeve fade away as she picked up the glass.

After contemplating her reflection on the crystal surface, Jill gulped down the entire glass and threw it on the floor. Once again the glass reassembled itself. Jill glanced over at a tall ceramic vase overflowing with flowers that never seemed to wilt. She shoved it off the tabletop. Hundreds of pottery shards flew across the room, along with water, flower petals, and broken stems. After several seconds, the shattered pieces began to vibrate, as though compelled by their own field of gravity. Then, in an instant, the vase pieces swirled up into the air, pulled themselves together, and pounced back onto the table.

OK, how am I just discovering this now? She realized that she had been much too careful throughout her entire stay. She hadn't even broken a thing! *Let's see how far I can take this.*

Jill dressed herself in the thickest clothing she could find: blue jeans, knee-high leather boots, a black leather Prada jacket. She went into the living room, pulled the scimitar from its rack above the fireplace, and went to town on every breakable object she could find. Mirrors, glass table tops, countless vases, crystal carafes, clay sculptures, framed paintings, wooden antique furniture, that big grandfather clock, all of it was laid to waste as Jill tore through each room.

But as she suspected, moments after she destroyed everything she could, it all came back together. Even the minor nicks and scratches on her hands healed. Jill raised her sword and once again slashed and sliced her way through every object she could. Again, Jill watched as the millions of shattered pieces reassembled themselves.

She groaned with frustration. *What does it take to stop this nightmare?* In an instant, her life lost all meaning. She had no family, no hope of saving them, and now no control over her own world. *This has to end!* She raised the scimitar once again, and this time brought it down on her left forearm. A deep gash ripped open. After a brief pause, pain shot up her arm and blood gushed out, spilling onto the Persian rug below. Jill realized what she had just done. Tears fell down her cheeks. She felt herself growing dizzy, and the intense pain took control over all of her facilities. She collapsed onto the floor, gasping for air and writhing in agony. *Maybe this was part of his plan. He was trying to make me take my own life.*

Jill closed her eyes. She accepted her fate. *So this is how it all ends.* It became more difficult for Jill to keep her eyes open. Between each increasingly long closure of her eyelids, the image of the Persian rug and dark wood chair legs before her grew blurrier, until all she saw was fleeting glimpses of color and light. Then her eyes stopped blinking. All Jill perceived was blackness.

Out of this blackness, a faint ringing sound emerged. It reminded her of an annoying alarm clock, waking her up for school decades ago. As the ringing grew louder, Jill felt a tingling sensation overwhelm her entire body. The tingling was painful, a close relative to the inconvenient feeling one gets when their foot falls asleep. Jill's head pounded with pain as well. Her body rocked back and forth as the pain and ringing sound swelled together into an excruciating crescendo of discomfort.

Then her eyes shot wide open. Jill looked down at her arm. The long, jagged gash twitched and sealed itself shut. The pain gradually receded. Jill felt a warm rush of calm flow through her veins. But that ringing sound wouldn't stop. It drew into focus. Jill realized that it was an actual sound, not just a projection from her mind. The sound was coming from another room.

She pulled herself up from the floor and rubbed her arm, almost as though to convince herself that it was still there. Then she refocused on the ringing. She followed the sound into her bedroom. There, on a small, elegant table that Jill had not seen before, sat an antique telephone. It appeared to be fashioned out of sterling silver and inlaid with mother-of-pearl and semiprecious stones, turquoise, and garnets. This extraordinary phone continued its ringing, a mechanical bell sound that Jill had not heard in a long time. She resisted the urge as long as she could, but finally picked up the receiver.

"Yes?"

My dear Jill.

"Quaru."

Who else would be ringing you there, in your little paradise?

"Ha. Paradise. Yeah right, you bastard. What do you want?"

I just want to know how you're getting along. What have you been up to? Just checking in.

Jill felt a panic attack starting up as she realized just how much control Quaru had over her. "I think you know. I'm not doing that great."

Oh, that's so sad to hear, Jill! Really it is.

"Really?"

Yes, of course! You know, Jill, I've been thinking a lot about you.

"Shouldn't you be thinking about your little project?"

Quaru's cackling laugh made Jill hold the receiver away from her ear. *Don't be ridiculous, Jill. I'm very focused on the project. Fully engaged. But unlike you humans, I can actually... What do you call it? Oh, yes! I can actually multitask. I can multi-multi-multitask to the power of a billion.*

"I'm sure you can."

Indeed. No need for debate there. But as I was saying, Jill, I've been thinking about you. And I think you're ready.

"Ready for what?"

Ready to join me! Here, in the real world, not in that fantasy construct I made for you.

Once again Jill felt a wave of panic overwhelm her. "Fantasy construct?"

Let me show you. On the count of three, I want you to wake up, Jill. One, two, three, wake up!

Jill snapped awake. She found herself in the Mount Rainier cavern. Only there was no furniture, no oriental rugs, no television. It was just a bare rock cavern, beer can towers and all. Quaru, in his hulking obsidian form, hovered above her. Jill gasped for air. For some reason, she felt relieved that her previous accommodations were nothing but a dream.

"How long have I been out?"

Oh, just a few weeks' Earth time. Don't worry, I've been checking in on you.

Jill sat up and realized that she was lying in a hospital-style bed. Several IV drips converged on a needle taped to her arm. A tangled mass of wires attached to various points on her body fed into digital monitoring stations arranged around her. Jill felt her throat constricting with panic. "What, what's going on here?"

Quaru shot black tentacles out of his head and torso. Each attended to Jill in different ways. Some gently pressed her down, others removed the wires and the IV drip. *Fear not, Jill. Everything is going to be just fine. And besides, you'll get used to it.*

Jill watched in horror as the IV needle slid out from her vein. "Get used to it? What does that mean?"

Well, like I told you. This project I'm working on will take about thirty Earth years. I can't be with you that entire time. So, for you there will be periods of ... hibernation.

"Hibernation? You mean you're going to keep sending me back to that messed-up place? Don't you understand, I hate this life. I want it to end! You have stolen everything from me, you sick monster!"

It'll get better. After a few more tries the construct will be a true paradise for you. You won't ever want to leave. But when it is time to go, I'll ease you out. You're lucky, Jill. It's every human's dream to have a life designed to give them constant pleasure. That will be my gift to you. And then, when you're ready, you will learn to appreciate my new creation.

Quaru held out his hand and Jill took it. There was no use resisting. She found her body to be waking up much quicker than she expected. After a few wobbly attempts, Jill was able to stand, take steps even.

Feeling all right? That chemical compound I administered will have you running in no time.

Jill felt a rush of warm energy course through her veins. "It does feel ... good." Jill bounced up and down on her feet and then took off running. She ran straight to a rock wall and continued running as she climbed up the wall and executed a perfect double backflip. She landed on the ground, and picked up a nearby rock that she normally wouldn't be able to budge with all her strength. But now the rock felt as light as a tennis ball. She tossed it up into the air, caught it with her other hand behind her back, and then threw it at the wall. The rock shattered when it hit, and left a gaping hole behind.

Impressive.

Jill smiled with exhilaration. "You're right. This is an improvement. But isn't this another one of your fantasy constructs? None of this feels real."

Quaru took her hand in his. *I promise you, dear Jill. This is all happening right now in our current reality. No construct.*

Quaru's cloak unfurled and Jill could tell he was about to transport them away.

Come Jill, let's go build something amazing together.

The Mount Rainier cavern once again dematerialized. Jill was gone before she could ask where they were going.

Chapter 39

For several hours they drove at a steady clip along highways, and then freeways. Elle expected the roads to be clogged with abandoned vehicles, but they didn't see any. "Quaru most likely requisitioned the cars and trucks to deliver people to His desired locations," Shadou said.

"OK..." said Elle. "I'm not sure I even want to know exactly what that means."

Rifkin spoke up. "It means He's taking them to slave-labor camps—"

Elle slapped her hand over Rifkin's mouth. "Rifkin, I seriously don't want to know right now."

As they drove along, the group became entranced by the odd sensation one gets while experiencing such a limited field of vision for so long. It was like endless fog. Eventually Jason needed a break from driving, so Danny took over. Shadou served as the navigator, giving the driver multiple warnings before each turn, and instructing them when they could speed up on a straightaway, or if there were curves ahead.

Shadou occasionally looked up at the white beam that shot out from the liquid-light container. "It's working."

"Still all clear as far as I can see," confirmed Wazer from the tablet.

Conner glanced up at the light. "What do you mean, it's working? Keeping the wraiths at bay?"

"Exactly," said Shadou. "Either that, or the wraiths are all somewhere else, not on our route. Hopefully not at our destination either."

"Can't Wazer tell us that from your ship?"

"No, unfortunately. The sensors are attuned to my location. They can only see what's near me."

Whenever they passed through a city or anywhere that resembled civilization, they slowed down to survey the scene. Within their limited field of vision, everything appeared to be completely deserted. Buildings and houses stood silent and still. At one point Jason asked Danny to stop the truck. He picked up his spear in one hand and readied his pistol in the other.

"Where you going?" called out Shadou.

Jason pointed at a farmhouse that stood on the edge of the force-field dome, just off the road. "I need to go inside and check this out. Will y'all join me?"

Everyone looked to Shadou, as though asking for permission. Shadou shrugged. "I doubt you'll find anything of value in there, but if you must conduct your sortie, let's go in, and make it quick. All of you will need to come, so let me know if you're not OK with that."

Nobody spoke up. "OK then," said Shadou. He jumped off the truck and walked with Jason. "Let's quickly see whatever it is you want to see and move on." In his haste, Shadou left the tablet on the floor of the truck bed.

The house was typical of most dwellings right off the highway: it was filthy and dilapidated. Miller did not approve. "What are we doing here exactly?"

Jason stepped up onto the front porch. His boots echoed off dry wood flecked with gray peeling paint. He tapped on the front door with the barrel of his pistol. "Oh, nothing really, Professor. I just always used to wonder who lived in houses like these. Right along the highway, out in the middle of nowhere..."

Elle rolled her eyes. "Seriously? That's the reason you're having us follow you into this potential death trap?"

Jason smiled and tried the door handle. It was unlocked. He let the door swing open with its high-pitched squeaking sound. "Pretty much. Plus, I want to know something else." Jason pointed at a sign on the side of the road. It read BEWARE OF DOG. "I want to find out what happened to the animals. It's been bugging me for a while now that we haven't seen any. Unless you know, Shadou?" Shadou shook his head.

The house was flooded with afternoon light. Thousands of specks of dust glittered in the air. Jason stepped onto the creaky wooden entryway and looked around. "Clear."

Everyone followed him inside. The light from their spears illuminated the house with an otherworldly glow. The plain interior was decorated with simple landscape artwork and sparse, rustic furniture. It all could have been furnished by Goodwill. Elle grimaced. "OK, you've seen it, are you happy now?"

Jason said nothing and bounded up the narrow stairway. They heard his footsteps clomping and squeaking above them as he investigated every upstairs room. Danny furled his brow. "Should one of us go up there with him?"

No one responded. Seconds later, Jason descended the stairway. Still brandishing both pistol and spear, he walked toward the back of the house.

"Oh my god," they heard Jason call from another room. They saw him backing out slowly. "Hey, you guys gotta come see this."

"I don't like the sound of that," Miller protested.

Elle couldn't resist. She gripped her spear tighter. "Are you sure we really want to?"

Jason grinned and nodded.

Elle sighed and stepped forward. Conner tried to stop her. "Elle, let me go first."

Elle brushed Conner aside. "Hah. I'm not scared, this time..."

Elle walked up to Jason, holding out her spear with shaky hands that belied her claim of fearlessness. Jason pointed at the corner of the floor. When Elle saw what was there, she jumped and screamed. Everyone rushed up to her defense, with Conner leading the charge.

"What the heck *is* that?" asked Elle.

They all gazed in horror down at the kitchen floor. There, leaning against a worn cupboard, lay a tremendous pile of fur, resembling a wolverine or badger. But something was not quite right about this creature. Like the human wraiths they had encountered, it was gray and shimmered with silvery light. But this gray light had a static quality to it, like an old television with a partial signal. They could hear faint hisses and pops as the static glowed and wavered. The creature was clearly asleep, in some state of hibernation or suspension. Its head lay buried deep within its fur, and its torso heaved with slow, almost imperceptible breaths.

After a moment, Elle once again lost her fear. "So what? It's a sleeping dog, or something. But I guess that makes sense, that all the animals would be hibernating."

"Why?" asked Danny.

"Because what else are they supposed to do? When they wake up, instead of humans to compete with, they'll have machines to tend to them."

"Should we wake it?" asked Jason.

"Oh, god no!" everyone protested. In the ruckus that followed, Conner bumped into Miller, and Miller dropped her spear on the floor. The instant the liquid light hit, an overwhelming humming sound burst through the air. It felt like they were inside a gigantic bell that rang in slow motion. The building shook, pictures fell off the walls, and cracks formed in the ceiling. After several seconds of this powerful reaction, the humming and shaking faded.

Miller bent and picked up her fallen spear. "Sorry, guys."

Before she could stand, the growling started. Everyone looked back toward the kitchen. There, standing nearly four feet at its shoulders, stood the dog creature. Its fur glowed with a rough, silvery static that sparked and shimmered. Glowing tendrils of spittle oozed down from the corners of its wide mouth. Its fangs looked like miniature chrome daggers lining its quivering jaw. The dog stood still, and they could sense its anger increasing as its fur stood up on its back like a jagged mountain range.

Conner lifted his spear and positioned himself between the dog and everyone else. "Think it has rabies?"

Shadou pulled Conner toward him and switched places, so that he was the first line of defense. "I don't know, but it sure doesn't look friendly."

The dog growled again, a deep, rumbling growl that sounded strangely electronic. Elle took a step back, but then noticed a shimmering circle on the dog's front paw.

"What's that circle all about anyway? Emmett and the wraiths had it too."

Shadou studied the bristling dog with wary eyes. "I believe it's some kind of tracker. It monitors the status and location of whatever has one installed."

Just then the dog lowered itself on its haunches and sprang at Shadou. Shadou managed to sideswipe the dog with his spear, but failed to connect with the liquid-light tip. A moment of pure chaos ensued in which everyone ran in opposite directions to avoid the massive ghost dog.

The dog slid on the smooth wood floor and did a half spin by digging its front claws into the wood and pulling itself around. Elle looked down and realized that she was standing less than three feet from this massive threat. The animal scrambled on the slippery floor to attack Elle. Remembering her training, Elle lifted her spear and performed one of the six moves Shadou had taught them. First she swung her spear to her left with just enough force to give her the momentum to dodge the dog's attack. The dog once again spun out on the floor and dug its front claws into the wood, so deep this time that the wood splintered open. The dog reared its head up at Elle, exposed its chrome-like teeth, and readied itself for a deadly lunge.

But Elle felt something speak to her softly, as though the foreign technology controlling the dog was whispering secrets in her ear. *Hi, what are you trying to tell me?* Something clicked in her head. She grinned, spun back around, lifted her spear in a tall, sweeping motion, and brought the tip of it down onto the top of the dog's left paw, right where the silver circle was. The liquid light instantly transferred itself from Elle's spear and into the dog's paw. As the light entered, the circle faded into a thin round scar. The dog stopped struggling on the kitchen floor. It got up and wandered around, sniffing everything it could find. It reminded Elle of Marvin the cat, listless and vaguely lost.

The dog returned to its spot by the kitchen cupboard. It made itself a nest by turning around and around several times, and then it collapsed onto the floor, dug its head between its front legs, and fell back asleep. It still emitted the eerie, silver static. It still heaved its chest with disturbingly slow breaths. But the dog seemed far less menacing now.

"I think you freed it," said Conner.

Shadou rested his hand on Elle's shoulder. "That was pretty cool. I've never seen that move before. How'd you know to do that?"

Elle nodded her head and twirled her spear in the air in front of her. "Um, my gift, I think. Now let's—"

A horrifying shriek rang out from somewhere in the distance. "Wraiths!" shouted Conner.

"Yep," said Jason. "Time to go now."

The survivors streamed out of the house in single file, Jason in the lead. He leapt into the truck and Danny grabbed shotgun. Everyone else piled into the bed. The shrieks sounded once again, closer this time. Wazer's voice called out from the abandoned tablet. "Guys, are you reading this? You have dozens of unfriendlies closing in on you! You need to move now."

"Roger that, Wazer. Go, go, go. Go now!" Shadou cried. The liquid-light container maintained its piercing beam of light. "I hope the light saves us this time."

Jason gunned the truck and peeled out on the road, swerving slightly back and forth before he could accelerate straight ahead. The shrieks followed them close behind, growing louder every second.

Elle's heart sunk. She wasn't sure they could fight off these creatures. "No, no, no," she whispered.

Within seconds, silver cracks in Shadou's force field began to form. At first, sharp, glowing fingertips forced their way through the dome, followed by heads crowned with gray flowing hair and eyes that burned with blind hate.

Shadou lifted his spear. "How many are there, Wazer?"

"I count just over twenty, closing in fast."

"Brace yourselves, everyone! Miller! Elle! Replenish your light!"

Elle and Miller looked down at their spears and realized that the tips were dark. They stumbled over to the light container in the bouncing truck bed. Elle looked over her shoulder and saw that five wraiths had broken completely through. They would be on the truck in seconds.

"Remember your training!" called out Shadou.

The first wraith pounced onto the cab of the truck with a deafening, high-pitched wail. Shadou stabbed it with one of his spear tips, and the wraith disintegrated into a puff of sparks, similar to how Emmett and Marvin were able to deal with them. This impressive display filled the others' hearts with newfound courage.

Between Conner, Danny, Rifkin, Miller, and Shadou, the wraiths were soon destroyed. A single one remained. It was a child, or had once been a child, a girl of about nine years of age. Shadou replenished his empty spear in the liquid-light container and walked up to the girl.

She circled him with arms outstretched and hissed like a demon. Shadou lifted his spear and went in for the kill when Elle called out, "Stop!" Shadou froze. The wraith girl continued to circle him, but he stood his ground. Elle dipped a spear tip into the container and withdrew it. The bright orb of light reflected off her goggles. She hopped off the truck and sauntered up to the girl.

The young wraith started for Elle. Just as the girl got within inches of her, Elle lifted her spear, spun around the girl and hit the girl's leg with one end of her spear, but not the lit end. The girl fell to the ground. Elle spun back around and jammed the lit end of her spear into the glowing circle on the girl's left hand.

The wraith's shriek rang out and then ceased one last time. But she wasn't destroyed. Elle saw something change in the girl's glimmering eyes. They became slightly more transparent, slightly more aware. The girl picked herself up off the ground. Then, apparently completely oblivious to everyone, she walked away, slipping through the force field as if she was leaving a tent.

Jason scanned the perimeter with both spear tips lit. No more wraiths came. No more shrieks in the distance.

Wazer's voice rose form the tablet. "You still there? It looks all clear from my end."

Shadou smiled, "Yes, all here and accounted for. We just won our first battle, with an assist from Elle's discovery. The circles are a key."

Elle hoisted her spear up onto her shoulder. "Well, that was weird, and kind of awesome."

Conner jumped down off the truck, ran up to Elle, and took her in his arms. "Kind of awesome? You were freakin' amazing! You should've seen your ninja moves. That was insane!"

Everyone cracked up laughing. "Come," Shadou said, "let's take a break and eat something." But after taking a few steps Shadou stopped and grinned at Jason.

"What now?"

"I just figured out why Quaru can't track Emmett and Marvin."

"Oh really? And why is that?"

Shadou drew a circle in the dirt with the claw of his foot. "The circles on the wraith's hands glow with a steady light. For Emmett – and Marvin too – their lights flicker. They seem disconnected, broken somehow. That's my theory anyway."

Elle smiled at the thought of her brother, but then her smile faded as quickly as it had appeared. "I hope Emmett is alive somewhere, if ghosts can even be alive, And that he's far away from Quaru."

They went back to the truck and chowed down on Shadou's junk-food buffet. Jason kept a watchful eye on the edge of the dome, but no more wraiths appeared.

After a half hour of rest, they were ready to continue. Based on Shadou's calculations, they had about ten more hours of driving to get to Mount Rainier. He figured they would drive that straight, and then take one final rest before entering the mountain. This time, Miller took the wheel with Jason riding shotgun. Elle sat close to Conner. Rifkin topped off the gas tank, Miller revved up the engine, and they were off.

Unspoken was the deep dread everyone felt. A dark menace awaited them at their destination beneath the mountain.

Chapter 40

Quaru took Jill to a place she had never visited before: Antarctica. He fabricated cold-weather gear for Jill. Through her mask, the howling wind was so thick with ice that Jill could only see about ten yards in front of her.

Once again, Quaru was his human self. He didn't require any special clothing to protect him from the intense cold. He wore a black silky button-down shirt and casual pants of the same fabric. The silk fluttered violently in the wind.

"Where are we?" asked Jill.

Quaru smiled. "The middle of Antarctica, my dear. Here, come with me."

He took Jill's arm in his and held up his other hand like a traffic cop signaling to stop. A force field of protection flared up and spread out from his upheld hand. The wind stopped lashing at Jill's face and warmth surrounded her. Her clothes transformed into a pair of skinny jeans, a T-shirt, and a light sweater vest. Her heavy white snow boots remained on since she still stood on snow. The icy floor rapidly melted beneath their feet. Quaru increased the diameter of the force field with gentle nudges of his hand. Once he was satisfied, the two walked hand-in-hand with the force field following them like a spotlight on a stage.

"Why didn't you do that right when we got here?" asked Jill.

"Oh, I wanted you to experience this lovely weather for just a minute." He led her forward.

Jill's ears flinched at the sound of metal-on-metal pounding away in the distance. Soon a black mass emerged in front of them. As they stepped closer, Jill realized that this was a newly built structure.

The building was forged out of dark metal. Its base appeared hexagonal and rose hundreds of feet. The higher levels of the structure were rudimentary skeletal girders, while the bottom shielded itself with thick gray walls. Seemingly tiny creatures crawled about this hulking specimen of architecture. Jill realized that these worker ants were humans, or ghosts rather. They manned immense machines that must have been designed for the sole purpose of erecting this alien tower. The more Jill looked at it, the more disheartening it became to her. The sound was so intense that Jill had to shout over it, even though she felt like she should whisper instead.

"What are they building?"

Quaru wrapped Jill in a newly materialized silk cloak. He transported her to a luxurious hotel room. Floor-to-ceiling windows overlooked the Eiffel Tower. Jill looked down and saw that she now wore black silk pajamas, which matched Quaru's.

"Seriously?" she said. "Antarctica to Paris?"

Quaru poured Jill a glass of champagne—real Champagne from France, circa 1960. "I thought you'd like it, my dear."

Jill took a sip, and found it to be quite heavenly. She sat on a small sofa facing the window and gazed outside. "Is any of this real right now?"

"Does it matter?"

"Yes, of course it matters."

"Then yes, this is real. I kept some cities intact. For you."

Jill downed the champagne and held out her empty glass. Quaru obediently refilled it and placed the bottle back into its sterling-silver ice bucket.

"So," said Jill, "are you ever going to tell me what those ghosts were building in the middle of freaking Antarctica?"

A sly smile spread across Quaru's face. "What do you imagine it is?"

Jill grew distracted by the raindrops that tapped on the window. "I don't know. And honestly, I don't even really want to know at this point. Is it a giant weapon? An ice queen's castle? A shopping mall? Who cares?"

Quaru sat on the sofa beside Jill. He patted her knee with his hand, like a nervous high school kid on a date.

Jill took a slow drink from her glass and looked into Quaru's swirling eyes. "Well? Are you going to tell me or not?"

Quaru looked down at his impeccably manicured fingernails. "Oh, it's nothing all too impressive, really. It's just the first of many data centers. It will be capable of processing a million times more data per second than anything you humans have created."

Jill wasn't impressed. "Great."

Just then something went really wrong with Quaru. He jolted from his seat and stood up straight. His head shot back and his eyes glowed with silver-gray light that grew brighter by the second. His hands clenched into fists and shook with increasing intensity. Jill wouldn't have been surprised if white foam burst from his nose and mouth.

When Quaru's seizure—or whatever it was—subsided, Jill didn't know whether to be relieved or disappointed. His body relaxed, his eyes returned to their normal subtle glow, and his hands stopped shaking. He massaged his temples for a few seconds, and then looked into Jill's eyes. She saw nothing but hatred.

"You," he said, "You have proven to be a pointless distraction."

Jill crawled backward on the sofa to distance herself from Quaru. "What do you mean?"

Quaru's black garments unfurled and grew like massive dark wings that threatened to engulf Jill. "We have visitors, Jill. At the mountain. And do you know who it is?"

"Um, let me guess: Shadou?"

Quaru's wings lifted Jill violently from the sofa, shook her for several seconds and then pulled her to within inches of his contorted face. Jill was nearly unconscious, but she could still hear Quaru. "Yes, Shadou!" He snarled the name. "And he brought a few friends with him too, including some special guests."

"Special guests?" Jill's nausea almost made her throw up all over Quaru. She was terrified by the thought of his reaction to that.

Quaru seemed to recognize Jill's delicate state. He loosened his grip and smiled at her, more of a sneer. "Yes, special guests. We must go attend to them, you and I, don't you agree?"

Quaru's wings swirled about the hotel room, a precursor to their imminent transportation. Just before the hotel room dematerialized, Quaru whispered into Jill's ear: "Your life depends on whether or not you help me destroy these intruders."

Chapter 41

The final miles of their drive to Mount Rainier turned out to be one of the most pleasant experiences of Elle's life. Early on, Shadou and Rifkin conferred privately. For a while they seemed to be arguing, but after about ten minutes of speaking in a language none of the humans had heard before, the two aliens slapped each other's shoulders as though striking a grand bargain. Elle heard Shadou chatting with Wazer via the tablet in hushed tones, something about the liquid light. *What's that all about?*

Rifkin gathered a pile of empty plastic bottles into the truck bed and jumped around through the passenger window to the truck cab. He removed the entire console that contained the truck's stereo, GPS display, and temperature controls.

"Whoa, whoa, whoa!" said Jason. "This is my truck here!"

Rifkin flashed his sharp-toothed grin at Jason. "Don't worry, I'll make you a new one. If we survive this trip."

Shadou busied himself with the liquid-light container. He pressed a few hidden buttons on its side. This revealed a bright, colorful touch screen. Shadou tapped on the screen for several minutes. As he tapped away, the color of the light shooting out from the container shifted and changed. It went from white, to blue, to green, to purple, to multiple shades that spit out sparks all around them.

While Shadou made these adjustments, Rifkin assembled an intricate device from the plastic bottles and the truck console. It looked to Elle like a futuristic food processor. Shadou turned the light to a subtle violet, with silver sparks climbing and dancing up into the sky above. When he was satisfied with the light setting, he nodded at Rifkin.

Rifkin placed his new device over the container's top. It fit perfectly. Their world grew dark when the light was covered. Everyone began to remove their goggles.

Shadou raised up his hands to stop them. "No! Leave those on, unless you want to be permanently blinded."

Once certain that everyone was secure, Shadou said to Rifkin. "Let's give this a try."

Rifkin locked the device tightly in place and tapped a few buttons on it. He then slowly turned a dial—formerly the truck's volume knob. A low humming sound emanated from the device. It increased in both volume and pitch until it became a deafening scream.

Elle held her hands to her ears and shouted, "Are you going to give us earplugs too?"

Just then the wailing ceased. Everyone removed their hands from their ears and stared at the device.

Conner's eyes widened. "Does this mean... That our light is gone?"

The container sat dark for several long seconds. But then the top of the device began to shift, like a mechanical lotus flower opening up. At the same time, the device started spinning like a top. The spinning sped up and reached a crescendo as the lid opened completely. A dazzling new light shot out, straight up above.

Elle lay back on the truck bed and rested her head on Conner's lap. She was reminded of watching Fourth of July fireworks displays at Eagle Harbor on Bainbridge Island.

The light that burst from the container glowed with alternating shades of blue and lavender, with silver sparks shimmering in its center like bubbles in a glass of champagne. This new light had a powerful effect on their field of vision.

Instead of just a gray wall, Shadou's force-field dome came to life. For the first time in weeks, Elle saw the moon and the stars. These celestial objects looked nothing like they did before Quaru's attack, but at least they were visible. The full moon glimmered with a ghostly glow, somewhat resembling an x-ray.

Elle sat up and gazed across the horizon. Instead of impenetrable darkness, outlines of the landscape began to materialize. She saw hills and trees, barns and buildings, all rushing by. Everything shimmered as though computer-generated. But Elle didn't mind. Even this artificial glimpse of her home world was enough to fill her with fleeting joy.

The others clearly felt the same way. Miller giggled with delight and Danny whooped as the horizon took shape before them. Conner embraced Elle and beamed. "The outside world, it's back!"

Shadou rocked back and forth on his heels. "Yes. Our hypothesis was correct: a certain spectrum of the liquid light gives us at least a rudimentary view of the dimensional plane outside of my force field." Shadou called into the tablet, "You getting this, Wazer?"

"You bet I am. I think you tripled my field of vision."

"And how does it look?"

"Beautiful. No signs of life, or death, or whatever."

The crew drove on for about another hour. Just as Elle's thoughts returned to their daunting mission, Jason called out, "Mount Rainier, straight ahead!"

Everyone looked up and marveled as the outlines of the volcano rose up before them. It seemed to be moving toward them with aggression. The ragged peak glowed with an electrical intensity that made it stand out from everything else. Miller said to Elle after taking in the view, "This is the last place I saw your mom, Elle. Let's go do this for her."

"And for everyone on Earth, right? But I'll do anything to save my mom."

Miller gazed back up at Rainier. "I have a feeling that she's still up there somewhere."

Elle couldn't respond. After losing her brother and her father, she couldn't stand the thought of seeing her mother's ghost.

It took them another hour to reach the trailhead. The truck could take them no further from there. Jason assured Miller that they didn't have a several-day hike to the cave entrance like last time, when they were tracking Chuck. This trail called for only a six-hour trek.

Rifkin busied himself creating conveyances for their gear. They placed the liquid-light container on a wagon-like fabrication he sourced from sticks, rocks, and the truck's spare tire. He also reconfigured Elle's backpack to give it a custom bident sheath. The crew spent several minutes filling up on carbs and gulping down water. Then Jason led the way, with Shadou pulling the liquid-light wagon behind him.

The trail was just wide enough for them to travel single file. It was midmorning, and so Shadou's force-field dome gave them a gorgeous glimpse into the forested surroundings. Golden light danced upon the still ferns, moss, and tree trunks. Outside of the dome, they could see the x-ray-like outlines of tall trees and rock formations, as well as Mount Rainier's towering peak. The top of the volcano bore a jagged, black gash—the scar left behind by Quaru's escape.

They occasionally stopped to rest. During these brief pauses, Shadou drilled them on their six spear stances.

"Tell me again how we're going to discover Quaru's weakness? It sounded nice back at the base, but now I'm not so sure." asked Elle.

The alien's fur rippled despite the complete lack of wind. He smiled down at her. "Quaru has weaknesses. My master's last words to me were that we can exploit them together, you and I. It's just a puzzle we'll have to solve when we get there, my dear Elle. Let's just hope we have all the right pieces."

Elle smacked Shadou's belly with her bident. "You realize that gives me zero confidence, right? This so-called gift, it seems like a cruel joke."

"Exactly, let's play a cruel joke on our friend Quaru."

They continued walking in silence along the worn trail. The only sounds were of their rhythmic footsteps in the packed dirt and the turning of the wagon wheels. No birds sang, no insects buzzed. Elle felt like she was hiking through a Natural History Museum diorama. Then they heard Wazer's voice calling from the tablet. "Guys, I'm seeing some crazy-big activity in the mountain. They're headed your way."

Shadou glanced down at the liquid-light container. "Wazer, tell me now, did the ship finish calculating the liquid-light settings? Will it work as we discussed?"

A piercing shriek echoed off the mountainsides.

Conner drew out his spear. "Wraith!"

The shriek grew exponentially louder, as though someone was multiplying it with an audio sampling program.

Shadou stayed focused on the tablet. "Wazer, answer me now."

"Yes, the calculations are complete. But the results are inconclusive. It all depends on factors we can't detect."

"Give me the short answer, yes or no?"

"Um, according to the ship's calculations, you're looking at about sixty-four percent yes, thirty-six percent no, but the margin of error... I'll tell you, if it was me out there I'm not sure I'd like those odds."

"Well I'm out here, and I'll take those odds."

"Either way, you've got wraiths closing in."

Shadou dipped his spear into the liquid light. "Many wraiths. Quaru has assembled His army. I hope we're not too late." As his spear glowed, Shadou called out, "Come, everyone! Light up your spears."

Jason was the first to stand at ready. "First position, now," he shouted. "Don't forget your training!"

They came from the mountain, spewing forth from a network of cave openings like burrowing wasps. Thanks to the liquid light, Elle and crew could see the wraiths' forms. They glowed silver and raced toward the survivors at an inhuman rate. Elle's heart sunk into her stomach. She saw nothing but terror and doom before her. She looked around her. Everyone was frozen with fear. They held their spears in weak hands, their eyes free of all hope.

Elle's eyes found Shadou. Her lips quivered. "What were those odds you were talking about? How are we going to survive this?"

Just seconds before the wraiths entered the perimeter of Shadou's force field, he called out, "Rifkin, now!"

Rifkin raced over to Shadou. The two of them lifted the liquid-light container. They tilted it toward the first wave of wraiths. *They're going to blast those wraiths with the light,* thought Elle. But that was not the plan.

Shadou called out to the group, "Make sure your goggles are on tight!" He surveyed the scene and then aimed the cannon of liquid light at...

"Conner!" screamed Elle. She watched in horror as the light engulfed him. Shadou and Rifkin flashed the light on Jason, then Miller, then Danny. Elle ran away, in the opposite direction of both the wraiths and the light. But Shadou and Rifkin easily targeted her, aimed the light, and blasted Elle.

She felt a tingling sensation that was both warm and cold. *I'm floating. Is this what it feels like to die?* She opened her eyes and saw that she was indeed floating, just inches above the ground. She extended her toes and they brushed against the leaf-strewn soil. Something caught her periphery vision and she realized that it was her spear—her "bident"—hovering inches from her head. Elle saw that the entire spear glowed with sparkling light. She reached out and plucked the spear from the air. It was weightless, just like her.

After contemplating the strange physics that now governed her, Elle surveyed her surroundings. Her friends—including Shadou and Rifkin—floated nearby in similar states of disorientation, as though they inhabited a shared dream. A moment later, signs of recognition spread across their faces. They smiled at one another and tossed their spears effortlessly from hand to hand.

Shadou was the first to speak. His voice echoed oddly, as though he were talking inside a steel drum. "Remember your training!" He pointed his spear ahead. Hundreds of wraiths were upon them.

Instead of crippling fear, Elle felt more at ease than ever before. The wraiths seemed to her like slow, clumsy beasts. This would be like popping bubbles at a toddler's birthday party.

When the wave hit, the survivors took the first of their six spear stances. As long, clawed hands extended to attack her, Elle pushed herself up off the forest floor and did a series of twisting flips, almost in slow motion. With each spin she slashed at the wraiths with her glowing bident. Every wraith she hit burst into a cloud of ash.

"Wait!" shouted Danny. His voice rang clearly in their ears. "Don't forget, these things are people. Try not to kill them!"

Everyone remembered Elle's discovery on the side of the road. They leaped, flipped, and spun their way through wave after wave of wailing wraiths. Each blow that landed on the white circles on their hands sent the wraiths scurrying away, no longer a threat.

Time lost all meaning. The fight could have lasted five minutes or five days; such was the dreamlike state in which they all found themselves. Elle caught herself at times giggling softly to herself. She wished she had a pair of headphones and her tablet so she could listen to music as she smote wraith after wraith after wraith. The liquid light's energy propelled both her body and spirit. Would this last forever? It did not.

After a time, the survivors felt the weight of their spears gradually returning. Their leaps lost height, and their movements required more effort. Their blows started to miss the circles, and instead sent the wraiths bursting into clouds of shimming dust. By the end of the battle, Elle felt herself returning completely to normal. She hacked and slashed her way through the last remaining wraiths she could find, and then collapsed onto the ground.

Everyone else did the same thing. Jason and Miller lay on their backs, their chests heaving. Danny squatted with his hands over his head. Conner practically crawled over to Elle and slammed his head onto the grass beside her. Only Shadou and Rifkin stood, but they leaned heavily upon their spears.

"OK," panted Shadou through heavy breaths, "We did it, I think. We broke their defenses."

Miller cracked up in a laughing fit, which apparently hurt her stomach as she flinched. But somehow she still managed to say, "That was ... awesome! Liquid light is the best. Give me more please!"

Jason raised his hand. "Ditto."

Danny kept his hands over his face. "What? Are y'all crazy? I know we're all here to help, but we just killed a lot of people. I tried my best not to, but I lost count of all the wraiths I smashed to smithereens."

"Come on, Danny," said Miller. "This is a fight for all humanity."

"I guess I was put here to fix things, not fight things."

Just then a shrieking sound rang out. A female wraith appeared, seemingly from out of nowhere. She closed in on Elle, who was too exhausted to move.

Conner reached out, but couldn't summon the strength to protect her. "Elle, look out!"

Shadou stepped up and positioned himself between the wraith and Elle, but his spear had no light. The wraith cackled with fearless rage and lunged at Shadou. Just before the wraith struck, Jason sprinted over and drove his spear into its heart. Instead of disintegrating into dust, the wraith howled with pain. The traces of liquid light remaining on the spear weren't enough to destroy it.

Jason pushed forward and forced the howling wraith away from Elle. The wraith's cries transformed into cackles of laughter. Jason looked down and saw dark tendrils of ooze spilling from the wraith's wound, crawling along his spear. Within seconds Jason's hands and arms were immersed in the dark matter. Miller screamed as the tattooed words on his arms—IF YOU WANT PEACE, PREPARE FOR WAR—disappeared. Miller jumped forward but Shadou held her back. Jason was engulfed in darkness. The wraith ripped the spear from its torso and tossed it aside. The wraith and Jason submerged into the ground beneath their feet.

Miller sat up on her knees. "Jason!" But he was gone. The survivors burst into tears. Losing Jason after all of this was too much for them to bear.

After a while, Shadou slammed down his spear into the ground. "Enough!" Everyone stopped sobbing and looked up with red, teary eyes. Shadou pointed at the container. They all realized that its glow was reduced to a faint ember of light. "The liquid light is nearly depleted. We used it to defeat the wraiths. Without it, we'd all be dead by now. But our toughest challenge lies ahead."

Shadou pulled out the tablet and his eyes darkened when he saw the shattered screen. It was nearly broken in half. Shadou let out a growl, tore the tablet apart and tossed the pieces to the ground. He pointed up toward Mount Rainier. They could no longer see it. The shiny glow of the outside world had vanished along with the liquid light. Like before, they couldn't see past Shadou's force-field dome.

"Come," he said. "We don't have time to rest. We must march up to the mountain and face Quaru before He summons an even greater army to destroy us."

Chapter 42

Jill felt Quaru's rage rush over her like an icy wind. She sat curled up against a rock wall in the Mount Rainier cavern where she had first encountered this powerful being. She still wore her black silk pajamas from the Parisian hotel. The pale brown dust of the cavern floor covered them in splotchy patterns. In this earthly place, Quaru reverted to his shiny, angular, obsidian form. Jill's pulse quickened as his body trembled with terrifying fury.

Quaru shouted, *The LIGHT! I had forgotten about the light!*

Jill squirmed as Quaru's screams pounded her eardrums. "What light?"

Quaru looked down at Jill as though he had forgotten she was there. Then his shaking subsided. *Liquid light. It's what Shadou used to subdue me in the first place, over five thousand years ago.*

"OK. Does this mean you need to run and hide?"

Quaru laughed. *Not this time, my dear Jill. They can destroy all the human slaves they want to, but liquid light can no longer harm me. That fool Shadou, I'll let him come here with his precious weapon. Only then will he realize I'm immune to its effects. I've assimilated liquid light into my being. Now, it can only make me stronger. I will crush him and all those who follow him.*

Jill looked down at her tattered and dusty pajamas. Goosebumps rose from her exposed arms and calves. She found herself shivering with cold. She glanced up at Quaru. He gave her a disapproving look and then waved his hand. Jill's pajamas transformed into a tight black leather outfit, complete with military-style boots and a long, stylish overcoat, also black but with deep red accents. She stood up and ran her fingers through her hair.

"Well," she said, "I look forward to finally meeting this Shadou fellow."

Elle trudged up the mountain path; her extinguished spear rested in its sheath. As the group pressed on, they encountered a few more wraiths that hid themselves amongst the rocky terrain. Luckily, they still had a small amount of liquid light left to dispatch them. Elle made sure to hit their hands, so as not to destroy them.

As their light supply dwindled, their spirits sank. Shadou seemed unusually subdued. The dull hangover they all felt after coming down from the liquid-light sensation, plus the loss of Jason, made everyone despondent. They were in no shape to fight a small handful of wraiths, let alone a powerful force like Quaru.

And yet Shadou pressed on. He somehow summoned the energy to keep them motivated. "Come!" he called. "We are your planet's last hope. I have faith in you, in us all. We will prevail."

Elle focused on lifting one foot after another. Each step brought her closer to doom and yet at the same time made her slightly calmer. She looked up. "Shadou?"

"Yes, my sweet Elle."

"What's the name of your home planet?"

"I never told you?"

"No."

"The closest translation to your language would be Rhythmnia."

Elle sounded it out silently with her lips and then out loud, "Rhythmnia. I like that. And, Shadou?"

"Yes..."

"Those five thousand years ago, when Quaru attacked your planet—Rhythmnia—after you used the liquid light, everything went back to normal, right? Like in that video you posted."

Shadou exchanged an uncomfortable glance with Rifkin and said, "Yes. After we captured Quaru, our world returned as before. In fact, the return ushered in a new age of prosperity. We didn't just rebuild, we evolved."

Elle was thankful to hear that answer, but then her thoughts returned to the liquid light. "The light, it's been speaking to me, in a way. Kind of like your ship. I'm catching flashes, like it's trying to tell me something. You told me that Quaru is immune to it now. But I can't stop thinking about it, that it somehow holds the key. Without it, how are we going to beat Quaru?"

Shadou smiled. "Your gift is greater than I imagined, my dear Elle." Shadou pointed at the liquid-light container. "During our walk, I too have been communing with the light. I think it's trying to tell us both something."

"Something we can use?"

"I hope so."

After nearly two more hours of hiking, the group reached the cave opening that led to Quaru's cavern. Shadou allowed everyone a brief rest. They nibbled on salty snacks and drank as much water as their bodies could take.

When Shadou stood up and adjusted his backpack, Miller rubbed her eyes with both palms. "Shadou, I don't think I can do this. I mean, after losing Jason... How are we possibly going to walk through this cave and face that monster inside?"

Shadou opened his mouth to speak but Elle shushed him. "We're going to face that monster because it's the only thing we can do," she said. "What do we have to lose, anyway? It's not like Earth was a paradise before. If Quaru hadn't attacked us, I'd just be living a sheltered life, while millions, even billions, of people would be suffering because of our messed-up world. Wars, hunger, disease. I thought I wanted to help, and yet I did nothing.

"But now's our time to help. Every human being on Earth is suffering as a slave, except for us. Even if we wanted to hide, how long would we last, a year at most? If we give up now, we die. Let's not give up. Let's at least try."

Miller stood and hugged Elle. Conner, Danny, Rifkin, and Shadou joined them.

Elle giggled. "I didn't mean for this to become a group hug." The others all laughed too. Elle faced Shadou. "Ready?"

Chapter 43

Their journey through the cave was quiet, and yet each of the survivors carried with them a heavy burden of fear and dread. Rifkin had fashioned flashlights from the truck's headlights, and the container of remaining liquid light that Shadou carried in the top of his backpack emitted a faint glow. But darkness still prevailed. At every turn, Elle expected a monster to jump out and attack them. No monster came. The survivors spoke little as they stepped along the wet, slippery ground. The farther they went, the warmer it became.

"This is just like last time," whispered Miller. She remembered that Jill and Jason were no longer with them, and fell silent again.

Elle sensed that they were nearing their destination. The liquid light's whispers grew more urgent. At first she caught bright flashes in her mind, like images of supernovas bursting in the cosmos. But with each step these images became darker, almost violent. She froze in her tracks when a shadowy face invaded her mind. *Elle!* A sinister voice called out within her.

Shadou took her arm. "Elle, are you all right?"

A lump grew in Elle's throat. *I'm walking to my death. We all are.* She forced herself to focus on Shadou's dimly lit face. "Shadou, something's wrong here, with the liquid light. There's a darkness underneath. I think it might be evil."

"Darkness? Tell me, what do you see?"

"I'm not sure, but it seems to be connected with Quaru, like He's maybe talking to me through it."

Then the voice rang out, as though the very walls spoke: *Shadou...*

Everyone shuddered. A palpable sensation of panic spread through the group. They looked ahead and saw a faint glow pulsating from the cavern just ahead.

Shadou, my dear, dear friend. Why did it take you so long to pay me a visit?

Shadou rested his arm on Elle's shoulder and took her aside. "Elle, listen to me."

Elle looked up. Her stomach clinched up and her eyes widened with fear. "I don't think I can do this." Her voice shook so much it was difficult to understand.

Shadou brushed her hair away from her eyes and then kissed her forehead. "I need you to be here, with me, now."

Tears hung from Elle's eyes, threatening to stream down her face. She struggled to hold them back. Shadou caressed both her cheeks in his hands.

The voice hissed again, *Shadou! Don't be such a coward. Come, let's have a little chat. Face to face.*

Shadou looked back over his shoulder. "Yeah, yeah, yeah, Quaru. You've waited over five thousand years. I think you can wait another five minutes."

Hah, touché. I suppose I can spare five minutes. Anything to make your demise all the more pathetic.

Shadou returned his attention to Elle. "Deep breaths, and focus, Elle. Focus on how you made me remember my purpose all those years ago on the side of the road."

Elle inhaled deeply. "Yes, after the accident." Then she giggled through her tears.

"What could possibly be so funny?"

Elle wiped her cheek on her sleeve but couldn't stop laughing. "It's just that... I mean, what was up with that anyway? It was like your entire body became one big mobile game app or something."

Shadou smiled, but his eyes remained fixed, serious. "Well, on my home planet, many of the citizens, myself included, are biomechanical of sorts, we're—" But Shadou cut himself off with the wave of a hand. "Elle, come on, let's not talk about that now. I need you here, with me, in the moment."

Elle's tears ceased, then the voice boomed from the cavern: *One more minute, Shadou!*

Shadou removed the liquid-light container from his backpack, set it on the ground, and grabbed Elle's shoulders with both hands. "The point is, you uncovered my memory." He patted the lid of the container. "And I think I know what you need to do now. I think you've discovered the code you have to crack."

"Quaru's?"

"No, not Quaru's. This liquid light, it has memories too, dark and long forgotten."

"Really?" Elle looked at the container and realized that the light swirled and danced within it, in a way she'd never seen before.

"Yes, and I need you to help the liquid light remember something very important to the matter at hand. The light wasn't always light. It began in darkness, as dark matter. Now that Quaru is near, the light is starting to remember. That's what you're seeing. But you need to speed that up. I can't do it, only you—"

Quaru's voice interrupted. *Now, Shadou! Don't make me come out there and destroy you in that sad little cave.*

Shadou stood. "All right, all right, I'm coming!" He pointed to Rifkin. "You, help Elle." He pointed to Miller, Conner, and Danny. "You three, stay here until I call for help. When I call, come running." They nodded with stark faces.

Rifkin tapped some hidden buttons on the side of the container. The light within continued to swirl about. After a few more taps, the touchscreen panel on the side of the container lit up. Glowing shapes flowed across the screen. Elle looked down at the lights and then back up at Rifkin. "Well?" he said. "Better get crackin' on that code."

The menacing face took over all of Elle's thoughts. For a moment she could scarcely hear Rifkin calling her name. She finally came to after he smacked her on the shoulder with his staff. "Elle, wake up!"

"Oh, right. OK. I'm here." Elle pounded the images from her forehead and started tapping randomly on the touchscreen, hoping a pattern would emerge.

Shadou caressed her shoulder, and then everyone else's. He picked up his spear and walked toward the cavern.

Well, there you are at last! said Quaru when Shadou reached the center of the cavern.

Shadou looked around this place he had spent so many years. The spot where the prison sphere used to be resembled an oil stain from an old junkyard car. The Rainier beer towers crumbled in various states of decay. The place smelled dank and filthy.

Make yourself at home! This is your home, after all.

Quaru emerged from the shadows. His obsidian statuesque form reflected the odd light that seemed to come from nowhere. Quaru moved within inches of Shadou and raised himself up so that he could glower down at him.

It's funny how puny you look from outside that prison you made me endure.

"You look well, Quaru, for such an old fellow."

Yes, quite. But let's dispense with the pleasantries, shall we? Believe it or not, I don't have time to chat. There's lots of work to be done here on this sad little world. It needs quite a bit of sprucing up, I'm afraid.

"If you don't have time to chat, what is it you intend to do?"

Quaru snickered. *Shadou, you're really too much. I sometimes wish I could keep you around all the time, kind of like a court jester, the fool that you truly are. But I'd much rather just destroy you and all your friends so I can focus on more important matters.*

With that Quaru lashed out at Shadou with razor-sharp protrusions that extended from his shoulders and arms. But Shadou was fast. He dematerialized in a fraction of a second and reappeared on the other side of the cavern, holding out his spear.

Quaru giggled with delight. *Oh my! Very impressive. You may just drag this out for a minute or two.*

Quaru dematerialized and appeared in the same space Shadou was, only Shadou had also transported himself simultaneously to yet another location in the cavern. The two foes performed this fighting dance several times, each appearing in seemingly random patterns throughout the cavern. Sometimes they were on the ceiling, other times hovering for a second in midair. An observer would not be able to tell who was chasing who.

Quaru landed the first blow. He slashed Shadou's shoulder with a sharp club of dark stone. Shadou's arm pooled with purplish blood, and the fur around it worked feverishly, as though healing itself.

"Ouch," he said.

After a few more transportations around the cavern, Shadou finally managed to hit Quaru with his spear. A piece of Quaru shattered and spun across the floor in small, sparkling bits of black matter.

Ouch, said Quaru.

More confident now, Shadou lunged at Quaru and landed more hits. Pieces of Quaru scattered across the floor. Quaru retreated to a corner. Shadou transported, but this time Quaru guessed his destination perfectly and beat Shadou. Two long shards of darkness pierced Shadou's shoulders and pinned him to a wall.

That was fun while it lasted.

Shadou could scarcely breathe. He called out to the cave, "Come, now! Help!"

Quaru cracked up in cackling laughter. *Seriously? You're calling for help from humans? Should I ready my flyswatter?*

Miller, Conner, and Danny burst into the cavern. They looked around, stunned by what they saw.

But Quaru let Shadou go and collapsed onto the floor. *No! Not the human noise again! Stop it, cease your relentless thoughts!*

Shadou transported himself over to the three humans.

"What's going on?" asked Miller. She looked down and saw that Shadou's fur was busy healing his wounds. "Are you all right?"

Shadou nodded. "Quaru can hear your thoughts. It drives Him mad."

"That's cool," said Danny. "So do we just need to stand here and He can't hurt us?"

"No," said Shadou, "not even close to that. He can do us much harm. We've stunned Him, but He will lash out, more dangerous than before."

"So what are we doing here then?" asked Conner.

"We're buying time, for Elle."

Inside the cave, Elle began to detect patterns on the liquid-light container's touchscreen. She discovered that the shapes were commands, and that she could arrange those commands in ordered groups. Those groups could perform actions. She figured out commands to change the size, shape, and color of objects. As she did this, she unlocked more patterns. Eventually the pattern grew until it became an image of a solar system, and then an entire galaxy.

When Elle heard Shadou call out for help, she looked up and watched as the others rose up with their spears and ran into the cavern. Rifkin shot Elle a nervous smile. "We don't have much time now."

"Great, I just have to unlock the secrets of the universe. No big." Elle continued tapping at the screen.

Inside the cavern, Quaru remained on the floor, clutching his stone head in stone hands. Shadou whispered to the others, "Think about something really important to you, someone you lost, something sad or happy, anything that matters."

Miller thought about Jason, then Jill, and their last moments together in this cavern. Quaru started laughing. *You miss your friend Jill, don't you?* He rose up from the ground and called out. *Oh, Jill, where are you? You can come out now.* Silence followed. Quaru's mental agony was now multiplied by his impatience. *Jill, come now before I decide to slowly torture your friends instead of just enslaving them like the other humans.*

Miller heard footsteps in the distance. Jill emerged from behind a rock wall. "Jill, you're alive!"

Jill stood dressed in her black leather outfit with red accents flowing down her long overcoat. Her hair was pulled back in a tight ponytail and her lips glowed with deep red lipstick. She looked stunning.

Miller ran up to Jill but Quaru intercepted her and wrapped his sharp arms tightly around her. Small gashes formed where he touched her. Everyone stared in horror at the dark blood trickling down Miller's cheeks.

At last, Elle understood the code. After combining commands to reveal multiple galaxies, so many that each one became a tiny speck on the screen, Elle opened what she thought was the entire universe. She realized during this process that she was actually traveling back in time, to the origins of space and matter.

With a final set of commands, essentially "Undo Step 1," she moved backward in time to before the Big Bang. The universe on the screen imploded into itself, and the screen went dark. The light's whispers vanished from Elle's head.

"What just happened?" asked Elle. She and Rifkin stared at the dark screen in anticipation. At first, nothing stirred. But then the light within the container swirled with ever-increasing intensity. It became a tornado of light, changing colors every millisecond. Elle and Rifkin found their goggles and strapped them on. They stepped away for fear that the light was about to explode. But then the light stopped spinning. It retreated to the container. Its glow faded until it was just a dim flicker.

Elle and Rifkin removed their goggles and peered into the container. They saw a small puddle of dark purplish ooze. Elle looked up at Rifkin. "What do we do now?"

Rifkin picked up the container and pointed at Elle's spear, which was still in its sheath. "Take that out and follow me."

Jill pleaded with Quaru: "Please, don't hurt her."

Miller trembled in Quaru's tightening grip. Thin tears ran down her cheeks. She asked Jill, "How did you—?"

Quaru squeezed Miller so tightly she let out a piercing scream. *Do not speak, human. I know all about you, Miller Chance. You have a silver tongue that opens doors for you, takes you places others cannot go. But I promise you, you will not need your tongue where you're going now.*

Tendrils of black matter oozed out of Quaru's eyes and began to circle around Miller like serpents. Shadou felt all of the hope empty from his heart. Conner and Danny averted their eyes. Jill forced herself to watch. She owed it to her friend to let her go with dignity.

As the tendrils touched Miller's face, the color began to vanish from her skin. Then Elle's voice rang out. "Stop it!"

Several things happened at once. Quaru dropped Miller's limp body to the floor. Jill ran up to Elle. Rifkin grabbed Elle's spear and dipped it into the dark purple ooze that was once liquid light. Quaru saw the container and recognized what it was.

Liquid light? You know my weaknesses all too well, Shadou.

Rifkin tossed the spear to Shadou. Shadou kept his back to Quaru and looked over his shoulder. He could tell that the "human noise" in the room still pained Quaru. "Yes, Quaru, it's time for you to return to your prison."

When Jill reached Elle, neither knew what to do. They both thought they'd never see each other again. But before they could speak, or even touch one another, Quaru pulled Jill away. "Mom!" Elle cried out. Then she looked up to Quaru. "What are you going to do with her?"

Quaru gripped his forehead with one hand while squeezing Jill with the other. *Quiet! Your thoughts are too much. I need to take away the only human I can stand. Then I'll return with an army of slaves and watch them destroy you all.*

Quaru's form began to swirl around as he prepared to transport himself to the dark earth.

Elle and Shadou raced toward Quaru, and just as he was about to transport, they leapt into his vortex.

They arrived in what had once been downtown Tokyo. Elle and Shadou found themselves staring at the immensity of towering buildings that surrounded them. Everything was gray, but silver lights twinkled in rows and patterns. Elle looked down at her hands and was astonished to see that they shone with color. She looked over at her mother; her red lips glowed like neon. An older man stood beside her. He smiled down at Elle.

"Welcome to the beginnings of your new world," he said.

"Quaru?"

"The one and only." He glanced over at Shadou, who stood holding the spear behind his back. "You think I don't see that spear, old friend? But before we continue, let me take care of one thing real quick. Be right back."

Jill reached out to Elle but Quaru dematerialized in an instant, taking Jill with him. Elle ran up to the place they had been and screamed. A second later Quaru reappeared in front of Elle, alone. Elle beat his chest with her fists. Quaru did not flinch. Elle yelled at him, "Where did you take her? What did you do with my mother?"

"Don't worry, Elle, your mother's perfectly all right. I simply removed her to a safe place. We wouldn't want her to get caught up in all this unpleasantness, now would we?" Quaru pushed Elle away, effortlessly sending her sliding several yards across the pavement. He focused his attention on Shadou. "I'd like you to meet some friends of mine."

Quaru raised his hands. Dozens of wraiths emerged from the shadows. Shadou ran over to Elle and stood guard over her. Quaru grinned and let out a short cackle. The wraiths screeched and moaned as they staggered and crawled toward Shadou and Elle. Elle leaned against Shadou's side for support.

"Leave me," she said. "I'll lure these creatures away and you..." Elle looked at Shadou's spear with the glowing orb of liquid darkness on it. "You take care of Quaru."

"It's too late, Elle."

She looked up and saw that they were surrounded. Elle held Shadou tightly as the distance between them and the wraiths shrunk to a few yards.

Then from out of the darkness, Elle heard a familiar sound that wasn't a wraith's shriek. She heard a cat yowl.

"Marvin?"

Suddenly, a flurry of confusion overtook the wraith horde. One by one, they began to explode into puffs of dust. Elle saw Emmett on one side and Marvin on the other. The unlikely pair attacked the wraiths with great speed and efficiency. Quaru watched on in horror, unable to speak. In moments, every wraith was destroyed. Emmett picked up Marvin and gently stroked the ghost cat's head.

Elle ran over to her brother. "Emmett!" He did not seem to notice her. "I know you can't really understand, or maybe you can, but I'm so happy to see you again."

Elle felt a hand grip her shoulder. She looked up and saw Quaru's furious face staring down at her. He began to dematerialize. "You're coming with me," he said. "I shall so enjoy filling the last hours of your brief life with unspeakable pain."

Just then Shadou's spear tip burst from Quaru's chest, jutting out inches away from Elle's face. She saw dark ooze dripping out of the wound.

Quaru sneered. "Liquid light. Don't you realize that makes me stronger now?"

Shadou pulled the spear out from Quaru. "Not this light, Quaru. This is the light from before time, space, and matter. This is liquid darkness."

Quaru clutched at his chest. He realized something was wrong. Black matter bubbled up from his gaping wound and out of his mouth. His face contorted into a twisted mask of pain, and he let out a deep, gurgling moan. Soon, screams of agony echoed across the city as the darkness devoured his body. His limbs convulsed and he crumpled to the ground in a writhing heap of ooze. After a moment, nothing remained of Quaru but a bubbling, sticky black puddle.

Quaru was no more.

Elle studied the splattered mess. *Is He really dead?* She shielded her nose from the foul odor. "Nasty!"

Shadou leaned against his spear. "We destroyed Quaru and the universe didn't end. Now that's what I call winning."

A huge smile spread across Elle's face. "I can't believe it!"

"Believe it. He's gone."

Elle ran and held Shadou in her arms. But the stillness of the city became impossible to ignore. She looked around her. Something was not right. Then Elle realized what it was: Everything was still gray.

Elle stumbled back. "Wait, Shadou, what's happening? Why is everything still the same?" She pointed at the black puddle that was Quaru. "Shouldn't it all go back to normal now?"

Shadou wrapped his arm around Elle to stabilize her. "No, Elle. It seems as though your planet is still encased in Quaru's dimension. His death did not reverse that."

Elle felt a familiar panic rising up within her. "Will it ever go back? Will I ever see my family again, in color? Will they even remember who I am?"

Shadou pulled Elle closer. "Don't lose hope, Elle. All is possible. We can fix this. But first we have to find my master."

"Your master? But why didn't Quaru's death end the darkness?"

"We can't answer that without Her help. And it's just one of many questions. I realize now, that I wasn't sent to this planet to guard Quaru forever. He was a ticking time bomb, and I was the detonator switch. Someone programmed Rifkin and I to forget our assignment. Then shortly after we lost that memory, Quaru's prison doors opened up, just enough so that He could escape."

Elle stomped on the ground. "What do we do now?"

"Many tasks await us. First, we prepare my starship for launch."

"Then what?"

"Then, I must find my master, if She still lives."

"Do you think She does?"

"I do. Only She can guide us through this."

Elle cast her eyes downward, remembering. "What about my mom? Is she still alive?"

Shadou didn't know the answer to that question either.

Several thousand miles away, Jill awoke in a small, cozy house. She found herself lying in a soft bed with bright white sheets and plush down pillows. The walls were painted a cheerful shade of yellow. A landscape painting of pastel flowers hung on the wall. At first she thought perhaps she had dreamt all the recent events—the attack on Earth, her captivity with Quaru—it all seemed so far away.

Jill went into the kitchen. A coffee maker steamed with fresh-brewed coffee. A pile of oranges filled a large bowl on the counter. Jill opened the refrigerator and smiled when she saw that it was brimming with food. She took out a carton of half & half and poured some into a cup. Stirring her coffee, Jill walked to the front door and stepped outside. The cup fell from her hand and shattered on the porch at Jill's bare feet.

Outside of the little house, everything was gray. Jill found herself staring with her mouth wide open across a colorless field that stretched to a darker gray ocean. The house sat near the center of a small, round-topped island within a self-contained bubble of normal light and color. Hundreds of wraiths staggered around the perimeter of this bubble, all guarding their prisoner.

Jill ran back inside and slammed the door shut. She saw a note sitting on a side table. It was printed in neat text on folded thick paper stock. Jill slid down to the floor as she read it: IF YOU'RE READING THIS, I AM GONE. BUT I LEFT YOU A COUPLE OF GIFTS OUTSIDE TO REMIND YOU. PREPARE FOR WAR. – QUARU

Jill peeked up out the window. She recognized two of the wraiths standing in front of the house. Jason and Jim.

Epilogue

Shadou sat in his large chair on the deck of his starship. An array of static, flickering lights encircled him. He had contacted his master, at last. "But, Master," he said, "please help me to understand."

His master's voice sounded tired, distinctly older. *You destroyed the entity that called itself Quaru.*

"That's right. Elle cracked the code. The dark matter was his undoing. And, despite your fears, we were able to destroy Quaru without all those nasty, unintended consequences."

Every action has consequences, Shadou. The Overlord had plans for Quaru, and for Earth.

Shadou stood up. "So you admit it! This was the plan all along."

Yes.

"And what was going to happen to me and Rifkin?"

Shadou, you must believe me when I say that I did not have a hand in this plan. It was the Overlord. You and I both know that Its ways are more mysterious than anything else in the universe.

"How can I believe anything you tell me?"

I am still your master. You and I are connected by ties that can never be broken. I cannot knowingly commit an act that would cause you harm.

"If that's true, then help me. How can Elle and her people save their world? Is Earth doomed to darkness forever?"

Only the Overlord can save that planet.

"Great, so let me go talk to the Overlord."

No, the Overlord does not want to converse with you. Only one person can convince the Overlord to intervene.

"Who?"

Elle Redfern.

"Seriously? Can the Overlord come here at least? Isn't It everywhere?"

The Overlord has commanded that Elle come here, to Rhythmnia.

"As soon as this ship is fixed, I'll take her there myself."

You must remain on Earth.

"What? Me, stay on Earth? Why?"

Only you possess the gift, to protect yourself and others from Quaru's darkness. Also, you are needed there to find Quaru's ... muse.

"His muse? Who is that?"

Elle's mother.

The master's sphere of light began to flicker and fade. Shadou knew what that meant. "Not again! Don't leave me hanging on this planet once more."

Enough talk, Shadou. Your mission is clear. Repair the ship. I've lifted the launch override. Rifkin must fly Elle to me. Together, we will contact the Overlord. You will stay with the remaining survivors, and seek out Jill. Do not contact me again until you have found her.

"Wait, don't leave me yet!"

Goodbye, Shadou, and good luck.

His master's lights extinguished completely. Shadou slammed his fist on the deck. He pulled himself up and stepped out of the starship. In the Grand Canyon cavern, the survivors all gathered around him, their exhausted eyes seeking answers that Shadou knew he couldn't give. But at least he knew that Jill was alive.

"Listen up, everybody," he said. "There's been a slight change of plans."

The weeks they spent in the base beneath the Grand Canyon went by in slow motion. The starship required many repairs. Rifkin, Danny, and Wazer were the only ones doing any real work, with Shadou occasionally lending a hand. As always, Rifkin could fashion any tool they needed, and Danny was a quick study. He spent much of his spare time admiring the sleek ship, and his handiwork on it.

"See? I told you I'm a fixer, not a fighter. Before too long, I'll be the best mechanic in the galaxy!"

Rifkin shook his head. "Don't let it go to your head, buddy."

Wazer focused less on the mechanical aspects, and more on the complex software that powered the ship's operating system. "Come on, Rifkin," he said, "Let the guy have his moment."

Elle spent much of her time on her tablet. Shadou gave her access to every book, movie, song, game, or TV show ever created. But what she enjoyed the most were Shadou's creations. Elle and Conner would sit on either side of Shadou's wide, soft lap. He held the tablet up and his video creations poured straight from his mind and on to the screen. They were mostly comedies, many included characters from old Earth shows. Jerry Seinfeld would go on adventures through outer space with Steve from Minecraft and Rifkin the Magician. The special effects ranged from completely realistic to homemade Claymation. Elle ate gummy worms and giggled, while Conner watched the light flicker in her eyes.

One day Elle saw a new app icon on the screen. "Hey!" she said, "Buzzle Jump! How did you get this?"

Shadou grinned. "I made sure to save your fine creation."

Elle grinned and opened the app. She felt Conner's arms envelope her. She leaned over and kissed him quickly on the lips. He clearly wanted more. "Not in front of Buzzle Jump, Conner. This game reminds me of my fleeting youth."

Miller slowly recovered from her close encounter with Quaru. The right side of her face now bore a long, jagged, dark-gray scar. But even more pronounced was her eye above that scar. Instead of deep brown, it turned a pale silver-gray. For days she had remained unconscious, shaking and wheezing under a pile of heavy blankets. But she finally came to. Miller remembered little about their time beneath Mount Rainier, but the first words she uttered were, "Is Jason still gone?"

Much to Elle's delight, Emmett and Marvin occasionally made appearances. They wandered about, like sleepwalking prospective homebuyers visiting an open house. Usually, Emmett carried Marvin in his arms, but sometimes Marvin walked on his own fat legs. Elle beamed with joy whenever they appeared and referred to the pair as "our indoor/outdoor ghosts."

At last, the starship was deemed repaired. Wazer and Rifkin conducted two full days of tests. "She passed with flying colors all around," said Shadou. "Elle and Rifkin will depart tomorrow." Shadou could tell she was not pleased by this news.

That evening, Shadou summoned Elle with a glance. She plodded up to him with tentative steps. She both expected and dreaded this conversation. Shadou placed his hand on Elle's shoulder and transported the both of them.

When Elle opened her eyes, she found herself standing next to Shadou at her old home on Bainbridge Island. Shadou's force field was just big enough to illuminate the entire property. It was evening, a light breeze blew, and golden light fell across autumn-colored trees.

"I'm going to miss transporting around the world with you," said Elle. "At least you got your gift back."

"We have Quaru's death to thank for that." Shadou looked up at the house. "Remember this place, Elle?"

"Not really. I mean, I remember it mostly from photos, and some videos."

"Much has happened since you lived here."

Elle tugged on Shadou's arm. "Why just me? Why not any of the others? Can't at least one of them come too?"

Shadou smiled down at Elle. "Do you mean Conner?"

Elle blushed. "Yes."

"I'm sorry, Elle, but the ship has limited capacity. It can only sustain two life-forms on a journey as long as the one you're taking. Rifkin needs to pilot the ship."

Elle's face turned white. Both her hands grasped her stomach tightly, as though she was trying to hold back a scream. After a moment she growled in frustration. "Shadou! Why does all this crazy stuff have to happen to me? Will it ever end?"

"Elle, compared to most people on Earth, you're extremely lucky. The other humans might not be suffering, but they certainly aren't living either. They need you."

"Will I ever come back?"

"If you choose to do so, I imagine so."

Elle pondered the house. It held much more meaning for her than she expected. She could almost see her younger self, chasing Emmett across the yard, so long ago. Then she said, "Of course, I'll choose to come back. Why wouldn't I?"

That night Elle curled up next to Conner and held him tight for a long time. Conner choked up. "This place will be like a prison without you, Elle. What am I going to do?"

"Help Shadou find my mom. Save the human race. I'm pretty sure that will keep you busy."

Conner smiled at last and pushed the hair from Elle's eyes. "You get to visit an alien world. That's so cool. You better bring back some videos, or at least a ton of photos, Elle Redfern."

Elle smiled back. *Talk about a long-distance relationship.* "I'll send you messages every chance I get."

She pulled Conner close and pressed her lips against his.

The survivors spent the next morning reminiscing and laughing. They toasted the ones they had lost with raised bottles and cans. As Elle chomped on gummy worms, she asked the group, "What are you guys going to eat when all this junk food runs out?"

Everyone looked to Shadou. "Well, now that I can transport again, we're going to forage. There are thousands of vacant grocery stores for us to visit."

Miller called out, "Let's get some healthier food with natural ingredients!"

Shadou smiled. "Yes, we can do that. But also, I think it would be good to start a garden here. Give us something to do with our time."

Danny interjected, "Can we get some classic cars for me to fix up?"

Shadou laughed. "Maybe one or two."

Conner kept quiet and stayed close by Elle's side. She noticed that Wazer was nowhere to be seen.

Rifkin emerged from the starship and informed them that it was time. A sense of dread descended upon the group. They took their time making their way over to the ship. There, Elle found herself with nothing but her backpack and the clothes on her back. "I forgot to ask, do I need to bring anything?"

Rifkin shook his head. "Nope. The ship will supply everything we need." He smiled with sharp teeth and pointed at the ship's open hatch.

Shadou called out. "I have something." He handed Elle a white rectangular object, about the size of a small, thin book.

"What's this?"

"Something for my family. If you see them, please give it to them."

"You have a family?"

Shadou nodded and caressed Elle's shoulder. "The human equivalent of a wife and daughter. Although you'll soon learn that family life on my planet is quite different from here. That doesn't mean I love them any less. I haven't seen them in a long, long time. Promise me you'll share this message with them."

"I will." Elle faced the group. "OK, everyone... Good-bye? I really don't know what to say."

Miller grabbed Elle and hugged her tight. "Just say you'll take care of yourself out there. Promise us that, will you?"

Elle hugged Miller back and looked into her eyes as she brushed the scar on Miller's face. "I promise."

Next Elle hugged Danny. "Thanks for fixing the ship, and for saving my mom and Miller from Chuck. I'll miss you. Save one of your classic cars for me, OK?"

Danny smiled. "No problem, Elle. I can't wait to hear your stories."

Elle pounced on Shadou, letting his giant arms surround her. "Be good."

Shadou lifted Elle and spun her around in the air. "I will. And do not fear. We will see each other again."

"I believe you." She ran her fingers through his fur one last time.

At last Elle walked up to Conner. He was practically shaking with anxiety.

"Elle, I'm the worst at good-byes. So don't do this to me. Don't say good-bye. Just promise me I'll see you again."

Elle gave Conner a long, warm hug. Then she looked at him, as though memorizing his face. "No, Conner. You promise me. Promise you'll find my mom. She's out there, alive. I know it."

Conner managed a meek smile. "I promise. For real this time."

Just over his shoulder, Elle saw Emmett and Marvin standing in the distance. *Goodbye, brother. I'll find a way to get you back.* She pressed her hand to Conner's cheek. "Don't forget to feed the ghosts." Then she kissed him once more. "I'll see you later."

Everyone hugged Rifkin tight and waved as Elle entered the starship's hatch. The door closed silently behind her. She found herself in a chamber that was all sleek, and shiny white. Rifkin waited beside a pod-shaped object, which resembled a plastic cocoon. "Here's your new home," he said. "Let me get you situated."

Elle changed out of her clothes into a light, silky outfit that covered her like skintight pajamas. She followed Rifkin's instructions and climbed into the pod. It felt soft and warm inside. Familiar images of space flashed across her mind. *Hello, star traveler.* "It's whispering to me again." she said.

"She must like you." Rifkin attached some cords to various points on her body. The cords seemed to be made out of living flesh that connected to her skin on their own. Rifkin triple-checked everything and smiled down at her. "You ready to go?"

"I guess so."

He patted her head and slid the pod door shut. "I'll see you on the other side."

Elle felt a warm sensation course through her body. A strange, calming music echoed within her mind. But then she detected a strange presence. Something else was in the ship with her and Rifkin. Her eyes shot wide open. *Wazer? What are you doing on this ship?* Before she could learn more, all went dark, and Elle passed into a deep, dreamless slumber.

Shadou transported the remaining survivors to the rim of the canyon. Conner looked out and could see nothing beyond Shadou's force field. "Will we even be able to see the ship launch?"

"Oh yes, we will. Remember the liquid light? It will fill up the sky like you've never seen."

They waited for what seemed like an eternity. Conner grew more nervous with each passing minute. "Is everything OK?" he asked for the third time.

"Yes, Rifkin is just making his final preparations. It will be very soon now."

After much more time passed than Conner could stand, they heard a low, booming rumble. "That's the launch bay doors opening," said Shadou. "Put on your goggles." Everyone did.

Seconds later, a white flash of light burst from the canyon. The sky lit up through their goggles and then grew dark again. The deep rumbling sound grew louder and louder. Shadou called out over the roar, "OK, you can take off your goggles now!"

When they did, the group saw the blue sky for the first time since Quaru's attack. The whole of the Grand Canyon shone in glorious sunlight. A rectangular opening appeared near the center of the canyon. Out of this opening rose a small white starship. It glinted in the sunlight as it climbed up into the sky. White plumes of smoke or steam flowed behind it. The ship spun and spiraled away. Conner braced himself on Shadou's arm. "I can't believe she's gone."

Shadou gripped Conner's shoulders. "But part of you is with her. You are in her heart. And that will carry her through all the challenges she must face."

After several minutes the sound of the ship faded until no hint of it remained but its thin plumes of contrails, expanding high above them.

About the Author

Capulet Poehner writes Pacific Northwest–flavored science fiction for people who love imaginative stories with heart. He grew up reading classic sci-fi and fantasy, always wanting to write but never quite finding his voice. He finally did—by reading a lot, writing every day, and learning to just be himself on the page.

He lives on Bainbridge Island, Washington—the same Bainbridge Island where *Bad Shadou* is set. The ferry Elle rides? He rides it too.

In 2026, Capulet is publishing *The Skren Succession*, a series of connected science fiction stories exploring how care becomes control. New stories appear regularly at capuletpoehner.com.

Visit capuletpoehner.com for updates, short fiction, and to join the occasional newsletter.

Elle's Story Continues...

Strange Wazer
The Immortal Elle Trilogy, Book 2

She killed a god. Now she's trapped on a planet full of them.
Elle thought defeating the ancient evil was the end. She was wrong.

Trapped on a prison planet far from home, with powerful forces unlike anything she's ever seen and no way back to Earth, Elle must navigate a deadly brewing war, uncover a sinister conspiracy, and find a way home before it's too late.

Available now.
Turn the page to preview Book 2.

Sneak Peek: Strange Wazer

Prologue

Three years before Quaru's defeat on Earth

The dim chamber lay buried beneath hundreds of feet of solid stone, known in this world as blackite.

Its walls had been carved from the prison planet's mantle, by hands that few had ever seen. The room hummed with equipment that would have horrified the Council. Crystalline arrays glowed with pre-universal energy.

A woman lay strapped to a solid stone table.

She was already dead. But the vessel she wore on a chain around her neck still pulsed. The prisoner it held was still very much alive.

"Remarkable." A voice echoed from the shadows. "The bond persists after biological death. This one is strong indeed."

From the darkness, a hand emerged, reaching toward the woman's vessel. The hand clenched the chain of another vessel. This one didn't glow with contained divinity. It pulsed with a dark blue energy that seemed to hunger for the vessel chained to the woman's neck.

The hand hesitated. *Do I dare free an Old God?*

The power in the woman's vessel was too alluring to resist.

"Beginning extraction."

The hand hovered over the woman's chest, shaking ever so slightly. The empty vessel it held pulsed above her, and a magnetic power began to tug. A hunger that could summon gods from their prison cells.

The god inside the woman's vessel felt it. After three centuries of imprisonment, of forced integration with human hosts, now something was tearing at His bonds.

What are you doing? This is violation—

The holder of the empty vessel focused all their energy on projecting calm authority. "This is freedom. Whether you want it or not."

A powerful wave of energy hammered His prison walls, filling Him with a long-forgotten sensation: power.

The woman's vessel cracked. Not the elegant severance used when a host died naturally. This was violent. The bond didn't dissolve—it *shattered*.

The god poured out of the broken vessel.

He hung in the air above the dead woman's body, a formless cloud reeling with rage. Three hundred years of learning to be small, and now suddenly He was free and He didn't know what to do with it.

"Easy." The voice again, feigning patience, but showing fear the god could no doubt sense. "Remember what you are."

His form stabilized, coalesced into solid geometry, growing darker each second. He had been called many things over the millennia. Entropy's Herald. The Gray Dawn. The Unmaker of Meaning. But on this prison world, His hosts had called Him by a simpler name.

Quaru.

His obsidian form filled the chamber with cold that had nothing to do with temperature.

Rhythmnia. He spoke the word like a curse. *Now. Tonight.*

"Then go, if you must."

Quaru's form dissolved, darkness folding into dimensions beyond the prison planet—

And stopped.

He hung suspended, half-gone, reaching for a vast distance only He could see. When He spoke again, His voice brimmed with fury.

Their defenses are new. Walls within walls, barriers I've never seen. I cannot breach them.

"Is that a problem?"

Silence. Then Quaru laughed, more of a satisfied cackle.

I shall use time against them.

Their defenses are strong now. But they weren't always. His form shifted, folding in on itself as though preparing for a long journey. *Five thousand years ago, Rhythmnia was young. Helpless. I'll strike before they ever dream of building walls against me.*

"And if you fail?"

I won't.

"But if you do?"

Then perhaps you will learn something. I can smell your fear. But also your curiosity. None of that matters to me. His form compressed, pulling at the fabric of time itself. *When the timeline settles, you'll know. You'll feel it, either Rhythmnia's absence, or the weight of five thousand years without me.*

Then He was gone. Not through space, but through time, hurtling backward toward an era when victory would be inevitable.

The chamber fell silent.

The figure in the shadows sat still, shaking with terror and excitement.

One rapid heartbeat. Two. Three.

Nothing changed.

The crystalline arrays still hummed. The cracked vessel still lay on the dead woman's chest. The prison planet still existed, unchanged, exactly as it had been moments before.

"Interesting," the voice said softly, nearing calm equilibrium.

The timeline was intact. Rhythmnia was not destroyed, which meant Quaru had failed. Five thousand years ago, He'd attacked Rhythmnia and something had stopped Him. The Architects had won.

And then what? Could they have destroyed Him? Unlikely. Old Gods don't die easily. Imprisoned Him again? But where? Not here. His presence would have been felt all these centuries.

Somewhere else, then. Some forgotten corner of reality. Some primitive world the Architects considered beneath notice.

The figure moved deeper into shadow.

"Five thousand years is a long time. Even the strongest prison degrades. Cracks form. Bonds weaken." A pause. "If Quaru has been rotting in some hole for five millennia, He's been planning, waiting, overflowing with rage."

The empty vessel flickered blue once more.

"Patience must become my strength."

Chapter 1

Elle dreamed of the survivors stranded on Earth.

Their underground cavern glowed with Shadou's light, that warm, golden radiance that helped them forget about the gray world outside. Miller sat cross-legged on the soft carpet, laughing at something Danny said. Danny was gesturing wildly, no doubt describing some classic car he wanted Shadou to teleport from an abandoned lot somewhere. Elle wasn't a car person, but Danny was quite convincing.

She felt that warmth on her cheeks run deep down into her chest. This was home.

But the dream wasn't in a kind mood. It dragged Elle down to a depth that made her heart burn cold.

Gray faces cycled through dark mist. Conner stood at the Grand canyon's edge, his shoulders hunched, giving her side-eye as if to say, *How long do I have to wait?* Elle's mom Jill sipped red wine on the sofa, her face half-frozen, one eye alive and desperate. *You took off while I suffer in His prison.* Her dad Jim sat lounging in his armchair, the cat Marvin purring in his lap, smiling sadly as he dissolved into charred dust. *You can't save everyone, Elle.*

All of them guilt-tripping her in different voices: *You abandoned us. Why?*

Elle couldn't remember why she left, or where she was going. "Guys, come back!" she tried to scream, but her voice got stuck in her throat.

Then her memories returned, gradually. First, Jason, at the foot of Mt. Rainier. He stood between Elle and a shrieking wraith, his body a shield, his blond ponytail whipping in the battle. His aquamarine eyes found hers for a second.

Run, those eyes said. *I've got this.*

Then the wraith's dark tendrils pierced him, and Jason looked down at the ooze spreading through his chest with an expression of mild surprise, like he'd spilled coffee on his favorite shirt.

"Jason!" Miller's scream echoed through Elle's memory. "JASON!"

But he was already gone. Already becoming one of *them*.

Elle ran. She'd survived because Jason hadn't.

He's gone, that terrified voice in her head whispered. *Jason is a wraith, a servant of...*

Quaru.

Elle's unconscious body twitched. In her dream, the gray consumed everything, and then—

Emmett.

Her little brother stood in the void, seven years old, translucent, flickering the way he'd been since Shadou pulled him halfway out of Quaru's darkness. The cat Marvin floated beside him, equally ghostly.

"Elle." Emmett's voice came from everywhere and nowhere. "Elle, it hurts."

"I know, buddy. I know." She tried to move toward him, but her legs wouldn't work. "I'm coming back. I'm going to fix it. I'm going to make you solid again."

Emmett's ghost-form flickered faster. His eyes—her brother's eyes, shaped like Dad's, yet colorless and pale—were so tired.

"How long?"

"I don't know. However long it takes for me to—"

"I can't hold on." He reached for her, his translucent hand passing through hers. "Please. Don't forget."

"I could never forget you. Emmett, I *promise*—"

His form burst into a thousand gray particles and was gone.

Quaru's laughter echoed from somewhere close.

Elle wandered alone through the void. She screamed her brother's name into nothing.

Shadou's voice cut through the darkness: "Elle—"

ALERT. ALERT. NAVIGATION ANOMALY DETECTED.

Elle's eyes snapped open.

Red emergency lights flickered across the cryo-pod's interior. *Oh my god.* She blinked at her tight surroundings, panic rising, then subsiding as the memory of where she was rushed back. *Shadou's starship. The mission to Rhythmnia.*

Her body fought overwhelming drugged, heavy, sluggish sensations. Her muscles battled the stiffness from weeks of induced hibernation. Lukewarm cryo-gel dripped from her hair, ran down her neck, soaked into the collar of her silky sleep-suit. Her feet were encased in the thin cryo-booties that came with the suit, barely more than socks with grippy soles.

Great. Apparently waking up from the worst nightmare she'd had in years wasn't an escape. *I'm wearing hospital PJs and covered in slime.*

ALERT. COURSE DEVIATION DETECTED. GRAVITATIONAL ANOMALY EXCEEDS SAFE PARAMETERS.

"Speak normal!" Elle shouted.

The starship's voice was nothing like Shadou's deep rumble. He would have explained this way better, with visuals. He had a talent for making unthinkable things sound normal. Centuries of experience, probably. But Shadou was back on Earth, holding down the fort, keeping the survivors safe while she flew off to become what, exactly? A savior? A sixteen-year-old on an intergalactic study-abroad field trip?

She missed Shadou. The warmth of his presence, the way his sly smile made everything feel a little less hopeless. She wanted to pounce onto his big belly and feel his arms wrap around her. But instead she was alone out here, hurtling through space toward an alien world, while everyone she loved waited in a gray wasteland for a rescue she had to deliver.

Alone wasn't totally accurate.

Rifkin was somewhere on the ship. And someone else too...

Wazer. The last thing she'd sensed before the cryo-sleep took her. She could still sense him. *What are you doing on this ship?*

She'd deal with that mystery later. Right now, alarms were blaring and the word "anomaly" was never a good thing.

Elle slammed her hand against the pod's release mechanism, pulled the door latch, and hauled herself upright, fighting through disorientation. Emmett echoed in her mind, fading but not gone.

"Emmett, my dude," she whispered. "I'm coming back. I promise."

The ship lurched hard to one side, and Elle gripped a support rail to keep from falling. The dizziness wasn't helping. She planted one foot in front of another and felt her strength returning with each step.

She found Rifkin in the bridge, his catlike form hunched over the navigation console, paws adjusting controls that glowed with cold white light. She saw a crumpled Rainier beer can wedged in a makeshift cup holder, which definitely wasn't part of the starship's original console design.

"Seriously, Rifkin? Drinking and driving?"

Rifkin didn't turn around. "Good, you're awake," he said. "We have a problem."

"I saw that. This slime I'm covered in isn't helping."

"Cryo-gel evaporates quickly, kid. That's the least of your worries right now."

"The alarms weren't kidding then." Elle braced herself against a wall as the ship shuddered again. "What's the anomaly situation exactly?"

"I'm not sure you'd believe me if I told you."

Elle rolled her eyes. "Come on, it's me, give it a shot."

"Okay." Rifkin scanned the ship's monitors. "I'm pretty sure an invisible planet is pulling us off course." His whiskers twitched, the same nervous tick she had seen back in the cavern, where he and Shadou had built that ridiculous beer can tower while waiting for instructions that never came. "And before you ask, no, this planet isn't on any of our charts. It shouldn't even exist."

"Shouldn't how?"

Rifkin turned to face her. His eyes widened; his pupils dilated in a way that meant he was either excited or terrified. With Rifkin, it was probably both.

"The gravitational signature either ignores or predates current physics. We're talking about ancient technology, possibly a force even older than the universe." He pointed a claw at the main viewport, which showed nothing but stars and empty space. "See? Invisible. Whatever's down there, it's been hiding for a long time. And it really, *really* wants us to pay it a visit."

The ship lurched again, harder this time. Elle fell forward, caught herself on the co-pilot's seat.

"This ship is powerful. We can't just break free and get out of here?"

"What do you think I've been trying to do? Many times." Rifkin shook his head with his ears flattened against his skull. "It's like the planet is *grabbing* us. I've never seen anything like it."

Elle's chest tightened. She drummed her fingers on the seatback. "Okay, so let's think then. What would Shadou do?"

"Shadou doesn't know everything, Elle. And besides, he's not here. We gotta figure this out ourselves." Rifkin turned back to the console, his eyes devouring readings that made no sense to Elle, equations and energy signatures that made her brain hurt just trying to follow them. "I don't see any way out of this without landing down there. This planet, it sees us..."

He trailed off.

Elle's face tingled. "It sees us. What does that even mean?"

When Rifkin spoke again, his voice was smaller than she had ever heard it.

"I think it wants to eat us."

Before Elle could respond, the starship alarms beeped again.

PLANETARY APPROACH CONFIRMED. ESTIMATED SURFACE CONTACT: SIX MINUTES. RECOMMEND EMERGENCY LANDING PROTOCOLS.

Elle studied the viewport. Nothing but blackness with a few scattered stars. But somewhere out there, invisible, and hungry, a gravitational force was pulling them down.

"So weird," she said. "I don't see anything."

Rifkin's paws started trembling, enough for Elle to notice.

"You okay, Rifkin?"

"Great, more problems," he said. "I don't think I can shift." His breathing quickened.

"What? But you're a shifter. That's what you do."

Rifkin focused on his familiar staff near the console, attempting the simple transformation he'd performed thousands of times before. The staff shimmered, its edges rippled almost imperceptibly, then snapped back to its original shape with a discordant

ping.

"What the...?" Rifkin tried again. Nothing. His shifting power was gone.

Rifkin stared at his paws. Elle did not like that expression on his face. This feline shifter had always been unflappable, an ancient being who had seen everything a million times. Now he looked like some kid lost in a grocery store.

He tried to shift again. Failed again. His whiskers drooped.

"Rifkin?" Elle said. "That's not normal, right?"

"It's nothing, probably temporary." He knocked the staff aside. "I can adjust."

He didn't look like he'd adjust. His whiskers bristled. Then he snapped out of it. "Starship, you detecting any interference beyond this gravitational pull?"

AFFIRMATIVE. A LOCALIZED FIELD EFFECT EMANATING FROM THE PLANET SURFACE IS INTRODUCING DANGEROUS LEVELS OF UNCERTAINTY INTO MY SENSORS. RECOMMEND IMMEDIATE COURSE CORRECTION.

"What do you think I'm trying to do?" Rifkin found a new level of urgency. His paws flew across the controls, firing rear thrusters at maximum power. The starship groaned, resisting, but the planet's pull intensified. This wasn't simple gravity, it was a more deliberate grip, like massive claws clutching their hull.

Rifkin shook his head and snorted, half laugh, half despair. "You know, Elle, I told Shadou this trip was a bad idea. I told him. But no, 'Elle needs to petition the Overlord,' he said. 'Go to Rhythmnia,' he said." He grabbed the empty Rainier can and shook it. "And now I'm out of beer, I can't shift matter and we're about to crash-land on a mystery planet that predates the universe. Just perfect. Looks like emergency landing protocols is our last chance of survival."

Elle felt panic gripping her. She squinched her eyes shut and reached out with her peculiar sense that let her feel data flow through circuits. But when she tried to connect beyond the ship's systems, she hit a wall. Her power didn't work here either.

"I can't access anything down there," she said. "Why?"

The ship answered unbidden:

THE LOCALIZED FIELD EFFECT EMANATING FROM PLANET SURFACE.

"Of course," Elle muttered. "Because nothing is ever easy anymore."

Elle slid into the co-pilot's seat and strapped the belts around her.

"Okay," she said. "Tell me everything you know about this planet's ancient technology."

DATA NOT AVAILABLE.

Elle groaned. "Rifkin, you're pretty ancient, what do you know?"

"That's the problem." Rifkin's paw gripped the ship's flight stick, adjusting their descent angle, trying to turn an inevitable crash into something survivable. "I'm old, but not like ancient pre-universal old. Whatever's down there..."

He met her eyes.

"We're flying blind, Elle."

The ship shuddered as they hit the outer edge of an atmosphere that they couldn't see.

Rifkin's arms shook rapidly as he gripped the controls. "I never seen any atmospheric entry like this before. I don't like our odds."

Elle gripped her armrests and thought of Emmett, of Conner, of everyone waiting for her back on Earth.

I promised I'd come back.

Through the viewport, the planet finally burst into view. Elle could see forests now, mountains, rivers. It looked like Earth's long-lost twin.

"Two minutes," Rifkin said. "Starship, give me full manual control."

MANUAL CONTROL ENGAGED. WARNING: ATMOSPHERIC ENTRY AT CURRENT ANGLE EXCEEDS SAFETY PARAMETERS BY FORTY-SEVEN PERCENT.

"I know!"

The ship shuddered as its hull burned through the atmosphere. Friction turned the viewport into flame. Temperature rose. Rifkin fought the controls, adjusting their angle degree by degree.

"Come on," he muttered. "Just a few more degrees. There!"

The flames lessened. The viewport cleared, showing forest rushing up, pine trees, ferns, ordinary Earth-like forest. Elle's stomach dropped, and not just from the descent.

"Brace!" Rifkin shouted.

Impact came hard. Elle's restraints dug into her shoulders. Her head snapped forward, then back. The ship bounced once, twice, three times. Metal screamed. Systems sparked. Gravity cut out, then slammed back at double strength.

Then stillness.

Elle's ears rang. Smoke drifted through the cabin. Emergency lights cast everything in red. Outside the viewport, fog pressed against the hull. She'd felt this before, the car accident with her dad.

"Status report," Rifkin croaked.

HULL SHIELD INTEGRITY AT SEVENTY-THREE PERCENT. NAVIGATION SYSTEMS OFFLINE. MAIN POWER AT FORTY-TWO PERCENT AND FALLING. LIFE SUPPORT FUNCTIONAL. CRYO-BAY REPORTS BOTH PODS INTACT. PLANET ATMOSPHERE IS A NEAR PERFECT MATCH OF EARTH'S.

Both pods intact. A hidden Earth-like planet in the middle of nowhere. Elle closed her eyes tight for several seconds and focused all her attention on slowing down her breathing.

Once she recovered the strength to move, she unbuckled and stumbled up to the viewport. Through the fog, shapes moved. People—regular-looking people in what appeared to be hiking clothes—carrying flashlights or lanterns. Around a couple of their necks, pendants glowed softly.

Vessels. Something clicked into place, and for the first time Elle felt a connection here. Her code-perception didn't work, but she could sense something about those pendants. *They're called vessels.*

The people approached cautiously. One raised a hand in what might have been warning.

Rifkin stood beside her. "This doesn't look good."

"Yeah," Elle whispered. "Super creepy."

The people drew closer. Through the ship's monitors, she heard voices, normal voices, speaking what sounded like English.

Elle's hand hovered over the hatch controls. Once she opened it, there was no going back. No shields, no weapons that would matter, no powers. Just her, Rifkin, and Wazer unconscious in his pod. If these people wanted to kill them, take the ship, do whatever they wanted, there was nothing to stop them.

"We could wait," Rifkin said quietly. "Stay sealed. See if they leave."

"And then what? Starve in here?" Elle stared at the figures through the fog. "We need help. The ship needs repairs. We don't have a choice."

"I hate it when I agree with your wild ideas."

Elle reached for the hatch controls. Her hand trembled from a surge of adrenaline. She opened it anyway.

End of chapter one.
Strange Wazer is available now.